The Summer Collection

Paul John Hausleben

Cover design, computer-generated graphics, and all artwork by Paul John Hausleben
Rear cover photograph and author photograph by Paul John Hausleben
Rear cover photograph of the author is by Ms. Alejandra Lopez

ISBN: 978-0-9886336-7-4

This is a work of fiction. Names, characters, businesses, places, events and incidents are either the product of the author's eccentric, strange and unusual imagination or used in a fictitious manner. Any resemblance to actual persons, living or dead or actual events is purely coincidental, and it was not the intention of the author.

Dedications

The Entire Collection

To sunburn, baseball games, hot-birds in the trees, fancy and not so fancy cars that we cruised in, fireworks in the backyard, those electric fans that buzzed around in my rooms over the years, and to sunny days and sultry nights. Thank goodness when October arrives!

The Dance

To the 1971 Japanese (the actual brand name begins with the letter T and ends in an A) sedan with the tricky doors. Long may you roll. I truly hope that the old man was wrong, and you did not return as a garbage can.

Hot Coals and Sparks

To the chap who sold us fireworks out of the trunk of his car in Paterson, New Jersey in 1974.

Flying

To Technical Sergeant William Howell Pierce, United States Army Air Force during WW-2, and his wonderful family. A true American hero with the 321st Bomb Group, assigned as a radio operator and waist gunner to B-25 low-level and medium bombers. He flew 63 combat bombing missions, over Europe, Africa, and Egypt. He was a Purple Heart recipient from some enemy "flak" sent his way. It is my honor to have the immense pleasure to have known you, Sergeant Pierce. God bless you. Thank you for the pleasure of listening to your tales of combat adventures, your wonderful sense of humor, for your guidance when I was a young man, and your friendship. Long may you fly and may all your takeoffs and landings be smooth.

DI DI DI DAH DI DAH

Unreasonable Expectations

To anyone who cannot ever forget the memory of someone special in their lives.

The Old Chair

To anyone who has an easy chair in the corner of a room that is full of memories and comfort.

Once in a Lifetime on a Summer Night

To Moonlight and Memories.

The Dance
Another story from the Adventures of Harry and Paul

Hot Coals and Sparks
Featuring the old man and other characters from the Adventures of Harry and Paul

Flying
Featuring Paul John Henson and Jeff Porter from the Adventures of Harry and Paul

Unreasonable Expectations
Another story from the Adventures of Harry and Paul

The Old Chair
Featuring Pastor Paul John Henson and Binky Hobnobber Henson from the Adventures of Harry and Paul

Once in a Lifetime on a Summer Night
Some words

Contents

Unreasonable Expectations

Acknowledgements

I would like to thank my entire family and as always, send an extra thank you and a tip of the captain's hat to Mr. Harry M. Rogers Junior. Special thanks to "Honest" Rafael Innis and Lydia A. LaGalla for the ideas, feedback, and inspiration for, "Unreasonable Expectations." Thank you to Pastor Donald F. DeGroat, Mr. Jeffrey Scott Pierce, the Pierce family, the old man, my sister Dottie, and my dear Mum. Thank you and a Frosty Mug Salute, a warm shout out, and an extra special thank you to the gang at 20 John Street. Somewhere down the line, I know we will all meet once again, and that will be one wild and crazy time.

Keep 'em cold because I am on my way!

"In July, in the hottest of the weather, if two cannot sleep alone, then one must sleep together."
John Henson Allcock
Date unknown

Preface from the Author

The story of how the book *The Summer Collection* became a published work reads as if it is a story in itself! It is very interesting how *The Summer Collection* evolved from a conversation, to the birth of an idea, into another book in the seasonal collections of my works. Initially, *The Summer Collection* is a book, in which I put together with a great deal of trepidation.

A casual conversation one day with a close friend was obtuse, and it was a sad lament that I currently had no further intention of writing any new stories or books. The novel *The Miracle Tree* had ended with the two characters of Harry M. Redmond Jr. and Paul John Henson in a very good place to leave them off, perhaps, forever. I felt that I had run my course, and I needed to concentrate on my photography and other priorities in my life. It was not that I did not have any stories left inside of my mind. I still had an endless array of ideas floating around in there, as well as a number of finished and unfinished drafts of stories and novels tucked away. In reviewing my library of work, I felt that much of it was inferior, and not very interesting to me. I also felt as though it was time to do something else. I did not say that I would never write again, I only said that I would not be currently working on any new book projects.

For those of us who understand the meaning of the catchphrase, I wanted to avoid the dreaded "Jumping of the Shark!"

My statement and my intentions greatly disturbed my friend. I was then encouraged by some pleading from my friend to continue, and while doing so, she made a subtle mention that although the novels that I had written, emotionally touched and captivated her, she confessed to also enjoying the seasonal collections of various stories because of how they invoked such powerful memories of her own past.

The Autumn Collection and *The Christmas Tree and Other Christmas Stories, Tales for a Christmas Evening* had been successful, and my friend emphasized how popular she felt another seasonal book would be with my loyal readers.

"A collection of summer stories would be wonderful. I am sure that even though you dislike the summer that Harry, Paul, and all the other fictional and non-fictional characters and persons, had many adventures in the summer. Just one time, I think you need to tell a truly, authentic, Harry and Paul story. Yes, Paul, you need to write a story that is almost one hundred percent true. I bet you have one of them inside of you," my friend preached to me as she coaxed me into thinking about another seasonal book.

At first, I dismissed her suggestion, but later in the day, I gave it some serious thoughts. Then, as so often happens in my life, I received some inspiration from an unusual source. This is where the story becomes interesting, because I am in many ways, very similar to the character of "Paul John Henson" and those persistent ghosts of the past never stop following me around. While working around the house, I tuned in a radio station for some ambiance, and an old song from the great Canadian folk-pop-rock singer Mr. Neil Young played on the radio station. It was a dynamic performance of the song, "Harvest Moon."

The song invoked memories in my mind of a summer dance of so long ago, and it was so powerful, in both lyrics and melody that I rushed to my computer, dialed up the corresponding music video, and confirmed my memories. The music video was wonderful, and it displayed a singer recanting his own memories of his youth, dancing with a pretty woman, while depicting a late summer night of memories.

I smiled inside because I knew that my friend was correct. I needed to tell the stories of summer and I have no shame in sharing that what followed in the next twenty-four hours or so were some of the most profound hours of my life. I typed and created the story contained herein this collection, and holds the title of, "The Dance."

I did take my friend's advice, and I created a story that while it is not one hundred percent true or authentic, it is at least ninety-five percent or so true! I typed and typed, and I have to be honest, I could not even consider sleeping until I completed the framework of the story. In fact, it had invoked such profound and powerful memories for me that I could not sleep for days afterward. It had stirred up memories of a lifetime in my mind and had affected me emotionally in such a profound manner that it bothered me for weeks after I had completed the story. It did not affect me in a forlorn or depressed manner, quite the opposite. It had caused intense exhilaration. The story came out of my memory banks, became reality right in front of my eyes, and then managed to stir up very deep emotions of a long-forgotten time.

Most of all, I realized that I had not jumped any sharks.

It was a magical time for me in the creative realm, and one that I may never feel again or ever try to duplicate.

I think because "The Dance" is such an authentic story, it made me recognize that we all reach a point in our lives, when we realize that perhaps the best times of our life are in fact, behind us.

Facing our own mortality is a difficult thing for any of us to consider.

The door to my summer memories was now wide open; therefore, the rest of the book flowed along rather easily. I have to say that the authentic theme sustained me throughout the rest of the book, and the rest of the stories have very strong elements of authentic truth to them.

Even though I dislike the heat and humidity, and

summer is not my favorite time of the year, it is a plethora of memories and good times for all of us! Summer brings us all outside for fun, on vacations, on adventures, and invokes some of the most powerful of our memories of holidays, families, and friends. It is a special time, when you place your work on a shelf for a week or two here and there, and we try hard to relax.

For me, summer is the time of the year that I look forward to the least, but I can never deny the happiness and adventures it has brought to me throughout my life. I admit that I cheer loudly and wildly, when October arrives, but I truly mean no ill will or disrespect to summer. I just want to say goodbye and hold on to the memories!

This book captures the adventures of the summer with both humorous overtones and heartwarming ways. Harry and Paul have returned once again, along with some familiar characters and some new characters too.

I have to admit that my friend was indeed correct when she surmised that some of our greatest adventures occurred in the summer. They sure did, and it is my wish that all of your summers bring to you golden memories, fun in the sun, and happiness.

I hope that this book, in some small way, helps to invoke some feelings for you, or returns you to a summer memory or two of your own. I hope that you enjoy reading this book as much as I enjoyed putting it all together. Thank you for reading it.

Paul John Hausleben

July 2014

Prologue

Summer is finally here! Wonderful, glorious, summer and all the joy it brings! The summer arrives and we all jump for joy! Yippee! Summer is here! We had all grown so weary of the cold, the snow, and the rain!

We all are now looking forward to the warm days, the splash of the pool, baseball, cold beer, lemonade, flowers, and roses in bloom, and happy bumblebees buzzing in our zinnias. Cutting the grass is a great exercise, and the yard work is wonderfully enjoyable! Days grow later, and the daylight ends framed with golden summer sunsets. We enjoy fireworks, outdoor music concerts, strolls downtown in the open markets and happy times off from work and school. There are those fantastic, fresh vegetables at the farmer's market such as giant watermelons, ripe-red-luscious-tomatoes, and baskets of golden sweet corn. Summer vacations and holidays. Romantic strolls along sandy ocean beaches, placid canoe rides on mirrored lakes, and gentle summer breezes that move our drapes and curtains on quiet evenings. The splash of fishing lures into the water, the cry of children at play, the flipping of hamburgers on the backyard barbeque grille.

All the joy and memories that summer brings to us all . . . it lives with us forever.

Yippee! Hooray! Summer is here! We love the summer! What a glorious time of the year.

Yet by the time that late August arrives, summer has worn out the welcome, and we are crying out for cooler weather. When will this heatwave end? I cannot wait for the cooler weather!

On those wicked, hot summer days, the sun rises differently, almost as if it is angry with us and is mean-spirited. You can easily determine that on some mornings, the sun is not playing around, and the heat of the day will cook, bake, and broil you. The birds hide, the breeze dies down and people flee to air-conditioned stores or the shopping mall, and dive into swimming pools.

By the late afternoon, you are soaking wet, your socks stick to your feet like duct tape, and you now suffer from a terrible case of "swamp butt." Then the nighttime comes, and it brings drippy humidity and bugs that chase you around for hours like relentless, little jet planes, while they try to suck all the blood out of your body.

You have sweat out of your fancy suit while stuck in a traffic jam on your way to that job interview, and you wonder if they will notice the sweat stains on your shirt! Your car battery exploded in the heat in a parking lot and you needed a tow. Just one week after a radiator hose had burst in the same heat wave. One more heat wave and your air-conditioning system will explode too, while the evil electric company sends a new bill every other day for bijillions of dollars!

The stupid grass needs mowing again, the hedges need trimming; the weeds have overrun the flowerbeds, those nasty wasps made another nest over the porch, and they stung little Johnny and Woofie the dog again!

The weatherman is on the television, waving at a weather map while a red warning scrawls ominously across the bottom of the screen. He warns of another dangerous thunderstorm on the horizon that could knock the electric power out again!

Oh yes, those stupid ass bumblebees in the zinnias are a pain in your ass. Your baseball team has lost twelve straight games, and the thunderstorm that rolled in late yesterday afternoon, knocked over all the rose bushes! Mothers send children outside to play, and dream of sending them all back to school someday very soon. To top it all off, if you have one more glass of lemonade your lips will fall off!

"I can't stand this heat! When will this wretched summer end?" You cry out in mercy and anguish, while walking as if you are a stiff wooden soldier while carefully shuffling along, in order, to allow your sunburned legs to heal.

Wonderful, happy summer and all the joy it brings! Yippee! Summer is here!

Golden afternoons, skipping through open meadows, gathering baskets and baskets of wild strawberries, singing happy songs, and filling your heart with joy and glee.

Wonderful, glorious, summer and all the joy it brings!

Oh, yes, and do not forget the terrible cases of "swamp butt" too.

The Dance

1

1971 Takajunky Model 10

"In the year 1971, when the first Takajunky model 10 was introduced here in America, by Takajunky Motor Works from Junko, Japan, the quality was something less than satisfactory. By the year 1975, though, the name Takajunky had come to exemplify quality, economy, and value. The company had come a long way from their humble beginnings."

I leaned forward in my chair, as the commentator on the television waved his arms in front of him over a red-colored, 1971 Takajunky Model 10 vehicle, displayed upon a rotating stage with the obligatory, beautiful blonde gal, clad in a bathing suit, standing and smiling next to the vehicle.

It was summer and the off-season for me. I was stuck in my apartment in Norfolk, Virginia, the home base for my new hockey team, the Norfolk Navigators, a club that I had joined just this past spring. I was sent to the team a little late in the hockey season, when the parent company of the Boston Bears bought my contract and moved me one-step closer to the big league. My agent told me that various scouts and coaches were following my progress carefully, and I was the heir apparent to the starting goaltender position with the Boston Bears hockey club.

In the meantime, I had to endure an assignment with the farm team here in Norfolk. My first half-year or so here, since my call up from the Albany, New York based, Flying Dutchman hockey club, had gone very well. I had performed well in the net, our team reached the playoffs, and we came close to a league championship. I had played well enough in the net to lead the league in goaltender stats for the playoffs. We had a good defense; we just could not score!

I was now resting from a groin strain suffered at the end of the year, and the team doctors had put me on a restricted work out regimen, to make sure that it healed before the season. I worked out lightly, three times per week, with the team and skated every day.

Life was grand when I was with my teammates or in the workout rooms; it was when I returned to my little apartment that the loneliness began. If I was not busy with hockey, the off times were difficult. It had been tough to leave my family and friends in New Jersey, and due to other circumstances, I was having a rough time emotionally.

In addition, this summer had been brutal in Norfolk. It had been swampy, hot, and humid, and every day was the same. The summer went on and on, for what seemed as if it was forever.

I was a cold weather guy, and I disliked the heat and humidity of the Mid-Atlantic Region of the United States. How I longed for the warm days and cool summer nights of my home in Paterson, New Jersey, where at least it cooled off a little at night, and you could enjoy a summer night in the backyard or on the back porch, without sweating to death.

This one Saturday afternoon, I was feeling particularly lonely and preoccupied with my memories. We had a very good workout on Friday and I had the weekend off to recover.

Bored and restless, I had flipped on the television to pass some time and collect my thoughts. I needed a break because I had to admit that my body had some slight aches and pains still nagging at me. In addition, my mind was exhausted.

I was not much of a television viewer, and other than watching my beloved ice hockey and some football games, I rarely, if ever, sat down to watch anything on the tube.

I had been mindlessly flipping through channels on the television, trying my best to burn away this lazy, hot, late July afternoon, when I mistakenly stumbled upon a boring documentary on the local public broadcasting television channel. The show that was on this afternoon was all about the early years of the introduction of foreign cars to America.

The previously boring program now had my interest.

The announcer continued, "Even though, the 1971 Takajunky Model 10 suffered from some early quality issues with tricky door latches, inconvenient and spontaneous leaks from under the dashboard heater cores, and poorly performing transmissions, the vehicle's overall reputation for economy and fabulous gas mileage, eventually earned, the vehicle a loyal following."

The announcer walked close to the Takajunky on display, the rotation of the stage stopped, and the beautiful gal in the bathing suit opened the driver's door for the announcer. As the camera zoomed inside the interior of the car, he continued with his description, "One of the earlier and most popular innovations, turned out to be the super deluxe, push-button, auto selecto radio! With a push of the button, the owner of the Takajunky could automatically dial into news, sports, and the type of music you desired. The radio would scan, tune the dials in a flash, and find your preferred selection for you in a split second. It was a fabulous technology for 1971!"

I leaned back, smiled, and laughed.

"Yes, it sure was," I exclaimed aloud to the entire room. You see, I could agree and testify with the announcer of the program, because I spent many a night in a 1971 Takajunky model 10, owned by my best friend, Harry M. Redmond

Junior. It was his first car, and the memories of this television program had stirred up came vividly rushing back to me.

Once more, the ghosts of my past came floating into my life, and they transported me back in time, to an adventure that Harry and I shared together in the early summer of 1975. This summer adventure led to a legendary incident that still lives on in the minds and hearts of all of us, and hangs in the air over Haledon, and Sussex County, New Jersey to this very day.

I flipped the "off" switch on the remote control, when the announcer moved on to speaking about some other type of automobile that I did not recognize. I leaned back in my chair and drifted off to sleep. . ..

December 28, 1973

Dear Debbie,

I hope you are having a great Christmas season. I have had a good Christmas season, and so far, I have to say that visiting Christmas Tree Mountain was the highlight of my holiday season this year.

Meeting you sure was wonderful too! The wild time that we all had from the Boryeungous that Ronzo whipped up this year sure made it interesting! For sure, it was quite an adventure for all of us. It was my pleasure to meet you, and as I promised, I wanted to write to you and stay in touch. I hope that we can continue to write and be friends. Maybe we can even chat on the telephone sometime. My grandfather's telephone number next door is 201-956-9738. I would have to let him know that I was going to use his telephone, or what time or day that you would call.

Please let me know. Thank you and I hope you will

write back to me.

Sincerely Yours,

Paul John Henson
182 Belmont Avenue
Haledon, N.J. 07508

I placed my pen down on my desk and sighed. This was the first letter that I had ever written to a gal. I was a nervous, fifteen-year-old teenager, writing a letter to a gal that I had met and had caught my eye just a week or so ago. Debbie Boatwright was my first crush, and I was now sailing uncharted waters. I signed it and folded the paper neatly into three folds. I stood up from my chair in front of the little shelf mounted on the wall in my bedroom, which I used as a desk. I went over to the top drawer of my dresser, and opened it up. There, tucked inside a little box that I kept in the top drawer, was a small piece of paper, in which had the home address for Miss Debbie Boatwright scrawled upon it. I took the piece of paper, opened it up, and studied it.

While I studied it, in my mind's eye, I could see her face, her clear, green eyes, and her hair blowing under her hat as she stood on the side of Christmas Tree Mountain this past December.

She captivated my young heart, and I could be wrong, but I do think she was interested in me, too.

Debbie Boatwright was the oldest daughter of Mr. and Mrs. Boatwright, who were the family that owned Christmas Tree Mountain in Sussex County, New Jersey. I had met her a week or so before Christmas, when I had visited the mountain along with a group of people from our neighborhood, and my best buddy Harry M. Redmond Jr. and his family, on their annual excursion to the tree farm in order to cut down Christmas trees.

Despite the now famous, "time bomb in the cupboard" incident, in which the men of our neighborhood took intoxication to a new level, after ingesting Harry's brother-in-law Ronnie "Ronzo" Boatmann's annual, home-brewed, whiskey concoction, I had enjoyed a wonderful time on the mountain. In fact, it had left me with a memory of a lifetime and it had begun my many adventures with my best buddy Harry and his wild and fun-filled family.

Debbie and I had shared some conversations, and in one particularly, poignant moment, we had shared a view and some words together on the top of the mountain, while we both overlooked a breathtaking sight of the snow-covered mountain top at Christmas time.

Before I had left to journey back to the city of Paterson, she slipped me her contact information, and asked that we stay in touch with one another. Now, despite the distance between us, I had decided to write her a short letter and see where it all went from here.

"Say Mum, do you have an envelope and a stamp that I could have?" I asked as I wandered out of my room and found my mother sitting at the kitchen table. Mum was sewing some holes in my old man's work socks and, with a bit of a puzzled look upon her face, she looked up from her work.

"Sure, in the right side, kitchen cupboard, Paulie. Are you writing for some hockey information?" Mum asked. It was unusual for me to mail anything, and since hockey was my passion and my sport, Mum assumed it had to be hockey related.

I stumbled a bit and fumbled, but decided that honesty was the best policy here, "No, I am writing to Debbie Boatwright. She is the gal that I met on Christmas Tree Mountain, when we went for the trees and all the men got bombed a few weeks ago, before Christmas." I was not overly comfortable right at this moment revealing that I was writing to a gal, but after all, this was my mum!

Mum smiled and said, "Oh, I see. Yes, I remember you mentioned her. In fact, you spoke about her quite a bit more than you did anything else for a few days afterwards. You mentioned her even a bit more than the time bomb in the cupboard that Ronzo prepared. Pretty, green eyes, if I do remember correctly. I guess she must be a pretty, little gal, eh?"

My mum was of English descent, and she had a particular way with words. The cultural challenge that my sister and I faced as we flipped and flopped between my old man, who was firmly of Paterson, New Jersey descent, and our prim and proper, English-born mum was certainly interesting. She was being careful now while she tiptoed around the fact that she had already known her son had a crush on some gal.

"Are you going to mail it today, Paulie?"

"Yeah, yeah, yeah, Mum. I am going to walk down to the mailbox on Burhans Ave with Skippy and mail it in there right now. Do you have anything else you want me to mail for you?"

"Yes, please take the envelope there on the shelf where your father keeps his newspaper. It is a payment for the electric bill, so please make sure it goes down the shoot, eh?"

"Sure. Will do," I said, as I sat down at the kitchen table. I took the note with Debbie's information out of my pocket, addressed the envelope to Debbie, double-checked the information for accuracy, put the letter inside, and sealed the envelope up. Mum watched me and smiled, but she did not say anything else, and she went back to sewing the socks. I waved goodbye, whistled for my faithful fox terrier, Skippy, hitched him to a leash, grabbed both letters, put on my vest and out the back door we went. It was a few days after Christmas, and it was overcast and cold. It had snowed lightly on Boxing Day, and remnants of some snow and ice crunched under our feet (and paws) as I made my way towards the mailbox.

We lived in the Borough of Haledon, New Jersey, about fifty feet or thereabouts, over the city of Paterson's northernmost boundaries, and the mailbox was located across the street from our house on the corner of Burhans and Belmont Avenue. We crossed the street; I opened the mailbox door and dropped the letters into the box. I opened and closed the door three times, and double-checked that the letters had indeed made their way down inside the box.

Looking down at Skippy, I mumbled to him, "Well, ole Skip, let's see what she says, eh?" Skippy looked up at me and wagged his tail a bit but he did not seem overly enthusiastic, perhaps he knew something in which I did not.

Now I just needed to wait.

And wait, I did.

After about three months, I was over the disappointment of coming home from school and asking Mum every day if I received any mail. Initially, the fact that Debbie Boatwright had not written me back was a devastating blow to my heart. However, in the big picture, I had hockey, an entire school of other teenage gals to take my mind off the crushing defeat, my best buddies Harry M. Redmond Jr. and Jeff Porter to hang with, and a host of other teenage diversions. In addition, being perfectly honest, I was only fifteen or so years of age, and you rebound rather quickly from these types of situations at that age.

Mum had watched me carefully during the initial "rejection" period, and she firmly stopped the old man in his tracks whenever he tried to tease me about the situation. My sister, who was about three years older than I, was sympathetic to my plight, because she had already fallen victim to a rejection from a potential boyfriend or two in her fledgling love life.

Soon, Debbie Boatwright was a faint memory in my teenage mind.

One day in late March, I arrived home from vocational school, wandered into my bedroom to change my clothes for a quick, street hockey shoot-around with Harry and Jeff, and while walking into my room; I noticed a letter sitting on the pillow on my bed. Skippy greeted me, and he jumped up on my bed and sat down while he watched me pick up the letter. It seemed as though ole Skip was interested in what the letter on my bed was about too. The dog did not mind curling up and settling in while he watched me carefully studying the letter. In fact, the way Skippy would lie around on it, it was as much his bed as it was mine. I looked at the return address and to my utter shock; I read that the letter was from Debbie Boatwright! I closed the door to my bedroom for privacy, sat down on the bed, and carefully opened the envelope. I peered inside and pulled out a handwritten letter. A letter composed upon a neatly folded piece of paper.

I unfolded the letter and read it:

March 22, 1974

Dear Paul,

I am very sorry that it has taken me so long to write back to you, but somehow it appears that our local post office here in Sussex County misplaced your letter. When I saw the postmark on the letter indicating that you mailed it shortly after Christmas, I felt terrible. I only just received the letter this week! Thank you for writing to me. I was thrilled to see your letter and sat down as soon as I received it to write you back. I also enjoyed the day when you, Harry, and the Redmond family, as well as your entire neighborhood, visited us here at Christmas Tree Mountain. I had a great Christmas, but the best part was meeting you.

I hope we can be friends. Maybe we can write to one another and speak when we are able to here and there. My telephone number, in case you can call, is 201-209-1798. I know it is a long-distance call, so it may be hard for you to call me. I look forward to you writing back to me. Once again, I am sorry about the long delay in your letter, and I am sorry for how long it took me finally to write back to you.

Sincerely Yours,

Debbie Boatwright

I dropped the letter and smiled. I had not been a victim of rejection, but instead, I was a victim of poor service from the United States Postal Service!

I felt honored.

Oh, oh! Maybe the letter and the electric bill payment had not gone down into the mailbox.

Hmmm, Mum never mentioned anything to me, but I had better not bring that subject up!

The old man immediately targeted me at the dinner table that night, as he teased me about my new girlfriend, and Mum, of course, defended me. I did not mind. After all, Debbie had finally written me back, and I had stars in my eyes.

The next day, I wrote Debbie back with a reply letter. In fact, we wrote, and we wrote, and we wrote. . ..

"Well, it does not look like much, does it, Paul? In fact, right now, it is a big hunk of junk, but hey, it is *my* big hunk of junk!" Harry laughed and smiled as he and I stood outside of his house in front of 20 John Street in Haledon, New Jersey. It was late May 1975, and we were looking at the first car that Harry had ever purchased. In fact, it was the first car that either of us had ever bought. I was saving my pennies for a vehicle and I had my eye on a used telephone service van that I had seen in the weekly auctions in downtown Paterson. I was still a few dollars short, but the old man promised he would take me to the auction once I had saved up the dough.

Harry's dog Cocoa, who was our constant companion as well as the world's smartest dog, sat on the sidewalk, watching and listening to us. As usual, he had his faithful squeaky toy, Piggy tucked safely in the grip of his mouth.

The car was a 1971 Takajunky Model 10, and Harry had picked it up for two hundred bucks, from some guy who lived around the corner from me on Tilted Hill. In all honesty, it was not a bad looking car for a seventeen-year-old guy to have purchased for his first vehicle. It was not exactly sporty, but it was practical. It was a four-door sedan, painted in a fairly ugly tan color, but it had good tires, low miles, (we classified any vehicle in our neighborhood that had less than two hundred thousand miles on it, as having low miles) and a clean interior. Even the seats did not have any tears in them. Overall, it was not that bad of a car, except for one small detail. Right at this particular moment, the car did not run.

Harry had just obtained his driver's license, and I was a few weeks away from taking the test to obtain mine. Right now, I was driving on a learner's permit. We both were firmly embroiled in the car, truck, hockey, and young ladies' phase of our lives now; indeed, it was a small circle of interest in which we kept these days.

That was all we thought about, and all we did.

We both were in a trade school and we had part-time jobs while we both were apprentices at our trades. Harry was working in Mr. Redmond's metal shop as a welder and steel fabricator, and I worked in an electric and electronics shop as a junior technician, and all around, "step and fetch."

We both felt we were on our way to success now!

"Yeah, yeah, yeah, I barely got it here from over in front of that bum's house who sold it to me, and the engine rattled and conked out. Now, the piece of junk will not start, it just makes a ticking noise and then dies out," Harry fervently complained, as he lifted the hood of the car and together, the two of us peered into the engine compartment. I heard Cocoa whimper when he heard that the engine had died out. Like I had said, Cocoa was the world's smartest dog, and he understood most everything that you said.

"Well, it could be the battery, Harry. I do not know that I have ever seen a foreign car under the hood, let alone a car from Japan. However, I sure learned a lot about working on cars, from working with the old man on our 1964 Putter Classic model 200 every weekend for the last ten years. Climb in and give it a try. I will watch and listen under the hood, while you try to start it."

"All right, twenty-seven. I will be pretty ticked at that bozo, if I wasted two hundred bucks on this pile of junk and it has some kind of major problem," Harry complained as he climbed in the car to start the engine. "Your old man warned me not to buy a car made in Japan, but I did not listen to him. Maybe I should have, he sure knows his cars."

I shrugged my shoulders while Harry climbed into the Takajunky and turned the ignition key.

"CLICK!" The engine made one big clicking noise. I spotted the pulley on the fan belt give a slight spin, and then it stopped.

I leaned out from under the hood, moved my long blonde hair out of my eyes, and yelled to Harry, "Turn the headlights on!" Harry nodded, and I leaned over to see the headlights burning bright and clear.

Oh, no! The battery is good. This does not look so good.

I pulled the oil dipstick out and the oil looked like varnish dripping from the stick. I smelled it, and it had a terrible odor. The residue on the dipstick smelled as if it was a mixture of burned oil and turpentine.

This was not good.

The big guy will blast off to the moon without a rocket ship when he hears the news. Not to mention, he will probably march back to the guy who sold him the Takajunky and beat him to a pulp.

I heard the radio playing inside the car and I walked over to see what Harry was doing. He was fiddling with the radio knobs and pushing buttons. Cocoa had jumped up inside the car and he tossed Piggy on the passenger seat next to him as he listened and watched Harry fiddle with the radio in the Takajunky.

"It does not start, but it sure has a cool radio, Paul. Watch this work if you find a station that you like . . . say this one here." Harry tuned it to the local radio station broadcasting the New York Bugs baseball game, and he hit the button. "Now watch. I will hit it again, and it will find another baseball game automatically!" Sure enough, the little dial indicator went up and down the radio dial until it found another baseball game. The radio stopped on that game and belted out the broadcast. "Neat radio, huh? The radio is an auto selecto! Look, the antenna even goes up and down too! Fantastic stuff," Harry was excited about the high-tech radio in his new Takajunky and he was remaining optimistic but too bad the car would not run.

He looked up at me and he must have sensed my less than buoyant demeanor was because his vehicle would not start.

"Why so gloomy? What do ya think, Paul? Is it just the battery?"

I tried a diversion.

"Cool radio, Harry, and a really neat antenna too! The interior is nice, not even a tear in any of the seats."

"Ya did not answer the question, Paul."

"Well, I dunno. I think the . . . engine . . . well, it seems like it is seized up."

Harry's eyes popped out of his head, and steam blew out of his ears! He rose up out of the driver's seat with his face turning red and his fists clenched.

Oh, no! This was not going to be good!

I attempted a last-ditch effort to diffuse the situation and to prolong the life of the chap over on Tilted Hill.

"Look Harry, I am not really sure, I am not an expert. I could be wrong. It just sounds and acts like an engine that my Uncle Ed had one time in some old pile of junk that he bought. When I went with the old man to check it out, the old man figured out his engine had seized up. However, this is a Japanese car, and I might be wrong. My Uncle Ed's car made a terrible banging and thumping noise under the hood before it stopped running. What did the Takajunky do before it stopped, Harry?"

Harry looked at me and screamed, "Oh, it just made these terrible banging noises and then a big thumping noise under the hood, Paul. That is all!"

Oops, wrong word selection there, twenty-seven.

"Oh well, I still could be wrong, Harry."

"Stupid, con artist, son-o-a-bitch! I am going back over there to get my money back and squeeze the living hell out of his face!"

I watched Cocoa pick up his Piggy, and he took off for the backyard of Harry's house. He did not want to be around when his master blew his cool.

"Whoa, easy there, big guy, let's see if we can get my old man to look at it first before you go doing something to land you in jail for six months."

"Six months, Paul? Oh no, I am thinking more like life in prison after I inflict some serious pain on this guy! Where is my hockey stick? I am going to butt end his face in!"

Just as Harry was losing his cool, we heard the big

engine of Mr. Porter's 1969 Galaxy Super Glide 500 roar up John Street as he turned the corner from Belmont Avenue. Mr. Porter was Harry's neighbor who lived at 30 John Street. He also was the father of our mutual friend, Jeff Porter. Jeff was always hanging around with us, until about six months ago, when he had taken up with a steady girlfriend. It had turned into a serious relationship, and although we still played some hockey on occasion with Jeff, he was either working, or he was with his new gal, and we did not see him as much as we once did.

Mr. Porter parked his car in front of 30 John Street, jumped out of the car, bellowed to his wife that he was home, and happily strode over to where Harry and I were standing. He was Cocoa's favorite person in the entire world, and the only known person who could get away with not having to engage in a sixty-two-hour game of "Fetch the Piggy." As soon as Cocoa heard the engine of his car roaring up the street, he was sitting on the sidewalk next to Harry and me. Mr. Porter always greeted us the same way for as long as we had known him, and this go around was not going to be any different. He carried in his left pocket some dog treats for Cocoa, and in his right pocket, he had a large brass bullet with the insides removed. Mr. Porter had drilled a hole in the bullet and hung his keys through the hole. Mr. Porter had been a radio operator and waist gunner on B-25 bombers in World War Two and his experiences stayed with him forever.

That story, dear reader, is for another time and place.

"Hey youse guys, bite the bullet," Mr. Porter said as he flipped a dog treat to Cocoa, and showed us his "key chain."

"Why so glum there, boys, you both look like you lost your teeth in a hockey game. Did you lose them?" he asked.

Since that was a realistic question, we knew we needed to answer it factually. We both shook our heads, and indicated that, "No" that our choppers were intact, for now.

Mr. Porter then noticed the Takajunky with the hood open and he put two and two together. He flipped Cocoa, another dog treat, while gazing at the Takajunky.

"Hmm . . . a new, used, car . . . or what appears to be a car, not bad looking, but something tells me that she is not running."

Harry moaned, folded his arms across his chest, and sat on the edge of the open engine compartment. He looked at the three of us and said, "Yeah, yeah, yeah, Mr. Porter. I just bought it this afternoon, from some clown over on Tilted Hill for two hundred bucks, and it seemed as if it ran solid. I heard a little knock in the engine but the charlatan said that it was normal for these Japanese engines. I bought it and when I got the car over here, it conked out. Paul seems to think that the engine has seized, so right now, this is just a pile of junk."

"Oh, I see. Tilted Hill, huh? Not too much good comes out of working a deal over on Tilted Hill. Now, Harry, I would think that a street-smart guy like you would have known that by now. I swear the older you two, and my boy Jeff get, the less brains, youse guys have. Anyway, I am sorry to hear about your luck. I think Paul's old man would be the guy to check it out for you, Harry. Everyone knows he is the best mechanic in the neighborhood. Did you call the old man to come over and check it out yet, Paul?"

"I will call him right now. He should be done with his dinner, and maybe, if he has not had too many Big Boulder beers, I can convince him to come over and check it out."

Mr. Porter nodded and said, "Well, sorry that I cannot help you boys, but engines are not my area of expertise. I am a flyer! My specialty is flying on low-altitude bombers, waist gunning, and being a radio operator in the big one! Engines that will not run, no, however, bombs over Europe, oh yeah! Right now, since there are no bombers available, I deliver fish in my seafood truck! I will see you boys later. In the meantime, bite the bullet!"

We waved goodbye to the always jovial Mr. Porter while he headed back to his house. Cocoa barked twice to say goodbye to his dog treat tossing pal. I walked inside of Harry's house and used his telephone to call my home, to see if I could convince the old man to come over and help Harry with the final diagnosis.

Two rings and the telephone picked up.

"Yeah, whadda ya want?"

"Hey Dad, it is me, Paulie."

"Yeah, yeah, yeahhhh, what's the matter? Did you lose another tooth in a hockey game? Do ya need stitches? C'mon over, I will get the needle and thread out of the drawwwah. I ain't paying that rip-off artist and thief, Dr. Salami, anymore dough for stitches!"

"Nah, nah, no games today, no lost choppers, and no stitches needed today. I had school and then I was working my regular job. Say, Dad, I was wondering if you had a minute or two if you could come over to Harry's house. You see, he bought a car today, and it is giving him some troubles. I checked it out and I think it is serious."

"Check out a car, huh? What kind of car did he buy?"

I paused for a second since I knew that foreign cars were not the old man's favorite thing. After the pause for courage, I piped in quickly, "Ah, it is one of them Takajunky sedans."

I waited for the explosion.

"TAKAJUNKY! Those are rice boxes! They are piles of junk! I told Harry not to buy one of those foreign heaps of junk. Do you two realize how many jobs are being lost in this country because of those crummy imports coming over here? They are recycled garbage cans, ya know. We send them junk steel and they make cars out of them. Years later, when they crush up those heaps of junk, they make garbage cans out of 'em again! What is wrong with this pile of junk?"

"Well, Dad, Harry said it was making some noises when he bought it, and when he got it home, it conked out. I think the engine is seized."

"Where did he buy it?"

"Some guy over on Tilted Hill."

I heard the old man sigh a long sigh on the telephone and he chuckled a little.

"What did he expect? Nothing good comes out of working deals over on Tilted Hill with some con artist clown. Wait 'til his old man and Ronzo get home. Harry's old man will kick his ass all over John Street. I swear youse guys, the older ya get, the less brains ya have!"

There was another patented, long sigh from the old man, to emphasize how inconvenient this was, to ask him to work on a "rice box" after a hard day's work, and cut into his Friday night, Big Boulder beer and the baseball game time.

I knew better.

He was not fooling me because I knew the old man's spirit. In fact, there was nothing that the old man enjoyed more than a battle with some old pile of junk in an attempt to revive it. My old man was the best backyard mechanic in the entire neighborhood, and his weekend battles with his 1964 Putter Classic model 200 were the basis of folklore and legends. He had rebuilt the car piece-by-piece from the ground up, not to mention that he had also glued the rusty body together, with mountains upon mountains of cans of epoxy.

Of course, I could not see him as we spoke on the telephone, but I knew right now his eyes were going back and forth in his head, he was licking his lips, and reaching for his greasy, New York Bugs baseball hat that he used when he went into, "car battle" mode.

"Ya know, the Bugs are playing the Flying Saucers tonight and Jim Beaver is pitching. You two dopes are cutting into my baseball and Big Boulder beer time here, (another long sigh and a dramatic pause) because you and that big goofball Harry do not listen. All right, I will grab my Substantial Industries tools and be over in a few minutes. Tell Cocoa that I ain't playing, any Piggy games will ya."

"Will, do. Thanks a million, Dad."

"Click." I heard him hang up the phone.

I went out the front door of 20 John Street, and bellowed to Harry, who was standing near the Takajunky waiting for my answer, "The old man is on the way!"

I rejoined Harry, and since I was not sure that he had heard me (because a huge crowd of neighbors now surrounded him) I told him again that my old man had agreed to come over as soon as he picked up his tools. I then warned him that the old man would beat him like a drum for buying a Takajunky. I looked around and noticed that we now had quite a crowd gathered around the Takajunky. A "new" car in our old, gritty neighborhood was a big deal.

Cocoa heard me mention that the old man was coming over, and he picked up his Piggy in hopes of enticing him into a game of fetch. Since Cocoa was the world's smartest dog and understood every word you said, I figured I better set the record straight right away.

"Sorry Cocoa, my dad has to work on the car. He will not be able to play any Piggy with you tonight."

Cocoa whimpered a little, dropped Piggy on the ground, barked twice, and wagged his tail three times to indicate that he understood.

The people of our neighborhood had returned home from work, it was a nice, cool, early summer evening, and folks were coming out to see what Harry had wasted, I mean spent, his hard-earned two hundred bucks on by investing in foreign cars.

Harold Clipclock came over; Joe Hinky-Doo came over

too, right after he took some time off from selling suspicious materials and "smokes" from his "ice cream" truck, the Nit-Nat kid's old man appeared, along with Mr. Manger, who was a stonemason and lived over on Geyer Street. Cricket Ware and Mr. Len also wandered over to check out all the excitement. Mr. Porter came back out of his house and along with Billy Healy, the two of them walked over to stare at the broken-down car. Soon, all the men were sipping cold beers, sympathizing with Harry over the pile of junk that he had bought, and they were all waiting for the old man to arrive.

Harry sighed when he spotted his old man rolling up 20 John Street in his big, four-door sedan as he was arriving home from the shop, followed by Harry's brother-in-law Ronzo, driving his prize 1967 rally sport Sonicmobile, with white racing stripes, the famous rally package wheels, and a crossed racing flag's logo on the front grille. What a car!

The entire crowd knew what was coming next, and although we had sympathy for poor Harry, it was still going to be painful. Mr. Redmond was a jovial guy. I only witnessed him one time ever become angry or yell, but he did have a way when you really blew it, of being, how shall we say, forceful in getting his point across!

"Hello! Wow, what a surprise! We have a party going on here in front of the house," Mr. Redmond said with a wide smile on his face. "What is this? Harry, did you buy a car without telling anyone? It looks foreign!"

Ronzo popped out of his sports car, took one look at the Takajunky, shook his head, and laughed as he gave his opinion, "That is one of those Takajunky cars. In fact, that is how I usually see them, alongside of the road with their hoods up!"

Harry mustered up a futile but brave defense, "Yeah, yeah, yeah, I bought it today, Dad, from some guy over on Tilted Hill, and now it won't start. Mr. Henson is on his way over to check it out, but it does not look good."

Mr. Redmond shook his head, tugged at his wavy, white hair and shook his large jowls, "Tilted Hill! Since you were a little jerk, I told you never to buy anything from anyone on Tilted Hill. Harry! Harry! Harry! Geez! Nothing good comes out of deals on Tilted Hill. It is full of thieves, thugs, hoodlums, and charlatans. Now that you are a big jerk, I swear the older you get, the less brains you have."

I think Mr. Redmond, Mr. Porter, and my old man must have compared speech notes.

"How much did you blow on this pile of junk?"

"Two hundred bucks, Dad."

Ronzo laughed, and Mr. Redmond shook his head.

"Did you go with him, Paul?"

Rather reluctantly, I shook my head no, indicating that I was not part of the dubious purchase and selection of the poor Takajunky. I disliked not supporting Harry in his moment of need, but I knew in my heart that I had to tell the truth.

Sorry Harry, but I was an honest teenager.

"No sir, I just found out about it when I came home from school and work today."

Mr. Redmond shook his head and spoke, "Well . . . Harry, why you would not bring Paul with you, is beyond me. At least, he would have steered you correctly."

On and on it went with a big, long lecture from both Mr. Redmond and Ronzo, while the growing crowd shook their heads in sympathy at Harry's plight.

Harry's sister Patty and his brother-in-law George (a.k.a. the Big Spike) arrived, and his oldest sister Linda (a.k.a. Linny) distributed beers and snacks to the now anxious crowd as they waited for the arrival of the old man. There was nothing that the Redmonds enjoyed more than a party, even if the cause of it was at Harry's expense for buying a pile of junk for two hundred bucks.

The news of Harry's purchase and ensuing troubles was spreading like a giant wildfire throughout the entire John

Street neighborhood. Mr. Orsini, who was the manager of the Foodworld on the corner stopped by when he heard the news, the butcher who worked for him also showed up after his shift ended, Mike the plumber rolled by, the homeless guy who lived in a box over on Geyer Street stopped by, and many others. Soon, a huge crowd had gathered in front of 20 John Street, all to see what the fateful outcome of Harry's ill-advised purchase was going to be.

Then we heard it, the gentle whir of an engine, somewhat similar to the sounds that a lawn mower engine would make, and then an occasional backfire in the distance. A slight whiff of burning oil and unburned fuel floated in the air, and we could hear some occasional, hollering, and yelling as a faint, "Move over and park that pile of junk, you stupid-ass," drifted through the air over in the distance. I knew that meant that some poor soul was stuck behind my family car, and finally, the irate driver was able to pass.

All these signs pointed to the arrival of the old man as he was behind the wheel of his beloved 1964 Putter Classic model 200 automobile. A quiet hush came over the huge crowd while we all turned to look towards the street corner of John Street and Belmont Avenue. Sure enough, amongst a few loud, "Here comes, Mr. Henson," and, "It's the old man," floating within the crowd, we watched as the 1964 Putter Classic model 200 turned onto John Street.

A long cry of blaring car horns, followed by car drivers screaming obscenities out their windows, arose. A line of cars that had backed up behind the Putter for twenty miles and ended downtown in front of City Hall in the city of Paterson roared by the old man as he turned off the main roadway. The old man shook his fist out the window at the drivers and fought back gallantly at the insults in the true, northern New Jersey fashion.

Up the road, he rolled, his mouth and entire face

frowning, his greasy New York Bugs cap on his head and his two hands gripped the top of the steering wheel, while he hunched over the wheel in residual anger at the verbal thrashing. The crowd parted like Moses moved the Red Sea, and they watched as he parked the Putter in front of the world famous 20 John Street. He shut off the engine, and it rattled to a stop, while the car coughed up a bomb of blue smoke and some puffs of smoked oil, and the driver's door swung open in a long, loud, painful squeak.

The old man had arrived!

2

It Lives!

The old man stepped out of the Putter, closed the door behind him, walked to the trunk of the car and lifted it open. He took a wooden stick that he kept in the trunk and propped the lid of the trunk open, (the hold open hinges had been broken for years. But why spend the money for them, when a stick worked just as well?) and he pulled out of the trunk, his trusty Substantial Industries, Super Deluxe, Whiz-Bang tool kit.

"Hey Dad, thanks for coming over," I greeted my old man. The old man nodded and said hello to the two hundred people who had now gathered around 20 John Street. He was like the sheriff in the old Wild West, riding into town on his white horse with a white ten-gallon cowboy hat on his head.

"Yeah, yeah, yeah. Whatever. Man, oh man, what are all of these people doing here, don't they know Jim Beaver is pitching tonight?" Cocoa came running over without Piggy; he did not want to risk getting the old man mad at such a critical moment.

"Hey Paul, do you want a Big Boulder beer or a Dingleberry?" Ronzo shouted as he stood over the cooler that Linny and Patty had set up on the sidewalk.

"Let me have a Big Boulder there, Ronzo. Those Dingleberries are way too sweet for me." Ronzo nodded, pulled a Big Boulder out of the ice and brought it over to the old man. After greeting everyone, shaking hands with Mr. Redmond, Mr. Porter, petting Cocoa, and greeting the rest of the gang, the old man turned to Harry.

Here it comes!

"What the hell is this bullshit, Harry? A foreign heap of junk!"

"Thanks for coming over, Mr. Henson. I know that I should have listened to you, and everyone else, about buying one of these foreign jobs, but it seemed like a good deal," Harry did his best to present a repentant spin on his already hopeless situation.

The old man looked at him, took a long sip of beer, and began his long speech. On and on he went as he pulled his tools out and set up his battle station. Lost jobs, rice box cars, junk made overseas, hard to get parts for, special tools, come back as garbage cans, on and on it went. Once the old man latched on to a subject, it was guaranteed to be long, drawn out, and painful.

This speech was no exception.

To Harry's credit, he took it like a man.

"Well, other than a pile of junk, let's see what we have here. Harry, one thing it ain't, is a good deal," finally the old man was ready, his eyes rolled a little in his head, he licked his lips, and I could tell that he was ready for battle. The crowd gathered in and watched as the old man hovered over the engine of the Takajunky. The Nit-Nat kids scampered up trees and hung from branches, in order to get a better look over the scene from higher up. The neighborhood beat policeman stopped by to see what was happening, and the battle was on.

"Hmm . . . oil stinks like turpentine, valve cover gasket is shot . . . ya got robbed, Harry, absolutely robbed. Hand me my big screwdriver, Paulie. Tie all that mop of your hair up will ya, it is getting in my eyes."

I pulled a hair tie out of my pocket and tied my long hair back while I handed the old man his giant screwdriver. We watched as he popped off the main drive belt and wiggled the pulley with his hands.

"Harry, jump ya lard ass in there, and see if you can crank this thing that youse guys keep insistin' is a car." Harry nodded, climbed in, and turned the key.

"CLICK!" Nothing.

A loud moan floated through the crowd. The old man shook his head, took the big screwdriver, and jammed it into the main pulley. He then motioned for me to grab a hold of it.

"Put your big mitts on it, Paulie, and pull down. You have the strongest hands in the world. See if you can turn that pulley even a little."

I nodded, grabbed the screwdriver, and yanked on it with all my strength. Sure enough, it moved, but not very much. The old man shook his head, leaned back into his Big Boulder beer, and took a long sip. He studied the situation for a few moments as the tension built. He then walked to the trunk of the Putter and we could see him moving things around and making noises as he looked for something he had in the stash in his trunk. The old man always traveled with a rolling stock of auto parts, tools, and supplies that would rival the greatest pit crews of any racetrack. The 1964 Putter Classic model 200 was slightly unreliable; therefore, he was always prepared to perform roadside repairs at any time.

Not a soul in the huge crowd asked him what he thought, or said a word, since the doctor was at work and no one wanted to risk disturbing him. The old man stood up as he apparently had found what he was looking for. He walked back from the Putter carrying two precious cans of Big Bob's, Special Secret Mystery, Lube-O-Oil, a large, heavy, lump-hammer, along with his beloved Substantial Industries, heavy-duty jumper cables. He turned the oil cap off the engine of the Takajunky and poured the contents of the cans down inside the engine.

The old man replaced the drive belt, looked at his watch as if he was timing something, and then said to Harry, "Get back in there and wait for my signal."

He then turned toward Mr. Porter and asked, "Say, Bill, can you pull that big Galaxy Super Glide 500 over here with that huge battery, and park it next to this piece of junk. I want to hook up my jumper cables to that big battery of yours."

Mr. Porter nodded and motioned for Cocoa to follow him. Cocoa loved nothing more than to be involved somehow in the action. Cocoa grabbed Piggy and the two of them were off. Quick as a flash, the big Galaxy with Mr. Porter at the wheel and Cocoa in the passenger seat, had been pulled up next to the Takajunky. The hood was open, and the jumper cables were hooked up to the Takajunky's small battery.

Ronzo brought another Big Boulder beer over and the old man popped the top off the can and took a sip. He looked at his watch, placed the beer can down on the ground, swung the lump hammer, and struck the face of the main drive pulley with a solid blow.

He looked over the hood and yelled, "Hit it, Harry!" Harry turned the key. The crowd leaned in, and held their breath, and we listened and we watched.

POW! POW! POW! The Takajunky engine turned over slowly, it cranked, backfired, and a huge bomb of dark, black smoke blew out the exhaust pipe. The smoke knocked over ten or twenty people and two Nit Nat kids, who were standing behind the car, before floating up into the air in a dark, black fog.

That cloud of black smoke still hangs over Paterson, New Jersey to this day.

The engine sputtered to life and knocked, clanked and clinked, but it ran. The entire crowd erupted in a deafening roar of claps and cheers. Hats were thrown in the air, Cocoa barked in celebration and tossed Piggy in the air, beer cans were touched together in celebration, and handshakes and back slaps were in order. Immediately, since it was a Friday night, Mr. Redmond ordered the barbeque grille fired up, and the big chief himself ordered a huge celebration cookout to begin. In typical Redmond fashion, the party would last well into the next afternoon. In a few short weeks, the swimming pool in the Redmond's backyard would open, and Harry's Resort will be once again, rocking and rolling for summer. Right for now, due to the resurrection of the Takajunky, a spontaneous celebration would suffice.

The Takajunky lives!

The old man was a hero, and he received a standing ovation and congratulations from the huge crowd.

Telegraph keys and news teletypewriters pounded crazily while they sent messages across America. Frantic newscasters on radio and television newscasts interrupted regular programming coast-to-coast, while the news broadcasts announced that the Takajunky lives. The United States Navy's Sixth Battle Group, afloat in the Pacific Ocean off the coast of Japan, received their orders to back off and now to turn away. The President himself, on the red hotline in the Oval Office, gave the order to stand down, and not to blow up the Takajunky factory off the map, for producing a pile of junk out of used trash cans, and sending it over to us here in Paterson, New Jersey.

Harry was thrilled, "Thanks, Mr. Henson! Thank you so much."

"Way to go, Dad," I said while I shook my father's hand. My dad was always my hero, and tonight, I was very proud of him.

"Yeah, yeah, yeah, well, ya owe me a can of Big Bob's, Special Secret Mystery, Lube-O-Oil there, Harry. Ya can only get it down at Sal Zucchini's store, and ya better hurry because it is summer now, and he will be pushing the tools aside and bringing out the swimming pools as a front to hide his normal operations," the old man said as he flipped the empty metal can to Harry, who caught it and studied the label.

"Sure, Mr. Henson. Tomorrow is Saturday and twenty-seven and I will be there first thing in the morning to buy you a bunch of cans! Thanks, again."

"Yeah, yeah, yeah, well, you better dump the oil and change it after a day or so, save your pennies too, because this engine is on its last gasp. Ya had better drop those cans off tomorrow or I am coming after you. I am heading home to watch the ballgame. I will see you, birds. Thanks for the beer, and next time, listen to me and buy American!"

I helped the old man gather his tools and gear. The old man, swigging the last drop of his beer, spoke with Ronzo, Mr. Redmond, and Mr. Porter, and accepted their congratulations for a job well done. We put all the tools and supplies in the trunk of the Putter, and the old man climbed in. A wave out the window, a turn of the key, a cough of blue smoke, a push of the button of the automatic transmission, a soft whir of the engine, and he was off at about five miles per hour, rolling into the sunset of a fabulous, early summer night.

The true American hero had confronted the foreign enemy, and the old man had won the battle.

In the distance, we could hear the blaring of the car horns, and yelling of obscenities out on Belmont Avenue as the old man turned onto the main road, gunned the engine, hit the Putter's top speed of about ten miles per hour, and he disappeared from our sight.

The old man's voice floated in the air, "Up ya ass, jerk! I *am* gunnin' the engine!"

3

Workin' a Deal

Saturday morning came, and bright and early, Harry and I were in the Takajunky, rolling down Tilted Hill making our way towards Sal Zucchini's famous, "store."

Now, of course, ever since the now famous "exploding pool" incident of Harry's Resort, we all had a special place in our hearts for Sal Zucchini and his "store." We were well versed in the ways of our little, New Jersey world. We knew that Sal was the one person that you did not ask many questions about, or speculate to others about the true nature of his business. After all, Sal's store was located in the heart of the heavily, Italian-American section of Paterson, known as the Riverside Section. Sal sold swimming pools for the summer, and tools, and various other "items" and parts for the rest of the year. His store was crawling with about four thousand Italian guys who were all wearing dark suits and sunglasses, so the actual nature of the operation, and who was the sponsor, was not really too difficult to figure out.

The Takajunky was running, but the engine sounded like a popcorn machine, or an even better description, was that it sounded like little "pops" of small caliper gunshots under the hood. The other interesting trouble was with the doors of the vehicle. We had noticed that when you hit a bump or other significant obstacle that made the car bounce, all the doors would fly open. Harry easily repaired the back doors by passing some rope through the handles to keep those doors closed, but the front ones we did not want to tie, for fear of not being able to escape in an emergency. We kept our hands on the inside handles, and once you were accustomed to the situation, it was rather easy to control.

The Takajunky had some interesting nuances, however, the radio was indeed very cool!

Harry turned the Takajunky into the parking lot of Sal Zucchini's store and slowly made his way to one of the front parking spots.

We immediately noticed two or three of the advance scouts of Sal's operation running across the lot at full speed, in full panic mode, and two of them crouched down behind a parked car. The other man was reaching inside of his suit jacket, as he too was running full speed across the front sidewalk of the store, then he dove behind a big, black, Galaxy 4000 sedan parked in front of the store! I elbowed Harry and screamed frantically when I realized that the Takajunky was attracting a lot of attention due to the suspicious noises coming out from under its hood.

"SHUT IT OFF! SHUT IT OFF! HARRY, THEY THINK YOUR CAR ENGINE IS GUNFIRE!"

Harry panicked when he realized what was happening, and he fumbled and bumbled, before he finally managed to shut off the engine. Slowly, the men peered out from behind their hiding places, when they had realized that the noises were nothing more than the hunk of junk engine rattling in misery under the hood of Harry's car.

We both breathed a huge sigh of relief.

Thank goodness, Sal's men did not "overreact."

We slowly opened the car door, made sure our arms and hands were fully visible, and made our way towards the front door. We were painfully aware of about fourteen thousand Italian guys in dark suits wearing sunglasses, who had descended from every nook and corner of the store and parking lot, to watch us very carefully. As we walked in the front door of the store, we ran straight into the familiar leader of the forward watch of Sal's operations. Even after all of these years, not much had changed. There he stood; it was the same large Italian guy, with jet-black hair, dressed in a fitted black suit and wearing dark sunglasses, even though he was inside. The only thing that was different now was that I was bigger than he was, and Harry was almost as tall as he was too.

The years had passed so quickly.

"Cannnahi helpah you?" The man asked with a thick accent. He then looked over the top of his sunglasses and we saw his face change.

Poof! Accent gone!

"Oh, Redmond Jr. and Henson. Youse guys had us shook up. Youse need to fix that car engine, man oh man, it is a . . . hazard. Hey, you two are getting so big."

I noticed that he held back a smile, and he waved at us to follow him.

He rambled a bit while we walked, "Henson, I hear you are becoming quite the hockey player there. No wonder youse are good. Henson, you are one big, strong, guy. I imagine we could use a guy like you and Redmond Jr. here in our . . . ah, ah, in our . . . store. We were expecting you. We just did not expect all that noise. How have youse guys been? How is your old man, Redmond Jr.?"

Harry quickly answered, "We are well. My old is too. Oh, I never did get your name?"

The large man ignored Harry's question.

"We just need a few cans of Big Bob's, Special Secret Mystery, Lube-O-Oil, mister big guy."

"Yeah, yeah, yeah, we know all about it, but Sal wanted to speak with youse guys when you showed up. He needs to work a deal with you. We are setting up the pools for the summer, but I will dig a few cans up for youse two guys, to replace the ones the old man used to get that pile of junk to run."

I looked out over the sales floor, which was actually a

large stripped out supermarket, with nothing but concrete and steel posts and row upon row of dreary fluorescent lights. There were about fifty or so workers, setting up various models of pools throughout the store. It looked the same as it did a few years ago, when we had shopped here to purchase the now famous exploding pool. The tools, auto parts, and other supplies had been all pushed aside for the summer. The big man waved for us to stop, and he disappeared behind a wall next to the main sales counter.

I was now panicking.

"Sal wants to work a deal with us, Harry? What kind of deal would Sal want with two, stupid dopes like us? This does not sound good, Harry," I tried my best to whisper, but I was afraid my nervousness was being overheard by Sal's henchmen.

"Calm down now, twenty-seven. Calm down and stop acting like such an old lady, will you! Do not go spinning off into old, lady land as you usually do. We are just here for a few cans of that Big Bob's oil stuff. Maybe Sal just wants to cut us a deal on them. Now calm down because here he comes."

Sure enough, from behind the wall, the man himself, Sal Zucchini, appeared! He looked the same as he did years ago. He was still a tall, lanky, older gentleman with a baldhead, dark, beady, black eyes, and a long, pointed nose. He was wearing a pair of black, thick-rimmed glasses. He nodded to us, sat down on his favorite stool at the end of the counter, and waved for us to come over. He then waved his hands in the direction of his right-hand man to indicate for him to go away. The big guy nodded to us and then to Sal, and he walked off towards the back of the store.

I was shaking in my work boots, and I am certain that Harry was, too. Sal looked at us over the top of his eyeglasses and his piercing stare went right through us.

He finally spoke, "Redmond Jr. and Henson. Nice to see

youse two guys. You need to fix that car of yours, Redmond Junior. It causes . . . unnecessary disturbances." Harry cleared his throat and went to speak, but Sal held his hands up to indicate that Harry should shut up, so Harry stopped cold in mid-voice.

When Sal Zucchini tells you not to speak, you listen.

"Look, I heard about the car deal that went down yesterday. This guy on Tilted Hill, this guy who sold you the car there, ah, Redmond Jr., he is, ah . . . how shall we say . . . he is now out of business. I had some of my boys stop by, and convince him that selling junk cars to teenagers who have very little extra money, and might just be down to their last nickel, was not exactly the career path that he should be following. When guys pull stunts like that in and around where I tend to do some business myself, it reflects very badly on us slightly, legitimate businessmen. I am sure youse understand."

We both nodded like stunned dopes as Sal continued.

"How is your old man doing, Redmond Junior?"

"He is fine, Sal, he is doing well, thank you."

"No more pool troubles?"

"No Sal, all is well."

"Cocoa and his Piggy are good?"

"Yes Sal, really good. We are going to take the cover off the pool this week, get ready for a big party on the weekend after Memorial Day. My dad, Ronzo, Mr. Porter, and Mr. Henson, all say Memorial Day is a day of honor, not a day for parties, so we always kick off the summer on the weekend after the holiday. My old man would like to see you, Sal. Please come by if you can."

Sal looked at Harry and smiled. He then waved his hands in the air and said, "Yeah, yeah, yeah, they are right about Memorial Day. You have to remember the heroes. That Mr. Porter guy is a real hero. A big, war hero, type guy. Your parents and your neighbors are all heroes. They take care of each other and they take care of their families, and their own lives. They are the most important people these days. A dying breed of people, who are good men and women, who work hard and keep old neighborhoods together. Honest people, who are kind and not mean-spirited. You cannot reward those kinds of people enough. Even Sal can never thank them for all they do every day. I try too, but I can never pay them back."

Sal's voice grew softer, and his eyes wandered away from us while he looked out over the sales floor of his establishment.

"I wonder what it will be like when they all move away, and youse guys grow up, and have families of your own? I wonder what the old neighborhoods will become?"

Sal looked at us with a stern look on his face, and I understood. This was the neighborhood where he lived and grew up, too. He loved it as well as the people who lived there, too. He was worried about the future evolution of the old neighborhood, and in looking back, Sal was correct in his prediction. In some strange way, he was the protector of all of it.

He continued with just the hint of a smile on his face, "You tell your father that Sal, says hello. He is one of the best—that father of yours. One of the best. It is a little difficult for me to go out in public these days. I do appreciate the invitation though. It is just when I travel, it is, how shall I say, a little cumbersome. I have to bring along my men and other stuff. I am sure you understand Redmond Junior. I would like to see him though and have a Big Boulder beer with him. Those Dingleberries that Ronzo drinks are a little too sweet for me."

Sal then looked at me.

I swallowed hard.

"Henson, how ya doing?"

"Fine, sir. Thank you."

"Big, strong, guy Henson. The word out there is that you are quite a hockey player too. Do you ever cut all that hair or shave, Henson?"

"No sir, not in a long time that is."

Sal nodded and rubbed his baldhead, and continued to speak, "Your old man is quite a mechanic. He is a good man, too. Hard worker. He never stops, but he always has time to help out people. He helps out people who are down on their luck. Youse two guys are lucky. Someday, you will realize how lucky you have been to have parents as you both have. You have the world by the balls, youse two guys. I hope you know that, men."

We both nodded.

Sal looked at both of us over the top of his glasses again, as he softly said, "Look, Sal needs to work a deal with youse two boys. I need your help with some jobs."

I swallowed hard, and I saw Harry swaying back and forth in his boots when he heard the words from Sal. This was unbelievable; Sal Zucchini was drafting the two of us into his operation! Visions of gunfights in dark Paterson alleys, and torturing people whom we had tied up to wooden chairs, and had lit matches stuffed under their fingernails, flashed in my head.

"I have some things, in which youse two guys can handle for me."

Oh, no!

"There are certain things that just do not cooperate with me or with my men anymore."

No cooperation. This was unreal!

I began to plot my escape. I could run fast. Faster than anyone here. I am sure that I could. However, what about poor Harry? The big guy was a lumbering oaf; he was not exactly fleet of foot. I could not leave him to a cruel fate of decimation at the hands of Sal and his henchmen. In addition, Sal would track us down for sure.

Sal stood up from his stool and he walked over to Harry and me. I could feel the tension in the air; I just did not dare steal a glimpse of Harry's face.

"I hear you boys are pretty good at the trades. The vocational school that you attend, as well as your fathers, have taught you well. I have this long, string of lights in my store that will not light up, and out on my loading dock, in my warehouse, I need this bolt welded on my dock plate. I think youse guys might be able to help me with these things. I have all the tools here that you need, even a welder. I just do not have anyone who can fix these things. My guys, they are good with certain things, but these types of tools are not exactly the kind of tools they use in their line of work. Can you boys help me out? I will make it worth your while."

Sal put his hand out for us to shake on the deal.

Whew!

What a relief, I thought it was the end of us!

Harry smiled and breathed a deep sigh of relief as he shook Sal's hand. I knew what the answer was going to be. There was no way that we would refuse Sal on a request like this one. In fact, on any request.

"Sure Sal, sure thing. We would be glad to help you out. Right, Paul?" I nodded my head and smiled as I carefully shook Sal's hand. I had a habit of shaking people's hands really hard and hurting them, so in the interest of self-preservation, I was very gentle with Sal Zucchini.

"Good, good, let me show you back here," Sal said while he waved for us to follow him to the back of the store. There, under the watchful eye of the numerous henchmen of Sal's operations, we examined the broken bolt on the loading dock plate.

After studying the broken piece for a while, Harry looked at Sal and told him, "This is nothing, Sal. A quick zip of the welder and I can fix this. Where is the welder?" Sal nodded at Harry, looked at one of his men, and snapped his fingers. Within seconds, a welder, some hand tools, a slag hammer, some welding sticks, and a helmet appeared. Two of Sal's men were pushing it into the location on a four-wheel dolly cart. They plugged it in, and Harry went to work.

Sal looked at me. "While Redmond Junior fixes the plate, come with me, Henson. I will show you the lights that do not work," Sal waved to me as he spoke. I nodded and followed him back onto the sales floor. About ten or fifteen of Sal's men followed behind us, all dressed in the same dark suits, with sunglasses on and emotionless expressions on their faces. Sal led me through rows upon rows of workers, assembling pools on the concrete floor as he readied his store for the upcoming summer season. Soon Sal's "workers" would fill the pools with water, the store would smell like strong chlorine, and the pool season would be well underway. We stopped under a long row of fluorescent light fixtures, in which not one single light bulb was lit up, along the entire stretch. All the other rows of lights in Sal's store burned brightly, but this row was dead as a doornail.

Sal pointed up at the unlit lights and said, "Here it is, Henson. Whadda need to fix it? If you are half the mechanic that your old man is . . . then this will be easy. Then again, if you cannot get the job done, then, I guess I do not need you, and I will take some other course of action." Sal stared at me intently as I looked up at the lights. Immediately, beads of sweat appeared on my forehead, and I felt them rolling down my face.

Oh, no! Sal does not need me!

Another course of action! I become disposable!

I had a vision of my feet cast in cement shoes, and Sal's henchmen throwing me into the Passaic River for failing on my light fixture repair mission. Oh, of course, Harry got the easy mission, welding some stupid little bolt.

The lucky stiff!

I had to receive the impossible scientific equation to solve.

Stay cool, Henson. You nailed your basic electricity

course with a one hundred percent on the final exam, think you dope. THINK!

I stammered and stuttered, "I—I—ah, need an electrical tester and a ladder. Maybe a screwdriver. . .."

Instantly, with a nod of the head, Sal's men brought the requested items. I kept forgetting that Sal's "store" sold tools, and besides that, it seemed as if the entire world was at his fingertips.

How I wished that the local Foodworld carried Big Bob's Special Secret Mystery, Lube-O-Oil. All we wanted was to shop for some special oil for the old man, and now Harry and I were fighting for our very right to survive.

How does this stuff happen to us?

I walked along the light fixtures looking for where the power feed wire entered into the light fixtures. I was now saying a prayer under my breath, and ran through my mind, every single lesson that my electrical shop instructor, Mr. Grossi, had taught us. Sal folded his arms across his chest, stared, and scowled at me. And all of his henchmen surrounded me, while I set the ladder under a light fixture that had the power coming into it. I climbed the ladder, removed the light bulbs, then the cover, removed some wire nuts, and tested the power feeder with the meter. The power was there; of course, it could not be easy and just be a blown fuse, or a tripped circuit breaker! I came back down the ladder and moved on towards the next light fixture. The sweat was pouring off my forehead like a river.

Sal looked at me and softly said to me, "Getting a little warm in here, Henson. It is going to get a lot hotter. Very, very soon."

All of his men nodded their heads in agreement.

I feebly nodded while I tested the power in the next light.

Okay. No power here. As I studied the wires, I spotted a black wire loosely hanging out of a wire nut connector.

I looked down at Sal and asked, "Sir, could you please

shut down the light switch that controls these lights?" Sal nodded, snapped his fingers and instantly a henchman was dispatched to the light switch on the wall. He shut it off and pointed back to me.

I tested the wire to make sure it was void of power, carefully remade the connection, replaced the covers on the fixture, and then snapped the bulbs back in. I slowly came down the ladder, looked at Sal, then back to the henchmen, then my gaze went back over to the single henchman standing by at the light switch.

The tension was incredible!

I said a quick prayer and motioned to the henchman by the switch. Sal folded his arms across his chest. It may have been my mind playing tricks on me, but I imagined that all the other henchmen were reaching for something inside of their suit jackets!

I softly whispered, "Please, God. Genesis, please God, let there be. . .."

The henchman flipped the switch on and all the lights sprung to life! They all flickered and snapped, but they all were burning bright and strong. I exhaled a long sigh of relief and wiped the sweat off my forehead.

Sal broke into a huge smile and waved at all of his men. "Nice job, Henson, nice job. You are a hippie, but you are a smart guy. You and Redmond Junior, youse guys have a bright future."

All I could manage to say was, "Thank you, sir. I am glad that I paid attention in electric class."

Sal waved, and he led me back up to the front counter where I met up with Harry, who was waiting for me there. Harry leaned over and whispered, "Thank goodness, we paid attention in school."

I nodded in agreement. I spotted a two-wheel hand truck with two full cases of Big Bob's Special Secret Mystery, Lube-O-Oil stacked upon it.

Sal smiled at us and said, "Here, this is for youse guys."

Sal pointed at the hand truck. "Give this to the old man. This should hold him off for a bunch of junk cars that show up in your neighborhood."

I piped in, "Thank you, sir. How much do we owe you for the oil?"

Sal sat back down on his favorite stool at the end of the counter, put his glasses back on top of his head, and shook his head.

He then spoke, "Nothing. I owe youse guys, and I want to hold up my end of the deal. I know how tough it is out there these days, so I want to help you with this bad deal on this car. My boys will drop a gift off at your house later. I think we might be closer to being even then."

"Oh no, please, Sal, we will pay you for the oil. Paul and I were glad to help out. The oil is enough, you do not owe us anything," Harry smiled and waved his hand in the air.

Sal frowned and pointed his finger firmly at us, "If Sal Zucchini makes a deal, then Sal makes a deal. I stand behind everything I sell, say, and do. Youse guys are good boys, from good families, youse work hard for a few dollars, and you study hard in school. That is important, and I feel bad about that jahbonni who sold you that pile of junk. That is why my boys and I, how shall I say it . . . we adjusted the situation over there on Tilted Hill. Sal will take care of youse guys. If I can ever be of assistance, then you call Sal and my boys, and we will take care of you." All of his henchmen nodded their heads at the same time. Harry and I were dumbfounded, and we both did not know what to say.

I finally mustered up some words, "Thank you, sir, we appreciate it."

"Look, Henson!" Sal yelled at me and I jumped out of my work boots. "Stop calling me, sir! Ya are too polite! You are like an old lady or something. Just call me, Sal. Sal Zucchini."

He reached out his hand, gave Harry his business card,

and smiled as Harry and I both took turns shaking his hand. He playfully punched us both in our arms as we passed him. "Be cool, youse guys," was all he said to us.

We followed one of his men, wheeling the oil out to the Takajunky. When we got out to the Takajunky, the man dropped the oil at the trunk and waved to us. Harry dug in his pocket, pulled out some crumpled-up dollar bills, and he handed them to the man.

The man looked at the dollars and smiled. He waved back at Harry and said, "Nah. Keep it. Ya got no extra dough. Like Sal said, youse two are good guys."

He turned and left. Harry unlocked the trunk, and he dropped the cases of the Big Bob's oil inside and closed it. We climbed in the Takajunky and Harry started the car up. We were both too shell-shocked to speak. Harry put the car in gear; we rattled and popped our way out onto River Street and made our way towards home. I looked over at Harry and asked him, "Did you make sure you welded the bolt really well, thirty-five?"

Harry shook his head in acknowledgement, "Sure did. The best weld that I ever made, twenty-seven. You could drive a freight train over that bolt. How about you, did you make sure those wires were tight and will last forever?"

"You bet, Harry. Best connections that I ever made." Harry smiled at me and we shook hands. Even in the adventures of Harry and Paul, this was a good one, and looking back over the years, we sure had some winners!

"Paul, your old man is going to be thrilled. Two cases of that special Big Bob's oil, this is like winning a jackpot!"

Harry then became a little reflective as he said, "Paul, you are the smartest guy I know. What do you think really happened to the guy who sold me this hunk of junk car?" Harry looked at me out of the corner of his eye while he continued to drive.

"I have a feeling that it is just as Sal said. He is out of business, maybe, in more ways than just selling cars." I saw

Harry crack a suspicious smile while I continued a thought.

"Do you know something, Harry? This was all so strange. A guy like Sal, you know that he knows a million welders and electricians that he could get over there with a snap of his fingers. There is so much more to this than just him asking two dopes like us to work on stuff in his store. Sal was testing us in many ways."

"What do you mean, Paul?"

"It is more than just working and fixing something, Harry. Sal may be a mobster, but he has a heart of gold. He takes care of people who he believes are important, who are integral parts of the old neighborhood, and who he feels that, somehow, sort of take care of him. I am curious as to what the gift is that Sal mentioned." I rubbed my chin as I thought about it. I still had my long hair and to add to my hippie appearance, I now had added a full beard. I had developed the habit of rubbing my whiskers when I was deep in thought.

"Well, I sure hope it is not another swimming pool," Harry looked at me and smiled. He handed me Sal's business card and I read it. All the card had printed on it was, "Sal Zucchini, Businessman" and a telephone number.

I put the card in my wallet.

We had no idea what Sal meant by a gift, but we were about to find out.

Harry pulled up in front of 20 John Street to see Mr. Redmond, Cocoa, and Ronzo standing on the sidewalk in front of his house, staring at a big wooden crate. Harry shut the engine off and it rattled to a stop as it shut down. We climbed out of the car and walked over to where the crate was.

"Hey, youse guys! What did you buy that is in the crate?" Harry asked them as we approached.

Mr. Redmond smiled and said, "We did not buy anything. The question is what did youse guys buy? A big truck pulled up in front of the house a few minutes ago.

The driver came to our door. He only spoke Italian, but I was able to understand that it was from Sal Zucchini for Harrya Juniorinin! You just missed him. The truck just went around the corner when you two boys pulled up."

"Well, I'll be," Harry mumbled as we walked over to the crate and all of us bent down and examined the contents. We all peered in and checked out the crate, which was about three feet by four feet, and had all kinds of Japanese writing and labels stamped all over it.

"I will get a few hammers and some crow bars," Ronzo reported, and he was off in a flash to the basement workshop to pick up the tools. Ronzo returned, and with a few bangs and a few tugs, the crate opened up. We all stared inside and saw that the contents had a protective covering over them.

Still mystified at the contents, we all eagerly pulled the packing away and tossed it aside. We all stood back in shock and awe, as there in front of us was a brand new, 1.0 cubic inch, Takajunky engine!

"Wow! It is a new engine for the Takajunky!" Harry was overjoyed. He looked at me and smiled as he said, "And all we did was weld a little bolt and fix his lights, Paul!"

I smiled back at my best buddy while we shook hands.

No, somewhere deep in my heart, I knew it was payment with a special purpose, for so much more than just that.

4

Cruising

The old man was thrilled when I returned home with the free bonus of two full cases of the precious Big Bob's Special Secret Mystery Lube-O-Oil.

It was like Christmas Day to him!

He was even more amazed when we told him how we fixed some things for Sal Zucchini at his store and then returned home to find out that Sal had dropped off the new engine for the Takajunky. When he had sufficiently recovered from learning of Harry's good fortune, I then asked the incredibly profound question, which was the question that the old man had waited his entire life for someone to ask him.

"Say Dad, maybe tomorrow after church, could you help us put the new engine in the Takajunky?"

The old man was sitting in his chair preparing to watch the New York Bugs baseball game on channel eleven, and he smiled a wide smile and his eyes flickered. To someone like my old man, who had battled for years and years to resurrect what seemed as if it were an endless collection of junky, old bombs of vehicles, this was a dream come true. Instead of struggling for hours and hours, just to loosen some frozen bolt from the front of a seized water pump, or peeling off leaky gaskets from oil-soaked valve covers, or jacking up vehicles on wooden blocks and ripping rusty, crumbling, exhaust systems out of old wrecks, and a myriad of other thankless, vehicle repair tasks, the old man had arrived. Finally, the old man had found the golden path to car repair heaven.

He actually had an opportunity to work on something new! A brand-new engine! This was not just installation of a new part, this was an entire engine, and it was shiny, clean, and not dripping with leaky oil and grease! In the annals of the old man's battles with cars in our neighborhood, this was a first. It was unheard of in the long history of the old man's famous car battles. A luxury. A free toll on the highway of broken-down vehicles.

He sat in his chair, staring ahead into outer space after I had posed the question to him.

"Dad, did you hear me? Dad?"

The old man sprung back to reality. A heavenly vision appeared in front of the old man's eyes. He was a new man, and the excitement was reflected in his voice, "Sure, sure, sure. Yeah, yeah, yeah, sure. I will be glad to help youse two guys. It will be easy, a slam-dunk, that engine is light. It is no bigger than a lawn mower engine. We will use those Substantial Industries ropes and chains that Harry's old man has, and throw them over the big tree branch in front of Harry's house. It will be just as we did when Mr. Redmond rigged up that system to pull the pool parts off the big truck from the shop. Pull a few bolts from the motor mounts, loosen a round or two of bolts in front of the transmission housing, some cables for the battery, some random linkages, a ground wire, and we will be all set. You need fresh oil and antifreeze for the new engine, make sure youse guys have plenty of oil and coolant on-hand. They do not ship new engines with oil. Even youse dopey kids need to know and remember that! We will be done in two hours. It is a piece of cake."

The old man leaned forward in his chair; he rubbed his hands together in glee and continued skipping along the pathway to car repair heaven.

"When I was a sergeant in the motor pool in the United States Army, we used to pull engines all day long. Say, grab me a Big Boulder beer from the refrigerator, and let me tell you about the time we. . .."

I retrieved the beer for the old man, handed it to him, sat down, and smiled at the old man. He was in car repair heaven; the least that I could do was to listen to another story from his United States Army days.

The next day after church, the old man and I rode over in the 1964 Putter Classic model 200 to Harry's house, and we began the engine replacement project. A small crowd of the neighborhood folks had gathered, but since it was still early on a Sunday, a good majority of the neighbors must have still been in church, or were sleeping off an overly ambitious Saturday night.

The day before, after the old man had finished telling me his military stories (two hours' worth, by the way) he had instructed me how to loosen up the most important bolts for the engine mounts, and the transmission housing. Harry and I worked on the Takajunky the rest of Saturday afternoon, and we had the car all prepped for the doctor to arrive to direct the operation. Harry and I possessed considerable tool skills now, we could handle certain tasks, and both my old man and Mr. Redmond trusted us these days to handle some heavier labor. Harry had parked the Takajunky under the big tree in front of his house, and Ronzo, Mr. Redmond, Mr. Porter, Cocoa, (and Piggy) were waiting for us in front of the house. After some greetings and pleasant exchanges, the work was ready to begin. It was too early for any beer, but Linny had prepared some coffee, and you can bet that the beer was on ice for a Redmond "new engine" celebration party later on in the day. Any excuse was a good excuse for a party for the Redmonds, and a new engine installation fit the bill just fine!

The old man peered in over the exposed engine of the Takajunky and smiled. He rubbed his hands together in delight, his greasy New York Bugs hat perched upon his head, his eyes flipping back and forth in his head like windshield wipers in a thunderstorm.

He was ready. The crowd gathered in and waited. The old man started the checklist.

"Did you two bananas, loosen all the bolts that I told you to?"

"Check, Mr. Henson."

"Replace the motor mounts?"

"Check, Mr. Henson."

"Did ya two pineapples, pull the battery cables, the engine mount bolts, the gas pedal linkages, the whoosie I warned you about that links the engine to the newfangled, watch-a-may-digger part or whatever they call it in Japan, and the cables for the grounds?"

"Yup. We got the whoosie."

"Heater hoses going through the firewall, the fuel line, and the radiator hoses?"

"Ah man . . . twenty-seven, we missed the heater hoses!" Harry shouted to me while snapping his fingers.

"Ya guys are bums! I have to check everything!" A loud moan went up through the crowd as they agreed with the old man's assessment of our grave and profound mistake. In reality, the old man would have been disappointed if he did not find something, or he did not have a chance to swing the tools. A quick spin of his ratchet wrench, a pry, or two with a big screwdriver, and a blob of Big Bob's Death Grip Tape to hold the heater hoses tight and prevent spilling too much antifreeze, and the old man had the heater hoses loose and ready to go.

He then scanned the entire engine. His eyes were darting back and forth while checking every detail. He licked his lips, and he then pronounced it good to go! The old man called for the ropes and chains, and Mr. Porter and Cocoa jumped into action to bring the Porter's Galaxy Super Glide 500 into place on the other side of the tree branch.

If Mr. Porter ever sold his giant Galaxy 500 vehicle, we may be all stuck, and no one in our neighborhood would ever be able to perform any heavy labor again!

We carefully strapped the chains around the Takajunky engine, and then we threw the other ends of the chains over the big branch of the huge maple tree in front of 20 John Street. We hooked the end of the chains to the bumper of the Galaxy 500. When the old man and Mr. Redmond gave the signal, the Galaxy backed up, and with a quick pull; the old engine was free and lowered to the ground!

Mr. Redmond should have patented his lifting method for gritty, New Jersey neighborhoods.

We carefully strapped up the new engine, and we all watched in awe, as the power of the Galaxy 500, lifted the new engine off the ground, and by the strength of the ropes and chains tossed over the tree branch, it hung in the air waiting for installation into its new home. The new engine dangled precariously over the bare engine compartment, while the now growing crowd held their collective breath, and gasped as the old man-made last-minute checks on every detail. When he gave the signal, Mr. Porter pulled forward, and with the assistance of Harry, Ronzo, Joe Hinky-Doo, Mr. Redmond, and me, we slowly and carefully guided the new engine into place. Previously, the old man had set a small floor jack under the car, in the base of the engine compartment. He now used it to lift the engine up and make fine adjustments to the final position of the engine on top of the motor mounts. A few cranks, a grunt and groan, and a heave ho or two, and, "plunk" the engine was sitting happily inside the mounts.

The new engine was in the Takajunky compartment and all of us, including the crowd, erupted into loud cheers!

Under the direction of the old man, it did not take us too long to replace all the bolts, replace the whoosie part, the linkages, the hoses, the cables, and replace all the parts and items that we had disconnected off the old engine.

The old man was in his glory, directing the battle from his command center, waving his arms, pointing at parts, giving advice, and checking every detail. In between, he told stories, stories meant to teach as well as to entertain.

"One time, in the United States Army, we had this old jeep. It had a water pump that always leaked and it was one, big, pain in the ass. ..."

It was becoming very hot now, especially hot for late May, and we were all sweating and wiping our brows and faces as the work went on. Summer had arrived, along with the new engine.

Soon it was finished, and the old man checked and double-checked all the work and the fluid levels. He smiled a little as he pulled the dipstick and checked to make sure we had filled the new engine with fresh oil, and he checked for our supply of antifreeze. I handed him some jugs of the fresh coolant, and the old man beamed as he added the fluid to the system.

We had passed the test.

The moment of truth had arrived, the crowd gathered around, and a quiet hush went over the entire group. The old man made the signal to Harry and without saying another word; Harry nodded and climbed into the driver's seat of the Takajunky.

Once more America paused, and all eyes of the entire country focused upon 20 John Street in Haledon, New Jersey.

Harry turned the ignition key, the engine fired off right away, and within seconds, it was purring like a kitten! It ran steady, smooth, and quiet. The old man studied the engine functions, made Harry put it in gear and back up a little, and then he asked him to go forward. He had Harry shut the engine off and he crawled all over the engine compartment while checking for fluid leaks or any other signs of troubles. Underneath he went, and then up to the top of the engine he popped, and then back underneath the car, and we could see his flashlight peering into every nook and cranny of the mechanical madness. He stood up slowly, wiped his brow, pulled off his greasy New York Bugs baseball cap, and smiled. Still, the John Street crowd remained quiet, since the patient was still in surgery and the doctor had not yet finished the operation.

The old man seemed satisfied, but he conveyed an ominous warning to Harry, "What you need to remember Harry, is to listen to me for once in ya life. Now, I tell ya, to take it easy on this car. The engine is new and strong, but the rest of the car is still old. Often, a new engine will put an undue strain on other parts, particularly the transmission. Do not be a cowboy out there!" Harry nodded that he understood and the old man pointed his pointer finger at Harry to emphasize his advice.

After careful study, the old man had Harry turn the Takajunky back on and run it until the temperature gauge came up. He then checked and topped off the coolant levels. The old man checked the engine and dashboard gauges one more time.

He stood up from under the hood, smiled broadly, turned to the crowd, and raised both of his hands over his head in victory.

The crowd went wild! A glorious cheer resounded and echoed throughout the old neighborhood.

Let the engine installation party begin!

And party we all did. All the rest of the day and well into the night, as only the Redmonds, Porters, Hensons, and the rest of the John Street gang could. A new engine party! A first, even, in the world of the Redmonds. The laughter still hangs over 20 John Street to this very day, along with a few, now-forgotten, empty, faded, Big Boulder and Dingleberry beer cans that rolled under a hedge row.

Another wonderful lesson taught to us and we had to add this one to so many more.

All too soon, the thrill of the victory faded. Life went on once again, even after new engines, parties, empty beer cans and victories, involving large maple trees and ropes.

We attended a vocational school, and were now attending our academic classes during the first part of the day, and then we worked at our trades for the final half of the day. We were cruising into summer, school was winding down, we had jobs lined up for the summer, and the excitement was on full blast. Unlike Harry, I still had no wheels, nor did I have a driver's license. Since I still had to wait for a little more time to pass in order to take my driver's exam, I took a bus to work, or sometimes, I hitched a ride with a fellow student who worked close to my place of employment, and I walked the rest of the way to the electrical shop. I even pedaled my old bicycle a few times when the weather was nice or I had no other transportation choices. You did not miss work back in those days, or you found yourself looking for a new position.

The entire week after we installed the new engine in the Takajunky was a blast. All we talked about all week at school were our plans for the weekend. Our world had changed. Now, we were living! Harry had a set of wheels!

Since we both worked on Saturday, staying out late on Friday nights did not work out so well for us. Saturday night was our night for adventure and exploration.

The new engine was running well, Harry was obeying the old man's mechanical advice and taking it easy on the Takajunky, and once we were accustomed to the doors flinging open on random bumps and bounces here and there, the Takajunky was not a bad little car. The big bonus was still that cool, super deluxe, push button, auto selecto radio!

I met Harry at his house on an early Saturday night after Memorial Day, and the plan was to cruise up to a large town on the outskirts of the city of Paterson called Wayne Township. There, we would cruise around the edges of the roller rink, the shopping mall, the park, and other haunts. The main mission was looking for chicks because it was summer and the optimum cruise time of the year.

Harry took one look at me and he frowned at my appearance, "Do you ever wear something different other than those old, canvas sneakers, a No Way tee shirt, (No Way was my favorite rock-and-roll band) and black dungarees? Besides, when are you going to cut your hair and shave, twenty-seven?" I looked down at my appearance and shrugged my shoulders. I did not think I looked that bad. Harry was dressed in a collared pullover shirt with loud prints, which was so common in the 1970s, and a pair of wide, bell-bottomed pants, held up with the classic 1970s wide belt with a big buckle.

Harry shook his head and said, "You will never pick up chicks dressed like that, Paul. I will show you what I mean. Jump in. It is going to be a great night!"

It was a fabulous, early June evening. The day had been warm, but the humidity was low. The sky was clear, and the sun was sinking now, but the air had cooled off nicely.

"Exactly what are we doing Harry, in order for us to pick up gals?" I asked what I felt was a reasonable question.

Harry frowned again. He waved his hand at me in disgust while he told me, "Can you stop being an old lady for just a few minutes, Paul? Look, have you ever seen in the teenager movies, where the big shot guys ride around in hopped up, hot rod cars, and cruise up and down the streets in front of the boardwalk on the beach, beeping their horns at all the gals, laughing, and playing loud music? The gals then jump in the cars, and they ride all around and have a great time!"

Harry's overly simple explanation of the art of cruising puzzled me. Since I had already received my daily Harry proclamation of being an old lady, I felt I had nothing to lose; therefore, I ventured out on the old lady limb and interjected some facts into our current situation.

"Got it. Well, sort of Harry. But we are not at the beach, and the Takajunky is not exactly a hot rod car."

Harry laughed aloud and shook his head.

"Yeah, yeah, yeah, the Takajunky is a hunk of junk, but at least we have a new engine and this cool radio."

A simple statement, and oftentimes, simple but plain truth really hurts.

We headed for Wayne Township, since Harry explained that we had a better chance with women from richer areas than where we lived, and this would be a fresh "crop" of potential chicks, since all the gals in our neighborhood already knew that we were bums.

Harry's logic was quite profound.

We rolled up the Hamburger Turnpike, which was a long, two-lane highway that led from the city of Paterson up into the suburbs of Wayne Township. Harry was blasting the progressive rock radio station WNEW 102.7 on the FM dial, from New York City over the Takajunky's radio, as he turned into the parking lot of the shopping mall.

"Now, sit back and look cool, twenty-seven. You need to be cool and calm. I will show you how this is done." I looked at Harry as he sat back in the driver's seat, slowed the Takajunky down, and rolled slowly along the main sidewalk leading to the front entrance of the shopping mall. He placed his hands on the top of the steering wheel, leaned back in the seat with his sunglasses on, turned up the radio, and tried his best to look like some movie star.

It was not working.

I felt like an idiot, so I just sat there.

Now, I would receive the label of delusional if I were to describe my best buddy Harry M. Redmond Jr. as a calm, emotionally controlled individual. He was over the top, dramatic, bombastic, overwhelming, enthusiastic, and emotionally charged up all the time. Nothing revved

Harry's engines up more than pretty, young women did; he was a tenacious and obnoxious pursuer of gals. Some older shoppers stared at us, shook their heads in disgust, some people pointed at the Takajunky and snickered, but Harry remained undeterred in his mission.

He suddenly sat up, grabbed my arm, and pointed as he screamed, "Oh boy! Look at those chicks over there, Paul! They are gorgeous!"

I looked around and did not see anyone.

"Where?" I asked.

"You know, Paul, for a great goaltender that can see a puck at one hundred miles per hour screaming towards your head, you are blind! Right over there!" Harry pointed towards two young gals about one hundred yards away, crossing the street to walk towards the main sidewalk of the shopping mall.

Harry must have chick radar to have seen them from this far away.

He stepped on the gas pedal, cruised right up next to them, and rolled up alongside of the two gals while they wiggled along the walkway. They were indeed very pretty, and they both were dressed in mini-skirts, and loudly colored, printed blouses that were popular in this era.

Harry was bug-eyed and drooling while he swooped in on his prey. He yelled at them through the open window, "Hey there, girls! How about taking a ride with us on this gorgeous summer night? My buddy and I are just cruising around looking for some fun, and we would love to hang with two gorgeous chicks like youse!"

I sank down in the seat. This was a little rough. I was way too conservative for this approach.

"Get lost, ya jerk!" The one girl said to Harry with an angry scowl on her face.

"Ah . . . ya are just playing a little hard to get, huh, baby?" Harry answered.

"You're an idiot, and your car is an ugly piece of junk!"

She stopped wiggling, put her hands on her hips and pointed at the rear seats of the lowly, Takajunky.

"Why do you have those ropes tied to the door handles of the back doors of your car? That looks so goofy. I am warning you that my boyfriend is a star football player on the Wayne Hills football team, he has a cool, brand-new, Sonicmobile, and he will kick your ass for hitting on us! Besides, we would not be caught dead in a car like that with two, loser jerks like youse guys!"

Ouch! This was not going too well.

I was about to discover an important, undeniable fact of trying to impress young gals. All teenage gals always had boyfriends with superior cars, lots of dough, and they were always superstar football players who could, "Kick our asses." Since we were loser hockey players, we never received as much respect as the glamorous football stars did.

Harry now knew that this quest was hopeless, and since he now had nothing to lose, he blasted back, "Ha! Football! What a pansy, la-la sport. My pal here is the greatest ice hockey goalie in the metro area, and you will see him in the big time someday. We eat football players for lunch. I can also guarantee your boyfriend will not kick my ass. Goodbye loser chicks! Your loss!"

I had to agree that the odds were low that her supposed boyfriend could kick Harry around. Harry was one big, tough hombre. Other than that comment, I honestly felt that the gal was pretty much on target with her comments. Harry pulled away from the sidewalk, miffed at his defeat for only a mere second or two.

Harry now strategically shifted gears quickly in his opinion and assessment of the previously "gorgeous" young gals. I would venture a guess that their rejection of his obnoxious advances had something to do with their new classification.

"They were not so hot close up, Paul. I thought they

were cuter until we got closer. Once ya got up close, they were not too swift. The one crabby twigeon had an awfully flat chest. Nice ass, but that was all. Ya agree?" I simply nodded my head. After such a rousing defeat, I was not going to disagree with the big guy.

"Harry, is this going to get people to call the cops on us? It is sort of like stalking gals. I am not sure. . .."

Harry shook his head as he told me, "Nah, nah, nah, there you go with the Mr. Nice Guy, Old Lady Syndrome, again, twenty-seven. Here in New Jersey, cruising is a way of life. It is a rite of passage for us guys. Cops ain't gonna do nuthin' about it. When they were our age, they did it too."

Weird Harry logic.

Most of the time, his wild logic and theories actually had serious elements of truth embedded inside of them. As the years passed, more and more of Harry's theories proved to be true. Right now, they just seemed weird.

The rest of the night went about the same way, with one crushing defeat after another. The sun had now set and this summer day was ending. Somehow, cruising in the Takajunky had not exactly transpired the way that the scenes in those teenage movies had depicted.

Beaten, discouraged, and downtrodden at our flawed, twigeon enticement plan, Harry and I decided to drown our misery inside the shopping mall, chomping down ice cream cones, while we sat together on a bench inside the food court of the mall.

"Hi, guys. Whadda youse doing?"

Harry and I had ice cream tumbling out of our mouths in shock, as two young gals had randomly walked up to us as we sat forlornly on the bench.

"Oh . . . ah . . . we are well . . . hey, just having ice cream here," Harry was shocked and his usually silken tongue tied up in collective knots at the explanation. Instead of all the stupid riding around like perverted hoodlum stalkers, all we had to do was sit on a bench and eat some ice cream cones to meet chicks.

"Hi, I am Janet, and this is my friend, Margie. Do you mind if we join youse guys?"

Harry, of course, recovered nicely. However, I still sat there like an idiot while ice cream mush drooled out of my mouth.

"Sure, sure, sure! I am Harry M. Redmond Jr. and this is my best buddy in the entire world, Paul John Henson. I know he looks like a hippie weirdo, but he is actually the best ice hockey goalie in these parts. I am sure you heard of him. He was in the 'Paterson Evening News' last week, with an article about some scouts who are watching him for some leagues in the fall. I am sure you read it!"

Harry was laying on the bullshit. He could sell ice to an Eskimo.

The two gals smiled, and Janet said, "No, hockey is not exactly our sport, but it is nice to meet you both." I stood up and shook Janet's hand, and then Margie's hand. "Wow, you are both big guys, but my goodness Paul, you did not look so tall sitting there on the bench," Janet said as she laughed and then winked at me. Oh boy, we were off to the races.

"Say, can we buy you some ice cream cones? Chocolate or vanilla?" Harry said with a big, wide, ice cream-laden grin on his face. They both asked for chocolate cones and Harry and I scampered off to buy them. Harry was beside himself with excitement!

He had hit twigeon pay dirt.

"I got Margie, and you got Janet. I cannot take women with thick glasses, Paul. Besides, I can tell that Janet is stuck on you already."

"How can you tell that she is stuck on me?"

Harry rolled over my potential question like a freight train, "They are gorgeous, twenty-seven! Did ya see that caboose towing behind, Margie? Can you believe this cruising stuff? I told you that cruising worked!"

"Well, Harry, I was just going to. . .."

I was about to tell Harry that we were actually sitting inside the mall on a bench, sucking down ice cream cones when we met the two gals, but why interrupt his moment of delusion filled joy. He blasted over me again anyway, "Oh yeah, twenty-seven! What a night! These chicks are super-hot!"

Now, while the two young gals were not unattractive, however, to label them as super-hot, would be a typical Harry M. Redmond Jr. over-exaggeration. Janet was short and very skinny. She wore thick glasses and had short brown hair. Margie was taller, a little rounder, with long, black hair down past her shoulders. They were both dressed in tie-dyed shirts and bell bottom dungarees. They seemed very nice, and they were both cute gals. Cute, I would concede, yes indeed, but to label them as being super-hot or gorgeous, might be a bit of a stretch.

We returned with the ice cream cones and the two of us paired off on our seating arrangements, as Harry had instructed. I sat next to Janet and Harry squeezed in next to Margie. Harry and the gals chatted up a storm. I sat calmly and injected here and there, but I was quieter. On and on, he rambled about every subject on Earth. Harry was in rare form tonight, blabbing about hockey, music, school, and our jobs, where we lived, (that did not seem to turn off the women's attitudes, which was a positive sign, usually when we mentioned the old neighborhood, women would run away in horror) and what we were planning to do this summer.

Most of the blabber was true, but Harry, of course, intertwined the yarns with wild embellishments.

"So youse gals, want to go riding in my car? I have a car, you know, it is not the greatest, but it has a cool radio and a new engine."

The girls seemed apprehensive at first, but Janet piped

up, "Well, we do not really know you that well, but you seem like nice guys. We will ride around the shopping mall parking lot for a little while."

Harry laughed and said, "Oh man, youse, have nothin' to worry about. Paul is really an old lady. He is also Mr. Nice Guy." Harry had a way of classifying me, which was not exactly the image that I would have wanted to project towards the young women.

Janet looked at Harry suspiciously and said, "We are not worried about, Paul!" Margie nodded in agreement at her friend's statement. Harry was a legendary womanizer already at the ripe old age of seventeen.

I could see that Janet was smart as well as very perceptive. We walked out to the parking lot and Harry showed the gals the Takajunky.

"This is your car?" Margie moaned. "Why do you have those ropes tied to the door handles?"

The girl's disappointment in the appearance of the poor Takajunky was deeply profound.

Harry slickly maneuvered away from the obvious, slight imperfections of the Takajunky, "Ah yeah, yeah, yeah, the door handles are a little tricky, but check out this cool radio."

I explained to Janet and Margie that we will need to hold the doors closed whenever we hit bumps because the doors would fly open.

"Once you get used to it, and hold the door handles tightly, then it is not so bad," I did my best to put a positive spin on the situation. I untied the rope and tossed the rope into the trunk. We climbed in, Janet and I slipped into the backseat, and Margie and Harry went in the front seat. Harry started the car, and he slickly diverted the attention from the junky vehicle to the cool, super deluxe, push button, auto selecto radio! Sure enough, Harry first tuned to a song by the Electronic Transistor Orchestra, and then with a push of the button, the radio dial went up and down and back again, and sure enough, the radio found another song by E.T.O! The radio slightly impressed the girls, but it was highly questionable whether it was enough to offset the obvious shortcomings of the Takajunky.

We took off to ride around the parking lot, and when we hit the first speed bump in front of the stores, Harry yelled out, "Grab the door handles!" All of us held the doors by the handles and quickly closed them tightly when they popped open.

"Are you sure that this car is safe, Harry? It seems like it is a crummy piece of junk," Margie had become a doubter in the quality of the Takajunky.

"Nah, nah, nah, it is a great car, Margie. It has a brandy dandy new engine," Harry tapped her on the arm to reassure her of the extraordinary reliability of the Takajunky. Right on cue, suddenly, Margie screamed and pointed at a yellow liquid pouring out from under the dashboard of the Takajunky. She quickly placed her legs up under her backside, and she sat on them while the fluid poured out all over the inside of the passenger compartment!

"Oh geez, the heater core has popped!" Harry yelled as he pulled the car over.

We jumped into action because this was an easy repair. I grabbed the tools out of the trunk, pulled the heater hoses, and bypassed the heater core under the hood. We used some old rags to mop up the coolant that had spilled inside the Takajunky and we were back in action. A minor, yet common, setback in the world of unreliable automobiles. My old man had taught me well, and I was following in his footsteps, as an expert in spontaneous, roadside repairs of junky automobiles. I even received a few accolades from the gals and a fluttering of Janet's eyelashes at my car repair skills. I guess I had impressed her with my quick actions, and it propped my ego up just a little.

Old number twenty-seven smelled a little like sweet

antifreeze, and Margie had coolant stains on her shoes, but in the big picture of Harry and Paul, it was not too bad of a situation.

After the passing of the excitement of the erupting heater core, and a half an hour or so of riding around the shopping mall parking lot, we were becoming bored stiff. Harry spotted the movie theater on the other side of the mall.

"LOOK! CRUISING WITH CRYSTAL ZIRCONIUM IS PLAYING! I WANT TO SEE THAT MOVIE! DO YOUSE GUYS, WANT TO GO SEE IT TOO? Harry was going nuts pointing at the sign for the movie on the marquee.

"Sure, we would love to see that movie, Harry!" Margie and Janet both were excited at the suggestion. I shrugged my shoulders; musicals were not exactly my favorite type of movies. I was always short in the cash situation, and I had not planned on a double date at a movie for tonight.

The movie Cruising was a musical starring the gorgeous and talented Crystal Zirconium, who was also a very popular singer at the time, and her costar was some greasy guy named John Revolting. It was about a group of teenagers in the 1950s that cruised around in hot rod cars and became involved in ordinary trouble with love and life. It seemed as if it was an appropriate movie for our current adventure. This was a typical lover's triangle movie involving teenage angst.

Harry worshipped Crystal Zirconium. He had a massive collection of all of her records, and now that she had branched out into movies, Harry was going even more nuts over her. I had to admit she was quite a beautiful woman, and she had a lovely singing voice, but I did not share quite the same zeal for her as Harry did.

We parked and walked up to the ticket booth. Luckily, I just received my pay from my job earlier today, and I did have a few extra dollars in my wallet. Between a few dollars for gas to give to Harry, the movie tickets for Janet and me, and the ice cream . . . I was now officially broke. Harry earned a higher wage than I did, and he was always better off in the money department than I was, so he was not overly concerned about the dough.

We paid for the tickets and sat down to watch the movie. Janet and I sat together; Harry was next to me, with Margie at his side. Harry bought soda, popcorn, and other snacks, and he immediately started eating, being obnoxious, and singing along with all the songs. He was being very loud, and Harry unabashedly broadcasted his undying affection and love of Crystal throughout the movie house.

The plot of the movie was annoying and simple, with Crystal's character being a "plain Jane" type who was trying to earn a date with the John Revolting character.

About three-quarters of the way through the movie, Crystal experienced a total makeover by her friends in a final, last-ditch effort to win over John Revolting, and she appeared on a staircase, singing some dumb song, while dressed in a skin-tight, black, leather outfit. In addition to her outfit, her hair, makeup, and other "features" had also undergone major enhancements.

She certainly was no longer a "plain-Jane."

She was singing as she alluringly walked down the stairs, her enhancements bursting out of the neckline of her dress, wiggling and jiggling, while sending every male in the movie house into a testosterone-induced shock. On the screen, John Revolting was stunned, and the entire movie house gasped along with him at her remarkable appearance.

I had to admit that Crystal did look very good!

That was the end of Harry!

He screamed and carried on like a wounded buffalo.

"SHHH, Harry, calm down man, calm down," I leaned over and tried to control him, as Harry pointed at the screen and held his chest at the sight of the reworked and enhanced Crystal.

"OH! FOR THE LOVE OF HEAVEN AND EARTH! OH, JESUS AND ALL THE MAJOR PROPHETS, SAVE ME!" Harry screamed and rolled around in his seat.

"Stop it, Harry. People think you are a jerk," Margie was doing her best to stop Harry from convulsing. It was hopeless, and despite my best efforts, and the efforts and demands of the two gals, the sight of Crystal had overcome poor Harry.

The skin-tight outfit and the sight of the enhancements had sent him to the moon without a rocket ship.

"Oh, my goodness gracious! SHE IS, TOTALLY GORGEOUS!" Harry screamed and bellowed as he then hit the floor of the movie house and rolled around under his seat. The ushers were running up and down the aisles, frantically checking people with their flashlights. They thought someone was having a heart attack!

That was it!

Margie stood up out of her seat. She stepped over Harry, pushed by me, grabbed Janet's hand, and pulled her friend out of her seat.

"Paul, sorry, but your friend is an atrocious idiot! I have a boyfriend whom I just broke up with and he is a superstar on the football team, and if he finds out I was here with Harry, he will kick his ass! And, furthermore, tell your dopey friend that his car is a piece of junk," Margie angrily told me as she pulled Janet along. "Come on, Janet, we can still take the bus home. Let's get away from these two lunatics!"

Janet shrugged her shoulders and said, "But, Margie, I like Paul. He smells like anti-freeze but he is nice and very good-looking too. Maybe we can. . .."

"COME ON!" Margie pulled Janet along.

Janet feebly waved goodbye to me as I waved goodbye to her, and I now directed my attention to coaxing Harry off the floor. He was strangely quiet now, and it appeared as if Harry actually had passed out. The movie thankfully ended, and it took me a long time to get Harry off the floor and out of the movie house. When I finally managed to extract him from the floor, he had a covering on him, consisting of sticky soda from old spills, bits of spilled popcorn, and chewing gum wrappers, which were randomly stuck all over his body.

A very kind woman, who explained that she was a nurse, came over to us. She gave me an empty popcorn bag and taught me how to revive Harry.

She very patiently explained to me while handing me the paper bag, "He has hyperventilated from the sight of the skin-tight outfit she was wearing. Hold this paper bag over his mouth and have him breathe into it to regulate the oxygen level to his brain. Crystal did the same thing to my husband when he saw the movie." Ah, hah! That explains it! The nurse was a veteran of reviving men from Crystal Zirconium, skin-tight outfit shock!

The manager came over to us and told us in a not so gentle manner to make sure that we never set foot in his movie theater again. "Youse, two idiots disrupted the entire movie house. We thought someone was dying. It was just your buddy's overzealous testosterone levels. Don't ever come back here, and if you do, then I will have ya arrested for trespassing!"

Crystal had done Harry in, and I held him up as he staggered to the Takajunky.

His heartbeat would be irregular for two days afterwards.

We never saw Margie and Janet ever again, but for Harry and me, it proved to be just another adventure to chalk up to experience.

Even to this very day, Harry will go for a medical checkup and the doctor upon examining him will say, "You are in good shape, Harry, but did any doctors ever tell you before today, that you have a little skip here and there with your heartbeat?"

"Yeah, yeah, yeah, doc . . . I know. Ever since I saw that movie 'Crusin' with Crystal Zirconium in that skin-tight outfit, her on the stairs, you know the drill doc," Harry explains.

The doctor leans back and agrees with the graphic testimony, as well as Harry's explanation for his medical condition, "Oh, sure! I have the same thing. I saw the movie too!"

As time passed along, we never really discussed the now famous "Crystal incident" all that much, but every once in a while, Harry would simply refer to it as "The time when he acted poorly in the movie theater."

Now that certainly was a sugarcoated (along with some gum wrappers, sticky soda, and some popcorn) description if I ever heard one.

5

The Invitation

I arrived home from school a few days after the famous "Crystal incident" to find a letter from Debbie Boatwright sitting upon the pillow on my bed. Debbie and I had written one another now for years, and we had spoken on the telephone here and there when we were able to prearrange the calls, and I had a few extra pennies in my pocket to pay the old man for the long-distance charges for the call.

In my house, no one rode for free.

Debbie and I had also spent time together during this past Christmas season, when I visited Christmas Tree Mountain once more with the Redmond family and the entire neighborhood, on the annual Christmas tree excursion. This outing, unlike the year before, thankfully consisted of a much more subdued, "time bomb in the cupboard."

Debbie and I shared a wonderful time, as well as a little hug, and even as Ronzo would say, "A smooch or two."

It was hard to have a long-distance romance, and I would say we were more as if we were glorified pen pals, rather than a boyfriend or a girlfriend, but perception is sometimes the reality. I sat on the edge of my bed, opened the letter, and read it:

June 8, 1975

Dear Paul,

I hope you are doing well. Summer is finally here, and school is almost out! I really enjoyed your last letter and the wild adventures of you and that crazy Harry! He is quite the fun character. If I remember correctly, I think you will be able to take the driver's test soon. I wish you good luck on the test! I know you will pass with flying colors!

I have a special favor to ask of you, which I understand ahead of time if you cannot fulfill. We have our end of the school year high school dance coming up in a few weeks, and I would love it if you could be my date and attend with me. It is the end of our junior year, and we all are excited about becoming seniors in the fall. The dance is on a Saturday night, on June 19, at 7:30 P.M.

I also have another favor, because my best friend, Emma Whackenfuss, has recently broken up with her boyfriend and she is without a date. She was very much looking forward to attending the dance. I am hoping that Harry would like to be her date and he would be interested in taking Emma to the dance. I have enclosed a picture of Emma in the envelope so that you can show Harry how pretty she is. Furthermore, she is a fun and happy person, who I think would get along well with Harry and his wild personality.

I know that it is a very long way for you to come out to Sussex County from the city of Paterson, but for this special event, and with the new engine in Harry's car, maybe you can make it. My dad said he wanted to pay for all of our tickets, and if you and Harry would come, it would be his treat. It sure would be a special time! I can think of no one that I would rather go to the dance with either than with Paul John Henson. Please call me (201-209-1798) or write back soon and let me know either way. Thank you.

Sincerely Yours,

Debbie Boatwright

I closed the letter, grabbed the opened envelope, and peered inside. Sure enough, I must have initially overlooked the picture. Inside the envelope, tucked in a corner, was a small photograph. Upon closer examination, I saw that it was a typical high school yearbook type of photograph. I pulled it out, and stared at a headshot picture of a stunning young woman, with flaming red curly hair, some freckles, and perfect teeth and perfect features.

Emma Whackenfuss was gorgeous! She had a strange name, but man alive she was a stunner! Now, Debbie Boatwright was quite a looker too, so combined, these two young gals must be the best-looking gals in all of Sussex County. I could not wait to tell Harry. This was going to be some kind of adventure! I stuck the letter and the picture of Emma in my pocket.

Two city slickers, heading out to the country to a dance, to date two gorgeous gals.

It was like a dream come true!

It was unreal!

I told my parents that I was going to grab something to eat over at Harry's house, and I went to fly at top speed out the back door of our house. The truth was that, right at the moment, I was way too excited to eat anything.

Mum stopped me as I went to fly out the back door, "Did you see the letter I left for you from, Debbie?"

"I did Mum, I did thanks! I have to go talk to Harry right away. Debbie and her friend have invited us to take them to a big dance at their school to celebrate the end of the school year!" My eagerness was revealing my feelings for Debbie, and I was spilling my excitement for the situation to my dear mum.

She smiled at me, and held my hand as she said, "Oh, that sounds as if it will be a grand time, Paulie. What a wonderful way to start the summer for Harry, for you and for those lucky young women. I dare say that they will be brought to the dance by the two most handsome young men in all of New Jersey."

The old man was reading his newspaper, drinking a Big Boulder beer, while sitting at the kitchen table as he waited for his dinner.

He looked up and laughed, "Ha! Youse two lovebirds are really going to fly all the way out to Sussex County for a dance with two farm girls, who stomp around cow pastures, ride horses, and raise pigs? Ya better not let Maureen Zipperelli hear that ya are chasing some country gal. She has been chasing you around for years, she lives right up the street, has a body that would knock a buzzard off a shit-wagon, is super easy on the ole eyeballs, and in my opinion, she is a pretty nice catch for some young buck." The old man hid behind his newspaper again, while he continued his diatribe of disbelief at my plans, "I love the logic there, twenty-seven. Hmm . . . I guess there are not enough young women around here to date and dance with, let's ride all the way to the Kingdom Come in a junk car for a date. Dating some local gals would seem to be a little easier on the old wallet to me!"

"Oh pooh, leave Paulie alone, dear. He and Debbie have been special friends for all of these years. I think it is very romantic." Mum came to my futile defense at the hands of the logical speech of the old man.

"Ha! Romantic, huh? It's stupid. That is what it is, not romantic. When that heap of junk car is stuck on the side of the road somewhere between Paterson and Sussex County, then that will be romantic!"

I laughed at the old man and his enthusiasm for my adventure.

"Nah, Dad, since you put the new engine in the Takajunky, it has not been running bad. Aside from the door troubles, and a few other issues, it will make it out there."

"Ya better hope, the transmission holds up, that is all I can say! I hear those rice boxes have special filters in the transmissions that clog all the time. I read in my 'Backyard Mechanics' magazine where the reverse gear works, but the transmission fluid does not pump enough to push any forward gears. You will be stuck in the middle of nowhere, trying to find a four-dollar filter, for a foreign car. Good luck with that." The old man looked up at Mum and me, then he looked back down to his empty dinner plate and he frowned.

"Geez . . . Joan . . . are us guys ever going to eat today or what?"

Mum smiled at me, shook her head at my father's legendary impatience, and she waved goodbye. I waved and out the door, I went. I sprinted to 20 John Street, and I was hoping the entire time that I would see the Takajunky parked outside the house, indicating to me that Harry had returned home from work. Sure enough, the car was there, and I could hear that the Redmonds were in the backyard, whooping it up on this warm June night. I could smell the familiar odor of the charcoal grill cooking food and hear splashing in the swimming pool in their yard.

Harry's Resort was a special place.

I turned the corner, and Cocoa immediately greeted me while holding his trusty Piggy. I could see that Harry's nieces and nephews were swimming in the pool, while Patty, the Big Spike, Mr. Redmond, Harry, and Linny sat on lawn chairs watching them. Cocoa followed me as I hustled to tell everyone the big news.

"Hey, Paul! C'mon in and sit down. You want a Big Bob's Griddle Frank?" Ronzo smiled at me and waved at an open chair.

"Sure, sure, Ronzo. Thanks. That would be great! Hey Harry, I have to show you and tell you something. First, I need to ask you and everyone else, do you think the Takajunky will make it all the way out to Sussex County?"

Harry answered, "Hmm . . . it should make it with the ropes on the doors and the new engine, twenty-seven. Why do you ask?" Harry was now intrigued.

Mr. Redmond was a bit more of a doubter; he rubbed at his chin and offered his opinion, "Even with a new engine that is pretty far for that heap of junk to go, Paul. All those hills out there, ya know. Tell us why you are so excited."

Even Mr. Redmond was now curious what the adventure could be. Now everyone leaned in to hear what was going on in our lives this time.

I was excited, and it was hard to hide it from my friends, but I started my explanation, "Well, I got a letter from Debbie Boatwright today, and she wants me to take her to the big end of the school year dance at her high school in a week or so."

Harry smiled at my good fortune and said, "No kidding, that is great. Debbie is a hot, little number twenty-seven, that is cool but. . .."

"Yeah, yeah, yeah, listen up, Harry. She also has a friend that she would like you to take to the dance. Her name is, Emma Whackenfuss."

Harry threw his arms up in the air when he heard the name of the gal, and he quickly dismissed the suggestion, "Ha! Emma Whackenfuss! No way, Paul! She sounds like some pig farming, country bumpkin, doggie chick that cannot get a date. Debbie is pawning her off on me so that you two can go to the big dance!" I was shaking my head as I reached in my pocket and pulled out the picture of Emma.

"I do not think so, thirty-five. Debbie sent me a picture of her." I took out the picture, and held it out as the doubting Harry, in an effort to confirm his theory, quickly snatched it from my hand. Harry took one look at the picture of the smiling, red haired Emma Whackenfuss and his eyes popped out of his head. Steam blew out of his ears and floated off the top of his head.

"HOLY SWEET WATER OF LIFE! SHE IS GORGEOUS! OH, YEAH! OH, YEAH! OH, YEAH, YEAH YEAH! FOR THE LOVE OF PETE! WE ARE GOING TO SUSSEX IF WE HAVE TO WALK OR ROLLERSKATE! I LOVE THIS! NOW, THIS IS WHAT I AM TALKING ABOUT!"

Cocoa picked up Piggy and threw him in the air in celebration, and he started to run around the yard barking. Ronzo came over from the grill. He looked in at the picture, and he let loose a long sigh, as he handed me the Big Bob's Griddle Frank.

"Holy smokes, she is gorgeous."

All the rest of the family leaned in and shook their heads in awe of her beauty, while I stood there beaming like a dope, with a stupid smile on my face.

Mr. Redmond took the picture from his son, stared at it, and whistled a low whistle, "That surely is some good looking, pig farming, country bumpkin, doggie chick, in that picture there, Harry. They grow them pretty up there in Sussex."

Harry was over the top in his excitement, and we immediately started to make plans for the dance.

Harry began pleading with me, "Call, Debbie, now! Call her now, Paul! C'mon in and use our telephone. Dad, say can we use the phone to call Sussex? We will pay you the dough for the call."

Mr. Redmond laughed and motioned to us as he said, "Please, go ahead, and call her! You two guys do not owe me anything. Just go use the telephone and make your plans. Tell Mr. Boatwright that I said, hello. Hey, Ronzo, toss me a Big Boulder beer. This calls for a celebration! I just cannot stand those Dingleberries. They are way too sweet!"

"Sure thing, Pop!" Ronzo smiled, reached in the cooler at his feet, and he tossed Mr. Redmond a beer.

Two love-struck teenage idiots stumbled over each other as Harry, and I raced each other, to make it into the kitchen of Harry's house to call Debbie Boatwright. I pulled the letter out of my pocket, noted Debbie's telephone number, and dialed the rotary dial of the telephone on the kitchen wall while Harry gasped in deep breaths of air while standing next to me.

"Dial, Paul, dial it quicker" I waved my hand in the air to calm the big guy down. He was being even more annoying than he usually could be.

"The dial only spins so fast, Harry. Calm down, will you? It is ringing now."

A happy voice answered on the line, and said, "Hello."

I quickly realized that it was Mr. Boatwright on the telephone line. He was always a happy guy. I had the vivid and somewhat skewed memories of when he was on his backside in a snowbank, with his feet sticking in the air, after consumption of the legendary time bomb in the cupboard, but I tried hard to put them out of my mind. Anyway, he was happy on that day for sure, but Debbie told me it was a bit on the rough side the next day for Mr. Boatwright.

Worshipping the porcelain god is never fun.

"Mr. Boatwright sir, hello. It is Paul John Henson. How are you?"

I was very nervous.

"Paulie, my boy! I am fine, doing great! I hear that we may be seeing you and Harry shortly! Oh boy, I will go get Debbie. She will be thrilled. I hope it is good news. Did you cut your hair yet, Paulie?"

"No, sir. I have not cut it."

"Shave?"

"No, sir."

Harry whispered and waved his hands in the air, "Cut the old lady chit chat. Get to the meat and potatoes!"

"Oh well, it is modern times, and each day and age has its own styles! I will get Debbie on the phone. It is always nice to speak with you Paulie. Despite the hippie thing going on, you are a nice, polite, young man. Mrs. Boatwright and I like you and are thrilled that you and Debbie are going to see each other. Hold please."

"Thank you, sir."

I could faintly hear some speaking in the background, and then what sounded like a person running across a floor, some dogs barking, and other strange background noises. Harry was pacing back and forth in the kitchen like a nervous cat. I heard the telephone receiver rattle around a bit and then Debbie's voice, "Hello, Paul! I am so glad to hear from you. Did you get my letter? I am praying that it is good news."

Debbie was obviously very excited.

"Yeah, yeah, yeah, hello, Debbie. I received the letter today. I am with Harry right now. Yes, we are making plans to come to the dance. We are attending for sure, Deb!"

Harry was right up next to the telephone now. He was trying to listen into Debbie's side of the conversation, while drooling all over himself.

"Oh, good! That is wonderful news, Paul! It will be a great time. Did Harry like the picture of Emma? She is very pretty, and she is so sweet, gentle, and kind."

I held the telephone away from my ear for a second or two while I pondered how I would answer Debbie's question. If I explained to Debbie that Harry was rolling around on the kitchen floor, with his tongue hanging out of his mouth, and his eyeballs spinning around, then that might be a bit far-fetched, but not an entirely, inaccurate assessment of his reaction.

In the interest of public safety, I decided to play it a bit closer to the cuff and remain on the conservative side.

"Well, he thought she was very pretty, and he is looking forward to the dance. Harry . . . is kinda, well, he is a little excited, and he absolutely wants to meet Emma."

"Oh, that is wonderful, Paul. This is going to be a great

way to start the summer. I know you do not have a vehicle yet, so will you be driving Harry's car up to Sussex?"

"Yeah, yeah, yeah, we will be coming up in the Takajunky."

"Will the car make it, Paul?"

The Takajunky's perilous reputation now reached far and wide.

"Sure, it will make it, Debbie," I boasted confidently. I then asked Debbie, "Say, Deb, what is the dress code for us guys for the dance?"

"Well, Emma and I will have dresses on. We will need to go and pick out some special ones now! Daddy will need to dig around for some extra money for me to buy something very special. The boys have to wear jackets and ties."

"Okay, got it. Harry and I will pick you up around six or so. Will that leave enough time to get to Emma's house and to the school?"

"Yes, that will be perfect, Paul. You have not cut your hair or shaved your beard, have you?"

"No, Debbie, I still look the same."

"Oh, good! Please do not tie all your hair back. I like how you look when you do not tie your hair back. I mean, you always look fantastic—but with your hair down you are so incredibly sexy! Anyway, thank you. I know this is a long-distance call, so I will let you go now. I am going to call Emma and tell her the fantastic news. I will see you then. Thank you so much! This is going to be the greatest time of our lives!"

We said our goodbyes, and I hung up the telephone. I turned to Harry and raised my hands over my head in victory. The big guy rushed in and picked me up in one of his famous bear hugs, and we danced and jumped around in the kitchen of 20 John Street.

"Paul, this may be our greatest adventure ever!"

I looked at Harry and smiled.

That is what I was afraid he would say.

6

The Revenge of the Takajunky

Picking out a dress jacket, tie, pants, and a shirt for the dance was easy. I only owned one set of dress clothes, or as Mum would call them, "Church clothes" or, in other words, a set in which a person could actually consider being, "dressy." I did actually own two white dress shirts and under the advice of Mum, I agreed to wear one and to carry the other shirt as a spare.

Mum told me in her wisest voice, "It will be hot in that gym, they will not have air conditioning, and after dancing around like a bit of a wild man from Borneo, you may want to wash up and change into a fresh shirt."

The lack of a wide selection of clothing options made the "what to wear decision" a simple process. I tucked my usual hippie attire of canvas sneakers and rock-and-roll tee shirts in the back of my closet just for one day. Harry was in the same boat. He might have owned one or two more shirts than I did, but not many more.

Attending formal dances with pretty, young women was not exactly on our "to do very often" list.

After the longest week in the history of humanity, the Saturday of the dance finally arrived. We only had two days of school left next week, and then the school year would end for us, too. With a combination of the dance and the end of school, to say that we were in high spirits was an understatement.

I had convinced Harry that we should leave early in the afternoon, to allow us enough time to account for a potential mechanical issue with the Takajunky. It would take us a little more than three hours or thereabouts to make it to Debbie's house, so we made plans to leave 20 John Street around one o'clock in the afternoon. Harry complained fervently, and of course, he accused me of "Being an old lady," but he did concede that I might be correct in my conservative approach.

Earlier in the week, the old man lent me a spare toolbox, and some of his most frequently used emergency repair parts and supplies for emergency car repairs. Just in case of a messy roadside repair, to protect my good clothes, he also gave me a pair of coveralls to work in, as well as a blanket to lie on the ground, and he also tossed in a few other necessities for roadside resurrections. Harry and I put it all in the trunk of the Takajunky. The old man's experience with long road trips and journeys at the wheel of junky cars was something that we highly valued.

I was dressed and ready to go. One last thing to do; I stuffed my emergency stash of a whopping thirty-five dollars in my wallet.

That was a fortune for me.

My suit was black with a white shirt, and I chose to go along with it, a black tie with some silver stripes in some type of haphazard pattern rolling through it. I am not sure it looked very good, therefore; I checked with Mum for confirmation. Once I received tie approval, I combed my hair, trimmed my beard a little, and polished my only pair of black dress shoes. Mum inspected me, took a few snapshots, and she pronounced me good to go. She said that I cleaned up nicely, kissed me goodbye, told me she was proud of me, and wished me luck. In a stroke of romantic genius, Mum had suggested Harry and I purchase some flower corsages for the women, and Mum reminded me of them. She took them out of the refrigerator, gave me a little foam cooler to keep them in and sent me on my way. Mum had suggested white flowers since we did not know the color of the dresses that Debbie and Emma were going to wear.

"White will match any color dress, in which the ladies decide to wear," Mum said.

Mum had bailed Harry and me out once again!

Harry's own mom had passed on when he was still young, and Harry's older sisters did a wonderful job in guiding and providing motherly advice to their brother, but in many ways, my own mum was like a second mother to Harry, and I am quite sure that Harry loved dear Mum too.

Even the old man said I looked good, he stuffed a ten spot into my shirt pocket, while he said, "Ya always need a haircut and a shave, but I must say that ya look good. I am telling ya two bananas that youse guys need to pay Debbie's old man for the tickets. You and Harry both need to buy 'em. It is the right thing to do, Paulie. You pay for your own dates. Be careful riding in that rice box too. Good luck. Remember what I taught youse guys."

I agreed with him, smiled and shook his hand, and the old man smiled back at me.

Out the door I went. While venturing off on another adventure for Harry and Paul.

It was another perfect summer's day. Clear and sunny, a little warm, but no humidity. I walked over to Harry's house carrying my foam cooler in one hand, my jacket slung over my shoulder, carrying my spare shirt in my other hand, which was pressed and hung on a hanger, while acting like some kind of big shot operator. Young guys did not very often; walk around wearing suits and ties in our neighborhood, so I attracted a bit of attention.

When I passed the corner gas station, the owner of the station, Vince Barroni, looked out, and shouted to me, "Looking good, Paulie! Have a great time. I hope the

Takajunky makes it!"

"Thanks, Vince," I waved, and thought how not too much remained a secret around the old neighborhood.

I was really just a little pistol and far from a big shot.

When I arrived at 20 John Street, it was the typical neighborhood gathering. This was big news for two poor schleps like Harry and me, to be wandering all the way out to the outskirts of New Jersey for a date and a high school dance. All the neighbors were curious, and they were out of their houses, hanging around to see what was going on, and to wish us well. Nit Nat kids hung off tree branches and some scampered up the tree trunks and sat in the crooks of the trees to get a better view. After all, this was a big deal, and the John Street gang was very easily entertained.

Harry's sister Linda commented on my appearance as soon as she saw me, "Oh, look! Paulie looks so handsome! He looks wonderful! The young women are going to faint!"

"I agree. I have never seen him dressed up before. He usually looks like some hippie bum or he is wearing goaltender equipment," I heard Mrs. Porter say.

Mr. Porter appeared next to his wife and whistled low as he said, "Wow, Paulie, all dressed up and on fire!"

I smiled at the comments.

A group of neighbors, Harry's sisters, Linny and Patty, and Ronzo, and Mr. Redmond, immediately surrounded me. The women were kissing my cheeks, telling me how good I looked, and the men wished me good luck. As we stood next to the Takajunky, the front door to 20 John Street moved a little. It moved to a slightly cracked, open position, and then . . . it glided open very slowly. First, a leg appeared, then another, then a quick whirl, and Harry spun around the door, and he appeared on the porch.

"Look!" Joe Hinky Doo pointed at the porch, signaling the arrival of Harry upon the scene. While we all turned around . . . the crowd let out with a collective gasp, then a quiet murmur, followed by a silent hush.

The hush overtook the crowd. The moment captured everyone's voices.

Harry stood on the porch, and he scanned the crowd, slowly moving his head back and forth. He posed, while he adjusted his tie and sunglasses, smoothed his hair over to the side, loosened his necktie a little, and turned on the ultimate cool vibe.

He looked like a movie star!

"Hello there, fans, admirers, and worshipers! Let me introduce myself. Yes, I am, right before your eyes, the world-famous Harry M. Redmond Junior," was all Harry said, followed by a wry smile and a quick lift or two of his eyebrows. He was dressed in a dark blue suit, a white shirt, a wide blue tie, and a big, wide white belt with a silver buckle. He wore highly polished white shoes with white laces, and a black tip on the end of the toes. His hair was freshly trimmed and combed with a fancy swirl to the side of his forehead. He moved slowly down the stairs, moving side-to-side, while he took the stair's one-step at a time, snapping his fingers together in unison with his alluring descent.

He was working the crowd into a wild frenzy.

Loud cheers and claps broke out amongst the neighborhood crowd, and everyone gathered around Harry to tell him how good he looked, and to wish him good luck, too. Neighbors posed with us for pictures, they snapped pictures of Harry and me together, and then each of us individually, and it turned into quite the event in the history of John Street.

And believe me, there were quite a few events!

Only here in this old, gritty, side street tucked into a forgotten corner of urban America could there be such camaraderie, and a collection of such wonderful people. If I lived a hundred lifetimes, what we all shared on that old street on a summer afternoon in the year of 1975, we could never duplicate.

It was very special. . ..

We took our jackets off and placed them on the backseats under the ropes holding the doors closed. I placed the cooler with the flowers on the floor in the back too, and we both laid our spare shirts down flat in the trunk, so that we did not wrinkle them. Amongst the fanfare, we climbed into the Takajunky, waved goodbye to the crowd, and off we went into what was perhaps going to be the greatest adventure yet of our short lives. What seemed as if it were the entire population of John Street stood in the middle of the street, and waved goodbye to us as we rolled off to Geyer Street and disappeared around the corner.

While we drove along, in the typical old lady fashion, I took out a small road map and I planned the route. First up the Hamburger Turnpike, then north on New Jersey State Route 23, then off to New Jersey State Route 15, and so on and so forth.

I was insufferable.

Harry, as usual, grew impatient with my attempts at organization, "Yeah, yeah, yeah, I know the way, Paul. Geez, we live in New Jersey. We ain't going to Alabama. Now listen, Paul, let's go over our hand and head signals, so us guys are on the same page. We need to be on the same page here and plan our strategy for a potential attack or an emergency escape. You never know when we may need to hide stuff from the girls, or some big, gargantuan guy wants to roll one of us. Look here, twenty-seven, if I twirl my right hand and roll my fingers like this here, then that means, I understand you and agree."

Harry demonstrated the signal as I nodded that I was on it.

"Now, if I tilt my head to the right side and wiggle my left hand twice in the air, that means to play it cool. If I make a type of duck quacking noise, like this in the air . . .

then that means we need to meet in the restroom to go over a game plan."

"A little weird on that one there, Harry, but I got it."

"If I make a running motion on a table or in the air with my fingers that means to take off and make a friggin' run for it!"

"That makes sense, Harry."

Harry was very excited; he jumped from idea-to-idea and flooded me with his hand signals and commands. I tried hard to memorize his special Harry and Paul hand signals. After all, they may come in handy in the future.

"I want to fill up here in this gas station, coming up on the right side here. We only need a few gallons. One thing about this pile of junk is that it does not use too much in the way of gas," Harry explained as he pointed to a gas station on the Hamburger Turnpike.

"Do you need any dough, Harry?"

He pulled into the gas station, stopped in front of the pumps, shook his head no, and climbed out. "Nah, keep it, Paul. You can buy the ladies something later."

A cranky, bent over old man pumped the gas, Harry paid him a few dollars, and we were off back onto the Hamburger Turnpike.

So far, so good . . . I thought.

Oh, oh, I should never think!

As we rolled up the road, the Takajunky suddenly lurched, lost power, and the transmission made a loud whirring noise! Harry was stepping on the gas pedal, but we had no power to the engine! We only had a loud increase in engine noise, but no propulsion. Harry glided over to the side of the road, amidst blaring horns and shaking fists of congenial New Jersey drivers.

We glided to a stop and now we were dead in the water. It appeared as if the transmission was history! It was a simple formula. No forward propulsion meant that there were not going to be any dances with pretty gals tonight for Harry and Paul. Our hopes and dreams were all spiraling down the Takajunky drain rather quickly.

Harry looked over at me, he frowned, and then he pounded the steering wheel in anger as he screamed out at the top of his lungs, "STUPID PIECE OF SHIT TAKAJUNKY!"

This was incredible. We had not even made it out of Wayne Township yet, and the Takajunky had already given up the ghost.

A million random thoughts ran through my head. I then remembered the prophetic words of the old man, "Ya better hope, the transmission holds up, that is all I can say! I hear those rice boxes have special filters in the transmissions that clog all the time. I read in my 'Backyard Mechanics' magazine where the reverse gear works, but the transmission fluid does not pump enough to push any forward gears. You will be stuck in the middle of nowhere, trying to find a four-dollar filter, for a foreign car. Good luck with that."

I looked over on the side of the Hamburger Turnpike and noticed a service shop on the other side of the road. It was open, and it had a big sign on the front that proudly proclaimed, "FOREIGN CARS OUR SPECIALTY. WE ARE EXPERTS IN TAKAJUNKY REPAIRS."

The owner of the shop must be a brave chap.

There was hope! I solved problems. That was indeed my specialty. I was not about to fold my tent so easily. Harry, however, was in a slightly different frame of mind. He bent over the steering wheel, and he was banging his head repeatedly on the top of the wheel.

The dire situation crushed the big guy's spirit. Visions of millions of red haired Emmas waving goodbye to Harry now danced in his head.

"Harry, please take it easy. Relax and take deep breaths. It is going to be okay. Because of my Old Lady Syndrome, we have extra time here. Stay with me, Harry. Please try the reverse gear."

Harry looked at me and he sheepishly nodded his head. He moved the gearshift, and sure enough, the car went into reverse.

It was that stupid filter! The old man was a genius.

"Harry, I know what it is. The old man told me how the Takajunky's all have a filter that clogs with dirt. The clogged filter then causes the car's transmission only to work in reverse. It cannot be that bad of a repair. Look over there on the other side of the road, there is a service shop." Harry looked over to where I pointed and nodded his head.

"The only trouble is that it is on the other side of the road."

Harry smiled a devilish grin. It was indeed a devilish and slightly fiendish grin, in which I had seen too many times before. Then it happened as the famous eye of the tiger appeared in his left eye.

Oh, oh! The eye of the tiger!

Now, it appeared in his right eye too! Defeat was not an option for Harry M. Redmond Jr. now.

I was in deep trouble.

"That is not trouble, twenty-seven. That is a challenge. Just get out of the car and stop the traffic, Paul!"

Visions of millions of red haired Emmas blowing Harry kisses filled his head now.

"Oh, Harry, I do not think we should. . .."

"Paul, get out of the car, take out that red rag that I keep in the trunk, wave it in the air as a warning signal, and stop traffic. We have come too far for you to be an old lady now! It is only one hundred feet or so. You can run like a deer, Paul. Now, is as good a time as ever for you to run!"

He made the little motion with his fingers that indicated it was time to run.

I nodded my head.

Harry was right. It was time to run.

I jumped out of the car, crossed myself, grabbed the rag, and ran out into the middle of the Hamburger Turnpike while waving the rag in the air like a lunatic. Cars skidded and slammed their brakes on and horns blared. People screamed obscenities out the windows at me while I mouthed repeatedly that I was sorry to them. Harry slammed the Takajunky in reverse, blew across the road, went over the center grass island, and turned the car up the other side of the road.

The only trouble was that the cars were now coming towards us. I ran as fast as I could in front of the Takajunky, waving my stupid red rag, as Harry steered the Takajunky backwards up the lane in the wrong direction.

It was a horrifying experience! Cars skidded, horns blared, cars spun like tops, but by the grace of God alone, we made it, and no cars collided or ran over the top of me. Harry made it to the breakdown lane; tore up the sideline backwards, whipped the Takajunky into the service station, and slammed the car to a stop in front of the service bay. An older man was sitting in a chair outside the bay door, watching this horrible scene unfold, and a young mechanic dressed in coveralls stood there too. The young man gawked at our actions with his mouth wide open.

I was painfully aware of police sirens in the distance. I had a strange idea that they were heading here.

The older man stood up and waved for Harry to back the Takajunky into the service bay. I heard him yell out to the young mechanic, "Pull the x two dash y four filter, off the shelf there, Billy. This will be the fifth one this week. Funny, how they never clog in this lane, it is always in that northbound lane."

Harry popped out of the car, and I stood there bent over at the waist, trembling, and trying hard to catch my breath, while shaking my head.

Harry smiled, tugged at his pants and said, "See, that was easy, there twenty-seven. I told ya so. Nuthin' to it!" I did not have the breath to answer Harry, and if I did, it would have been ugly.

"Do you have dough, boys? You two jerks look like you are going to some fancy party or something," the older man asked while simultaneously insulting us, and standing there with a wrench in his hand. We nodded. Harry showed him some bills in his pocket, and the old man signaled to his partner to jack up the car. "I will have you boys on your way in a jiffy. All of these rice boxes have the same troubles."

"Ya okay there, Paul? Ya sure are huffing and puffing a lot there. For a professional athlete, I would think you might be in a little better shape. Nice work, though! Ya still can run fast there, twenty-seven. Ya are amazing!" Harry patted me on the back as we watched a police car pass by us with the siren blasting and tearing down the Hamburger Turnpike, obviously in search of backwards driving cars. Luckily, we had safely tucked the broken-down Takajunky inside the service bay, hidden from a policeman's eyes.

"Harry, I swear, I may be an old lady, but I swear if. . .." The two of us watched the police car now tear up the other side of the road in the other direction. We watched as the older man was true to his word. Within a few minutes, they replaced the filter, and the Takajunky once more, smoothly shifted into all the gears, forward, and reverse. We were back in action and thankfully, this turned out to be only a minor delay.

On the surface, it was an inconsequential delay, however, it was about to take a turn for the worse.

Harry beamed at the old man and asked him, "How much do we owe you there, old timer?"

"No trouble, fancy guy. That will be two hundred and fifty-two dollars."

The both of us almost lost our eyeballs.

"WHAT ARE YOU NUTS, PAL? I ONLY PAID TWO HUNDRED BUCKS FOR THE ENTIRE CAR."

Harry had the eye of the tiger back, so I stepped in front of Harry and held him back as I explained, "Sir, my old man told me that filter is only worth about four dollars. It took you ten minutes to replace it. That seems a bit high."

"Ha! Sorry, hippie, but you should have had your old man replace it. It is a Saturday afternoon, and I dropped everything to fix the car on an emergency basis, so you two birdbrains can get to your fancy party," the old man said with a sneer.

The younger mechanic pulled the Takajunky out of the service bay and jumped out of the car. He walked over to us while he was smiling and nodding his head. He now held a wrench in his hands and then dangled the keys to the car in the air in order to taunt us.

"Ya better pay up punks," he threatened. "Or, else." He tapped the wrench into his hands.

Harry clenched his fists, and I held him back with my arm.

I looked at the older man, then at the younger mechanic and said, "You were sitting on a chair and hanging around when we pulled in. I did not see any other repairs going on here." I then pointed at the younger guy and said, "As far as you go there, you little twerp, I really think it is better if we do not go there, pal. We may look fancy, but it can get ugly with us really quick, so quit with the threats!"

He looked at the size of Harry and me and realized the error of his ways. He took my advice and dropped the wrench act rather quickly.

While the old mechanic watched us, I reached in my pocket, and pulled Harry aside, "I have about forty-five bucks, Harry. We can offer him that and see if he goes away."

"No way, Paul! He is shaking us down. This is unreal." Harry shook his head rather adamantly in disagreeing with me about paying off the crooked mechanics.

"What choice do we have, Harry? Time is now ticking

on us. Right now, we are still ahead of the game, but if we have to wait for your father or mine to bring us more money, it is going to be too late. I say, it is worth a shot."

Harry looked at both of the rip-off mechanics and then back to me. Harry now agreed and he mumbled, "I guess . . . so we can get out of here, I agree. Go ahead and try it if you want. I would rather just bust his head open, but you are right . . . go ahead, Paul and try it."

I nodded and turned to the older man, "Sir, here is forty-five dollars. I think that is more than fair. I think we can call it square now."

To our shock, the older man shook his head and grinned again, "Nope, you boys are going to be late for your party. I already told you how much you owe me. If you cannot pay, then I think I will flag down that police cruiser and show him where your car is. Ya know . . . the car that he is looking for that seems so hard to find."

This guy was evil. He was now blackmailing us!

"You can use the telephone in the shop there to call your parents for more dough, but no dough, then no keys!"

Just as Harry and I huddled up, we spotted out of the corner of our eyes, a big, black, Galaxy 4000 vehicle with blacked-out windows come roaring down the Hamburger Turnpike, and we watched as it pulled into the driveway of the service shop and it screeched to a halt. Right behind it, another big, black Galaxy 4000 with blacked-out windows pulled up and stopped behind the first car. We all turned, looked, and our mouths dropped open, when the big guy who stood guard in front of Sal Zucchini's, "store" jumped out of the front door of the first car, and stood next to the back door of the Galaxy 4000!

He looked at Harry and me from behind his dark glasses and nodded.

Four more of Sal's men jumped out of the doors of the second Galaxy 4000 and surrounded the first car. They all were dressed in dark suits with their usual sunglasses on, and they scanned the entire area while they were watching everything.

"Holy shit, twenty-seven! It is Sal!" Harry yelled and poked me in the side.

The mechanics walked down the driveway close to where Sal's men had parked the Galaxy cars, when suddenly, Sal's men held their hands up in the air in an abrupt warning for them to stop.

They stopped.

The big guy opened the rear door of the first Galaxy and, out of the car, jumped, Sal Zucchini! He looked at Harry and me and smiled. He adjusted his tie, smoothed his jacket, adjusted his necktie, and made sure his sunglasses were tight on his head. Sal then walked slowly towards us while his henchmen surrounded him.

"Redmond Jr. and Henson. Youse boys, look like a million bucks. Ya look great in suits. I never would imagine youse guys cleaned up so nice."

"Hey, thanks, Sal. We sure are glad to see you!" Harry said as Harry and I shook his hand.

The big guy nodded at us and we shook his hand too.

Still smiling widely, Sal explained, "I heard that youse guys are going to the big party and dance. Two pretty girls, man, what a day for youse guys. However, it seems as though you have hit a slight snag in your plans here. Ahemmm . . . as you may remember, due to the nature of some of my business, I tend to keep an ear to the police radio. My boys heard the call come in of a Takajunky going backwards up the Hamburger Turnpike, with some long-haired hippie dressed in a suit and tie, running out in front of it. We knew it was youse guys in some kind of trouble. Now, I also know that there are two bums on this road, who like to shakedown folks, and how shall we say . . . try to take advantage of situations. That is where Sal Zucchini steps in . . . to organize these types of situations. I can assure you that the boys and I can take care of this situation."

Sal turned towards the two dumbfounded mechanics and smiled. He and his henchmen walked slowly towards them as Sal said, "Now, listen here, these two boys happen to be associates of mine. I hear there is a little question of a repair bill that is, how shall we say . . . a little, artificially inflated. There is also a little matter of holding back car keys. Keys, which actually belong to my associates. Let's see, a four-dollar filter, ten minutes of labor. I think fifteen dollars is more than fair. If you feel otherwise, then perhaps we need to step around in the back and have a chat or two. I am sure after you and my boys talk for a while, you will adjust the service repair bill, as well as see the error of ya ways. You see, I am sure you want to keep your little shop here intact, and explosions that go off and blow-up establishments in the middle of the night for no real reason, are a terrible . . . tragedy. The police and the newspapers always say it was some kind of leaky gas can, but us guys, well, we know there can be other causes too. People who take advantage of two, good, young men who are on their way to having the time of their young lives, are how shall we say . . . let me choose the correct word . . . expendable. Yes, I like that word . . . ex . . . pend . . . able."

The two mechanics were now shaking in their boots.

The older one finally had the nerve to speak up, "Yes sir, fifteen dollars is more than fair, Sal."

Sal roared in and got in the older man's face, "Sir, to you! Only my friends call me, Sal! And, let this be a lesson to you two characters, who take advantage of hard-working and honest people. Bums like youse bums, will always get what ya deserve. Somehow, and some way, it will come back to bite youse square in the ass and the score will always come out even in the end! Guys like youse will lose. Remember that, the next time you try to shakedown someone. In the end, it always comes around to get you."

Sal whirled around and pointed towards me. "Henson,

go ahead and give this bum the fifteen dollars!" Sal waved for me to join him and pay the older mechanic the dough.

"Sure thing, Sal," I said as I reached in my pocket and gave the older man the money. He took the money, tossed me the car keys. The two of them ran back into the shop, slammed the door, and put a "CLOSED" sign in the front door. Sal smiled, adjusted his necktie once again, and he and his men turned and walked back to the Galaxy.

Sal met us next to our cars; he shook our hands and smiled while he told us, "I do not want to hear any thank you from youse two guys. For this situation and our . . . intervention, or for the new engine for the car. Not a word. I still owe you. These kinds of small-time punks, who operate like this, are a real nuisance to me. Now, youse boys have a great night and get up there to Sussex. I would ride you myself in my limo, but it is out of my territory. I am sure youse guys understand. Stay cool, youse guys. Stay cool."

He playfully punched us in our arms. We all waved and turned away to walk to our vehicles. Sal was climbing into the backseat of the Galaxy when he suddenly popped back out and yelled in my direction, "Henson!"

I turned back to Sal and answered him, "Yes, Sal."

"For a tough guy who every once in a while, acts like an old lady, you run fast, and have extraordinary courage. I admire a guy with guts, Henson. Ya should try hard though, not to make a habit of running down busy roadways. It can be unhealthy for ya, Henson. Also, I know you worry about everything. Please do not worry about the police cars running up and down the road. I have taken care of that situation too for youse guys. Stay cool, Henson and Redmond Junior. Remember, when Sal Zucchini says that right now in your lives, you have the world by the balls, that he is right. Sal stands behind everything he says, sells, and does. You two are both young guys, tough, handsome, and alive! I know that tonight you will create memories that will stay with youse guys forever. Have the time of your lives, youse guys. The time of your lives."

"We will, and I will do my best to stay out of busy roadways, Sal." He nodded, smiled, climbed into the car, and as quick as a flash they were gone. Harry and I climbed back into the Takajunky and we were on our way.

"Paul, Sal is right when he says you are sometimes an old lady, but man oh man, you are the best old lady I know!" He reached over, put his big arm around my neck, and squeezed me.

"Thanks, Harry."

I smiled at my best friend while I pondered the opinions of my personality traits shared by Sal Zucchini and Harry M. Redmond Junior.

In a strange sort of way, for once, I felt it was actually a compliment.

7

The Dance

Despite the slight delay due to the revenge of the Takajunky, we still were way ahead of schedule. My advice to leave plenty of time to account for "issues" turned out to be solid advice. Soon, the haze and soot of our home city of Paterson was in our rearview mirror, and the beauty of the rural side of New Jersey on a June afternoon was all around us. The Takajunky did not have any air conditioning, but today, we did not need it. We rolled northward, with the windows rolled down, the radio blasting music, the wind rushing through the car, and the little engine happily humming along. We made our way up and down rolling hills and through the country highways and byways, and we held onto our doors whenever we hit a bump or two.

New Jersey has it all, from seashores, to sports, to old, worn-out cities with smokestacks that touch the sky, to mountains, to mobsters. It is one of the most fantastic places on Earth, it really and truly is. No matter where I roam, or where I would end up in life, I always take a piece of this special place with me in my heart, in my accent, and in my soul.

We turned off the highway and before we knew it, we were riding up the familiar country road that led to Christmas Tree Mountain. How different it looked from our Christmas time excursions. Now, the mountain was all dressed in summer splendor! Green, rolling cow pastures, bordered with split-rail fences and trimmed in elegant forest lines, created a stunning backdrop to the barns and farms that lined the dirt roadway for miles.

It was a gorgeous scene for a glorious summer day.

I looked at my watch and we were a little early, but not too bad. It was about five thirty or so, we had timed our trip very well indeed. We pulled into the driveway at the base of the mountain, and there it was in front of us, the scene of the famous runaway Christmas tree and the prodigious time bomb mixture. The gravel path leading up and down the side of the mountain, now had a cover of bright, green grass poking up here and there through the gravel base, and flowers waving to us in the gentle breeze, rather than my previous memories of frozen ice and snow rimming it. The Boatwright's farmhouse sat off to the side, and the barn was off at the end of the wide end of the main drive and pathways. Two or three dogs came running out to greet us, wagging their tails and barking. I think they were looking to see if Cocoa had come along with us. A chicken or two, followed by a family of quacking ducks, escaped from the barn, and they ran around and wandered close to us to see if we had any tidbits to feed them.

"Nope, we are not in the city of Paterson any longer, are we, eh?" I teased Harry, while gathering the foam cooler with the flowers in it from the car. We walked together to the front door of the farmhouse.

Mr. Boatwright appeared on the porch, waving to us. He walked down the front steps to greet us.

"Hello, Paulie! Hello, Harry! Nice to see you, boys! Glad that you made it safely. Hey, that there rig of yours is not such a bad, little car, there guys!"

If he only knew.

"Wow! You guys look great. Like two movie stars. The girls will be thrilled." We greeted him, shook hands, and followed him into the house.

I pulled Mr. Boatwright aside, before we went inside his house. I said, "Sir, we would like to pay you for our tickets.

Harry and I want this to be our treat for the girls. I am sure you understand."

"Paulie, it is only ten dollars for all of you to go to the dance. I do, however, understand that you want this to be your event, so I will humbly accept your offer."

Harry handed Mr. Boatwright a five-dollar bill, and I did the same, then we walked into the front door of the farmhouse and stood in the middle of a large, living room that included the largest stone fireplace and hearth, in which I have ever seen.

The Boatwright family members were very similar in personalities and their mannerisms as the Redmonds were. They were carefree, happy, hardworking, and just plain old-fashioned fun. Dogs ran around barking, cats peered at us from lofty posts in and around the living room, and Debbie's younger sisters and her brothers pointed at us and giggled.

Two city slickers out in the country. We were fish out of water.

We greeted Mrs. Boatwright, who had us sit down in the living room, while she served us both a wonderful drink of homemade lemonade. It tasted cold and delicious!

A hassock fan sat in the center of the floor and gently moved air around the room. All the windows were wide open, and here in the mountains in the country, God provided the air conditioning for you!

Mrs. Boatwright told us that Debbie was almost ready, and she and her husband chatted with us as we enjoyed our drinks. She beamed in exuberance, I suspected she was very proud of what could have been her daughter's first, "real" date with a young man, because as she sat there smiling, Mrs. Boatwright went on and on, speaking with Harry and me about how handsome we both looked. She leaned in when she was out of an earshot of her husband, and she whispered to me that she loved my hair and beard, and no matter what the future styles might be, that I should never cut it or shave. We were sitting there chatting and laughing when I heard a door open at the top of the stairs and then close.

"Oh, good! That must be Debbie now," Mrs. Boatwright said, as she grabbed her camera and put it up to her eye. We all stood up to greet her. Sure enough, Debbie Boatwright appeared on the top of the staircase.

Debbie smiled, waved, and she looked at me and mouthed, "Hello there, Paul."

I heard Harry whistle low and hard.

I was stunned at her beauty, but I did manage a rather feeble wave while the flashbulbs snapped and popped, capturing her slow and elegant descent down the stairs. Her brown hair hung down long past her shoulders. It was longer than I had last seen it when we visited for Christmas. She was dressed in a light blue dress with some type of white frills around the hemline which stopped just before her knees. The dress had matching white trim around her neckline, and she had a little flower in her hair. She wore a white pearl necklace around her neck, with a set of matching pearl earrings. Debbie wore white low-heeled shoes on her feet, and then there were those eyes . . . those fantastic green eyes! She walked down the stairs while her family, followed by Harry and me, broke into a round of loud applause. She walked over by me, and gave me a hug, and signaled for me to bend down (Debbie was fairly short, but I was now pushing six feet four or so) she took my hands in a clasp, and she gave me a kiss on the cheek, as the cameras continued to snap and pop. Debbie Boatwright was a beautiful country gal for sure, and she had captivated this city slicker's heart.

Once I recovered from Debbie's grand entrance, I reached down into the cooler, pulled out the corsage, and nervously pinned it upon Debbie's dress. My hands were shaking like a leaf. Mrs. Boatwright stepped in to help me and she put the final touch on my rather awkward efforts, as Harry and Mr. Boatwright ribbed me at how nervous I was acting.

This romance stuff was not so easy!

Debbie loved the flowers, the corsage turned out to be a huge hit, and earned me another kiss. This one was gently upon my lips, and a whisper in my ear about how handsome I was!

Harry winked at me when he saw how big a hit the flowers were with Debbie, and he knew that Mum had hit pay dirt with her suggestion.

Thank you, dear Mum.

After some more chatting, a few more pictures, and well wishes from her parents, we were off. While removing the ropes from the rear door handles, I explained to Debbie about the tricky doors of the Takajunky. Unlike most young women who, when they first were introduced to the Takajunky, Debbie did not frown or have a look of disdain upon her face. She simply smiled as we explained some of the Takajunky's special features. In preparation for picking up Emma Whackenfuss, Debbie and I climbed in the backseat. Debbie sat close by my side, but still within arm's reach of the opposite door handle, as we pulled out of the driveway waving to her family on the front porch. The backseat of the Takajunky was not the ideal environment for couples to snuggle up close to one another.

"So, did you have a nice ride up here, guys?" Debbie asked with a smile.

I saw Harry look back at me in the rearview mirror, and he smiled. I almost started to tell her the actual story, but I stopped short. After all, who would not believe that we broke down on a highway, I stopped traffic, Harry drove his car backwards on the roadway, we had the car repaired, a guy tried to rip us off, and a New Jersey mobster who is our friend, and has a heart of gold saved us from the grips of evil.

What is there not to believe?

Someday, I swear that I will write all of these adventures down, and people can decide for themselves whether they are true or not. Until then, I just said to Debbie, "It was good, Deb. Nothing to it."

"Oh good, I am glad there were no adventures."

That's correct, no adventures. Just the adventures of Harry and Paul.

Debbie gave Harry directions to Emma's house. I reminded her to hold her door on a bump or two, and in a short while, we were pulling into the driveway of another farmhouse.

Harry was a nervous wreck now, while his excitement was building for his pending meeting with the gorgeous Emma Whackenfuss. He was blabbering on and on from the front seat about some unrelated subject, pushing buttons frantically for music that he thought would be "cool" and complaining that all he could tune in were radio stations, playing country and western music.

There would come a time in Harry M. Redmond Junior's life, when country music would be a huge part of his lifestyle, but that is a whole other story for some other time and place. Right for now, he was working himself into a hormone driven frenzy.

"Harry is a little excited about meeting, Emma," Debbie observed. "He is not going to be disappointed. Emma is such a nice, sweet gal."

I nodded my head as I pictured a happy, little gal dressed in a flowery dress, skipping in and amongst the farm meadows with a basket in her hand, as she picked wild strawberries from the summer fields that lined these meadows on the sides of the roads for miles.

Sometimes visions in our minds can mislead us in such strange ways.

I would like to say that this house looked different from the Boatwright's house, but that would be a bit of a stretch. I suppose that if Debbie Boatwright had the opportunity, and she came into our neighborhood, she would say the same thing about our houses. They all looked the same! We parked, climbed out of the car, and walked towards the front door.

While we walked together towards the front door of the home, Harry looked at us and asked, "Do I look all right, youse guys? Is my hair, okay?"

Debbie smiled but did not answer. I told the big guy, "You look fine, thirty-five. A movie star, you look like a movie star. Relax. It is going to be fine."

I thought about how I had never seen Harry so nervous before.

"Be careful of the cow and horse piles, boys," Debbie warned as she casually pointed towards the ground. Harry shrugged his shoulders as he looked at me and I pointed down, too. We dodged a few piles here and there, but Harry seemed to be mindlessly plowing along, oblivious to anything but the vision of Emma Whackenfuss stuck in his mind. An unhappy rooster came running out of a side corner when Harry stopped and came too close to a group of chickens wandering around. He chased Harry all the rest of the way to the porch.

"Geez, feisty little sucker! Little red, son, o' a," Harry said as he sprinted away.

We climbed onto the porch, and before we could even knock, an extremely tall man opened the front door. He was dressed in a plaid farmer's shirt, had no hair, and he wore a toothless grin. When I say he was tall, I do mean tall! Even with my height, he towered over me. Behind him, an entire collection of giant people came running. A tall woman, a tall younger gal, and a tall teenage boy. They all were like trees!

"Well, come on in there, Debbie and your city slicker friends," the tall man shouted. He led us into a large living room, not unlike the living room in the Boatwright's home.

"The flatlanders are here to pick up, Emma Lynn!" I

heard one of them shout as they all came barreling into the living room to gawk at the big-city slickers. The tall man reached out his hand, bent over, and shook Harry's hand as Harry stared up into the stratosphere to look up at the man.

"Howdy there, young, flatlander, city slicker, movie star guy. I am Arthur Whackenfuss. I am Emma's pappy, and this here is my wife Emma, my son Artie, my other daughter, Emma Annie, and the dog over there barking at ya is Art!"

Harry shook his hand and mumbled, "Geez, what do you people eat around here that makes you grow so tall? I am hearing that youse guys are very original at the old name game too, huh?"

"What's that young feller? Speak up!"

"Oh, I said nice to meet you and your family," Harry fudged his way through it.

Harry introduced me to Mr. Whackenfuss and the rest of the group as we made the rounds through the family. They seemed nice enough; it was just that they were all so tall that it was hard to focus on anything else.

"I reckon you stepped in a cow pile there, young city slicker. Ya tracked it all over our house," Mr. Whackenfuss said as he pointed down with a frown at Harry's fancy white shoes that had the cow, "mush" all over them.

"Now, we have cow doo-doo all over the place." We all tried not to laugh as Harry struggled with the big lumps all over his fancy shoes and all over the place.

Harry tried hard to explain, "Oh, wow, my goodness! I am so sorry. It must have happened when the rooster chased me. We do not have cow piles to worry about in our neighborhood, just piles of other stuff."

"Oh yeah, yeah, yeah. I reckon that Artie the rooster is a crabby one!"

I did my best to help Harry as Mrs. Whackenfuss handed him a rag. Debbie and I tried to clean his shoes up, but I soon gave up, took his shoes off, and tossed them outside on the porch.

Harry's movie star image was taking a few hits here.

"Oh, do not worry, we will clean it all up after you city slickers leave and you are done messing up our house," Mrs. Whackenfuss told it, as it was.

"Why are you not wearing any shoes? I thought all big city boys wore shoes."

We all were distracted by the cow pile situation, and had not heard the approach of another person, until we heard her soft voice behind us. We turned around to see a gorgeous gal standing in front of us, pointing at Harry's feet.

It was Emma Whackenfuss!

She was just like as she was in the picture. She was perfect, with gorgeous, tumbling, red hair dangling past her shoulders, a perfect figure with all the parts and pieces in the right places, enhanced by a form-fitting, black, low cut in the ole neckline dress.

Now, I will do my best to describe Emma's chest area, and still keep these words within a decent and somewhat vague, but factual description. You see, her somewhat controlled and captured chest projections bulged out of the top of the neckline of her dress. Harry's eyeballs now were as if they were laser beams, while he focused only upon that particular region of her body! She wore a pair of black, low-heeled (thankfully) shoes, she had a wonderful smile with perfect white choppers, and a tiny, gold necklace framing her very long neck.

She looked just as gorgeous as she did in her headshot picture. A little ole country girl she was not! My vision of a happy little gal dressed in a flowery dress, skipping in and amongst the meadows with a basket in her hand, as she picked wild strawberries from the summer fields, was slightly flawed.

She looked like a million-dollar chick from Las Vegas.

The only thing that was not readily apparent from viewing the picture was that she was six-foot bijillion or so in height.

"My goodness, Debbie. Emma is quite tall," I said to my five-foot, sweet, little, country gal.

Debbie nodded, leaned in, and deadpanned, "She was captain of our championship basketball team, Paul. We were undefeated."

I would not have expected any other result. The other teams most likely just forfeited the games and stared at Emma.

Harry was jaw-locked at her beauty, as well as her height, hair, figure, and other rather robust, "features." I could have been wrong, but I think his right eyeball was spinning clockwise in his head, and his left eyeball was spinning in the opposite direction. He also required a wheelbarrow to carry his tongue around in now.

Locked deeply in a testosterone and hormone imbalance haze, Harry finally managed to recover; he reached his hand out and mumbled, "I stepped in cow doo-doo outside, when I was chased by Artie the whacko rooster, so we ditched my shoes on the porch. I already tracked the lumps all over your entire house. You can smell it in the heat now. Hi, Emma. I am Harry M. Redmond Junior. Are you for real?"

Emma smiled, stared Harry up and down, and said, "I am real, Harry. In fact, all parts of me are real, there, big feller. You will do just fine. You are a cutie all right. I am glad to see you are at least six foot and not some little twerp. You have a chest as big as mine, a nice tight ass, you look as if you have the build of a tank, and you are not a patsy ass. I like that."

She then grabbed Harry, hugged him tightly, whipped him around like a rag doll, leaned him over, and gave Harry a big, lip-locked kiss while simultaneously latching both of her powerful hands firmly upon Harry's backside.

The entire Whackenfuss family cheered and clapped as they encouraged Emma on her mission to reduce poor Harry to a quivering pile of his former self. I thought about how I might have to haul a comatose Harry back to Paterson, and check him into the emergency room of the hospital for that pesky, irregular heartbeat, originally induced by Crystal Zirconium and other lovely ladies.

Harry was now plunged into intense and immediate love.

"My, she is a tad bit on the aggressive side, Debbie," I commented to my date in a low whisper, while bending down next to her ear. Debbie smiled and she kissed me gently on the cheek.

"Yes, Emma does speak her mind, Paul."

I thought about how she not only uses her lips to speak.

Now that Emma finished destroying Harry, she looked at me and smiled.

Oh, oh!

"Wow, you are a tall one there, Paul. Only a few inches shorter than me. I hear you are quite the athlete. You look strong. Maybe we can go one on one someday in some hoops, or afta' lookin' at ya, some other kinds of activities."

"Well, I do not go too much for playing basketball, now, hockey is really. . .."

Emma ran a ramshackle over the top of my stammering, "You are gorgeous too. Great athletic body! Big arms, solid chest, nice ass, and a little pop in the front groin-u-lars too. Ya packin' sum heat there. Handsome, tough guy, goaltender. Love the hair and beard! I bet you can run and go all night if ya reckon ma meanin'. Debbie has nailed a winner with you, there all right. Hot looking guy, Deb!"

She then walked over, high-fived an embarrassed Debbie, and pushed me a little to test my strength as she laughed. I could not help but think, where was the sweet little gal that Debbie had described?

We took some pictures all together, with her family,

with Harry, and then with Debbie and Emma. I had to admit; I have seldom seen two gals that were more gorgeous together. They were striking in their collective and contrasted beauty.

Harry borrowed a stepstool and pinned the corsage on Emma's dress, while she chuckled as Harry dangled nervously near her very large and highly exposed chest region!

After the fanfare, it was now time to take off.

We picked up Harry's shoes off the porch, scraped at them a bit, and all headed towards the Takajunky. I noticed that when she thought everyone was preoccupied with cow piles and doo-doo removal, Emma quickly ducked around the corner of the porch of her home, she picked something out of the shrubs alongside the house, and she placed it into her purse. I could not tell what it was, but I thought it was unusual. Everyone had their eyes peeled for the status of a certain resident aggressive rooster, and they did not notice Emma's quick exit.

However, Paul's goaltender eyesight noticed.

We checked carefully for Artie's whereabouts, and made a mad dash to the car while dodging cow and horse piles. The entire Whackenfuss family stood on the porch and waved goodbye to us.

Their heads were scraping the top of the porch ceiling; I swear they were.

We gave Emma the rundown on the nuances of the Takajunky's tricky doors, Harry showed the gals the super deluxe, push button, auto selecto radio, he started the Takajunky up and put the car in gear, and off we all were to the dance.

The sun had lowered in the sky now, and as we drove west through the June night, the western sky was ablaze with reds and oranges that glowed along the horizon.

"GRAB THE DOORS!" was the standard war cry as we drove off on the bumpy country roads to our next adventure.

It was a rather short drive to the high school, and in no time at all; we pulled into the parking lot of the high school, parked the car, and made our way to open the doors for our dates.

When we jumped out of the car to let our dates out of their seats, Harry leaned over and whispered, "Emma is unreal, Paul. She almost broke me in half with that hug, and I thought her lips were a vacuum cleaner on my mouth!"

I really did not know how to answer him, so I just smiled. He forgot to mention her death grip on his backside, but I was quite sure that he would eventually recall that fact, too. We let our dates out and Harry locked the Takajunky. Actually, I do not know why he would lock it, since it was overly optimistic that some poor soul would actually want to steal the car. Debbie took the tickets out of her purse and handed them to all of us. All over the parking lot and the school property was a slow migration of nicely dressed, young people, making their way towards the front doors of the high school. Harry commented to me in a low voice out of earshot of our dates, about how many pickup trucks we could see parked in the lot, along with a few farm tractors. He also noted how many of the guys were wearing big straw hats!

This was a large school, it covered a tremendous geographic area of Sussex County, and I imagined that an awful lot of teenagers were going to attend this dance.

I was correct.

We checked in with the administrators and chaperones running the event, showed them our tickets, and received a table assignment along with those stupid, sticky nametags that you have to stick on your clothes, which say, "My name is such-and-such." We all tossed them away as soon as the chaperones were not looking. They were holding the dance inside the high school gymnasium, and the organizers decorated it very fashionably, in the typical manner of a high school dance. There was music equipment set up in a corner of the gym, with a short chap standing next to a record player, an amplifier, and a tall set of speakers. A silver microphone was set upon a tall stand on the side of the speakers. The short chap was studying boxes and boxes of records while some country music bellowed out of the speakers.

Harry pointed at him and whispered to me, "I guess that is the entertainment, twenty-seven." I nodded as we continued to walk into the gym.

The gym was huge, but it was overflowing with attendees. This was quite a popular event! Emma and Debbie were certainly grabbing their share of attention, not only for their stunning appearances, but for the fact, they were hanging on the arms of two "flatlanders." Gazing at the nametags of some of the guys and gals, I noticed that an awful lot of the last names on the tags were similar, as well as repeated with many of the same names, "Smith, Jones, and White.

These were the types of moments that the master showman, Harry M. Redmond Jr. lived for. He strutted into the gym (we had managed to scrape off all the cow doo-doo off his fancy shoes) worse than Artie the rooster in his barnyard of hens. He still was wearing his movie star sunglasses, he had Emma's arm looped through his, and he was in his glory, envisioning that every single person in the entire gym was focused solely upon him and his date.

This time, he might have been correct.

There was an open area, which I surmised was an area set aside for dancing, and it was located directly in front of the speakers, numerous tables and chairs assembled in a dining area, and food tables lined the rear wall of the gym, offering a selection of food and drinks. Some large paddle fans softly moved some air around in an effort to keep the gym cool.

We sure appreciated the cool breeze from the fans!

We arrived at the table that our tickets had assigned us to, each selected a chair, and we all sat down. As we chatted, four guys and four gals showed up, stood next to us at the table, and stared at us with dopey smiles on their faces. My assumption was that they were also going to join us at our table. They looked like nice young people; the guys wore quality suits, all dark blue in color. In fact, they were all identical. On their heads were propped some straw hats, and around their necks they hung bolo ties, and the gals were dressed in flowery, printed dresses. In fact, they were all identical dresses, too.

One of the guys, who wore a big, wide-brimmed straw hat with a black band, stood in front of us and said, "Well, golly gee whizzers, weeze'all get to sit with Emma and Debbie and the city folks. Boy, you gals sure look pretty in them there dresses tonight. Howdy y'all, I am Billy Ray Smith. These here, are my brothers, first there is Bobby Ray, and then Timmy Ray, and that there, handsome feller, is Jimmy Ray. Our dates here are Becky Sue Jones, and her sisters, Debbie Sue, Linda Sue, and Tammy Sue! Nice to meet y'all!"

I watched Harry slowly shaking his head in amazement at the names of folks here in the farmlands of New Jersey. Harry leaned over and asked me, "Paul, are you sure that we did not drive to Alabama?"

Billy Ray smiled as we all greeted them and we all shook hands. I did not want to admit it, but all of them looked identical.

"Ouch, boy oh boy, you city slickers are strong ones! At first, I reckon ya looked like you were nothing but a long-haired hippie to me, but I reckon with that handshake, ya can break a few people in half," one of the young Smiths shook his hand in the air, after I shook his hand.

"Oh, I am sorry, Jimmy Ray. I guess that I do not know my own strength sometimes. I play a lot of sports and I guess I work out too much."

The young man frowned and corrected me, "I am, Timmy Ray."

"Sorry."

It was all a bit confusing.

We all sat down at the table and made small talk. It was obvious that since they discussed a great deal of school-related issues, and general discussion of local events, Debbie, as well as Emma, knew the Smiths and the Joneses. The gals stared at Harry and me, and they all pointed and giggled. Debbie sat there smiling and holding my hand, while Emma hung on Harry and laughed in his ear as Harry began to tell some mystical tales of our adventures in the big city. He turned up the Harry magic, flung his big arm around Emma, kept his one eye glued upon her chest area, put his mouth in gear, and it was full-speed ahead. Emma was captivated while he turned on his silken tongue and typical Harry magic.

I looked around to see if there were any Eskimos in attendance who might have been a bit short on some ice for their igloos.

"I reckon y'all are crazy! You city boys are a barrel of fun! We are going to have a tractor pull in the parking lot after the dance. You city boys are invited." One of the Smith boys announced.

Harry guessed at his identity, "Thanks, there Tommy Ray, but we have other plans."

Harry was wrong.

"I am, Timmy Ray. We do not even have any brothers named Tommy. Our uncle is Tommy Ray!" Harry shook his head at the confusion. But we were about to leave the world of mixed-up names, because we watched while a school official strolled across the floor with some papers in his hand. He stood in front of the gym, grabbed the microphone, and read a long list of rules and regulations, including where and how they planned to conduct the tractor pull, and a host of other warnings, along with the strict penalties for any infractions. He mentioned something about cows and horses, but I did not catch all of what he was exactly saying.

Soon it was time to dance!

Finally, the party had started!

Harry and I both had visions of slow dancing in the middle of the floor, with our lovely girls held closely in our arms, as they stared at us starry-eyed, while they were lost in romance!

Of course, we were wrong.

"Time to line up for a square dance, y'all!" Some big guy with a straw hat on his head yelled into the microphone.

The entire population of all the farms in Sussex County, New Jersey, rushed out onto the dance floor. Our gals enthusiastically grabbed us, and out we went onto the floor. Luckily, old number twenty-seven was not too bad out on the dance floor. After some slight missteps, I was right in the swing of it. Harry followed my lead, and soon the "city boys" were high stepping along with the country boys!

"Oh, Paul, I had no idea you were such a dancer! You are great!" Debbie was thrilled as I wiggled and wobbled in a haphazard, Paterson style do-si-do. I did not want to shatter her dream of a special lifestyle, and tell her that they do the same move in a polka, so I just smiled.

"Paul is the best dancer that you will ever see there, Debbie. All those goalie moves on the ice make him as loose as a goose. He can bend in ways that most people have never even dreamed of!"

In a rare image drift, Debbie whispered to me, "I will keep that in mind," as she winked at me.

After we square danced, it was off to line dancing, and then we moved into a freestyle hoedown of some sort, as a bunch of country boys and gals danced and hopped in the middle of a giant circle of clapping partygoers.

After much coaxing and a strong combined push from Emma, Debbie, and Harry (mostly Emma since she was a strong one!) I suddenly found myself in the center of the giant circle. I stood there embarrassed until the crowd cheered and chanted me on. I conceded defeat, pulled a hair tie out of my pocket, and tied off my long hair. Once I fell into the beat of some kind of fast fiddling music, I broke into an "improvised Paterson jam" and the rhythm and tempo turned me into a dancing machine! The crowd cheered widely and the music stopped. Emma and Debbie rushed in and held my arms up in the air in victory as the crowd clapped wildly.

"You won, Paul! When the music stops, the judges have picked the best hoedown dancer," Debbie told me as she stood on her toes and motioned for me to bend over, so that she could kiss my cheek.

Won? Won, what? Hoedown dancer? I have no idea what I was exactly doing out there. I thought I was acting like a jerk. Harry stood on the sideline, roaring with laughter at the entire scene.

A smiling, older man with very few teeth, and one small blob of short hair stuck on top of his head like a rooster, carried a big trophy over to me, and handed it to me as the cameras snapped and popped. The trophy had a large wooden base that proudly held a plaque proclaiming me as the winner of the "Highland Hills High School Hoedown Dance of June 1975."

"Here ya go, there long-haired, hippie guy, city slicker, flatlander, who needs a haircut and a shave! I reckon we never have seen anyone dance like that! You must have learned that from stomping on them there, big, roach bugs that live in the big city!"

Where did these people come up with this stuff?

Harry was making duck quacking motions in the air, and I remembered that meant we had to head for a restroom mission. After jumping around like an idiot, I was sweating hard now, and thanks to Mum, I knew we could pick up our spare shirts, wash up, and change in the restroom.

We politely excused ourselves, grabbed the trophy, and made our way towards the front door to go to the car. We explained to one of the chaperones where we were going, had our hands stamped, listened to a speech about bringing back in any, "City slicker, type contraband" and we headed for the car. I did receive some congratulations on my dancing skills, which I found to be quite hilarious; when you consider that, I was clueless as to what I was really doing.

Harry and I stepped out into the parking lot. The summer nighttime air felt cool and crisp. It was a welcome change from the warm gym. It felt wonderful!

"This is some fantastic time, Paul. I cannot believe that you won that stupid contest. What exactly in the name of hell were you doing out there?"

"Harry, I have no idea."

He laughed and put his arm around me as we walked closer to the Takajunky.

"These girls are the prettiest ladies that I have ever seen. Did you check out that dress and that chest on Emma! Whooo weee! She is something else. A little tall, a little strong, but man oh man, she is something else. Debbie is a knockout too, Paul. I could do without all this hayseed and coverall stuff, and the cow doo-doo on the bottom of my shoe, but this is an incredible time. These country bumpkins, in their own way, sure know how to party."

"I agree that it has been quite the time. The night is still young. I just hope and pray we do not have any more hoedowns. My legs may fall off."

We grabbed the spare shirts, put my trophy in the trunk, and headed off to the restrooms to wash up and change. In a few minutes, we were fully refreshed, dried, and cleaned up. A quick return trip to the car to drop off the old shirts, and soon we were heading back to our ladies and the table.

It seemed as though the Smiths and the Joneses had wandered off to the tractor pull, and the table was now all ours. Thankfully, it now was a slower pace, as people were eating and relaxing and the wild, fiddle music had faded to a backdrop of softer, country music with some sad sack chap, with a fake drawl, crooning on about a lost, hound dog and a pickup truck that would not start. We met back up with the gals, prepared some food plates for them, as well as for us, and we sat down to eat. The crowd of locals now treated us as if we were celebrities, with guys and gals coming over to us to ask us questions and to meet us.

Harry was in his glory. On a trip to the food tables for refills, Harry and I met up with the short chap who had been playing the music.

He looked up at us as he stood in the chow line, smiled, and said to me, "What exactly was it that you were dancing out there, hippie guy? To me, you looked like an idiot jumping around out there, but to these bumpkins around here, they ate it all up and gave ya some dopey trophy. Youse guys are two fish out of water here. You do know that, don't you?"

We recognized the accent, and special, insulting language highlights, and we smiled back at him.

"Dennis Martini, 52 Wayne Avenue, Paterson, New Jersey," he proudly announced, while we both took turns shaking his hand.

Martini continued on, "Paterson, that is, until my old man moved me out here for stupid, country living, and the quiet strum of banjos to lull you to sleep at night! Man, it is nice to see some city boys from the old, home city rather than some country bumpkins. I will say those two women of yours, are the prettiest gals in the entire school. How you two bums got dates with them, well, you both sure are lucky! I'm warning ya though, to keep your eye out for Emma's old boyfriend, he is not very happy about youse guys being here with her. He is a big meathead, captain of the football team and all. Some big, farm boy, with a brick for a head."

We knew that he was captain of the football team. It just had to be. I bet he drives a nice car, too.

"He also has some fancy Sonicmobile, so he thinks he is hot stuff," Martini added.

Yes! Right again!

We nodded our heads and thanked our fellow Paterson comrade for the inside scoop.

Harry sensed an opportunity.

"Wayne Ave, huh? Over by the Great Falls and Libby's, hot-dog joint. Say Martini, I imagine that a Paterson guy like youse is, ya must be sick of all that foot-stompin' and hollerin' music. How about some good, old, weepy-eyed rock-and-roll ballads for some slow dances, so we can snuggle up with our ladies on the dance floor? I saw you had quite a collection of records there. I am sure an old Paterson boy has some good stuff stashed away in those boxes."

"Yeah, yeah, yeah, but these cowpokes and farmers will faint if I played any of them. I am so sick of this country music that I could scream, but anything else that I might decide to play, would go over like a lead. . .."

His voice drifted off, as Harry had whipped out a twenty-dollar bill and was waving it in the air in front of Dennis. His eyes followed it while he smiled.

Oh yeah, Dennis was from Paterson!

"Balloon." He finished his thought, smiled, and Harry slipped the twenty into his shirt pocket.

"You are on my payroll now, Martini. Deal?"

"Deal! I did not get your name."

"Harry M. Redmond Jr., is the name! Deal maker, welder, womanizer, general horn-blower, tough guy, hockey player, and overall windbag. But, all in all, there Martini, when it all shakes out, I am not a bad guy. This long-haired guy here is Paul John Henson, the best dancer and ice hockey goalie in the entire metro area. Stay tuned, you will see him in the big time someday. I guarantee it. Watch for my signal to key up the tunes there, Martini."

We completed the deal and we headed back to the table. We finished eating. Harry waved to Martini, who waved back. We grabbed our ladies as the music started, and the slow dance was on! A loud moan and a groan went up from the foot stompers, but it was out of their hands. After all, where we came from, a payoff is a payoff, and a deal is a deal.

We snuggled up and danced, and we danced, and then we danced a little more. Now this was more like it. Starry-eyed ballads, weepy-eyed ladies, and magical times. Yes, it was a wonderful summer night dance, and memories to last a lifetime.

Pure, simple summer magic.

Emma and Harry pulled in tight and he had one of the biggest smiles on his face that I had ever seen. You see, due to Emma's height, and Harry's height, he "lined up" right where he wanted to on Emma's body. Debbie and I danced the night away. Once she followed along, she was an excellent, slow dancer. I also had the opportunity to stare into those wonderful green eyes.

Martini had taken good care of us; after all, he was a Paterson guy.

We took a break from dancing, and the ladies followed us to the food table to pick up some drinks. Harry and I were filling our drink cups, when ten or so large young men with straw hats on their heads, and mean scowls on their faces, suddenly surrounded us.

A huge guy with large shoulders, a big chest, jet-black hair, and some kind of drool coming off the side of his mouth stepped forward. He looked at me, and then at the girls, and then he focused his eyes upon Harry.

I had a bad feeling as I felt we were about to meet the

meathead in which Martini had warned us about.

"Go away, Billy Joe White! We do not want any trouble with you and your football team friends. We broke up, and it is over! Harry is my date tonight, and Paul and Debbie are here together. Now, leave us alone," Emma warned him as she shook her finger in his face. He just smiled and ignored Emma as he stepped closer to Harry.

Yes, it was the meathead.

Debbie grabbed my hand and whispered to me, "Oh no, Paul, this is so bad. These are all the star football players from our high school team. Billy Joe was all-county this past year. He is the star player on the team. He is very mean and strong. He is Emma's old boyfriend!"

Yes, we knew that too.

Billy Joe Meathead walked over and pushed Harry squarely in the chest and he said, "Get lost, city boy! Emma is my woman and you and your long-haired, hippie, dancing machine, idiot friend are about to get your clocks cleaned."

I saw that familiar glimmer in Harry's eyes appear.

It was the eye of the tiger.

Defeat was not an option now.

Now, the truth of the matter was that Harry and I had fought many a hockey war, both on the ice and off the ice. We, in our past, were beaten up, bruised up, sewn up, won many battles and lost a few too. Billy Joe had just made a very grave error. You see, Harry was correct; we did eat football players for lunch. There was only one trouble, there were two of us and eleven of them.

Not good. We were not that hungry.

"Relax, Deb. Stand over there with Emma and be ready to run. Do you both have all of your stuff?" Debbie and Emma nodded to indicate yes to me.

"Good. I have a feeling we are about to make a quick exit. Remember, they may be football players, but they have never met two, street smart, tricky, hockey players from Paterson before." Debbie nodded, and she and Emma followed my instructions.

I stepped in close to Billy Joe, and his friends surrounded us. Harry looked at me, tilted his head to the right side and he wiggled his left hand in the air twice. Hmmm, these Harry and Paul's secret signals have come in handy!

Now, I just have to remember what the stupid sign was that Harry just sent me!

Harry frowned because he could tell I did not get the first one, so he repeated it, while he wrapped his arms around his body and made believe he was shivering.

Got it! I guess he could have just told me that fact, but anyway, Harry wanted me to play it cool. I should have known that Harry had a plan.

I towered over Billy Joe, and I think he was more than a little surprised when he saw my size and the look in both of our eyes. I pushed my shirtsleeves back a little to expose some muscles in my arms. This was all a game of typical testosterone-laced, male posturing, of which we were well accustomed to from playing in hockey games, but it would buy us a few seconds that we sorely needed. I could sense that Billy Joe's confidence had faded just a wee bit.

Harry smiled when he saw Billy Joe's apprehension towards me. I spotted him spin his right hand and twirl his fingers to me to make sure that I understood he was going to make a move. I had seen this one before as Harry tapped the edge of the punch bowl to signal to me what his plans were. Ronzo had taught us an old trick at a wedding reception once, when Ronzo needed to "cool down" a drunken relative who was out of control, and was grabbing all the women's backsides at the reception. Harry was way too smart not to know the odds were bad on this one. The night would be ruined by a brawl, and in a strange sort of way, he knew the meathead was right. Emma was a fabulous woman, and she was worth fighting for to win back.

Harry knew that he would do exactly the same thing.

Harry whipped up some quick poppycock, "One trouble you have there, drooling mouth, brick-headed, farm boy, is that you have underestimated the odds. You see, we might only be two guys, and you have your whole football team of clunk heads here to back you up, but we are hockey players, and Paul here is a goalie. He eats pucks for lunch and well . . . I eat footballs."

As Harry spoke, I diverted their attention with a false quick move, while Harry slipped a five-dollar bill out of his pocket and tucked it under the edge of the punch bowl. The punch was clear, and the bowl was a clear glass bowl, so it appeared as though the bill was floating in the liquid.

"Say, will you look at that? Some jerk chucked five bucks in the punch there."

Harry peered in and pointed at the bowl. He had deadpanned his delivery perfectly as the big dope fell for it and the meathead looked over the top of the bowl. Harry made the running sign with his fingers. I grabbed Emma and Debbie's hands, and we took off!

Harry grabbed Billy Joe Meathead by the back of the head and dunked him straight down into the punch and swished him around good and hard in the ice-cold liquid! Harry was a strong guy, and he picked Billy Joe's head up numerous times, and then sent him back into the bowl for a few good "rinses." He and his buddies were so stunned; they did not even fight back. Harry then grabbed his five-dollar bill back, and he took off behind us, while the stunned football team tried to recover from the humiliation of their superstar!

Out the doors we flew, laughing, and the girls screaming in joy! Past the stunned chaperones, out the front doors we flew, while we ran to the Takajunky.

"Pray that piece of shit Takajunky starts, twenty-seven! God listens to you, Paul! Start praying!" I could hear Harry screaming behind me.

I was already praying.

The football team and their blockhead leader had recovered, and they were in full pursuit now. We unlocked the doors, jumped in, and Harry started the engine.

Thank you, Sal, and thank you to the old man.

The Takajunky started right up.

Now realizing that we had escaped in our car, the footballers headed for their own vehicles to chase after us. That is when we found a faithful ally had come to our rescue. You see, the Smith brothers had been watching from afar. They had started their tractor pull, and the brothers were all riding around in their tractors in the parking lot preparing for the contest. A quick wave from one of the brothers, (I was not exactly sure which one it was, and I was not about to guess!) and they had strategically blocked in all the football player's vehicles with their tractors!

We escaped into the summer night, and with a beep of the horn and a wave, we bid farewell and thanks to our farm boy pals! Off we drove into the night, two Paterson, New Jersey, hockey players, two fantastic, gorgeous, young women, and one old, crummy, piece of junk car with doors that flew open on bumps. We did not care though; we were having exactly what Sal Zucchini had predicted.

You see, we were having the time of our lives.

8

Moonlight and Memories

"That was incredible! You two are a riot! I haven't had so much fun or laughed so hard for years. Harry M. Redmond Junior! Where have you been for seventeen years of my life?"

Emma Whackenfuss reached over and gave Harry a kiss as he desperately tried to remain focused on the road.

"I never have seen Billy Joe been made such a fool of. He will never live it down!"

"Billy Joe needed to cool down youse guys, so old Harry cooled him!" Harry explained between kisses and laughs.

Debbie was still laughing, and she reached over, took my hand, and we shared a long and passionate kiss.

It had been quite a night, for sure.

"Go down this road and then turn here, Harry," Emma gave Harry driving directions.

She had a plan, too.

We turned up a dirt road, and we held on tightly to the doors as we bounced and bumped along. The night was clear and cool now, and the sky was lit up with a nearly full moon. Mr. Moon hung over the roads, pastures, and meadows, providing the only light for us, other than the headlights of the Takajunky. There were no streetlights here amongst the farms and pastures of Sussex County.

"Stop here, Harry."

Harry stopped the car inside of a little dirt cutout in the road at the top of a hill, overlooking a long, open meadow, which rolled out in the darkness below us. We climbed out of the car and walked over to look at the view. I put my arm around Debbie as she shivered a bit in the cool summer night air.

It was breathtaking. The moon illuminated the landscape, and some faint lights from farmhouses were poking through the night, twinkling at us here and there. An occasional car's headlights passing on the main road below flickered through the trees. The air was cool and crisp, and the evening's summer breeze gently blew across our faces.

Emma reached into her purse, smiled, and giggled as she pulled out a bottle of Bumpkin's Farm Apple Wine. I now knew what she had stashed away in the shrubs next to her house.

"Emma! You didn't," Debbie laughed and pointed at the wine bottle.

"I sure did, Debbie. Pappy will not miss it!"

Harry grabbed our emergency blanket from the trunk, which we had just in case we had to lie on the road to fix the car. He spread it out across the hood of the car so that we did not get dirty. The four of us spread across the hood of the Takajunky, sharing sips of wine from the bottle, laughing, telling stories, and staring up into the moonlit sky.

The moonlight blocked some stars, but I sure knew where to find some.

All four of us had them in our eyes.

We played the radio, we danced on occasion on the side of that meadow, feeling the night together, and feeling the joy. I think we all were just a bit tipsy, and perhaps just a touch silly, but we did not care. We shared wine, laughter, and some hopes and dreams together, all on a summer night.

It was late now, and all too soon, it was time to head home. Magical times on a summer night when you are young always end too soon, but the memories linger on forever.

We climbed back into the car and we rode back to Emma's house. Debbie and I kissed her goodnight, and we all hugged one another together. Harry walked her up to the front door, and they were gone for a long time.

Debbie and I did not care. We took full advantage of the time alone.

Harry returned, a little disheveled, but smiling for sure!

It was now off to Debbie's house, and first, a tearful goodbye for Debbie with Harry, and then a slow walk for Debbie and me to the front door of the porch.

There were just a few lights on inside the Boatwright's house. I am sure lurking somewhere inside were Debbie's parents. We did not care as we embraced and then kissed passionately on the front porch. I spotted even in the darkness, some tears rolling down Debbie Boatwright's face.

"Hey, Debbie. Why are you crying?" I asked her.

She smiled and said, "Because this wonderful night is over, and I do not know when I will ever see you again, or have this much fun again. You are a special, young man, Paul John Henson. I wish tonight would never end."

Debbie was a smart gal. She knew how young we were, how far away I lived, and how time, life, and space had a habit and way of drifting people apart.

I wiped her tears away and smiled as I whispered, "And you are a special young gal. Whenever you want to see me, Debbie, you will still be able to find me. It will be just the same way that I will always be able to remember and see you too."

I stopped speaking, turned towards the darkness, and waved my hand over the view from her porch. Debbie wiped some of her tears away and stared at me with her sparkling green eyes while waiting for my explanation. I dabbed at her eyes with my handkerchief and dried her remaining tears.

I then continued to explain, "On some summer night someday, when you spot a nearly full moon hanging in the sky, close your eyes, dream, and the moonlight and the memories, will allow this special night to return to you in your mind forever and forever."

She smiled at me. We kissed again. I waved goodbye, and told her that I would write to her next week. I heard the door to her house open and close behind her as I walked back to the car. I opened the door, climbed in, and closed the door. I looked over at Harry, and he smiled and we shook hands.

"Oh, yeah, Paul! The time of our lives!"

I had to agree.

We drove the long ride home, sharing memories of the day, as well as, of the night, Sal's rescue of us, the punch bowl incident, the hoedown dance, my stupid trophy that we could hear rattling around in the trunk, Dennis Martini, and the beauty of two country gals from the farmlands of New Jersey.

We were such a long way from Paterson, New Jersey, both in distances, and within our minds and souls.

When we ran out of stories of the dance and our latest adventure to tell and recall together, Harry created a little more confusion for me. Since our hand signals had worked so well, Harry felt we needed to have a few more for strategic use in future situations. Harry went on and on demonstrating new hand signals, as we laughed and conjured up wild Harry and Paul scenarios where they might come into play.

Hey, you never know, but in reality, I just became even more confused, while Harry added a few more special Harry and Paul secret signals and signs to our playbook. We had to admit to being physically exhausted, but the adrenalin of the day and night lingered and fueled us along. In the many countless adventures of Harry and Paul, this one certainly was very special.

The early morning light was thinking about touching the next day. You could just see the faint signs of the sunlight on the horizon as we rolled into the city of Paterson. The Takajunky had done the job, and this old car was very special to us now too. The end of the ride was quiet. We were now even more exhausted; the adrenalin had finally given out, and we had spoken about our adventures and hand signals all we could until another day.

We knew that in the world of Harry and Paul, there would be another adventure right around the corner. There always will be, you see Harry and Paul adventures never really end. The years may pass, but they go on forever, as long as there are memories, dreams to dream, fun-loving people who enjoy life and care for one another in special ways, stories to tell, roads to travel, music to hear, dances to dance, and love to give.

They go on and on until the end of all time.

Harry dropped me off in front of my house at 182 Belmont Avenue. I grabbed my trophy, my dirty shirt, my foam cooler, and I closed the car door. I waved goodbye to Harry; I told him I would see him tomorrow, and he waved and pulled away. I climbed the stairs to my porch, turned the key in the door, and made my way into our living room. It was now close to four in the morning; I was dead tired and dragging my backside behind me.

The old man was sitting in his chair in the living room and he looked up at me. He had been reading his latest copy of *Dark Secrets* magazine. He shut the light off over his chair, took off his reading glasses, and smiled at me.

"Hey chief, ya look like you had quite the time."

"Hey, Dad. Yeah, it was something else. It was great."

"Good, good, I am glad youse guys are home safe. That is a long ride. Did that rice box run all right?"

"Well, for the most part. We had some trouble on the Hamburger Turnpike, but I will tell you about it tomorrow. I am kind of beat right now. Reading your 'Dark Secrets' magazine, eh? Any good articles this month?"

"Yeah, yeah, yeah, one, or two. One good one about how these big, evil retailers will be sticking some new-fangled electronic gizmos inside stuff to track what you shop for in the big stores. Another article is about how someday we will have television sets that are so thin, ya can hang them on the wall of ya livin' room. You know, save the floor space. Mum will like that, because she won't have to pull the television out to clean behind it every day. But I tell ya, it is all to make 'em cheaper and charge ya more dough. It is all about the money, ya know. Seems like every place ya turn these days, has a new, evil shadowy figure hiding behind the corner to watch what you are doing."

I nodded my head and mumbled, "I guess, Dad."

The old man nodded, and pointed at my trophy as he asked, "Whatcha win?"

"Oh, some dopey, dancing trophy for a hoedown dance or some kind of dance like that. To be honest, I didn't even know what I was doing. I just kind of winged it."

He nodded and smiled.

"You were always a great dancer. Did you and Harry pay Debbie's old man for the tickets? It was the right thing to do, ya know."

I nodded and mumbled, "Yeah, yeah, yeah."

"Did youse guys and gals steal away a few beers?"

I was an honest guy and the old man was a smart cookie. I suspected that he had attended a few of these events too when he was my age.

"Nah, just a few sips of wine from a bottle that Emma hoofed from her old man, but not too much."

He nodded and smiled again as he said, "That won't hurt you. As long, as you keep your head on and do not go crazy. Say, get some sleep. I will see you tomorrow."

"Thanks, Dad, and hey, thanks again for fixing the Takajunky. Harry and I do appreciate all you did for us."

"Sure, Paulie. Get some sleep."

I waved and made my way to the bathroom. After a quick shower, I climbed into bed. Skippy looked up. He moved over, and he let me into the bed as he went back to sleep.

"Hey, Skip. Goodnight pal."

He did not even move.

Sleep came easily as I drifted off, with visions in my head of cows, mad roosters, Sal Zucchini, irate, meathead boyfriends, hoedown dances, rattling, old cars with trick doors that flew open on bumps, tractors and chickens, and of course, a certain gorgeous young woman with a blue dress and a flower in her hair.

As best as I can remember, Harry never saw Emma Whackenfuss ever again. Sadly, I never saw Debbie Boatwright ever again either. We still wrote to one another for quite a long time, and we may have spoken on the telephone once or twice after the big dance.

I do not remember.

The last letter I received from her, she told me how she had gone off to a university in the Midwest, her folks had sold Christmas Tree Mountain, and they had moved to a smaller house in Pennsylvania and retired.

Then, for whatever reason, we lost touch.

I am sure she met some nice young man along the way, and forgot all about Paul John Henson; she was too pretty and wonderful not to have.

A year or two after the dance, I went off to play professional ice hockey, and travel a long way from the old neighborhood so dear to my heart. Shortly thereafter, I met the woman of my dreams, and my life changed forever.

That is indeed a whole other story for another time and place.

I do think that you never really forget your first love. It is a rite of passage from your youth to one of the first steps towards being an adult. You may tuck the memory of the experience away for safekeeping, but it never really goes away. I think God keeps a section open in the hearts and minds of all people, to remind everyone of how great a gift he has given, when he gave us all a song of love, hope, joy, memories, and dreams. God gives us special friends such as Harry M. Redmond Jr. too.

I woke up from my nap and shook my head. I thought to myself, 'My goodness—what powerful memories and vivid dreams.'

They had affected me profoundly.

The television was still on, babbling away with some story of a chap climbing around the side of some hillside, poking in the ground with a shovel. I stood up, climbed out of my chair, stretched, and shut the television off. I looked out the window of my apartment and saw that the heat of the day had passed, and it actually looked as if it was going to be, for a change, a nice summer night. They were rare here in Norfolk, Virginia; let me tell you, as they were usually sticky, sultry, and nasty.

It was about seven or so in the early evening now. My goodness, I must have been tired, I had slept the afternoon away!

It was no wonder my mind wandered during my nap. These were lonely times for me, the off-season in hockey, trapped in some ungodly place full of heat, humidity, and mosquitoes, on the road away from family and friends; it was a bit rough. To compound my thoughts, I had not spoken with Harry M. Redmond Jr., in many years, ever since he had suffered a terrible tragedy in his life. On top of that, every day of my young life, I missed a certain young woman named Ms. Binky Hobnobber, but that is also another whole story.

Now that I was awake, what was I going to do with the rest of my night?

Looking out the back door of my apartment, I saw what appeared to be a nearly full moon trying hard to shine into the approaching night sky.

I suddenly had an idea.

I remembered a bottle of wine, which I had bought a long time ago for a forgotten occasion, and I had tucked away in a corner of my refrigerator. Rarely did I even drink a glass of wine, so the fact that it remained untouched for so long in my refrigerator was not surprising.

I grabbed a small transistor radio (since my jeep did not have a super deluxe, push button, auto selecto radio) an old blanket, and the bottle of wine and a wine glass. I walked out the back of my small apartment to my old jeep, which I always parked in the rear driveway of the complex. I climbed in, started the engine, and turned the jeep around to face the sunset and the moon hanging off in the sky above the horizon. Spreading the blanket out on the hood of my jeep, I popped open the bottle of wine with a corkscrew, tuned the radio to some music, and jumped up on the hood of the jeep.

I took a long sip from the bottle to test it while I relaxed and enjoyed the special summer evening. I recalled my words to Debbie Boatwright on her front porch, poured a little wine into the glass, lifted my glass in a toast to her, smiled, and looked up at the moon.

Yes, despite the loneliness, challenges, and occasional sadness, life is good, and so is a touch here and there of moonlight and memories.

THE END

Hot Coals and Sparks

1

Snowy Pictures and Sparks

"Now, if you knew what was good for you, you would man up, pay the extra money, and subscribe to cable television as the rest of the modern world does. It is a wonder that your house actually has running water and electricity. I swear all those blows to your head from hockey pucks have affected your brain wave functions," Mr. Hobnobber stood shaking his head at me as he watched me fiddle with the dial on our old television set.

I always enjoyed a visit from my in-laws, and in particular, my wonderful chats that I shared with my father-in-law, Senator William T. Hobnobber. My wife, Binky, and I had invited her parents over to our house for a Fourth of July picnic and celebration.

Binky was in the kitchen with her mother, preparing some food for the cookout we had planned, and my father-in-law was with me in our living room, watching me try to adjust the old television that we owned. I was in the final months of seminary, and Binky and I were on a tight budget as school slowly ended for me after a long haul. We had a small house that we had rented since we got married a few years back, and once I graduated, we were optimistic that we would be able to upgrade our lifestyle.

Until then, I would have to suffer at the hands of Mr. Hobnobber, and his oftentimes harsh observations of my bargain basement ways. Binky had grown up in an affluent lifestyle, as Mr. Hobnobber had been a successful attorney before he ventured into politics. But my loyal wife was very content in our small house and she was satisfied with our present life together. Of course, nothing was good enough for Binky in the eyes of her dear father!

"I sure hope we can watch the Crumbley's Department Store fireworks on this old relic of a television set. Since you invited Mrs. Hobnobber and me over here for this Fourth of July picnic, my expectations would be that I would be able to view the fireworks tonight as we enjoy a nightcap together. I love when they play the overture and the big fireworks explode. It stirs my patriotic heart! Say, when exactly are you going to stop going to school, graduate, and actually work for a living? It seems to me that this endless education of yours would eventually end. Maybe, if you actually had some type of gainful employment, you could afford to give my precious daughter all the finer things in life that she deserves, instead of this hippie lifestyle you lured her into with all of your hair, beard, and wild music. Besides, we do not even have any air conditioning here. It is going to be a million degrees today, and all we have are these ridiculous fans blowing hot air around."

The words jumped into my throat, but they just stopped short right before leaving my mouth. I was just about to say all of his ranting and raving was adding to the volume of hot air floating about, but the words did not quite come out.

The thought was sure there though.

I stood up and smiled. Even a holiday gathering never actually caused my father-in-law to ease any pressure off me. He had only been here for ten minutes and already my father-in-law was beating me like a drum in a marching band.

"Look at that lousy, snowy, picture on the television," Mr. Hobnobber complained, and pointed at the television set.

"Relax, relax, Dad Hobnobber. I will just need to go into

the attic to readjust the antenna up there. I will be right back. Please, Binky will mix you a nice, strong, Scotch on the rocks, sit here, and I will make sure that channel four tunes in clearly, so that you can watch the fireworks tonight," I attempted a vain effort to cool down my exploding father-in-law.

"Antenna! Ha! Who still utilizes such antique technology in these modern times? I am continually amazed as to the level of balderdash that you can whip up as a smokescreen to cover up your ineptness at lifestyle management. This is absurd. I imagine you will run into Marconi himself up in your attic too." Mr. Hobnobber waved his hands in disgust towards me as I turned towards the staircase. He then turned towards the kitchen and yelled out, "Dear Binky, your hippie husband is going into the attic to fix the antenna. When are you going to give up on him, and move back home darling, so you can watch a real television set?"

I heard Binky call out to her father, "Come in the kitchen, dear Father and leave Paul alone. I will mix you a nice, strong, drink. He will make sure the television picture is clear for watching your precious fireworks tonight. Once Paul fiddles around with the antenna, and has it working better, we will cook the hamburgers and hot dogs. You do realize that Paul and I have much better things to do than watch television at night!"

I saw Mr. Hobnobber stop short on his way towards the kitchen, as his mind wandered. His daughter's roundabout insinuation was sure to set him off now. I smiled, but I knew it was time to exit, stage left.

I scampered up the staircase to head for the antenna in the attic and ran smack into some ghosts from the past, right there on the staircase.

Right there in front of me!

I stopped and smiled.

"Oh geez, for the love of Pete! This is not that complicated youse guys. Dorothy, you watch the television screen, and relay to your mother how the picture looks. Honey, you stand at the base of the stairs and yell to your father. Pop, you stay at the top of the stairs, listen for Joan's instructions, and then relay to Paulie. Paulie, you hang out Gramp's bedroom window and yell at me which way to turn the stupid antenna according to what the rest of them tell ya!"

My old man pointed, as he divided our family up into a relay team that started at our old black and white television in the living room, and ended at my grandfather's bedroom window overlooking the roof. We had asked too many questions about the process and collectively gotten on the old man's short nerves. The plan was for the old man to climb out on the rooftop, loosen the mounting bolts, and spin the television antenna to pick up a better signal so the old man could watch the baseball game. My sister Dorothy, or as I called her, Dottie, would relay to the rest of us when the picture became clearer as the old man spun the antenna around. This was a common ritual that the old man undertook at least two or three times per year, when some thunderstorm, windstorm, blizzard, or an ice storm, would come along, and as the old man would say, "Knock our antenna flewwie" and cause a poor, quality picture.

It was a Saturday afternoon, a few days before the Fourth of July holiday, in or around 1974 or so. I was in and around fourteen years of age, watching and learning, a long-haired hippie kid on the road to discovery. Even learning how to adjust television antennas on rooftops was interesting to me. I still wore my hair long, tied it all in the back of my head, wore black canvas sneakers, and now I was proud of the fact that just a little faint line of a beard had appeared upon my face. I was a teenager, life was exciting, and this was just another classic adventure with my old man.

The old man was making a big deal at the snowy picture that had crept in on channel eleven, which was, of course, the station that broadcasted his beloved New York Bugs baseball games out of New York City.

"Now, do youse bunch of bananas have it this time?" The old man asked, but none of us dared to ask another question, even if we did not understand the instructions. Mum always said the old man was last in line when God handed out patience. I actually think that he was next to last because my best buddy Harry M. Redmond Jr. was just a little worse than the old man was in the old waiting department.

"I have to see the Old Timer's Day game on the Fourth of July at Bugs Stadium. I wait all year for that game, and the stupid antenna has to go out! I also want to see the Crumbley's Department Store fireworks on television from New York City. I love when they play the overture and the fireworks are going off."

The team divided into battle stations, and when we all were in our designated positions, the old man climbed out the bedroom window, and he jumped out onto the rooftop of our house, and crept along, until he reached the antenna. He had stuck various wrenches, screwdrivers, and other tools into his pockets, and he held them close to make sure none of them rattled around and tumbled out.

"Piece of shit antenna, every time it rains or a little puff of wind comes along, it spins around up here like some kinda stupid-ass windmill."

I could hear the old man proclaiming his love for this mission as he moved along the roof. I watched while he loosened the bolts and spun the mast, holding the antenna around a little in the mounts.

"Which way is New York City, Paulie?" He looked over

at me as I hung my head out the window. I pointed east towards the sun, and he nodded.

I heard Gramps yell, "No good, Paulie boy. Tell him channel eleven is snowy!"

"Channel eleven stinks, Dad!"

"How about now?"

The old man spun the antenna a little.

"How about now, Gramps?"

Gramps nodded and relayed the question along. Down in the deep recesses of our house I heard my sister say something, but I could not make it out.

The information made the way up the chain, and Gramps yelled back, "Bloody well, perfect right there!"

I knew my sister had not actually said that, and I heard my mother yell at her father for saying the word, "Bloody" in front of the children. Gramps and my mum were English, and my grandfather's colorful language of his native country oftentimes got him in a "Spot of trouble here and there."

I cleaned the relay language up a bit, as I yelled to the old man, "It is perfect right there!"

He nodded and yelled to me, "Tell them to try the other channels!"

I relayed the information back to the gang. This was worse than old Indian smoke signals. There had to be a better way than this. Back the information came that all the channels were good now except for channel four and thirteen. We spun this way and that way until the old man's patience finally gave out.

"OH GEEZ! MAKE UP YOUR MINDS. I AM COOKED OUT HERE ON THIS DAMN ROOF!

In the interest of self-preservation and peace, we decided collectively that it was now good enough. And the old man tightened the bolts, slid his way back over to the window, and climbed back in the house.

"Geez, my head is cooked from sitting out there," he

complained as I helped him with the tools. We all gathered back around the television set and all the channels looked good. There was a little ghost shadow on channel four, but it was not so bad. Channel 13 tuned in rather weakly, but that was a public broadcasting channel out of Newark, New Jersey and we seldom watched it, anyway.

Mum was concerned about channel four, which was the channel that broadcasted her favorite soap opera on every weekday afternoon. She looked at the old man, batted her eyes a little, and said, "I do enjoy my afternoon show on channel four, dear. You know, *'Nights of our Lives'*. Do you think the little ghosts will go away, my dear?"

The old man stared back at Mum and shook his head. Back on the roof, he went and the words that he utilized during this part of the mission still float in a dark obscenity cloud over the top of 182 Belmont Avenue in Haledon, New Jersey to this day.

I have heard they have drifted a little towards the east since then, but not too much.

After another hour or so of fiddling with the antenna, we finally came to a compromise as to which of the channels were clearest on the screen. Mum appreciated the old man's second efforts and after making an incredibly big deal about the entire job, the old man forgot all about it, because the time had come for the New York Bugs baseball game to come on. He settled into his chair, cracked open an ice-cold Big Boulder beer and sat back to watch the big game.

"This is going to be a good one honey, Jim Beaver is on the mound, and he has been riding a hot streak," he yelled out to the kitchen to where Mum, Gramps, my sister, and I were sitting around the kitchen table having tea and some snacks.

"That is nice, dear. What team are they playing, Paul?" Mum asked. My mum did not actually care a hill of beans about baseball however, she made believe she was a little interested to humor the old man.

"Those stupid-ass Flying Saucers. I can't stand the manager of the Saucers. That crybaby boo-boo McGee. His brother stinks as an announcer, and this crybaby, was a jerk when he played too."

"That is nice, dear. Enjoy the game."

Our fox terrier, Skippy, made a guest appearance, and he lazily wandered into the living room to sit next to the old man and listen to the game too. I had a limited interest in baseball. It was not my favorite sport because hockey ruled my world, but since it was the summer, and almost the Fourth of July, in the interest of tradition and good, old, American holidays, I would catch a game or two, here and there.

It was hot and sticky now, and we did not have any air conditioning. That is unless you could count the windows being open, and the four hundred and sixteen, electric fans that spun around in every room of our house.

Soon our living room filled wall-to-wall with the voices of Blabber Viscardi, Johnny Mclaughy, Ralph "The Rocket" Lenard and Bob McGee as the play-by-play announcers for the New York Bugs. The announcers were just as if they were old neighborhood friends.

You could hear the opening remarks by Bob McGee floating amongst the gentle whirring of electric fans buzzing around our home, "Welcome ladies and gents to the Bronx in the great state of New York, and welcome to Bugs Stadium, for another exciting afternoon of New York Bugs baseball. Yes, on a fantastic summer afternoon here, the Bugs take on their bitter rivals, the Flying Saucers out of Beantown. We have Jim Beaver on the mound for the Bugs versus Sidewinder O'Leary. . .."

After finishing my tea, I wandered into the living room too and sat down in a chair next to the old man to watch the game with him. "Any score yet, Dad? I asked him.

"Nah, nah, nah, not yet. The game is on the line here,

though," the old man answered as he licked his lips and adjusted the Bugs hat on his head.

I looked at the line score flashing on the bottom of the screen while the audio buzzed on the television. There was no score yet, it was only the bottom of the second inning. I was puzzled as to exactly why the game would be on the line in the second inning. However, what did I know? I was a hockey player, and the old man was a baseball expert.

Just when you settle in for traditional, old time enjoyment and an afternoon of America's pastime—disaster strikes! The old man was intense as he was leaning in, sipping his beer, clutching his Bugs cap on his head as Jim Beaver had the Flying Saucers best hitter, Bobby "The Crusher" Phillips, locked up with a two ball and two-strike count.

The intenseness of the moment captured me too. I leaned in, caught up at the moment, while I listened to the announcer, the great Blabber Viscardi and his call of the game.

"Beaver looks in for the sign, the windup and the pitch. And, and, and he delivers. . .."

BANG! POP! POP! POP! POP!

POOF!

Skippy took off like a rocket ship. The noise had him running for his life.

There was an early firework display in our living room!

The television screen went dead, the picture faded to a small, white dot in the middle of the picture tube, and the sound faded away. The voices and pictures faded slowly away into oblivion.

No more, Blabber Viscardi, Johnny Mclaughy, Ralph "The Rocket" Lenard and Bob McGee, only a dead television set! It was all gone, except for a faint whiff of ozone and a slight burning smell that lingered in the air.

The old man jumped up from his chair, his Big Boulder

beer went flying onto the floor and he yelled out, "What the hell happened to the TV? Did he strike Crusher Phillips out or what?" The old man ran over to the television, and started to fiddle around with the knobs behind a metal lid in the front of the television, and he then beat on the top of the wooden cabinet.

Our American Blabber model, X6-12 television, was very old. In fact, old was not actually a very accurate description, because the word, "Ancient" was the exact word that the television repairman used when he last serviced the set. It was a black and white set, housed in a large, blonde colored, wooden cabinet, with brown speaker grille mesh that covered the front speakers. It had large metal knobs that stuck out all over the front of the set, and in true Henson family tradition; it was slightly unreliable. The television perpetuated the ongoing Henson tradition of the old man to keep things past the normal life expectancy that average folks usually kept items.

On an average, the old man kept most everything, twenty or so years past the normal life expectancy. People would accuse the old man of being rather thrifty in his nature, but the old man was careful to correct people who accused him of that personality trait. You see, he would tell folks, there was indeed a huge difference between being thrifty and being poor. Thrifty implied that you had money to spend.

I stood up, walked over to the old man, and offered up a factual observation, "Dad, I thought I saw and heard some sparks and popping noises come out the back of the set. Do you smell something burning?"

Mum, my sister Dottie, Skippy, and Gramps came running into the living room as the old man nodded his head, leaned over the top of the television, and started to sniff deeply in the back of the television.

"Something is on fire in here, Paul. Smells as if your bloomin' telly is on fire," Gramps observed as the old man frowned and pulled the plug on the television set.

It was now a unanimous observation that the television had fried, and it was about to be declared as having gone, "Flewwie." The old man stood up and put his hands on his hips. His eyeballs rotated around in his head, sort of rotating in rhythm to the pulsating tom-tom drums on the side of his temples. Once again, Skippy took off for greener pastures, and Mum, Dotty, and Gramps retreated to the kitchen.

"This stupid, damn piece of shit television has gone flewwie! Quick, Paulie, run and get my radio out of the bedroom. I need to listen to the game! Run!"

I took off like a flash to pick up the radio out of my parent's bedroom, because the old man was now very excited and upset about missing his beloved Bugs game. I was now praying that Jim Beaver had struck out Crusher Phillips as I reached to pull out the wall plug behind the nightstand where my parents kept an old (ancient) table radio. This radio was also very old; in fact, it was older than the television set, if that was actually possible. I carried the radio back into the living room; the old man grabbed it and plugged it in. He sat the radio on the table next to his easy chair and he turned the radio to the "on" position. He feverishly tuned the dial to 770 on the A.M. band and he waited for the tubes to warm up.

It always took forever for the tubes to warm up.

"Oh geez, c'mon! How stinkin' long does it take for a few tubes to warm up!" The old man was not a fan of the warming-up period of old electronics.

I was still praying as I heard the radio crackle to life. The old man slid the tuner back and forth as the voices became clearer.

A tweak of the tuner knob and the voice of Ralph "The Rocket" Lenard came in loud and clear. Ralph had moved over into the radio booth to cover the game and he blared loudly into the microphone, "Yeah, yeah, yeah, the Bugs are now down one to nothin,' due to that monster home run that Crusher Phillips put into the right field bleachers. That was a one of a kind shot. Let me tell you folks, you do not see homers hit like that every day. Once in a lifetime shot there by Crusher Phillips, the ball bounced off the billboard behind the seats. Ya know, the billboard advertising for Dingleberry beer. I have to say that I prefer Big Boulder beer myself. Those Dingleberries are way too sweet! I cannot ever remember someone hitting the billboards before! I bet Jim Beaver would like to have that pitch back!"

Oh, oh, this is not good.

I slowly walked towards the kitchen and said, "I will get a dish rag to clean up the beer, Dad. I will be back."

The old man stood up from his chair, and he bellowed out, "YOU HAVE GOT TO BE KIDDIN.' A ONCE IN A LIFETIME HOMER AND I MISSED IT! CRUSHER HIT THAT STUPID-ASS BUM BEAVER'S FASTBALL INTO THE DINGLEBERRY BEER BILLBOARD. FOR THE LOVE OF PETE, I HAVE NEVER SEEN A BALL HIT THAT BILLBOARD! JOAN GIT ME THE PHONE NUMBER FOR THAT STUPID HANK'S TV REPAIR SHOP!"

"Yes dear, calm down it is just a television set."

Even in the kitchen, I could detect a faint smell of high voltage laden ozone and an acrid burning smell floating in the air. It was a little early for a firework display, but the old man had set off a few sparks as a prelude to the big celebration.

I am sure it was not exactly what he had planned, but after all, a spark is a spark.

Happy birthday America.

2

Psst . . . Want to Buy Some Fireworks?

"Mr. Henson, I hate to tell you this, but your flyback transformer is gonzo."

"Flyback transformer! That sounds like a part ya just made up, Hank. If you are gonna rip me off, then at least make up a fake, phony, and fraudulent part with a name that makes sense."

I sat in a living room chair along with Skippy, who was sitting next to me as we both watched the battle scene unfold. Hank had agreed today, in what was likely to be a huge mistake on his part, to stop by and check out the television set on his way home from his repair shop. He had apparently only agreed after the old man gave him a long sob story about the New York Bugs and the Old Timer's Day game on the Fourth of July. We had listened to the rest of the game on the radio, and the old man was not in the best of moods. The Bugs and Jim Beaver had not just lost the game this afternoon. Destroyed would be a better word to describe the loss.

Now, the old man was on a roll. Not only had the Bugs been plastered but also his beloved, American Blabber model X6-12 television set had blown up in a spectacular pillar of smoke.

He hovered over the back of Hank, watching his every move as Hank worked on the television set. The old man continued his illustrious legacy of battling with repairmen, storekeepers, retail managers, and a virtually endless stream of other folks, who he knew were plotting how to extract the last coins from his pockets and the last dollar from his wallet.

Hank from Hank's Television Repair Shop had been coming to our house for years to service our old relic of a television set, so he was a well-seasoned veteran in my old man's endless retail and service shop conspiracy theories and patented speeches. Hank just shook his head, picked up his tools and high voltage tester, and tossed them back into his tool and tube caddy on the floor in front of the television set.

"You know something, Mr. Henson? I agreed to come out and check your set as my last service call of the day on a Saturday afternoon, because for some odd reason, I really like you. I really do, but I am not exactly sure, why it is that I subject myself to this punishment every few months or so. Although, I must admit, a visit to see you is almost worth it for the comic relief alone, Mr. Henson."

"Well, whatever there, Hank, but you just ripped us off on a repair last month, and now the television is flewwie again. You must have planted some kind of a time bomb in the set to guarantee it will blow up in a week or two. I read about all the tricks youse guys pull in this business, in my June copy of 'Dark Secrets' magazine. Yeah, yeah, yeah, sticking little pins inside of the parts so they blow up, and putting higher voltages to parts, so they blow up down the road. It is all being watched now by the government."

Hank reached into a silver clipboard he had on top of his toolbox, and glanced at some papers as he said, "Hmm . . . let's see here, Mr. Henson, yes, in-deedy. I put an audio output tube in this set on January the third of this year, and it is now July. That is not last month, but I forgot that there is a Henson time zone in this world. Henson time seems to revolve at a different speed and pace than the rest of the entire world. And yes, I admit that I am being followed right now by government agents, who hide behind dark sunglasses and watch television and radio repair guys."

Hank was hitting back pretty hard. The old man screwed his mouth up in his usual corkscrew mode, which indicated that his initial battle plans had failed, and he was regrouping on his strategy.

"All right, Hank, let's cut to the chase here and lay your card's face up. How much is this part that does not exist going to cost me to replace," the old man conceded the fact of which he would not publicly admit to anyone; Hank might just know a little of what he is talking about in regard to flyback transformers.

"I will be honest, Mr. Henson, the flyback is big bucks. They go in the summer because of the heat and humidity, which get in the copper and make them burn and arc. You do not have air conditioning here, and it has been hot so far, this summer, so this one just blew up. The transformer is one of the main parts to produce the high voltage to run the picture tube. Unfortunately, I think you are looking at sixty-five to seventy bucks and on a set this old, I have to say that it is not worth it."

"Old! This set is not old, Hank. I just bought it a few years back! Your old man sold it to me.

Hank shook his head and said, "Mr. Henson, my dad has been retired for fifteen years now. This is a model X6-12, and the American Blabber company just came out with the color model X62-249. I hate to tell you, but they consecutively number their models. This set is old. Then again, I look around here and see that you still drive that same 1964 Putter Classic model 200, the radio there is an American Blabber model from thirty years ago, so once more, Henson time is different from the rest of the world."

"Seventy bucks, geez, Hank, that is some major coin. Let me take a look in there and see what this fleaback transformer looks like."

"Flyback not fleaback, Mr. Henson."

"Yeah, yeah, yeah, whatever there, Hank. Show me what you are pitching here. I still am not convinced that this is not some kind of rip-off."

In northern New Jersey, there is a large population of what we would have commonly called on the streets, "chronic mispronunciation guys." My buddy, Harry M. Redmond Jr. and I were very aware of the population, and one of the neighbors of Harry over on John Street was one of the worst of the bunch. He was a tall man named Clifford McWhiffy, who worked with our friend, Jeff Porter's father. We called Clifford by his nickname, which was, "Cliffy," and he would never pronounce any names or words correctly. Nonnative northern New Jersey speakers would require a translator to converse with Cliffy as he rambled on and on in some unknown gibberish. The story of Cliffy, I will leave for another time and a set of words, since he was a legend, and his adventures would fill many pages in order to tell his story correctly.

The old man was also a member of the "chronic mispronunciation guy's club," although his talents were more in the less common, "I heard it my way, so that is the way that I am going to say it," type of subgroup, rather than the more common, "I just totally speak gibberish group." One or two glaring exceptions were the city of Chicago, Illinois, which the old man insisted was spoken, "Shercargo, Illynoise," and pizza pie, which was converted to, "Pizzer pies." It did not matter if you were ordering one pizza pie; it was always plural to the old man. With our dear Mum and Gramps being English, they combined their linguistic efforts, desperately trying to teach us to speak proper "King's English." The old man would easily thwart their efforts, as our father was the connection for Dottie and me to speak good, old-fashioned, authentic, New Jersey street slang.

"Here is the flyback transformer . . . right in here," Hank pointed. My curiosity was now aroused, as well as Skippy's, as we both wandered over to peer inside, too.

"That is the flying transformer? That black thing there is

seventy bucks! It does stink as if it burnt up in there, Hank. It smells a little like my wife's pot roast, after she cooks it for forty hours so that no one gets sick. I admit that there may be a slight chance that you are right, but ya got to charge that much for that blob of wires?"

"It takes forever to install. There are lots of wires. It is complicated."

"Ha! I could put that in, even if I wore a blindfold! I just put a steering box in the Putter, which Vince here at the corner Golf service station told me that no one could do!" Skippy and I spotted a large, black, wheel-like transformer with a large wire sticking out of the top of it. It smelled as if it had cooked and it looked melted. Skippy sniffed and turned his nose up at the odor and took off.

I agreed with our family dog.

Hank shook his head as he picked up his clipboard and started to write out his service invoice. He was still shaking his head as he said, "You may be a good car mechanic, Mr. Henson, and I bet you are a good one, in order to keep that pile of junk in your driveway running, but there is no way you could put a flyback transformer in."

Oh, oh!

I spotted the old man's ears wiggle and twitch. His eyes went beady and determined, and his fists clenched a little. I knew that was the look that he would get when he sensed a mechanical or repair challenge loomed on the horizon.

In the old man's eyes, Hank had just thrown down the gauntlet.

The old man firmly believed that he was fully capable of repairing any mechanical devices, electrical devices, plumbing fixtures, or any other inventions made by mankind. I had a strange feeling that he just included a flying transformer, a fleaback transformer, and a flyback transformer in the same repair category.

"Say, Hank, where can I buy one of these flyer transformers?"

Oops, I forgot the flyer transformers.

"Flyback, Mr. Henson, a flyback transformer. You can find them down at Jersey Electronics on Goffle Road in Paterson. You just need the model number. Good luck to you, if you think you can do it, Mr. Henson. By the way, that will be six dollars and eighty-five cents for the service call. If you go for the repair, I will give you credit for the service call charge."

"WHAT! Hank, I swear ya a bum! Seven bucks for a service call! Youse guys are all the same. . .."

The next day, the old man had a half-day off from work, because the shop where he worked closed early for the day before the Fourth of July. Right after work, the old man and I were in the 1964 Putter Classic model 200, riding down together to Goffle Road to Jersey Electronics. The old man had picked up the gauntlet and accepted the challenge.

I knew that he would. He was not going to miss Old Timer's Day for the New York Bugs and his Crumbley's fireworks for a mere obstacle such as a burnt fleaback transformer.

The next day was the Fourth of July, our family was having a big backyard barbeque, and I would be running between our backyard and a big shindig over at Harry's house. This was a big holiday for us, and we were all excited. Gramp's sister, our beloved Aunt Alma, was due in later from Florida, along with her daughter, the famous Cousin Pat. Aunt Lois, who was Mum's kid sister, and her husband Uncle Ed, was also coming over, so it was a big family day for all of us.

I loved when Aunt Alma and Cousin Pat would visit. Aunt Alma was "English" having not come over to America permanently until just a few years ago. She married a chap who owned shoe stores in Florida and a few in the United Kingdom, but they had finally settled in America in their later years. Aunt Alma was vibrant, full of humor, pretty, fun, and a wonderful woman. She spoke some Welsh and she would teach me words here and there, and I loved sitting with her, while listening for hours to her tell of her life and adventures. Aunt Alma was now a widow, and she traveled all over the world and tried very hard to convince her brother to join her on her travels. Gramps would have none of any such nonsense as he complained that his sister would always pick some, "Horrible, bloody hot, bug infested, place to visit that no self-respecting Englishman would ever consider visiting on a holiday."

Aunt Alma usually fled the terrible heat of the summer in Florida, and spent a good deal of July and August staying with Gramps in his second-floor apartment above us. She would then visit upstate New York, to stay with her daughter, Cousin Pat, to enjoy the fantastic autumn weather in New York, until she returned to Florida in late October.

Cousin Pat was a much, much larger version of Aunt Alma. She was a large woman, and she was gorgeous. Her facial features were perfect; she had perfect bone structure and clear, blue eyes. She was one of the prettiest women that I had ever seen. She was also full of life and fun. She had come over to America with her mum and father and met a man who operated dairy farms in upstate New York. He sadly passed away a few years ago, and Cousin Pat now traveled a little with her mum and stayed on her farm in New York. Cousin Pat was for lack of a better description; very large, she was in fact, huge in girth and size. Full of enjoyment, she spoke really loudly, snorted, howled, and whooped with laughter at everything, and was a whirlwind of excitement.

She weighed an enormous amount of weight, and the old man prepared feverishly in advance of her visits. He would reinforce chairs, our living room sofa, and the toilets in the bathrooms. You see, in addition to her large girth and size, Cousin Pat was a legend for her clumsiness too.

She was like a human wrecking ball as she plowed into things, broke wine and drinking glasses, beer mugs, tipped and tripped over furniture, and destroyed almost everything she touched. Mum, Gramps, and the old man would put away family heirlooms and other sensitive items for weeks in advance of her visit. Mum would serve drinks and food to Cousin Pat in the plastic versions of cups, tableware, and glasses to try to prevent some accidents. It was all part of her persona and, in a very strange way, a part of her charisma, too.

Preparing for a visit from Cousin Pat was similar to the preparation for the arrival of a blizzard or a hurricane.

We pulled into the parking lot of Jersey Electronics, parked the Putter Classic model 200, and the old man and I walked into a maze of parts, wires, and electronic components as far as the eye could see. In front of us, in a labyrinth of complicated electronic wonder, were rows upon rows of parts, equipment, and an assortment of general junk. All of it was all stacked, lined up, and organized to fill up every corner of the store. There were antennas on display hanging from the ceiling here and there. The store had a distinctive odor of plastic and metal. A big, sweaty guy was standing behind the counter and he looked up at us as we walked into the store. He had a towel around his neck to wipe his face. An electric fan was set up upon the counter and was blowing on him, but it seemed to be a fruitless effort to keep this enormous and gelatinous chap cool. As we approached, I saw that he wore a uniform shirt with "Mike" stenciled above a pocket that held about twenty-nine pens, and a miniature screwdriver with a magnet on top of it.

"Whadda youse boys need?" Mike asked.

"I need a flying backwards transformer for this model television set," the old man said to Mike, the sweaty counter guy, as he handed Mike a notepaper with the numbers written down upon it.

Mike looked at us as if we had two heads, so I jumped in really quick in order to weed through some confusion, "A flyback transformer. We need a flyback transformer there, Mike."

"Oh, okay, thanks for the translation hippie kid. You must be hot with all that hair," Mike said as he wiped his face with his towel. I was not a big fan of summer and heat and humidity, and I could really sweat a lot too, but Mike made me look like an amateur. He looked as if someone just hit him in the face with a fire hose. Mike's towel was high on the disgusting meter and it left little doubt to the fact that it had been a hot day, and even though it was now almost four o'clock in the afternoon, it still was hot.

"Hey, are you boys in the trade? We are wholesale to the trade only, ya know," Mike pointed up to a sign above the counter proclaiming the store policy.

"Well, yeah, yeah, yeah, chief. I am in the trade . . . I am a machinist if that is what you mean. Hank sent us down here, Mike. You know him for sure, he is a rip-off artist, charlatan, and crook, ya know, the owner of Hank's Television and Radio Repair shop," the old man testified as to our ticket for entry into the secret, inner circle, and exclusive world of electronic repair. I knew that was not what Mike wanted to hear as far as our qualifications go, but it must have been a long, hot day for the big man.

He studied us for a few seconds, wiped his face again, waved his hand in the air, and mumbled, "Oh, what the hell. Now, let's see here. . .. HOLY SWEET WATER OF LIFE! AN AMERICAN BLABBER MODEL X6-12!" Mike screamed as he looked at the note with the model number on it. "This set is older than dirt! Did you ride here on a dinosaur or what?"

Mike laughed as he picked up a dirty and torn book from the counter and started to thumb through it. The old man did not say a word, but I knew he was not thrilled with Mike's outward shock and jokes at the advanced age of our television set. Mike was studying the book, thumbing through pages, and he wrote a number down on the note pad.

"Hmm . . . we may actually have this part. I see that it crosses into a Thordawson X72 dash 123 niner. I recognize that number. I sold one of those about twenty years ago. Wait here."

Mike wandered back into sections of rows upon rows of steel shelving behind the counter, and he reappeared holding a part in his hand.

"Well, I'll be. We do have one," he said with a smile. He blew a layer of dust off the box, placed it on the counter, and opened it. We all peered inside and sure enough, it looked like the flyback transformer inside of our television set, well, without the smell and burned appearance that is.

"Ten bucks plus tax pal," Mike said with a smile. "Youse guys are going to put this in? Flybacks are tough, ya know."

"Yeah, yeah, yeah, we can handle it. I just finished putting a steering box in that 1964 Putter Classic model 200 out there," the old man pointed at our family car sitting in front of the store.

Sweaty Mike leaned over the counter, and looked out to where the car was parked, while drops of sweat poured off his forehead and dripped onto the countertop, "Wow, my uncle had one of those hunks of junk cars years ago. Looks like everything you have, except for this hippie kid here, is kinda old there, pal."

The old man was in a rare, "I will forgive the insults of the store clerk mood," so he let Mike ride on that comment. Actually, Mike was sweating so badly that it just was not worth it.

We paid him, grabbed the part, thanked Sweaty Mike, and took off.

"Geez, I do not think I have ever seen someone sweat that bad," the old man said as we stepped out of the store and headed for the car. "I would've debated him and called him out for some of those comments, but I was afraid he would sweat on us." I nodded my head in agreement. As cool a store as Jersey Electronics was, I just wanted to bail out of there too. It was hotter than Hades in there.

Jersey Electronics was next to a fast food, hamburger and hot dog joint. The store was located on a main drag that led outside of the northeast side of the city of Paterson, and into a small borough on the outskirts of the city. It was a busy road, and as we walked towards the Putter Classic model 200, I became aware of a short guy, wearing dark sunglasses, parked along the edge of the parking lot on the other side of where we had parked our car. He was carefully studying folks as they moved about in the fast-food restaurant's parking lot. He sat on the trunk of his car with his arms folded across his chest. I tapped the old man's arm and pointed him out. The old man nodded as we both knew, he was a typical, New Jersey street guy selling something out of the trunk of his car.

We just knew it.

He had the look, and growing up on the streets of this gritty, old, urban area had refined my skills in identifying what I needed to be aware of, and in some cases, steer clear of too. Sometimes, what they sold out of their cars was of interest, sometimes it was pure trouble. Most of the time, it was something illegal, or how shall we say, it might come under the slightly shady category of, "obtained under some kind of questionable procurement circumstances."

After all, this is New Jersey, and street deals are a way of life here. It is the same as breathing and eating. As we walked closer, and the old man was about to put the key in the car door, the shady guy spotted us and he stood up.

He walked close to us, looked over his shoulder, and then around in all directions, waved to us to come over, and spoke in a low voice, "Hey youse guys . . . psst . . . youse guys want to buy some fireworks?"

As soon as the old man heard the word, "Fireworks" his ears wiggled and twitched and his eyes widened. I can tell you there was not much the old man enjoyed more in this world than setting off some fireworks. Since New Jersey had outlawed fireworks a few years back, the old man was not the same person. Sure, he would set off some boring sparklers that fizzled and sparked a little, but something was missing from his Fourth of July celebrations. The television exploding the other night, provided the old man with some unwanted, but slightly interesting, sparks and sizzles. But it was boring in his big picture of patriotic, American, explosive lust. It was the true explosions in which the old man craved! The booms, the bangs, the running away as he lit the fuse, the smell of gunpowder, the hiding from the policemen as they cruised up and down the front of the road we lived on, while they tried to figure out where that bottle rocket came from was all part of the Fourth of July to the old man. It was, in his opinion, positively un-American that the State of New Jersey outlawed fireworks in the first place.

In a classic ploy, not to allow the shady character peddling the fireworks know that he was very, very, interested, (which would of course, elevate the prices) the old man played it cool, as he casually answered, "Well, I don't know . . . maybe. Whatcha got there, chief?" The old man waved me over as his body language changed while he strolled over towards the peddler. I knew my father really wanted to sprint over, make him lift his trunk lid, while he panted and drooled over the pyrotechnic assortment that, undoubtedly, the peddler had strategically hidden in his magical trunk.

"C'mon over here, pal. You and the hippie. I have got all the good stuff. Here, here, just take a good look in the trunk here, pal," the shady peddler waved us over as he unlocked the trunk of his car, and revealed a cornucopia of explosive desire. Our eyes popped out of our heads, as there in front of us, in full frontal, naked display, was every currently illegal firework device known to mankind. The shady peddler waved his arm over the trunk in delight at the amazing collection of explosions he had managed to gather for sale.

Only in New Jersey could you go for a part to repair your television, and next to a fast-food joint, run into some shady guy peddling fireworks out of the trunk of his car.

It was amazing.

The old man immediately turned to me, handed me the flyback transformer (fleaback transformer), grabbed me by my shoulders, and firmly said, "Here hold the fleaback transformer. You keep your winky, dinky, doo mouth shut. You are always way too honest and have old lady tendencies. I know this is illegal, but I swear that if you tell your mother!"

I was already nodding my head in agreement. I received the transmission loud and clear. The look in the old man's eyes told me everything that I needed to know. My lips were sealed.

"Here you go, pal. Everything you need to light your neighborhood on fire for the Fourth of July and have the coppers comin' for miles! Cherry bombs, m–eighties, ash cans, ladyfingers, sparklers, fizzlers, shaker bombers, skyrockets, bottle-rockets, dipsy doodlers, Roman candles, Paterson candles, black snakes, blue snakes, Catherine wheels, zippers, spinners, poppers, floppers, and zingers. I have tanks that shoot cannonball fireworks at your wife when she yells at you. I have airplanes that drop bombs, ground spinners, helicopters, pinwheels, and flares. I have rockets that blast off and explode in loud bursts, and rockets that explode in fountains of colors. Ya name it and I have it, pal!"

The old man rubbed his face with excitement and anticipation. His eyes were going back and forth in his head as if he was watching a tennis match. This was better than he could have ever wished for and imagined. The shady peddler knew he had a true fireworks lover and connoisseur at his storefront. I mean, actually, in front of the trunk of his car. He could smell the sale.

The old man always kept in his wallet what he commonly referred to as "Beer money" or in some cases; he called it, "Emergency money." He had a little zipper compartment on the side of his wallet, in which he put this stash of dough. I am sure it was money that he hid from Mum in some way, shape, or form. Money was tight for us, and to blow a bunch of hard-earned dough on fireworks would be a difficult sell to Mum, so into the reserve fund he went. He was going to fly under Mum's financial radar for now, but deep inside, he knew that Mum would eventually ensnare him in her net of money wasting criticisms. It was worth the hit the old man knew he was going to take. We are talking about fireworks here, you know!

"I do not know, chief. This stuff looks expensive," as he reached for his wallet, the old man strategically laid the initial groundwork for the negotiation process to begin. The old man leaned over to me and whispered, "I am going to use my beer money here. I will pick up just a few things here and there to add some fun to our party."

It was indeed a convincing justification, because in my opinion, mere beer money was actually in some strange way, "different" than regular money was. Beer money's true destiny always is to procure frivolous things; after all, the old man always told me you only rent beer, tea, and coffee.

The shady peddler looked over the top of his trunk and around the car, keeping an eye out for the law. He was now anxious to make the sale and move along, "Look pal, we do not have a lot of time here for hard core negotiation. Youse guys have me exposed here. I am out in the open, and this stuff is not exactly legal ya know. Tomorrow is the big day.

I am down to the wire now, so I need to unload this stuff. I will give you a good deal, so let's cut the chit chat, and pick out some stuff."

The old man rubbed his hands together in glee. Not only did he find the mother lode of fireworks but also the guy was desperate for a deal. His usual hard-core negotiations and painful, long, drawn out, hand wringing would not be required. The old man nodded, looked in his secret wallet compartment, and pulled out fifteen dollars. The stage was set.

"Give me all you can for fifteen bucks, chief, but I need at least two skyrockets and the ash cans in the mix . . . and a few of those wives shooting, tank thingys."

"Hmmm . . . yeah, yeah, yeah, fifteen bucks, I can give ya some good stuff," the shady peddler said as he gathered up what seemed to be one of each item and dropped them all into a paper bag. "Now, you do know these ash cans are the equivalent of a quarter stick of dynamite pal. Be careful!" The shady peddler warned us as he dropped a few silver-colored devices with green fuses sticking out of the top of them into the bag.

"Yeah, yeah, yeah, chief. I was lighting off fireworks when you were still peeing in your diapers," the old man dismissed the warning.

I thought it was strange how a guy riding around the streets of Paterson, New Jersey with a trunk load of fireworks on a hot summer night, which could blow up four or five city blocks, would suddenly become overly safety conscious.

I admired his roundabout concern for our well-being.

The bag was full. The old man gave the shady peddler guy the fifteen dollars, and the fireworks "salesman" closed the trunk, waved, and jumped into his vehicle. In a flash, he was off, he tore across the parking lot, and we watched from a distance as he stopped on the other side of the parking lot of the fast-food restaurant. He jumped out of the car, carrying two license plates in his hand. He then proceeded to unscrew the plates on the vehicle and switched them around with the replacement ones.

Once more, he was off in a flash.

It really was remarkable.

The old man shook his head and said, "Geez, the guy works harder at being a crook, then if he went and got a job, and made an honest living."

I had to agree.

Life in New Jersey was different, and the education that you received growing up here was worth a million dollars.

We jumped in the 1964 Putter Classic model 200 with our flyback transformer and our little bag of explosive tricks. The old man started the car up, and we rolled off into the late afternoon summer sunset. Now, we just had to hide the fireworks from Mum, put the part in the television, and celebrate our nation's birthday.

Sounds simple, eh?

Well, nothing in the life of the Henson family was ever simple.

3

Back on the Air

"Paulie, go get my soldering iron, the socket set, a flashlight, a pad, a pencil, some masking tape, and the radio solder. We will put this part in and be watching the New York Bugs game by seven o'clock."

We had returned home, hid the stash of fireworks in the garden shed, had a quick bite to eat, and now the old man was back, and focused upon the task at hand. A challenge was a challenge, and the old man would never back down from any repair. Once someone presented the idea, or suggested that he could not fix something, then I can assure you that it was all over. My mother had fretted and tried her best to talk him out of the undertaking. She sensed that this could spoil the mood for the holiday, and with our relatives visiting, she was doing her best to make sure the holiday spirits were lively. Mum also strategically and carefully hinted that there was also the possibility of burning our house down, injury by electricity, or other hazardous factors in the replacement of the flyback transformer. The old man scoffed at all of these ideas; he would have none of any such talk of failure. No matter what, he was determined to watch his New York Bugs, Old Timer's Day game and his fireworks on this television. There was no question in his mind that he would succeed.

By the time that I returned with the requested tools, the old man had thought of ten more tools that I needed to go back down into his basement workshop to pick up. This was the equivalent to the construction of a great battleship or a bridge. There were never enough tools.

Mum, Dottie, and Gramps had retreated to the kitchen to help Mum while she prepared some food for the big picnic tomorrow. Skippy was hanging out there too, looking for a tidbit or errant blob of something that may drop within his reach. I thought how the food preparation was actually a smokescreen to hide from the old man's repair mission. Despite the newly ordained, yet still novice, television repairman's outstanding confidence, there remained a great deal of doubt in and amongst my family as to this undertaking by the old man. No one else was brave enough to hang out with me and watch, so I was alone now to take one for the team. Electronics was not exactly in the old man's standard repair repertoire, so the doubts were understandable. Sometimes these types of repairs went south rather quickly, and turmoil and strife were the end result. I did not mind, as I provided emotional support and I learned some new, "creative" words for use in a street hockey game with the guys over on Geyer Street.

"Hold this flashlight, Paulie, and hand me the flat blade screwdriver. No, no, no, c'mon, wake up and shine it over here, you pineapple. What are ya blind?" I quickly adjusted the light to where the old man was pointing. The old man had unscrewed the television chassis from inside the cabinet, removed all the knobs, and pulled the insides out to see where the wires for the transformer were located under the cabinet.

"This is a piece of cake! I know that damn rip-off artist, Hank, was just exaggerating about how tough it is to replace this to get me to pony up the dough! I will mark each of these wires with the masking tape, number them, draw a diagram, and cut them in half. Then we just wire the new one up according to the colors and our marks," the old man said while his confidence was building. It seemed as if it was a very organized and reasonable plan for me.

"I just need to get this big wire off the picture tube here. Hand me that big screwdriver." I handed my father a big screwdriver, and he placed it under a big, red wire and . . . BANG! POWWWW!

A giant spark flew out of the wire, the old man fell backwards on his backside, his Bugs baseball cap toppled off his head, and he rolled around on the floor behind the television!

"DAD!" I screamed as I checked on him, and he seemed to be surprised, but he was all right. He sure had scared the living daylights out of me. The rest of the family came running in from the kitchen to check on our status.

"GEEZ! HOLY SHIT! Where did that come from? The television is unplugged! I am all right! I am all right!" The old man was waving in the air and standing up now to reassure everyone that he was still alive and well. I retrieved his Bugs hat and handed it to him.

It was a hard lesson in electronics, as we had now learned that a picture tube held an electrical charge, long after it was unplugged.

Mum ventured into the turbulent waters once more and Mum said, "Maybe, dear, honey bunny, lovie . . . you should reconsider and call Hank. This is awfully dangerous and I am not sure you can. . .." She stopped short when she spotted the glare on the old man's face. My sister, Gramps, and Mum scurried off because the mere suggestion that the old man, "Did not know what he was doing," was not going to work.

The old man looked at me, took his Bugs hat off, and pushed his hair back on his head under his baseball cap. The giant spark had shaken the old man and knocked him down, but not deterred him. He stood up, shook his head back and forth a few times and he said to me, "Ya think that jerk, Hank would've told us about that red wire thingy. He was hoping that spark would knock me on my tookus when I touched it. It was a booby trap!" I nodded my head in acknowledgement of the old man's latest conspiracy theory.

It was never worth disagreeing with him.

The old man was still mumbling as he bent back down to resume his work, "I wonder where he put the spy camera. I read in my 'Dark Secrets' magazine, that all television repairmen put a special device inside of the television set, so the people in the television studios can look through the picture tube and see inside your house. They make extra dough off the installations and the big companies work payoff deals with the repairman. That is why I never let them see anything in the living room other than a regular household setting. I am telling you, Paulie that this modern technology is scary these days."

I thought how our house was anything but a "regular household setting," but still, I found it hard to swallow that Hank had implanted spy devices inside of our television set. Nonetheless, *Dark Secrets* was the old man's favorite magazine, (other than the *New York Bugs Yearbook,* but that only came out once a year) and it fueled his belief in his endless conspiracy theories.

It was part of his magic.

"You know, Paulie, the article in 'Dark Secrets' that I read last month, suspects that a lot of this spy activity comes from Russian super spies posing as ordinary civilians," the old man reported. He stood up from behind the television and pointed at some diagonal wire cutters that he wanted me to hand to him. Now, this was the 1970s, and the Cold War was on in full force, but somehow that theory seemed a bit far-fetched for even the old man to swallow.

"I do not think they have gotten to Hank just yet though," he added as I heard him clipping wires in the back of the television.

Well, that was certainly good news to know that our friendly neighborhood television and radio repairman was not under the covert employ of the Eastern Bloc.

It was now becoming warmer and increasingly more humid in the house, so I moved one of our numerous floor fans over to a table, so the air would move around a little more in the tight corner where the old man was working. We did not have air conditioning, not even some classic "window shakers" you would see stuck in windows here and there throughout our neighborhood. We did, however, have a multitude of fans, and the quiet whir of their blades as they spun around is still a fond memory for me of a hot, summer night.

My father asked me to plug in the soldering iron and hold it in the air between uses to make sure we did not burn the rug in our living room. I sat on the floor next to the old man as he clipped wires, joined them together, and soldered them individually, according to his diagram. I marveled at his skill, while he easily worked through his plan, cutting and joining what seemed to be an endless array and a maze of wires, and he quickly mounted the new transformer in place of the old one. He handed me the stinky mess of a melted, old transformer, and it smelled so bad that I quickly placed it inside of the box, which had contained the new transformer, and I pushed it aside. The air filled with the distinct odor of melting solder as the old man soldered the wires and then wrapped the splices with electrical friction tape. While he worked, he taught me what he was doing, carefully showing me how to make the connections, then how to melt the solder until the joint was shiny and hard. It was a valuable lesson, because I went on to an apprenticeship in a trade school, and then between other occupations, I ventured into an on and off career in the electrical and electronic business.

Those occupations and the stories behind them, I will leave for another set of words and tales for another time.

When the old man asked me to try the soldering exercise on my own, then I jumped at the chance. I tied my long hair behind my head with a tie that I always kept in my pocket and leaned into the work. It was fun, and the memories of working with my father on projects such as these would last a lifetime. The time passed quickly, and perhaps, because of the foreboding warnings of Hank as well as Sweaty Mike, we thought the project would be a lot worse than what it actually had been. Before we even realized it, the wires were connected and double-checked for accuracy, the new flyback (or fleaback, flyer, or flying backwards transformer, and several other old man variations on a theme that was used during the project) transformer had been installed, and the chassis was slid back into the television cabinet.

It was the long awaited, decisive moment. The moment of nerve-rattling anticipation, and nail-biting tenseness.

It was time to plug the television in and try it out.

Oh, boy! If it did not work, then I needed to run for it.

I plotted my escape route as I gathered up the forty-two-thousand tools we utilized during the installation on the new transformer.

The old man looked at his watch and proudly announced, "Look, we are done in time for the first pitch. I might want to miss it though. The Bugs are home, and they are playing the Cleveland Pale Faces. That bum Fritz Robertson is pitching tonight for the Bugs. By the first inning, the other team's batters are usually going around the bases like hands on a clock. Say, honey! We are done. We are going to plug in the set and see how it works. Youse guys should come in and watch." The old man was now signaling and bellowing to the kitchen for Mum and the rest of the gang to come out of hiding, and check out the main event.

From the far reaches of the furthermost corner of our home, I heard Mum squeak out a feeble and half-hearted, "All right, dear."

Slowly, with great fear and trepidation, Mum, Gramps,

Dottie, and even Skippy crept into the living room and gathered around to watch the results of the newly acquired electronic skills of the old man. They knew, as well as I did, that if the television set erupted into flames and sparks, then it would quickly become a bad scene, and this would be the first television set to land on the moon without a rocket ship.

The old man was smiling broadly . . . for now.

He reached over and plugged the set in, then reached for the on and off knob and gave it a turn. To say there were a few crossed toes, fingers, and paws in this room would have been a gross understatement. I imagined and prayed that gathered together somewhere in a special corner on Earth, there would be a rabbi, a priest, a bishop, an Indian medicine man, a witch doctor, a magician, and all of them were chanting and praying. Then as an extra good luck measure, please add legions of angels strumming harps as they sat upon the clouds, in order to coax the television into working. We all cautiously leaned in, as the audible "click" of the on and off knob made the connection and the power lights and dials glowed.

So far so good . . . no fires, flames, ozone smells, or sparks.

The old man stood in front of the set with his arms crossed in front of his chest as he tapped his shoe on the rug. The tubes were warming up. It always took forever for the tubes to warm up.

As we stood there watching and waiting, I heard a little, high-pitched noise in the back of the television, then a faint glimmer of brightness flickered on the screen, and then some sound! Yes! Some sound!

The old man leaned in and flipped the channel selector to channel eleven. He listened and waited while looking down at his watch to confirm the time. I heard the familiar voices of Blabber Viscardi, Johnny Mclaughy, Ralph "The Rocket" Lenard and Bob McGee, blabbing through the golden mesh covering the speaker on the front of the television cabinet. The entire family leaned in and waited. The anticipation was agonizing! Suddenly, a flicker on the screen, the picture tube flickered to life and, and, and there it was!

A picture!

The Bugs versus the Cleveland Pale Faces on our screen in living, black and white.

"YES! YES! YES! UP YA ASS, HANK! I DID IT! I DID IT!" The old man fist-pumped in the air in joy.

"Joan! Get me a Big Boulder beer to celebrate! Yes! Eat my dust, Hank, ya big bum. Seventy bucks, my ass."

The old man accepted the gauntlet, dealt with it, and Hank had been soundly defeated.

The old man let loose with a "song of joy" at the sight of the restored television as the entire family jumped in the air and cheered. Even Skippy ran around the living room, barking at the sheer excitement and joy of the situation. I high-fived the old man, and Dottie and Gramps hugged him to congratulate him on his conquering of the pesky fleaback or flying backwards, or whatever it was called, transformer. Mum came over, hugged the old man, and then gave him a big kiss right on the ole smacker! Now, she could watch *Nights of our Lives* again.

Time may pass, other repairs may be completed, and seemingly insurmountable obstacles overcome, but in the grand scheme of things, there was only one old man.

In addition, I was proud to say that he was my father.

The euphoria of the television repair would carry over for at least the first couple of seconds of the New York Bugs game. It lasted until the cleanup hitter for the Cleveland Pale Faces; Mitchell "Muscles" McGirk, blasted a first inning homer off Fritz Robertson that seemed as if it circled the Earth four times and the baseball, he had hit landed right in front of our house in the middle of Belmont Avenue.

"Oh geez, for the love of Pete! This Robertson is a bum. My aching ass. Why, oh, why, is he still in the big leagues? Drunk and pitching underhand, I could do better than this bum could! It is a wonder the fleaback transformer did not blow up again. Geez, Joan! Get me another beer," the old man was holding his head in agony as Muscles McGirk circled the bases, while blowing kisses to the angry, home crowd. Mum came running in with a cold Big Boulder beer for the old man to ease the shock and pain of the home run.

The New York Bugs were cooked; where was Jim Beaver when we needed him?

By the eighth inning it was dark outside. The Bugs were behind twelve to one, Muscles McGirk kept going around the bases like hands on a clock, and the old man had concluded that this game was a lost cause. He now had a few Big Boulder beers racing around inside of him, in order to ease the pain and despair of Fritz Robertson's pitiful performance on the mound for the Bugs. I sensed he was a little adventurous in his nature. I watched as the old man stood up from his chair, flipped the television off, and looked over at me.

He had a mischievous look in his eye as he said, "Say, Paulie, Mum is taking a shower, Dottie is in her room listening to her loud, ear shattering, rock–and-roll records, and Gramps has had more beers than me. It is dark out and it may be a good time to test out some of those fireworks we bought." He smiled and waved to me as he added, "Hey, make sure Skippy is asleep in your room, and then meet me out in the backyard. Sneak in the kitchen drawer and grab a book of matches too." I quickly moved into action. After all, tomorrow was the big day, and a test of the fireworks was in my opinion, a very smart thing to do.

After checking on Skippy and confirming he was asleep, I walked out the back door of our house and met the old man in the backyard. Our part-time pet and the resident neighborhood stray cat, Pussface, immediately ambushed us. He came walking up the back sidewalk, simultaneously meowing loudly at the appearance of the old man. Pussface was a stray tomcat who wandered the neighborhood looking for handouts and mooching sleep time on our back porch.

Ever since the old man saved him from freezing to death one Christmas Eve, many years ago, he loved the old man, and he hung around our house as if he was our pet. Pussface was an ugly cat. Some people would say he was an orange tabby, but it actually was very hard to tell. His head was three sizes too big for his body, he was full of battle scars from fighting with Skippy and other animals and his tail was mostly gone from collisions with cars.

He was a mess.

In many ways, though, Pussface epitomized the typical New Jersey tough guy. Despite the circumstances, he fought on, and the old man would not admit it, but he loved the old cat. The old man also knew Pussface's main weakness. You see, some folks might find it strange, but Pussface the cat loved beer. He was the feline equivalent to a neighborhood hobo.

"Oh geez, Pussface. Where ya been all day? Hiding from Skippy and the heat, I bet," the old man said as he reached down to pet him as Pussface rubbed up on the old man's leg to say hello and meowed loudly. The old man knew Pussface was very smart, and all he was looking for now was to mooch a good night of sleep on our porch, a few scraps of food, and a dish of beer.

The old man explained to the old cat, "Look, Pussface, we are going to be making some noise here in a few minutes and it may shake ya up a little. I would say it would scare some fur off ya, but since you have very little left, then I guess it will not matter too much. C'mon, I will get you some beer and we have a few chunks of ham leftover. I will be right back, Paulie. He will be asleep in a few minutes."

I nodded as I watched Pussface happily follow the old man onto the back porch.

It was drinking time!

I stood there in the backyard, waiting for my father to return. The night was sticky, moist, and still quite warm. Our backyard was stuck on the edge of the city. It was located on a busy street and it never really became completely dark. The lights of the streetlamps that lined Belmont Avenue kept my backyard lit, and the noises from the rolling of the cars, trucks, city buses, and other vehicles that passed by the front door, was something I had grown accustomed to over the years. A few lightning bugs flew out of the grass here and there and floated into the air, signaling to a mate with a glow and a flicker of light. They floated and danced before my eyes and flew into the tree above my head. A number of other bugs responded with a flash of light here and there, and I had no doubt they would be successful in their missions. It was a little too early in the month for an abundance of lightning bugs to be out. It was sticky and hot enough for a few of the bugs to appear this evening, but by mid-July, our yard would fill up with them, floating and illuminating while they were dancing in the summer nights. When my sister and I were younger, we would chase and capture them in glass jars, study, and then release them.

Tonight, I simply watched and wondered at God's great creation of such fascinating creatures, and I dreamt of fireworks.

I could hear an occasional "bang" and "boom" going off in the distance. Another one or two went off around the corner from us, and even in the haze of the streetlights, I could see the sky flash here and there in conjunction with some explosions. It seemed as if the entire city of Paterson as well as the Borough of Haledon was warming up to celebrate our nation's birthday.

I looked over at the apartment house next door to us and

could see the flickering of televisions behind the drawn shades, and even with the competing road noises, I could hear the gentle whir of fan blades spinning around in various apartments in a gallant, yet futile effort, to keep the occupants cool.

A middle-aged couple named Ada and Al occupied the apartment that was closest to our house. They were a bit on the odd side, and the old man had occasional battles with them over various situations. I always found them to be rather friendly. I could have done without ramming into the side of Al's car, while riding my bike one day when I was about ten years old, but that is a whole other story for another day.

The farthest unit on the end of the apartment house had an older woman living there, named Mrs. Grudley. She was an elderly woman, a widow, and she was a bit of a crabapple. She would generally open her window, yell out, and complain about everything anyone did around her apartment. She would even give the landlord a piece of her mind when he would try to cut the small area of grass that was between our house and the edge of the apartment building. She would complain that his mower was loud, and that dust was getting into her apartment. The landlord would throw his arms and hands into the air as if to ask her what alternative solution he could possibly offer to her, in order to remedy the situation of having to maintain the grass. Mrs. Grudley was a tough, old bird, and I would just smile and say, "Hello" to her when I ran into her on occasion. I would see her on the sidewalk, walking to the Foodworld supermarket, or walking on Belmont Avenue here and there, and getting on the number fourteen city bus to go into downtown Paterson, but she mostly kept to herself except, when she yelled at you. She usually scowled at me, but occasionally, when I ran into her, she would nod her head and mumble something back. Mrs. Grudley usually sat right next to the side window of her apartment, staring out at the world and scowling.

I heard Mum and Gramps say that she did not own a television, but she preferred to listen to the radio and read books. That made sense, because on nights and days such as today, you could see her by the window reading by the glow of a lamp, while a radio played soft music in the distance. I thought that she was rather lonely as opposed to being a crabapple, however; I generally always tried hard to find the positive side of people.

The old man reappeared with a smile on his face, carrying a beer bottle and a flashlight. He came down the back steps and said, "Pussface will not hear a thing. He sucked down half of this bottle, ate, and curled up in the corner of the porch. The beer will make him pass out until tomorrow morning. He is just an old, drunken bum. Let's go get a few bottle rockets and we can use this beer bottle as a launcher for them."

The old man was excited at the prospect of a few random explosions to dull the pain of the tragic loss by the New York Bugs. He tilted the bottle back, downed the rest of the Big Boulder beer and the bottle was ready to go. We scurried over by the garden shed and pulled out the bag of fireworks. Even with only the glow of the street lamps on Belmont Avenue, I could see the eager anticipation in the old man's eyes.

This was finally the moment that he had been waiting years for arriving!

"Here, you hold the flashlight, Paulie. Hold it here so that I can pick out some bottle rockets." I held the flashlight as the old man selected about five or six bottle rockets from a pack of about fifty or so that were in our bag of tricks. He was fumbling with a rubber band that held the red wooden stick ends of the rockets in a tight bundle to bind the bottle rockets together. For someone who might have never seen a bottle rocket before, the perilous device consists of a medium-sized firecracker mounted on a wooden stick, which was about a foot or so long. You placed the stick inside of a longneck bottle, (Dingleberry beer came in longer necks than Big Boulder did, and the empty bottles would be perfect, except for the fact that we never had any empty bottles because everyone refused to drink them) position the bottle towards a clear sky, light the fuse, and get away. The first charge propels the rocket a hundred or so feet in the air. The firecracker then explodes on the second charge for a big bang for your buck. The appeal about bottle rockets was not only the fact that the excitement level was high, but they also were very cheap in cost.

"Too bad, we don't have a Dingleberry beer bottle, Dad. Those Big Boulder bottles are kind of short and the rocket could flop over," I decided to point out the flaw in our beer bottle selection.

"Ah, stop being an old lady. Harry is right. You are such an old lady, worrying about everything. I was setting off bottle rockets before you were born. It is not worth drinking one of those Dingleberries even to get the bottle. They are so sweet that they make your mouth regurgitate. Even Pussface hates them."

After that description of consumption of a Dingleberry, I could see the old man's point. I did not exactly understand it, but I could still see his point. I also could never understand why we always had a six-pack of Dingleberries in our refrigerator. It was a mystery.

"Now, hold the flashlight. Here we go! I hope your old lady is watching television."

The old man set the first bottle rocket in the beer bottle. He carefully adjusted the angle of takeoff for an open view of the sky over the top of the abandoned restaurant's parking lot, in between the tailor shop roof, and the sign for the old parking lot for the restaurant, (there were a few obstacles here in the city) he struck a match, and lit the fuse.

"FIZZZZZZZ! FIZZZZZZZ! WHOOOOSSSEEE!

The rocket popped off, launched into the night sky, up over the top of the parking lot, it flew into the darkness. Somewhere—somewhere—somewhere—where is it? It soared over towards Tilted Hill.

"BANG!"

There it was!

"Fantastic!" The old man shouted. "Get me another one, Paulie." I picked another bottle rocket out of the pack and handed it to the old man. The same drill and another bang. Pyrotechnical mania now overcame the old man. He was in his glory! Smoke, gunpowder, a faint flutter of paper from the exploded rockets filtered down from the heavens on top of us like manna from God. After we launched about five or six of these bottle rockets, we were stunned when a bottle rocket appeared in the sky and exploded above our heads! It had come to us from the direction that we had launched our rockets.

"Hey, some jerks must be shooting back at us!"

The old man realized that we were under "attack."

"Hand me one more." He set it off, and sure enough, one more launched back in our direction. The old man was about to set a rocket in the bottle when he chuckled a little and said, "Time for a little modification, Paulie. We're gonna knock these jerks out of the sky. Us guys used to do this when we were kids. Hand me a little pack of those ladyfingers and one of those ash cans, would ya? They are the smaller ones there. The ash cans are the big, silver guys."

The old man pointed at a small pack of firecrackers in a pale red wrapper. I held the flashlight as the old man carefully opened the pack and untangled a few of the small firecrackers from a maze of fuses. He carefully unwound three or four of them and with an extra length of fuse; he tied them, along with the ash can, to the top of a bottle rocket. As he worked on the modification, a few more rockets came over and exploded above us. Our enemy was still shelling our Henson defense fronts. The old man carefully set his newly created missile into the bottle and was about to light the fuse when it tipped over and fell on its side. The weight was too heavy for the now top-heavy bottle rocket.

"I got it. I got it. Don't worry or tell me the bottle is too short, will ya. I know what I am doing," the old man said as he waved at me to keep my trap shut about short-necked bottles. He set the bottle back up and carefully steadied it. Now, confident that it was ready to go, he lit the fuse and smiled as we stood back and watched.

"This will get them," the old man proudly proclaimed.

"FIZZZZZZZ! FIZZZZZZZZ!"

Just before the vertical takeoff, the bottle started to fall over! In horror, we both watched as the bottle tilted, spun around like a top, and, "WHOOOSSSSEEEE!" Off the bottle rocket took off into the darkness in the complete opposite direction, towards the apartment house!

"Oh, geez! Shit! DUCK, PAULIE!" The old man waved and screamed as we hit the ground. We both watched in utter despair and helplessness, as the telltale fuses of the bottle rocket allowed us to track it in the darkness, and watch as it flew in the air, and then right in front of old lady Grudley's apartment window, it let loose!

"BANG! BANG! BANG! BANG! BOOOMMMMMMM!" It seemed as if the entire world shook and windows rattled for miles.

Oh, no! This is not very good.

Would you believe happy birthday America?

We watched as every light in the entire apartment house came on. Every window, every floor, every single apartment in the entire building, with every single resident sticking their heads out of the windows and screaming collectively into the night, "WHAT WAS THAT? CUT IT OUT YOU JERKS! WE ARE GOING TO CALL THE COPS

ON YOU DAMN IDIOTS!"

The old man waved to me to stay on the ground and he put his hand up to his mouth for me to remain quiet. Our enemies over on the other block, of course, were unaware of the slight malfunction that we had suffered in our artillery detonations, and they continued to launch bottle rockets in our direction. They must have heard our massive explosion and decided to pound us with sheer volume now. I could see the flashlights of the nearby residents poking out of their windows as they flashed into our yard while the apartment house folks tried to locate the source of the firecracker launching. Since the bottle rockets were coming over from the other block, it seemed as if we were off the hook, and the culprits were determined to be the gang from a few blocks over on the Tilted Hill.

I heard Ada scream to her husband, "Al, tell the cops, it is coming from over on the other side of Gabby's restaurant near Tilted Hill!"

We crawled along the ground, like soldiers avoiding gunfire on the battlefield. We moved strategically in between flashlight beams dancing around our backyard projecting from the far reaches of the apartment house next door.

The old man came over and whispered to me, "Hey Paulie, grab the bag, the matches, and the bottle. Then let's head for the front door. They will not be able to see us on the other side of the house."

I nodded and did as the old man said. We crawled along the ground until we were safely around the side of our house.

This was about to get a lot worse because I now could hear the wailing of police sirens in the distance.

"Run! Head for the front porch, Paulie," the old man was coaching me along in our escape plan. We made a mad dash for the front door, ran up the steps, and dove onto the front porch just as a police car rolled by the front of our house.

This was nuts! We were hiding out on our own front porch!

We peered over the top ledge of the porch railing, and we could see two police officers looking around towards our driveway and using the searchlight mounted on the patrol car to check the backyard of our house.

Just when it seemed as if they were going to get out of the patrol car for a closer check, our enemies from the next block over sent one more poorly timed salvo our way and it popped in the air above our house. The policemen had tracked it the entire way. I could see the officer in the driver's seat point in the air and then in the direction of Tilted Hill. He then slammed the car into gear and sped off in the direction of the launch.

We were off the hook. I guess that we had won the game of aerial combat. I wondered if the chaps over on Tilted Hill were now running and hiding on their front porches, too. The old man leaned up on the wall of the porch and sighed. He took his New York Bugs hat off, smiled at me, and laughed.

"Mum must have dozed off or she would be ripping me apart by now. Gramps and Pussface are half in the bag, and Dottie plays her records so loud she would not hear it, anyway."

"I wonder why ole Skip is not barking, Dad?"

"As long as he is on your bed, that dog sleeps like a log. I swear he would sleep through anything." The old man was laughing now as more police cars sped down Belmont Avenue in the direction of Tilted Hill.

"What a great day, Paulie, and tomorrow we can have more fun!"

Between my old man and my buddy Harry M. Redmond Jr., I had learned to keep a very broad definition for the word "fun" in my dictionary. The old man had now fulfilled his explosion quota for the night. He was ready to pack it in for the day.

I smiled back at him as he reached over, shook my hand, and then pulled me close to him for a hug. I heard a few more pops, bangs, and explosions going off in the distance.

Yeah, yeah, yeah, I know, happy birthday America.

4

A Henson Fourth of July to Remember

The Fourth of July! America's birthday, fun, hot dogs, hamburgers, hot coals in the grill, baseball, beer, hot days, sticky nights, barbeques in the backyard, and visits from relatives for backyard fun, including a visit from the legendary Cousin Pat. Despite the adventures and fun of the previous day, my father sprang into action relatively early. The old man had been up since dawn, preparing the forward Henson defense front for a visit from Cousin Pat. He knew that he would need to have his tools ready, his stock of epoxy, his tubes of all-purpose glue and all weapons of his repair arsenal would be required to repair the damage that Cousin Pat could inflict, as she made our way around our family home. She was like a wrecking ball swinging on the end of a crane boom.

I always had to get up early anyway, because ole Skip needed to be let out and do what doggies do, so I joined the old man in the living room as he double-checked his television repair.

"Hey, chief. Did ya sleep good?" The old man asked, as I nodded to indicate that I did. "You did not say anything to your old lady, did ya, about last night? You are always too honest and get us both in trouble. I swear instead of being a hockey goalie you should go in the ministry."

"Nah, Dad. I will keep my mouth shut. How is the television working?"

"Good, good, the big game comes on around one or so, and I expect Uncle Ed and Aunt Lois to be here around noontime. Uncle Ed wants to see the Old Timer's Day game too. I love when they introduce the players onto the field. Blabber Viscardi sets up the microphone behind home plate, and he says a few words about each player when they run out of the dugout and line up along the baselines. It is a piece of cake, cuz, I guess everyone ahead of time! When Big Foot Garumba comes out of the dugout, the crowd goes wild!"

When he played for the New York Bugs, Big Foot Garumba was the old man's ultimate hero. He was a giant, hulking brute who had hit home runs that are still orbiting the Earth to this day. The old man had never emotionally recovered from his hero's retirement from baseball.

The man said, "Sure wish, ole Big Foot could come back, the Bugs need him. Most of these bums nowadays cannot hit their way out of a paper bag. Say, I let Pussface out already, and I hid the fireworks back in the shed early this morning. I tucked them around the corner inside the front doors there. We still have tons of them left. The two skyrockets are in there, lots of ash cans, some more bottle rockets, ladyfingers, and those two tanks that the crook told us shoot little cannonballs out of the turret. We can shoot some off again tonight. I promise not to modify any of them."

The old man smiled at me. He shut the television off, and we walked into the kitchen.

"Yeah, yeah, yeah, I think that may be a good idea, Dad." Mum was working at the counter in the kitchen making hamburgers for our cookout. She was making the burgers out of what my parents and everyone else in my neighborhood called, "chop meat." As I grew older and traveled around the country, I realized the rest of the country called it "ground beef." I also always found the meaning of the word "barbeque" to be different from the rest of the world as opposed to the Tri-state area in and around New York City. The majority of the world knows barbeque to be a particular type of meat dish, a sloppy mixture of pork, chicken, or beef soaked in some kind of smoke-flavored sauce. I found that fact out when I was living in Norfolk, Virginia, playing ice hockey for a team based there and I received an invitation to a cookout in a teammate's yard. When I slipped up and called it a "barbeque," everyone looked at me as if I had four eyeballs. To "youse and us guys," it meant you were having a cookout on a grill in your backyard. The New Jersey, New York, and Connecticut areas are one of the most fascinating places on the planet. The lingo and nuances go with me forever.

"Did ya get the chop meat at Aldon's butcher shop, Joan? I hope you got the high test, the last time, you were a cheapo, and you got that fatty stuff and the flames from the grill caught the tree on fire above the grill," the old man said as he watched over my mother's shoulders as she made the hamburger patties.

"Yes, dear. I bought the chop meat at Aldon's shop and the butcher told me it was very good quality. I also picked up a pack of Big Bob's Griddle franks. I know how you love those hot dogs. I suggest that this year, you need to set the grill in front of the shed, that way it will be away from the trees and it will not be on the pathway where people will walk. Cousin Pat is coming, so we have to make sure she stays far away from the grill."

I looked over at the old man for his reaction, and sure enough, his eyes widened in anticipation of Cousin Pat's arrival. I would say that his face reflected a combination of horror, in addition to a little fear.

Gramps arrived for morning tea and breakfast, as did my sister, and soon we were setting up the backyard with extra chairs, tables, and we were making other preparations for the big barbeque. The old man had his charcoal grill out, his can of Big Bob's jet fuel, super-enhanced, atomic powered, lighter fluid, and he was preparing for the great American holiday. He did follow Mum's advice and set the grill up in front of the shed and away from the trees.

I always found the Fourth of July to be fascinating, since my Mum's side of the family was of English heritage, and here we were celebrating our independence from the English Crown. It was a long time ago, but in my eyes, the whole holiday celebration was to a certain extent rather strangely conflicted. I did break away and bounce back and forth to Harry's house and checked in with him and his family for their big shindig too. I told Harry about our fireworks adventure of the previous night and he swore he heard the boom and wondered where it had come from!

Their parties were always a blast, and I loved being over there for these types of events. I needed to be careful this holiday, since this year, was a special holiday gathering of relatives at our house. I did not want to face the wrath of Mum for skipping out on a visit from them. At noontime, Uncle Ed and Aunt Lois arrived, and soon the party was on. Aunt Lois was my mother's kid sister. She was a short, pretty, very English looking gal, with a wonderful sense of humor, and Uncle Ed was a tall man who also was a ton of fun. Skippy loved Uncle Ed, and he ran around the house like a racecar whenever he showed up and then hung out with him the entire day. For some strange reason, of which I never really understood, Uncle Ed always insisted that Skippy's name was "Ralph."

The Big Boulder beer cans were now popping open, and soon, we gathered in front of the television to watch the introductions for the big Old Timer's Day game live from Bug stadium. Even Gramps, who was an English football (soccer) league fan (Nottingham Forest was our team) sat down to watch the dramatic introduction period to the game.

To provide an appropriate backdrop of exaggerated male achievements, the old man wove an intricate and drama-filled tale of how he installed the "flying backwards" transformer amongst the precarious danger of electric shocks and sparks. The sparks and shocks parts of his tale were certainly true, but the old man, fueled by an extra intake of Big Boulder beer, exaggerated the rest of the tale. For example, I am not exactly sure our guests believed the part where the old man arm-wrestled Sweaty Mike at the counter, in exchange for a slight discount off the price of the replacement part.

The voice of Blabber Viscardi once again filled our living room, "This player was a New York Bug for ten years and he held down the shortstop position. His fame spread far and wide after his key hit in the 1964 World Series when he drove in the winning run off Lefty McClure that iced the game for the Bugs in the ninth inning! Number ten. . .."

Before Blabber Viscardi could complete the long-winded introduction, the old man jumped out of his chair, spilled some of his beer, and shouted, "Billy the banjo Hoppleburger!"

"Billy the banjo Hoppleburger! Number ten!" Blabber Viscardi confirmed the old man's prediction.

"Ha! Told ya! Hoppleburger was a bum, but he did get that one key hit!"

On and on it went; one washed up, dried up, old, former New York Bugs player after another, wobbled and trotted out to the baselines, with Blabber Viscardi announcing their names, along with a short biography of the player. Staying remarkably consistent, the old man guessed a good percentage of the players even before Blabber Viscardi could finish the description.

Finally, the big moment had come. The coveted, dramatic introduction of *the man.*

The old man leaned in, along with Uncle Ed, and they waved their hands in the air for everyone to stop talking as Blabber Viscardi began his introduction, "Folks, this man is a legend. Born in the wild jungles of Borneo, he honed his muscles and skills by lifting giant, tree trunks and carrying them on his back in the wild jungles as a young boy. He moved to Newington, Connecticut, as a young boy, when his dad took a job in some supermarket sorting pineapples. There, he learned the American game of baseball, and the rest of the legend lives on forever!"

The crowd was going wild and the old man was jumping around the living room as the excitement built. The dramatic announcing skills of Blabber Viscardi had worked everyone into a wild frenzy!

Viscardi pointed out in the far reaches of New York Bugs Stadium, and the camera panned and zoomed in on an old high-rise building far beyond the outfield bleacher seats.

"He is the only man ever to hit a fair ball out of Bugs Stadium, when he smacked the baseball nine hundred and forty-six feet, and seven and one-quarter inches. The baseball went right through the top, right hand, corner of that fifteen-story window on the sunny side of that big apartment building. Yes! Way out there, folks, he hit the homer! It went clean through the window of apartment number fifteen-sixteen, knocking a poor man unconscious, while he was sitting at his kitchen table, eating a bologna sandwich with mustard on white toast and while drinking a much-too-sweet Dingleberry beer."

I thought, my goodness, what intricate details. Blabber sure was dragging this one out.

"He hit a total of eight hundred and fourteen home runs, and ten thousand and two hits. Knocked in twenty-six thousand RBI's, two stolen bases, ten league MVP's, elected to the Hall of Fame on the first ballot, four World Series MVPs, ten gold gloves, hot-damn, he even sold hot dogs in the stands between innings, (Blabber got caught up in his own emotions and he slipped up with a little profanity) here he is the great and powerful and legendary—number seven—Poindexter, Big Foot, GARUMBA!"

Poindexter? That was his real name. A guy who was born in the wild jungles of Borneo, whose first name was actually Poindexter.

This was unreal.

Nostalgic emotion overcame the old man and Uncle Ed. They both were now standing up, while clapping and hugging each other, as the tears rolled down their cheeks.

"GARUMBA! YOU WERE THE BEST!" They shouted together.

Gramps stood up from his chair, tugged at his pants, and wandered off towards the kitchen as he mumbled, "It seems like a big batch of bloody nonsense to me over some dried up, old prune of a chap who can barely run anymore. Back home, we would have just started a bloomin' riot at the football match, knocked the seats down, and all met at the pub to tip a few and continue the brawl."

My sister Dottie also stood up, and followed Gramps, Aunt Lois, and Mum, while they all collectively commented, "This is dumb."

I thought how that summed it up rather well.

The old man tried in vain to summon the family back and drum up interest, "Hey, where are youse guys going? Now they play a game against the old timers from the Shercargo Purple Socks." Skippy and I stayed and endured the shouting and yelling of the game, as some old chaps huffed and puffed and sweated their way through the action. Of course, Big Foot Garumba smacked a homer to finish it all off, and the old man and Uncle Ed went nuts.

The Old Timer's Day game had just ended when we heard a terrible hullabaloo and bumping noises out on the front steps.

The old man jumped up from his chair and shouted, "That must be, Aunt Alma and Cousin Pat!"

We all had heard the noises, and we rushed to the front door. The old man and Uncle Ed flung it open, to see Cousin Pat, fallen head over a teakettle at the bottom of the front steps, holding our front railing in her hands! Cousin Pat was laughing, so the first indication was that she was not hurt too badly. Aunt Alma was leaning over her, trying her best to assist her.

Aunt Alma looked up as we all rushed to help and she called out, "Oh, goodness! Pat is a wee bit on the clumsy side. She seems to have tumbled down a bit here. Oh John, Paul, Eddie, and Paulie boy, can you please help me get her back upright? Pat does weigh a wee bit!"

"I am fine! I am fine. My huge backside broke my fall. I wobbled a bit, dear Mum, and the railing came loose when I grabbed it to steady myself. I am fine."

We all grabbed Cousin Pat, tugged, and helped her up. She did indeed, just as Aunt Alma described, "Weigh just a wee bit." The good news was that she seemed fine, except for a slight limp on her right ankle.

Mum spotted her cousin limping and shifted into her nursemaid mode, "Oh my Pat, you have twisted your ankle a bit. Please bring her inside and put her on the sofa. Dottie come along. We need to prepare a cold compress with some ice to take down the swelling."

We helped Cousin Pat inside and plopped her on the sofa in the living room. The sofa creaked and groaned, and the cushions sunk down to the floor as the frame buckled from her enormous weight.

"Oh my, this sofa is as if you are going to sea, Paul," Cousin Pat said as she sank down to the floor. The old man frowned as he clandestinely checked the sofa for collateral damages. As Cousin Pat iced her ankle, the delayed greetings started. After such a precarious start, the party was still on.

"I will procure from my cupboard, my special bottle of Canadian rye whiskey, Pat. A shot or two of that will dull your pain a bit, and you will be dancing around by this afternoon lovie," Gramps said as he went up to his apartment to obtain the magic tonic.

I shivered at the mere thought of Cousin Pat dancing about while destroying everything in her path.

Aunt Alma greeted everyone, then she turned to me and smiled.

"Paulie boy, come here and let me look at you, dear boy. It is going to be a wonderful summer. I can teach you a bit more Welsh, dear lad. Come and give Auntie Alma a huggie. I see how you are so tall and even more handsome now than on my last visit. You remind me of my Cousin Percival in Nottingham. He was a rough and tumble bloke. He was a football goalie in his younger days. Now, he is a bit of a dried-up old prune, he just sits at the pub, swallowing gallons upon gallons of dark ale, passing gas, and telling tall tales of his past glory, sort of just as your own father now does." Aunt Alma smiled at me, and she held her arms open, while I thought how I wished Aunt Alma could have picked another relative for me to resemble, rather than poor, Cousin Percival. Then again, I always wondered what happened to old goaltenders!

Aunt Alma continued on, while motioning me closer and saying, "I hear you are quite the player in goal. I do not know a bloomin' thing about hockey, but it is much the same as soccer. I plan to go to Toronto this fall before I return home. We have a cousin there and we all plan to visit. Pat and I want to see a hockey game too! We hope that dear Pat's backside will squeeze into those seats in the arena. I wish I could drag your grandfather with me, but my brother is a bit of a lump these days. Rwy'n dy garu di."

My goodness. That was some speech. Aunt Alma was indeed a classic character. I came over, bent down and gave Aunt Alma a hug and said, "I love you too, Aunt Alma. It is nice to see you too."

"Oh, Paulie boy, come over here and greet me, too. I hear your Welsh improving a bit. I cannot get my big backside up off the sofa right now, but it has been a long time since I have seen you," Cousin Pat was signaling to me, so I went over and gave her a hug too.

It was a little tough because there was quite a bit to hug.

Aunt Alma then greeted Dottie and everyone else. She was dressed in her usual brightly colored dress. This time it was green, and she wore her traditional white pearl necklace, her large horn-rimmed glasses, and white pearls in her ears for an earring selection. She was very pretty, with flaming red hair and a wonderful smile. Cousin Pat's hair was not as deep of a red in color as her mother's hair, but it was close.

These were wonderful people, full of life and enjoyment.

Not a single time, in all of their visits, can I ever remember any of them, ever being despondent or angry. In fact, Cousin Pat even took the tumbling down a set of stairs in stride. What an example of how to enjoy life that they both portrayed for my sister and me. It was a joy to know them and have them as relatives. Years later, I would realize just how lucky I was as a young man to have shared my life with folks such as all of them.

The living room was warm now, and the fourteen electric fans the old man had spinning around, thankfully drowned out the baseball game on the television. He kept a close eye on the progress of the game, and he was thrilled to see the Bugs were actually winning the regular game after a bold triumph in the Old Timer's Day game.

Gramps returned with a hit or two on the Canadian magic and Cousin Pat magically restored to full health. Uncle Ed helped her off the sofa and Cousin Pat teetered and tottered while she leaned upon Uncle Ed and me as we moved the party to the backyard. It was cooler outside now than it was in the warm house. There was just a slight breeze in the haze of the afternoon.

The old man was ready to fire up the charcoal grill. The distinct odor of lighter fluid filled the air. I stood on the sideline and watched him while he doused the coals with the volatile fluid and hurled a match into the mix.

"WHOOOSSHH!"

The flames shot into the air and the coals cooked under the flames. The old man had stuck the old table radio in the open window close to the grill so that he could keep an ear on the game. Even a block or two away, I could hear the yells, shouts of joy, and the "clang" of a horseshoe or two echoes over to our yard from the Redmond's house, and the world famous, Harry's Resort. I would head over there later because that party would go on for days; therefore, there was plenty of time.

Pussface, the cat, hung off in the distance looking for a sip or two of beer. He made an occasional appearance, being very careful not to come too close to Skippy. It did not matter; Skippy was too hot to battle with his archenemy right now, anyway. He sat down next to Uncle Ed, panting, drinking water from his dish with his long chain hooked around his collar, just in case he decided to give Pussface a chase. We all listened and watched as the family gathered in a circle of lawn chairs under the shade of a tree, shared some beer, sodas, wine and iced tea, and chatted about every subject you could actually cover.

Aunt Alma told of her travels to Barbados in the spring, and Cousin Pat told us of a blizzard she rode out in Saratoga County in upstate New York this past winter. It was a magical discussion. I listened and took mental notes for future stories and tales to pass along when the time was right. The old man would add a colorful story or two here and there and share his latest theory or two from his *Dark Secrets* magazine. He hinted at a special treat for later, of which I knew what he was speaking, but the rest of the group was puzzled as to what he meant.

Gramps leaned in as he sucked down a Big Boulder beer, took his handkerchief out of his pocket, and wiped his brow as he said, "Wheeewww. Bloody hot! I think each year it becomes hotter and hotter. How I wish to be in a nice, cool place with a little breeze. You cannot even sleep on days such as this. I say, Alma, that this reminds me what we would say back home when it was hot."

Aunt Alma looked at her brother and chuckled as she disagreed, "Oh, John, you are quite the character. This is not hot, nor was it hot in England. Now, John, where I live in Florida that is hot! What did we say back home, my dear brother? I cannot recall. I am indeed, quite puzzled."

Now, it may have been as my father and Gramps would say that perhaps one, two, three, too many beers had induced my grandfather's next statement, or it may have been just the actual saying, but he leaned in and said, "In July, in the hottest of the weather, if two cannot sleep alone, then one must sleep together!" We all leaned our heads in and then shook our heads as we tried in vain to understand what Gramps had just said. Mum asked him to repeat it, and he did.

My sister guessed, "Oh, Gramps, you mean sleeping in bunk beds."

He took another swig of beer, shook his head as he smiled and answered Dottie, "Two, do not sleep alone or sleep together in bunk beds." The discussion went on and on, with no clear conclusion other than I had to agree with my grandfather. I would take a nice, crisp day with a cool breeze anytime!

As good a puzzle as the English riddle turned out to be, I think the highlight of the discussion came from a positively beer-induced speech of Gramps, as he told of a letter he was diligently composing to the Queen of England.

Gramps perked up, cleared his throat, and told us, "In light of this holiday, when you people here in this wonderful country had so gallantly decided to seek your independence, all over a small quarrel of some taxes on inferior tea, I dare say that it has recently turned into a bit of a mess. I have already written to the President of the

United States to seek improvement of the current state of affairs. If I do not see some type of satisfactory response, then I will finalize and send along a letter, in which I have asked the Queen of England to consider the reinstatement of the former colonies to the British Empire, and to proclaim bygones to be bygones. I am afraid that the chap in the Oval Office has a bit more trouble to contend with these days, and therefore just in case, I will retain my dual citizenship in both of these great countries."

I thought how I hoped that he really was just under the influence of a bit of the suds and that he was not actually going to write a letter to the Queen of England with such a plea. A thought or two passed through my mind of the Queen of England reading Gramp's letter, then dispatching some of her agents across the pond to consider the situation!

Gramps then wobbled a bit, and he sat down at the table while signaling to Mum.

"Say, Joanie dear, how about another one of these Big Boulders? Please love, not one of those Dingleberries they are too bloomin' sweet." Mum handed her father a cold beer from the cooler as he stood up again, and this time, he called for a toast. Cousin Pat struggled out of her chair, tipped over her wine glass and broke it. Aunt Lois handed her a replacement for the toasting.

Gramps cleared his throat again and proclaimed his toast, "Here is to the United States of America! It has been good to me and to my family. When I look around here, and see how far we have come, I know that despite my love of England, there is no place I would rather be than right here. God bless America and long may her flag fly! Here! Here!" A rousing toast transpired.

No one could have said it any better.

In the background, the old man cheered and tossed a beer down his throat while he was struggling with the flames from the hot dogs and hamburgers. He shot water from a plastic spray bottle on the coals to calm the raging inferno.

"Geez! I thought you bought the good stuff! THE DAMN FLAMES ARE GOING TO COOK MY ASS!"

Despite the intense struggle with the flames, the food was cooked, and we all sat around a table in the backyard and enjoyed the traditional fare of hot dogs, hamburgers, corn on the cob, cold salads, and chips. Pussface and Skippy shared a few food scraps here and there, too. Pussface managed to coax a few dishes of beer out of the old man to wash the food down with, too.

There was something special about food cooked on a hot charcoal grill on a Fourth of July day. It had an unmistakable flavor as well as an aroma to it that was unforgettable to your mind and your taste buds. The New York Bugs had pulled out the victory, so the old man and Uncle Ed were in even higher spirits than before. We cleared the table and packed the food away. The grill sat in the corner in front of the shed, still blazing hot, as the old man tried to peddle to everyone, one or two of the remaining, now pulverized, hot dogs that sat smoldering upon the top grill screen.

The afternoon was waning now, and the hot sun was sinking lower. Soon the heat of the day would have passed and the night would bring some much-welcomed cooler air to northern New Jersey. Mum and Aunt Lois served some tea and coffee, along with some traditional English desserts, some gelatin, and fresh fruits, such as melons, pineapples, and watermelon.

It was quite a meal and everyone was stuffed . . . well, almost everyone.

Disaster in the crazy world of the Henson family can strike at any moment. After many experiences of minor and major magnitude, I always knew to remain prepared. Looking back now on this incident, I sometimes think it was a missed opportunity for us that in light of my grandfather's passionate, stirring, patriotic, speech about America, the old man did not dash into the shed, reveal to the world his surprise stash of explosive joy, and shoot off a skyrocket in honor of America at the culmination of the speech.

Perhaps fate would have dealt us a better blow if he had. On the other hand, perhaps not.

Cousin Pat succumbed to the lingering smell of the smoldering hot dogs on the grill. She never actually filled her massive body with food.

"I will have one of those last hot doggies on the grill there, Paul. I will get it, I need to move about, I can feel my ankle getting stiff," Cousin Pat rose slowly out of the chair and waved towards the old man, who was still sipping a beer, and chatting with Uncle Ed and Gramps.

"Nah, nah, nah. Paulie, get Cousin Pat that last hot dog. Let her sit and rest," the old man was instructing me.

Cousin Pat waved back as I had jumped up to get the hot dog, but it was too late. "I got it, Paulie boy. I am fine," Cousin Pat proclaimed. At first, she staggered and wobbled on her sore ankle, but she became a little steadier, as she first picked up a hot dog roll from the table, then she made her way towards the grill. Her intent focus was upon the consumption of grabbing that remaining hot dog.

As we all watched in horror, she reached for the hot dog with the tongs, and her ankle caved in under the tremendous weight. She staggered, twisted, and knocked over the grill!

"OH MY! OH MY! I AM SO SORRY," Cousin Pat bellowed out as she snorted, coughed, and choked.

She managed to catch her balance, but the grill went flying and hot coals and sparks flew in the air. The old man, Uncle Ed, Gramps, and I jumped to react, but I froze in horror as we watched some hot coals roll and tumble inside the open garden shed door!

It was as if time stood still for a few moments. The old

man turned towards me in what appeared to be slow motion while he looked at me in shock.

He and I both knew what was behind the door!

Oh, c'mon! There is no way that our luck could be so bad, not even in the world of Henson could that have happened. There is no way in a million chances that one of those hot coals or sparks could have landed and tumbled just perfectly, in the perfect location that it would have ignited a fuse. . ..

"FIIIZZZZZZZ – FIIIZZZZZZ – FIIIZZZZZZZ"

On the other hand, perhaps the odds were slightly better than we initially thought.

The telltale sign of pending liftoff sent a shock wave of doom throughout my mind and body. The old man waved his hands in the air, ran towards Cousin Pat, and grabbed her.

"RUN! RUN! RUN! EVERYONE RUN!" The old man screamed to a puzzled crowd of relatives, as he tugged in vain at Cousin Pat.

Gramps looked puzzled as he put his hands on his hips and asked, "What is that bloody fizzling noise?"

The old man waved at him in desperation while tugging on Cousin Pat.

Gramps continued to ignore the warning, "I say, old boy, have you had too many beers? Why are you screaming about now? I hear some kind of peculiar fizzling and crackling noise."

"FIIIZZZZZZZ – FIIIZZZZZZ – FIIIZZZZZZZ."

The old man gave up and screamed, "DON'T WORRY ABOUT THE BLASTED DAMN FIZZLING NOISE, POP! RUN! FOR THE LOVE OF PETE! RUN!" I tried to reach the old man to help him move the mountainous Cousin Pat, but I realized that it was in vain, so I just dove on top of them, and we pushed her to the ground and covered her up.

Uncle Ed put the dots together. He grabbed the rest of

the women, unhitched Skippy's leash, and heeded the old man's warning. He screamed as he ran with the group towards the back door of the house, "I know that noise from my time in the United States Marine Corps!"

"What is it Ed, what is going on?" Aunt Lois was asking as the puzzled women sprinted along with him.

Then borrowing a page from the English playbook, he yelled, "Just bloody well run!"

Gramps spun around and, realizing it was a bad scene, he ran and hid under the table.

"FIIIZZZZZZZ—FIIIZZZZZZ— FIIIZZZZZZZ."

I thought about how this was taking so long for the fuses to burn. Perhaps they were duds, and nothing was going to happen. Yes, that was it . . . the fireworks were all duds.

I was wrong.

"BANG! BANG! BANG! KABOOOOOOOMMMM! POP! KABOOOOOOOMMMM!"

First, the door blew off the front of the shed, and then on the next explosion, the top of the shed blew cleanly off. Deep in the recesses of my mind, I remembered the shady peddler's warning, "Now, you do know these ash cans are the equivalent to a quarter stick of dynamite there, pal. Be careful!"

The old man whispered to me as we huddled on the ground over the top of a stunned Cousin Pat, "Must have been the ash can, only two more to go!"

A skyrocket blew out the front door of the shed, and it zoomed across the lawn and over the top of the table where Gramps was hiding.

I heard him yell out, "We are under attack! It is worse than the bloody Germans threw at us in the big one!"

It flew across the top of the table, trailing colors and sparks, and it stuck in a tree between our house and the apartment next door, while exploding with a loud boom and a spray of awesome colors.

"BANG! BANG! BANG! POP! POP! POP! POP! BANG!

BANG! BANG! POP! POP! POP! POP!"

Bottle rockets flew in the air, and went in every direction, ladyfingers went off, followed by an exploding array of dipsy doodlers, cherry bombs, Roman candles, Paterson candles, black snakes, blue snakes, Catherine wheels, zippers, spinners, poppers, floppers, and zingers. Then, after a slight lull in the action, another wave came as the backyard was filled with explosions, sounds, and colors of igniting of drop bombs, ground spinners, helicopters, pinwheels, fizzlers, sparklers, and flares. I watched in awe, as a half in the bag Pussface the cat ran for his life in terror, while one of those little tanks rolled across the ground. The tank chased him as it shot cannonballs out of the turret at the poor, drunken cat. Then another tank emerged from the shed and chased the poor, drunken tomcat in the other direction.

"BANG! BANG! BANG! POP! POP! POP! POP!"

"BANG! BANG! BANG! POP! POP! POP! POP!"

"KABOOOOOOOMMMM!" The sides of the garden shed now collapsed in on one another in slow motion.

One more ash can to go.

Then it suddenly stopped.

A huge, smoke-filled haze floated in the air above our backyard, and a cloud of gunpowder hung over our heads. Spent and destroyed paper from exploded fireworks, floated from the sky like a ticker-tape parade and rained upon our backyard. We rolled around on the ground and tried our best to help the stunned and confused Cousin Pat to her feet.

"What in bloody blue blazes happened? All I wanted was one more hot dog," she kept repeating over and over.

Gramps stuck his head out from under the table, looked both ways, and stood up. He brushed off his pant legs, pointed at the pile of rubble that used to be our garden shed, and put his hands on his hips as he observed, "I say, Paul. I do think that you might be bloody well in need of a new garden shed there, old bean. Oh well, look on the bright side. The doors were a bit rusty and now you do not have to paint the bloody thing."

The rest of the family had been hiding inside the house, and now that the explosions had passed, they came rushing out to check on the rest of us. As we checked each other for casualties, we then became aware of the apartment house next door. Every single resident who was home was hanging out the windows of the apartment house. They were all clapping and cheering loudly. Some were waving American flags in the air, some were waving to us, some residents were whistling, and most of them were yelling in our direction.

"GREAT SHOW, PAUL!" Ada screamed from her apartment window as she cheered us.

"THE BEST!" Mr. Kindler yelled from his first-floor window.

"LOVED THE SKYROCKET THERE, PAUL! TOO BAD ABOUT YA SHED THOUGH!" Charlie Jenkins shouted from his basement apartment window.

"FANTASTIC, PAUL! I LOVED THE TANKS CHASING PUSSFACE!" Al yelled while waving his American flag from a window next to his wife.

Then, in a sudden and unexpected deviation that caught everyone off-guard, and an extreme break from her legendary and traditional crabbiness, the window to Mrs. Grudley's apartment flung wide open, she stuck her head out, waved a small American flag and yelled at the top of her lungs, "GOD BLESS AMERICA!"

I realized as I stood there amongst the smoke, haze of gunpowder, smoking hot coals and sparks, and the remnants of what used to be our charcoal grille and our garden shed that Mrs. Grudley was correct. Where else could you buy a part to fix your own television, in order to watch some guy on the tube who was born in the wild jungles of Borneo, and who now was an American icon?

Where else could you have a cookout in your own yard, with relatives who originally came from every inch of the globe, and then blow up your own garden shed with illegal fireworks bought in the trunk of a car from some shady crook?

Only in America.

Then it happened. A stirring moment of patriotic emotion overtook us all. It began in one of the first-floor windows and if I remember correctly, it spread to the second floor of the apartment, then the third-floor windows, then the fourth floor, a faint note at first, then it grew louder, while more folks joined in, "God bless America, land that I love. . .."

Soon, we all joined in, and before you knew it, the entire backyard and the apartment next door filled the air with the song, as we all stood as one in celebration of the day and our great country. At the ending of the last note, the old man remembered that he still had one more skyrocket that had not gone off. He turned and dashed into the debris of what used to be his garden shed, fished around in the smoke and rubble, and emerged with one last hurrah. He carefully set it in the middle of the yard, cautioned everyone to stand back, and lit the fuse.

"FIIIZZZZZZZ WHOOOSSSEEEE!"

Up it went. Hundreds of feet in the air, and, "KABOOOOOOMMMMM," it exploded in a loud bang, and a rain of colors, to the backdrop of cheers of the entire neighborhood.

God bless America, indeed.

That night in front of the television, while we all watched the Crumbley's Department Store fireworks in living black and white, under the quiet hum and the backdrop of forty-two fans, the old man leaned over to me, and he whispered just out of earshot of dear Mum, "You know, Paulie. I still have one more ash can. . .."

He smiled at me and gave me a playful push in the back.

5

Happy Birthday America

It was terribly hot in the attic, and I realized that all of this running up and down the steps was fruitless. It was just making me a sweaty mess. Every adjustment that I made to the antenna resulted in an even worse picture on the channels that I was trying so hard to improve. I decided to steal a page from the old man's playbook that all of those ghosts whom I had met on the staircase had reminded me of.

"Now, Binky, please, you stand here on the top of the steps and yell to me what Mom Hobnobber says. Mom, you listen to Dad Hobnobber, and relay and yell that info to Binky. Dad, you tell us when the picture is clear. This is not that complicated, youse guys."

They all started to nod their heads in agreement that they all understood the instructions loud and clear. Oh boy, I knew that a nodding round would last a long time whenever it consisted of Hobnobbers, so I decided to get ready for the adjustment. We divided into our battle stations and I climbed back into the stifling hot attic loft. I turned the antenna slightly, here and there, while trying hard to determine which direction New York City was from Great Falls, New Jersey.

"How about now, Binky?" I yelled.

From the deep recess of the hot loft, I heard the relay chain go on and on and back and forth.

Binky yelled back, "Channel four stinks, twenty-seven." I knew my wife was relaying the exact language from her father.

I turned the antenna a little east and repeated my call, "How about now, youse guys?" I waited as the relay chain went down the line. The answer came back as I wiped the sweat from my brow.

"Perfect, leave it right there, twenty-seven. Dear Father says that it is a perfect picture on every channel," Binky yelled back to me.

I repeatedly crossed myself for some element of forgiveness, tightened the bolts, and smiled as I whispered very softly, "Bloody well, perfect."

Now, if I only had one more ash can. . ..

Happy birthday America.

THE END

Flying

During the course of our lives, we pass by and encounter many people. We meet them every day, in the corner store, at work, in the supermarket, and at the gas station. Their faces pretty much look the same, some are black, some are white, some have long hair, and others have no hair at all. Some are tall, some are short, and some smile, while others seldom do. Their actions may be similar and the hustle and bustle of daily life may cause them to be lost in the mix forever. Do we ever stop and think about them?

I mean, really think about them?

Where they have been, what they have seen, whom they have met, or what they have accomplished? Are all of their stories the same? Are they all moving endlessly from point to point without a purpose?

I doubt it.

I know for a fact that everyday folks have special stories to tell, and some of them would surprise you as to where they have been, what they have seen, and what they have accomplished.

In the whirlwind that has become our lives, we need to stop and think. We need to take a minute or two to ask folks about where they have been, and what they have seen, and what they have experienced. I think in many ways, the greatest stories this world has ever known are now being lost forever. Lost in a world of technology. Lost in a world of modern technology and complexity. Where sharing a beer together on a warm summer night on the front stoop and front steps of your house and telling yarns of the past has become lost. It is lost in a web of complicated mumbo-jumbo and electronic hooey, which removes the human factor from so much of what we shared years ago. Everyone has a story to tell, it is a shame that nowadays; we choose not to share stories as we did years ago.

Life was sure a lot simpler back then.

I also know that some of the folks that you pass every day are heroes. They do not tell you that or advertise the fact, but they are. At one time in their lives, they put their lives out there, on the line for the things in which we all believe in, enjoy, and take for granted every day. Now, mind you, dear reader, I am not writing about the baseball star who won the most valuable player award last year, or the quarterback who thinks he is hot stuff, and won the championship last year while being paid millions of dollars.

I also do not mean the rock-and-roll star that may strut around on stage with half of their body exposed under the disguise of "entertainment" while many disillusioned people drool over them.

No, I am writing about a very different type of hero. The ones who blend in with the walk and the talk of everyday life, the ones who at one time of their lives, put aside their own hopes, dreams, and ambitions to answer the call that they were destined to answer.

In the meantime, you would never know it, because while they are heroes, they sometimes wore a fantastic disguise, and in my case, myself, and many other people, thought they actually just drove a seafood delivery truck around the streets of Paterson, New Jersey.

The telephone rang in our little house in Great Falls, New Jersey, on a late Saturday afternoon in July 1986.

"I will get it Binky," I shouted as I picked up the

telephone. I knew that my wife was down in the basement collecting the laundry, and I wanted to make sure she heard me, and did not rush for the telephone while I picked it up.

"Hello."

"Hey, Paulie . . . it is, Jeffrey. Jeff Porter calling."

"Oh hey, Jeff, it has been a little bit of time since we spoke. How is your dad doing?"

"Well, that is why I am calling you, Paulie. I hope you can help me. My dad is not doing so swift. . . ."

Jeff's voice choked off for a bit and wandered. He returned to the line, a little weaker in voice, but he was making an effort. I knew this was not going to be a pleasant conversation.

"It is not good, Paulie. He was in the hospital last week and they sent him home with hospice care, they come and stick him with needles all the time. Needles, and pain medications, that is what it has come down to these days, Paulie. It is ugly now, my dear, old friend. I am afraid he is coming to the end of the road. My mom is a mess."

I felt my heart sink. Jeff Porter was actually my oldest friend. I knew him even before I met Harry. We had been friends even before he moved from Oxford Street in Haledon, New Jersey, to 30 John Street right next to the world famous, Harry M. Redmond Jr., where the rest of the story is as they say, "History."

Jeff and the entire Porter family were amongst my oldest and dearest friends. As young men and boys, Harry, Jeff, and I were inseparable, until we were around sixteen years of age or so. It was at that age when Jeff met the gal whom he eventually married. From that point on in our lives, Jeff was, understandably, always busy with her.

Jeff surely had taken the correct course; because the two of them went on to marry! No one could argue that Jeff had chosen well by picking a pretty gal over hanging with two ugly mugs from the old neighborhood.

Jeff's father, the world-famous Mr. Porter, was one of the most remarkable men in which I have ever met, and I trembled a little at the mere thought of what he was now going through.

"I am so sorry, Jeff. I really am. How can I help?"

"Well . . . Paulie, things have been rough for quite some time. Dad has not been working and the funds are low, you know the veteran medical care takes forever. I am afraid that church going has never been our strong point, Paulie. I was hoping you could help me with some pastoral care here for my dad, now that, that . . . ah, he is well, he is going to need it. I spoke with my mother and she said to call you. She said Paulie would know what to do. You always know what to do. I was hoping you could come over, and you know . . . pray and help Dad move on . . . to the next step."

I did not really know how to answer. Sure, I was now in my second year in seminary, but I was hardly qualified for this type of counseling at this point in my career or education. I had only now briefly studied in class for this level of end-of-life pastoral care, and I could not in good conscience with my calling serve communion without an ordained pastor present. I had an idea, though, of what to do next.

"If I remember Jeff, you and your folks are Methodist. Isn't that, right?"

"Yeah, yeah, yeah, Paulie we know you are Lutheran, but it does not matter . . . we have not been to church in forever. However, you are correct. We are Methodist if we are anything."

"Jeff, no trouble. I will be there for sure for you, and for your family, but I am not quite qualified yet. I will need some help here. I have an acquaintance. A pastor. A wonderful man who is a Methodist pastor. He stepped in with some kind words one day at a time in my life, when I sorely needed some inspiration. Jeffrey, I know he will help us, because he is part of the brotherhood, my friend. His dad was a flyer in World War Two. Low-level and medium bombers too. B-25s to be exact."

I heard Jeff sigh on the telephone, as the words choked out of his mouth, "Yeah, yeah, yeah. The brotherhood, Paulie. Can you call him and come over, Paulie? I do not know if Dad will last the night." I was now aware of my wife Binky, who was standing next to me, listening intently to the conversation. She knew the gist of it and she came over, put her arms around me, and held me tightly.

"I will be there, Jeff. Just as soon as I can, my friend. I will call Pastor DeYoung right now."

"Thank you, Paulie," was all I heard as he hung up the telephone line. My hands trembled and shook as I turned and hugged my wife.

She whispered with her head resting upon my chest, "I guess it is Mr. Porter's time, twenty-seven. It is time for him to go flying one last time."

I nodded as we held each other for a long, long time

I found the number in my file for Pastor Donald DeYoung and dialed his number.

He answered on the first ring.

I explained to him the situation, and he understood. Yet at first, Pastor DeYoung remained slightly hesitant at my request.

"Paul, I do think you can handle this, son. You need to give yourself a little credit. . .."

I didn't mean to be abrupt, but I cut Pastor DeYoung off in mid-sentence.

"Mr. Porter was a flyer, Pastor DeYoung. B-25s, waist gunner and radio operator. World War Two, sixty-three missions. Europe, Egypt, and Africa."

The line became quiet for a few seconds.

I remembered some words that I had heard so long ago and I smiled as they all came back to me.

"You see, there is this certain thing about a military

brotherhood. An unwritten rule of a fraternity, a bond for some people that lasts beyond lifetimes, beyond normal human relations. It comes because of service, service to freedom, service to what is right, just, and kind. Those who have served know it all too well and the honor of it extends beyond just those who I call my brothers. It extends to family. It extends to friends. It extends to all people who recognize sacrifice in the purest form. If only, it extended to all of humankind. Maybe war would no longer exist and peace would reign."

"What is the address, Paul? I will get dressed and meet you there as soon as I can. I will bring my communion kit."

You see, Pastor DeYoung knew of the brotherhood and the honor too.

I gave him the information, and we hung up. I went off to change into a black suit and tie, grabbed my old Bible, kissed my dear Binky goodbye, and I was out the door. As I jumped in my old jeep, a million memories came rushing back to me. I could see Mr. Porter singing, "Silver Bells" at the top of his lungs in front of a frowning New Jersey State trooper as we all sat together in the bed of an old truck filled with Christmas trees. I could see him working a barbeque grill at Harry's Resort cooking hamburgers and hot dogs, while wearing an Uncle Sam's hat for the Fourth of July, and there he was, putting a tricky horn that played Christmas songs when you pushed the horn button on his Galaxy 500 Super Glide. I saw him dancing with Mrs. Porter on the patio behind Harry's house, swinging and swaying to big band dance music. Clearly, in my mind, I recalled Mr. Porter arguing with an umpire at our little league baseball game. Then the umpire proceeded to toss him out of the game for debating a strike call, and then made him sit in his car in the parking lot for the rest of the game. There he was, right in front of my eyes, with Cocoa right next to him, sweating bullets as he used his giant Galaxy Super Glide 500 car to pull out car engines and pool parts with ropes tied to the front bumper of his car.

Then there was his laugh. It was a belly-shaking laugh and a twinkle in his eyes. There were so many memories and ghosts of the past that haunted me. Memories of growing up in the old neighborhood, and meeting special people such as Mr. William H. Porter.

"You see, youse guys—the flak from the Gerry's at-at guns was coming from the ground, and we were flying so low that it was ripping right through the skin on the plane. I had this here gun, ya see, and I was just firing blindly out the hole in the plane where I saw flashes of light on the ground. I had a set of cans on my head, over my ears, but to be honest, the noise of the engines was so loud that I could not hear anything. The Morse code key was strapped to my leg with a little leather strap, but I had no intention of tapping out a message or even listenin'. I had this thick glass in front of me where I sat as a radio op, so I could see out for positions. I was just blazing away with the machine gun fire. I knew the flak had hit me. I felt some sharp pains in my shoulder, around my waistline, and along my arm, but I pushed the trigger until the barrel of the gun was glowing red in the daylight. I could feel the warmth of the blood running all over my arms, but I just kept firing. It was all I could do, youse guys," Mr. Porter explained, while he took another sip of Big Boulder beer from the can he was holding, and he smiled at us.

It was a sultry and hot summer night, in August 1976, and Mr. Porter, Harry M. Redmond Jr., Jeff Porter, Cocoa the world's smartest dog, Harry's old man, and Harry's brother-in-law, Ronnie Boatmann, sat along with me on the front steps of 20 John Street in Haledon, New Jersey.

Mr. Porter continued, "I was reminded of it because today is the day. I guess you could say it is the anniversary. August 18, 1944, we were over Toulon Harbor in Southern France and we nailed them all. We nailed a battleship, a sub, and a cruiser. I saw three or four of our bombs land dead on the battleship. We were supposed to be a medium bomber and heck, most of the time we were so low that you could throw a baseball from the ground and hit us. I felt bad, because I knew ole Captn' Floyd had been hit badly in the copilot seat, but there was nothin' anyone could do . . . we were all, how shall you say . . . tied up!"

"Weren't you scared, Mr. Porter?" Harry asked, as Mr. Porter took another swig of his beer.

"Sure, I was a mess, Harry! But you do what you have to do, when your life is on the line. The way I figured it was, the guys on the ground with bombs flying out of the sky and landing on them, was pretty shook up too. Hey Ronzo, you went through Tet in Nam, you know the feeling."

"Yeah, yeah, yeah, Bill, but I was boots on the ground. No way that I was getting up in those planes and flying around in the sky. At least on the ground, I could use my street smarts and run." Ronzo gave him an honest explanation of his experience in Vietnam during the Tet Offensive.

"Me too, Bill. I was infantry when I was in Europe, and I always walked next to the tanks. They were pretty nice to have along," Mr. Redmond commented.

Mr. Porter nodded, leaned on the fence, swigged the last of his beer, and motioned to Ronzo to hand him another beer out of the ever-present beer cooler.

"Big Boulder beer, Bill, or a Red and White Label?" Ronzo asked with his hand on the lid of the cooler.

"Big Boulder beer, Ronzo, those Red and White Labels ya drink are way too sweet. Paulie, your old man, was in Korea, if I remember right," Mr. Porter said as he opened the new beer can.

"Yeah, yeah, yeah, he was a mechanic in the United States Army, in the motor pool. That is where he learned to fix vehicles and engines so well, Mr. Porter," I answered. Mr. Porter nodded and smiled at the mention of where my dad had learned his legendary car repair skills.

"Say, Dad, tell us guys the rest of the story. So, what happened over France?" Jeff asked his dad.

"Oh yeah, well, we lost one engine, Captn' Floyd was hit bad, and the other pilot who, if I remember right, was a battlefield comm officer from California, took over. I think his name was David, but his last name escapes me. He was a great pilot, and even with one engine, those B-25s could fly. Captn' David got on the squawk box and he says to us guys in the gunner boxes, I am gonna line 'em up for you boys! Gonna be flying right even with those damn Gerry guns, so let 'em have it, men! He pulled the plane up high, then circled back around and flew in low and right over the river, and he went right under some bridge above the river! What a flyer he was, and then we had clear shots at the Gerry's at-at guns lined up on the river. The tail gunner and I hit them dead on, tore them up, and when the other pilots saw what Captn' David did, a Brit pilot followed us, and they let them have it too! Then another, and then another. Right under the bridge, and we tore the livin' hell outta of them bastards. All ya could see in the hills where the guns were located—was flying stones and fire. The English flew the B-25s too. Maybe some of your mum's relatives, Paulie." Mr. Porter and the rest of the group stared at me, knowing my English heritage on my mother's side.

I shrugged and said, "May have been, Mr. Porter. I would have to ask Gramps and Mum."

Mr. Porter laughed at my quizzical reaction, and he continued his tale.

"We made it back to base. We flew into England rather than back to North Africa. The plane was a mess, but those B-25s could take the flak like no other plane ever made. We landed, or sort of belly landed as best we could, and fell down and kissed the ground. Man, oh man, we kissed the ground, let me tell youse guys, we kissed the ground. Sixty-three missions that I flew and never did see anything like that day. It was a rain of gunfire. It was wall to wall from the ground. We were sitting ducks in the sky. Ten of ours went out, fifteen of the English, and seven came back out of all of us. . ..”

His voice trailed off, and Mr. Porter became less animated.

“Seven planes are all that made it back. We cut Captn’ Floyd out of his seat, but he was gone. He was gone. A great guy too. He gave me a pet spider monkey when we were in Africa together. For an officer, there was no one better. He was a regular guy. I used to feed that monkey everything that monkey could eat anything. He was our mascot in our barracks along with my bulldog, whose name was Odivie.”

He took a swig of beer as we all leaned our heads in and listened. The sky was starting to grow dark, and twilight was upon us, as the sun had sunk lower since Mr. Porter had started to tell us his war story. It was still warm and sticky. Mr. Porter wiped the sweat from his forehead, and he sat down on the edge of the porch steps.

His voice was soft and low now, and I am sure there were tears in his eyes along with the sweat as he told us, “It was a bad scene, youse guys. It was really bad. All of us were hit, and Captn’ David, he actually had a ton of blood from both his own wounds, and blood and brains that splattered on him from Captn’ Floyd. Ugly, really ugly. I was hit all over, but some English surgeons dug all the metal out of me, stitched me up, gave me a few days off, a trip to a pub or two in town, and a Purple Heart. Our group, the 321st bomber group, they gave us a d-u-c for the mission and the Brits, got something from the Royal Crown, but I cannot remember what the hell they call it.”

“What is a d-u-c, Mr. Porter?” I asked, as I sensed he needed a break from the emotion.

“A Distinguished Unit Citation. It comes from the top, the highest award a unit can receive when you display as I remember it, gallantry, determination, and esprit de corps in a mission that was under extremely difficult and hazardous conditions. It is like the Medal of Honor given to an entire unit."

"Wow, geez . . . Mr. Porter, you are a hero," Harry said with a smile.

"Nah, youse guys, it is just like Ronzo says that you do what you have to do. The whole world was going up in smoke, so you did your part. You did what you had to, well, to, save all of this." He waved his hands and arms over our neighborhood. The neighborhood was old, gritty, and rundown, but it was ours!

We all understood.

"I miss them all so much. Captn' Floyd, Kenny, James, Roy, Jake the snake, Captn' David. I owe them all my life in one way or another. I just wish I could see them all one more time. You know . . . to thank them. Thank them for doing what they had to do too. I miss flying too. As bad as it seems, it was so peaceful. Those B-25s were noisy, so your ears would feel as if they were going to drop off your head. But flying, yeah, yeah, yeah, flying was where I felt the best. Higher, higher, and higher, blue skies, white clouds, warm air rushing in my radio op window. It was a feeling of letting go. All of your ties and troubles on the ground, did not matter. It was all gone when I was flying."

He wiped the tears away from his eyes as he swigged the beer.

Jeff was smiling broadly at his father's story. It was a son's pride.

Mr. Porter stood up and looked at us. He said, "You are all part of the brotherhood of flyers. All of youse guys, because of relations or being friends with me, not to mention the fact that Ronzo, Harry Senior, and Paul's old man have been there in combat too. We all made a pact to tell our stories forever. As long as we all tell the stories, they will never die. All those guys who did not come back, their stories of commitment live on through youse guys, and guys like me who did come back. You see, there is this certain thing about a military brotherhood. An unwritten rule of a fraternity, a bond for some people that lasts beyond lifetimes, beyond normal human relations. It comes because of service, service to freedom, service to what is right, just, and kind. Those who have served know it all too well and the honor of it extends beyond just those whom I call my brothers. It extends to family. It extends to friends. It extends to all people who recognize sacrifice in the purest form. If only, it extended to all of humankind. Maybe war would no longer exist and peace would reign. It is what we do."

I raised my hand and said, "Count me in, Mr. Porter."

"Me too," Harry yelled out and then he was followed in our uneven oath by Ronzo, Jeff, and Mr. Redmond and even a bark or two from Cocoa.

Mr. Porter then tilted back the last drops of beer.

He wiped his eyes once more, and smiled as he said, "Thanks, youse guys. Hey, it is late, and that seafood delivery truck needs to roll by four in the morning. Thanks for listening."

He took out his famous "key chain," which was a large caliber brass bullet with a hole drilled in the end, through which he passed his car and house keys. He bent down, patted Cocoa on top of his head, and said, "Hey, bite the bullet, youse guys." Mr. Porter then turned and walked towards his home.

"Hey, Mr. Porter." I called out as I stood up and gave him a very poorly executed salute. I then yelled out, "Thank you!" He smiled and waved back as he headed to his house at 30 John Street.

I pulled my old jeep onto a main drag and shifted gears as I headed in the direction of the Porter's house. It was more than just a few miles away from my house, and it would take me a bit of time to arrive. On the way, the memories would just not stop coming. The ghosts of my past were chasing me down the road and not allowing me ever to forget. It was part of my life that in a roundabout way I feared, but also cherished.

"Come on, smash the top of the television, Paulie and get channel four to come in clearer."

I stood up and fiddled with the fine-tuning knob, as the directions from Harry did not seem to be the actual way to tune in the old television set. Channel four came in clear, and I sat back down. It was close to the top of the hour and the entire neighborhood was crowded into the living room of the Redmond's house at 20 John Street in Haledon, New Jersey.

"Bill, did they say which segment it was going to be on?" Mr. Redmond asked Mr. Porter.

"Nah, Harry, just that I would be on tonight's show," Mr. Porter answered. It was a hot July night, in and around 1977 or thereabouts, and we were all crowded into the Redmond's living room to watch the only color television set in our entire neighborhood. This was a monumental night as one of our own, Mr. William H. Porter, was a celebrity! This was a historic event in the history of the old neighborhood! The entire neighborhood was here to watch in living color, a television show called Real Persons that aired stories of actual, "Every day, ordinary persons" and tried to make celebrities out of ordinary people telling their own stories.

A few weeks earlier, Mr. Porter and Mrs. Porter had attended an air show in New Jersey, and there on display, was an actual B-25 bomber aircraft, such as he had flown in World War Two. Mr. Porter was climbing around inside, reliving his memories, when a television crew and interviewer from the show spotted him. After a quick chat, some paperwork to sign, and a few disclaimers, the management of the show told Mr. Porter that they would like to interview him while filming it for the program. The producers had called, told Mr. Porter that the segment would air on tonight's episode, and the news had spread like a wildfire throughout our neighborhood. Now, we all were crowded into the hot living room at the Redmond's house to watch, while Mr. Porter became a television star! Every fan in the entire neighborhood was spinning around in the windows, on the floors, and on tables in a vain effort to keep everyone cool.

"All right, all right, here it comes, so now, shut up everyone," Ronzo yelled at everyone while the music started and the host came on the air.

"On this evening's show, we relive a memory as we begin the show tonight with an interview with a true American hero. A man who flew sixty-three missions in B-25 bombers during World War Two over Europe, Africa, and Egypt. We ran into Technical Sergeant William H. Porter at an air show in Sussex County, New Jersey, while he sat inside an actual B-25 they had rolled out onto a runway for the air show. There, Sergeant Porter told us his incredible story from his days of service in the United States Army Air Force in World War Two."

The entire living room stood up and cheered as sure enough, Mr. Porter appeared on the television in Harry's living room!

In living color, too!

A handsome young man, who was the interviewer, sat down in the cramped quarters inside the airplane with Mrs. Porter standing off to the side with a mile-wide smile on her face.

"So, Sergeant Porter, what exactly did you do here in this seat? I see a radio and a seat here. . .."

"Well, there should be a very large gun here, too. I was a waist gunner and radio op, and I guess they had to remove the gun for obvious reasons. It was a big one."

The interviewer cut off Mr. Porter and asked, "How many times did you fly, sir?"

"Sixty-three missions. Once over France at Toulon Harbor, we almost did not make it back. The at-at guns from the Gerry's tore the plane apart." Mr. Porter stood up and pointed at locations that were still vivid in his mind of where the bullets had ripped through the plane's fuselage. "Bullets ripped through here, here, and here. Some of the flak hit me in my arms, my waist, and my shoulder. I could feel the blood running out of me. Bullets and shells flying all over . . . killed our copilot, and we lost one engine too. We flew under a bridge with one engine! We needed a better shot to knock out the German's anti-aircraft guns to take them out, so the other pilot, Captn' David, flew under the bridge. He was an amazing pilot. I shot until the barrel of my gun was red from heat. I shot all I had. Then the Brits flew behind us and they blasted them too! We took all of the guns out, and a battleship, a submarine, and a cruiser. Us and the Brits!"

The interviewer shook his head, as he too could feel the emotion of the situation.

He asked, "Were you frightened, Sergeant Porter?"

"Sure was! I was scared out of my wits! What are your options? I was about your age, son! You are flying through a rain of enemy fire coming up into the sky from the ground. I did what I had to do, though. I did it, along with my brothers in arms, so that young people such as you are, could, well . . . do what you are doing right now, son."

Mr. Porter put his hand on the young interviewer's shoulder and you could see the emotion in the young man's face as he continued the interview.

"Thank you for your service, Sergeant Porter. What else did you do here?"

Mr. Porter went on for a few minutes and explained the controls, various radio knobs, and duties as a radio operator and waist gunner that he had performed. We all listened intently because this was fascinating reporting. Regardless, if it was Mr. Porter on the television screen, or some other stranger, it was captivating.

As the interview drew to a close, the young man asked Mr. Porter, "Even though this was a long time ago, I can feel your memories are still very powerful, Sergeant Porter. What would you like to do more than anything else as you sit here reliving a time in your life that must be so vivid?" The camera zoomed in on Mr. Porter's face, and you could see the tears forming in the corners of his eyes.

His mouth quivered, and he finally spoke. "Yeah, yeah, yeah, I want to see the brave men that I served with one more time. I want to thank them for what they did for me and for our country, in fact, for the entire world. I want us to go flying together, one more time. I miss them all so much. Captn' Floyd, Kenny, James, Roy, Jake the snake, Captn' David. I owe them all my life in one way or another. They are all part of the brotherhood, and as long as those who remain continue to tell the stories, I feel we all go on somehow. You see, young man, there is this certain thing about a military brotherhood. An unwritten rule of a fraternity, a bond for some people that lasts beyond lifetimes, beyond normal human relations. It comes because of service, service to freedom, service to what is right, just, and kind. Those who have served know it all too well and the honor of it, extends beyond just those whom I call my brothers. It extends to family; it extends to friends. It extends to all people who recognize sacrifice in the purest form. If only, it extended to all of humankind. Maybe war would no longer exist and peace would reign."

The young man conducting the interview lost all of his composure as he reached out, shook Mr. Porter's hand, and struggled to say, "I could not have said it better sir, in fact no one could."

The show then cut to a commercial.

There was not a dry eye in that living room at 20 John Street on that hot summer night, and I am sure across America too.

I arrived at the Porter's house and pulled my jeep into the driveway. Jeff Porter appeared from the side porch of the home and waved to me as I shut off the engine. I sighed deeply, grabbed my Bible, and stepped out.

This was not going to be easy. When I decided to enter the ministry, the last thought that I could ever imagine was that I would have to provide end-of-life guidance to such a close and dear friend. It was the one thought which had never entered my mind.

"Thanks for coming so soon, Paulie," Jeff said as he met me and the two of us shook hands. "He is going downhill fast, Paulie. You will not recognize him. The nurse from hospice was just here, and she gave him some pain medication. He drifts in and out of sleep and mumbles, but it is not really very good at this point." Jeff Porter looked down at the ground and then back up at me with misty eyes. "I do not think it will be too long."

I placed my hand on his shoulder and gently squeezed it to acknowledge his pain.

"I understand, Jeffrey. Pastor DeYoung will be here any minute now. I asked him to bring his communion kit. I hope we can serve your dad. I think this is Pastor DeYoung now." Sure enough, a little compact car pulled up and parked in front of the house. Pastor DeYoung had spotted us standing there, and he quickly turned into a space along the curbing of the street. Pastor DeYoung shut off the engine. I saw him fumbling around on the front seat of the car as Jeff and I walked over to it.

I had met Pastor DeYoung a few years back when I had first returned to Paterson, New Jersey, after retiring from playing professional ice hockey. I was struggling with my future, the loss of my gal Binky Hobnobber, and my best friend, Harry M. Redmond Jr. was still wandering out there somewhere lost in grief after his wife had passed away. I met Pastor DeYoung in a random meeting on a street around the corner from my small apartment, and we struck up a conversation. He had helped me to deal with a difficult time in my life, and for that, I was always grateful. We struck up a friendship of sorts and even though he was a Methodist, and I was Lutheran, we shared a bond. God once more had a plan and Pastor DeYoung was part of that plan for me.

Those stories are better off left for future words and stories, but suffice it to say, God always has a plan for you.

"Hello, Pastor DeYoung. Thank you for coming on such short notice. It is good to see you, my friend." We shook hands as he stepped out of his vehicle. I helped him with his communion kit, his Bible, and some papers and books that he was putting into a briefcase. Pastor DeYoung was a short man, around fifty years of age or thereabouts, with a dark black beard and thick-rimmed eyeglasses. He had a warm smile and was a gentle, caring soul. You could see it in his eyes. He was dressed in a traditional black suit and clerical white collar.

"Sure, Paulie. I wish it were under better circumstances, but it is nice to see you, my young friend."

"This is my friend, Jeff Porter. Pastor De Young, please meet Jeff Porter. Jeff and I have known each other for a very long time." Jeff and Pastor DeYoung greeted one another and shook hands.

"I understand your dad was a B-25 flyer in World War Two, young man, and that he flew quite a few missions in the big one."

"Yes, Pastor De Young. Sixty-three combat missions."

Pastor DeYoung shook his head and whistled a little. "Quite a few, son, quite a few. In fact, I have not heard of someone flying that many in quite a long time. My own father was a chaplain assigned to the Army Air Force in World War Two. He flew a few too. I know of both the pain and joy of combat flying, son. I remember the stories. They are special. . .." Pastor DeYoung drifted off. "Paulie tells me that you and your family are Methodist."

"Well, yes. I guess we are Methodist, if we are anything, Pastor DeYoung. I have to confess that we have not been to church in quite a long time. I feel bad about that . . . but we called Paulie, because we knew that he would know what to do."

Pastor DeYoung was not a stern or judgmental pastor. It was not his style.

He placed his hand on Jeff Porter's arm and said, "I understand, and God does too, Jeff. Church attendance is anywhere you would like it to be. Church can be in your heart, in your mind, in your backyard. You have done the right thing, Jeff. Please, let us go and see your father now." The three of us walked into the kitchen of the Porter's home and I greeted Mrs. Porter, Jeff's wife, Debra, and Jeff's older brother, Steve. It had been a bit of time since I had seen them, and we lingered for a while.

Mrs. Porter was a dear, sweet woman, who I also had a bundle of memories associated with. She did not say much as the tears rolled down her face, but we hugged for a long time as she whispered to me, "Thank you, Paulie. Thank you for helping us."

We made our way to a back bedroom in the house, and Pastor DeYoung pulled me aside from the family before we entered the room.

He mumbled, "Excuse me," to the Porter family, and he spoke quietly to me, "Paulie, have you studied end-of-life counseling yet in seminary?"

"Just a little here and there in class, Pastor DeYoung. Not much though," I answered.

He nodded his head and said, "This is going to be difficult for you, since you are all old friends. We can do this together, along with God's guidance. We will commune with Mr. Porter and the family as best we can. He does need to be coherent though. I am sure we will break some rules of both our churches, but I know it is not the first time for you to break some rules, Paulie."

He smiled at me because he did know of some of my past history. I shook his hand and smiled back. I knew I was about to receive a better lesson than a hundred classes in seminary. We entered the bedroom, and it was a rough scene for me to handle. I had to admit that I was shocked at the appearance of Mr. Porter. He was in bed; pale, gaunt, and thin. I tried my best to remember him in my mind's eye, as I knew him for all of those years. We took some chairs and sat down next to the bed.

Jeff leaned in and spoke. "Dad, Paulie is here. Paulie and a friend of his, Pastor DeYoung." Mr. Porter's eyelids flickered a little but remained closed. Jeff looked at me, and I nodded my head in acknowledgement.

"Hey, Mr. Porter it is, Paulie Henson. I am here with a good friend of mine, Pastor Donald DeYoung. We would like to chat with you for a bit."

Mr. Porter still did not move or even seem to hear my voice. I had an idea and turned towards Jeff.

"Where is the key chain, Jeffrey?" I asked.

Jeff smiled; he reached inside a dresser drawer and fumbled around for a while inside of it. He pulled it out and handed me the keys while Pastor DeYoung and the rest of the family watched.

"Oh my, I see, Paulie. A memory of some sorts. That may work," Pastor DeYoung said with a grin.

I took the key chain, gently opened Mr. Porter's hands and fingers, and placed the key chain in his hands.

"Hey, Mr. Porter . . . bite the bullet."

Mr. Porter's eyelids flickered again as we watched his hands feel the key chain in his hands and a smile came over his face. He spoke very softly, in almost a whisper, as he opened his eyes and looked at me.

"Paulie . . . yeah, yeah, yeah, bite the bullet, youse guys."

I leaned over the bed, held my hands over his, embraced them tightly, and I smiled.

He smiled back at me.

We quickly prepared the communion table, while Mr. Porter was awake, and Pastor DeYoung and I shared the liturgy and prayers. We served Mr. Porter a wafer with wine by Intinction, and he managed to eat a small piece of the wafer and accept the sacrament. We then all shared in the Lord's Supper with the rest of the family, as Pastor DeYoung pointed out Bible verses for me to read aloud to the group. After properly putting the communion kit away, we all prayed for quite a long time, and then sat in silence next to the bed. Jeff's wife and his brother comforted Mrs. Porter while Jeff, Pastor DeYoung, and I watched as Mr. Porter slowly drifted away.

As the hours crept on, he was growing weaker, but for some reason, he still was holding on. His will was strong, but you could tell that the pain, even with medication, was immense.

"Bill, say, listen . . . my dad was also a flyer in B-25 bombers in World War Two," Pastor DeYoung spoke into Mr. Porter's ear. The three of us studied his reaction, and Pastor DeYoung encouraged me to speak when we saw his eyes flicker again. He whispered to me, "Carry on, Paulie, he is holding on, but the Lord is waiting for him. You need to help him move on, Paulie. That is our role here. We need to ease his suffering and let him know it is time. Shake free some memories, Paulie. Think, then help him to let go."

My mind was blank for a moment. I think it was the grief; it was the pain of the situation, but I knew that Pastor DeYoung was correct. It was the core of our faith. I prayed for strength, for the right words, and a memory came back as I leaned in and spoke.

"It is time to fly, Mr. Porter. Time to go flying once more. Higher, higher, and higher, blue skies, white clouds, warm air rushing in your radio op window. It is now time to let go. All of your ties, pain, and troubles on the ground will not matter. It will all be gone when you go flying."

Mr. Porter opened his eyes wide and stared at us with a

smile breaking out on his face. He spoke weakly, but clearly, "Flying . . . oh yes, Paulie, it is where I need to go."

"We all love you, Dad!" Jeff yelled as he held his father's hands, with tears streaming down his face as the rest of the family rushed in.

Mrs. Porter grasped her husband around his neck and kissed his cheek as he closed his eyes once more. He reached and touched his wife's face with one hand, then dropped it quickly down to his side.

Then he took a few deep breaths, and he spoke clearly and strongly as he moved his other hand over the key chain, he still held.

"I see them all! Captn' Floyd, Kenny, James, Roy, Jake the snake, Captn' David. There they are . . . to go flying with me."

He took a final, deep breath. His body shuddered, and Mr. Porter went flying once more.

We sat in silence for a very long time as the grief overtook us all. Pastor DeYoung and I made the proper telephone calls to the hospice to make the final arrangements for a doctor to arrive. He waited for the doctor to arrive and Pastor DeYoung and I explained to the doctor the end of the life situation. We then called the funeral home and made the final, painful arrangements. The Porter family asked Pastor DeYoung to perform the funeral, of which he agreed to do for them, and he exchanged contact information with Jeff and Steve to prepare the schedule.

I walked with Pastor DeYoung to his car and thanked him for his assistance and the lessons, which he had taught me.

"You did well, Paulie. That was a tough one for you to deal with at such a young age. In this career, you and I have chosen, you will learn to run the avenue in both directions. You will baptize precious babies and see old folks such as Mr. Porter off to their rewards. It tests your emotions and your faith. You are a strong one, Paulie. You will pass the test of time and faith. You will make a great pastor." He put his arm around me as he sensed how difficult this afternoon had been for me.

"I can also tell that man was very special. He was a courageous hero, Paulie. Maybe, if it were not for brave people such as Mr. Porter, then we would not be standing here right now. Or perhaps, we would be speaking German." I nodded my head in agreement, shook his hand, and thanked him once more. He climbed into his car and he was gone. I knew he was correct in his description of Mr. Porter. If not for him and many other folks, then how different this world would be.

This long summer day was ending. The heat was giving way to a calm summer breeze that gently rattled the leaves in the trees. It was a welcome prelude to a wonderful summer night to come. Summer heat, glorious sunsets, and gentle breezes all combine to warm, and then cool your soul.

I walked slowly back to the side porch of the Porter's house and spotted Jeff sitting on the steps. He pointed down to a beer he had set on the steps for me. I smiled, took my suit jacket off, and loosened my tie as I sat down next to him.

"Gotcha a Big Boulder beer, Paulie. Those Red and White Labels are way too sweet."

I laughed and popped the top off the beer. "Here is to your dad, Jeffrey." We touched our bottles together in a salute and each took a long swig of beer. It tasted cold and good.

"Is your mom doing all right, Jeffrey?"

"Yeah, yeah, yeah, I had the doc give her something. She is asleep. Debra and Steve are watching her. Thanks again, Paulie, for everything."

"Sure, sure, sure. You are welcome, Jeff. I really did not do anything."

"Oh, yes you did. It is amazing how the peace comes after the pain, Paulie. Both for my dad and for all of us. It is such peace right now that I feel," Jeff said as he looked over the top of the bottle while downing another sip.

"That's how God designed it, Jeff. I know it is hard to take right now, but your dad is in an exquisite place right now. He is flying once again, and that is where he always felt the best. He always told us that. You remember?"

The tears were now rolling down Jeff's face, and I reached over and put my arm around him, while I pointed in the sky to an airplane flying out in the distance in front of us. The lights were flashing in the darkening sky as it circled closer to Newark Airport.

"That must be one fantastic reunion in Heaven right now, Jeffrey . . . Captn' Floyd, Kenny, James, Roy, Jake the snake, Captn' David, some British pilots, and Technical Sergeant William H. Porter."

"No doubt that they are tearing up the joint, Paulie. Hey, bite the bullet," Jeff said as he reached into his pocket and pulled out the key chain. I placed my hand over Jeff's and we held the key chain together in our clasps.

I smiled as we sat together, and we shared a lifetime of memories on those porch steps, and more than a few beers on a fabulous summer evening.

As long as I will live, I cannot thank heroes such as Mr. William H. Porter enough. All the simple things we take for granted in which freedom brings to us every day, comes as a result of the efforts of soldiers such as Mr. Porter who answered the call, and rose up from the ranks of ordinary people to defend what is right, just, and kind.

It is not much, but the least I can do is to tell the stories. Since we were all part of the brotherhood, then I will do my best to carry on the tales of their efforts. I was still part of the brotherhood of flyers. We all had made a pact to tell these stories forever. As long as we all tell the stories, they will never die. All those soldiers who did not come back, their stories of commitment live on. You see, there is this certain thing about a military brotherhood. An unwritten rule of a fraternity, a bond for some people that lasts beyond lifetimes, beyond normal human relations. It comes because of service, service to freedom, service to what is right, just, and kind.

To quote what Mr. Porter told us all on that summer night so long ago, "Those who have served know it all too well and the honor of it extends beyond just those who I call my brothers. It extends to family. It extends to friends. It extends to all people who recognize sacrifice in the purest form. If only it extended to all of humankind. Maybe war would no longer exist and peace would reign. It is what we do."

Thank you for your service and for what you did, Mr. Porter. You see, I learned as a young man growing up on those gritty, but special streets of Haledon and Paterson, in northern New Jersey that true heroes wear covert disguises, they blend in, and you cannot really see or notice them. I am not speaking of the movie stars, or the athletes, who score touchdowns on Sunday afternoons, or the multitude of other so-called heroes that we pretend are so important or real these days. We make heroes out of such strange people these days.

I am speaking of the heroes that you cannot detect. You see them every day, in the store, driving their cars, walking the streets of your neighborhood. They do not advertise it, earn a bank full of money, or flaunt their experiences.

They are in disguise.

For me, one of the greatest heroes that I ever met, pretended to be a seafood delivery man, and drove his truck around the streets of Paterson, New Jersey for more than thirty years.

Hey, bite the bullet, youse guys.

THE END

Unreasonable Expectations

1

Harry Works a Deal

I was strolling through a sporting goods store in the local mall, killing time, while I was bored stiff on one late summer afternoon. For some reason that made no real sense, except to once again relive some memories. I wanted to check out the latest in hockey equipment. I found myself mindlessly wandering around, trying to find the aisle in which the store displayed their selection of hockey equipment.

I was on my heels a bit these days, having recently returned to my home city of Paterson, New Jersey. I returned home after retiring from professional hockey due to a catastrophic knee injury and some resulting surgery this past year.

Now, it was just this awful loneliness that I had to deal with day after day.

My best buddy, Harry M. Redmond Jr. was out there in the world somewhere. I had not heard from him in many years, since his wife passed away tragically and he took off in his grief. The love of my life, Ms. Binky Hobnobber, also had left me, and I had no idea where she ended up either.

Now, my professional hockey career was over, and I wondered where I was going with my life. I could not shake the past; it followed me around and haunted me at every turn. For some reason, after I retired from hockey, I returned to the area where I grew up, and I thought about how I had made a huge mistake. I should have started anew, and maybe the memories of the past would not have followed me to the new location. I just could not figure it out though. The lure of the old neighborhood was just too strong, and for some unknown reason, I had found myself back here once again.

It was very strange.

It was a few days before Labor Day and the summer was happily drawing to a close. Weather wise, for northern New Jersey, it had been a terrible summer, full of heat and humidity, and it had been difficult to enjoy the season. The last place I lived in for a full summer was in Norfolk, Virginia, and let me tell you, that was a sticky and hot area of the country. The one thing, which I think that I was looking forward to most of all in returning to New Jersey, was a break from awful summer weather.

I was wrong. This summer in New Jersey was terrible!

I was not a big fan of heat, bugs, and humidity anyway, but this particular summer had been even more difficult to struggle through and endure. I had a thought that Mr. Harry M. Redmond Jr. was indeed correct, when he would call me an old lady and complain that for such a rough, tough, hockey player, I was such a pansy la-la and an old lady when it came to the heat of the summer!

Thoughts of Harry went back and forth in my head, and as I walked up and down the aisles, I suddenly found myself in front of a display of fishing boats, and I realized that I was in the fishing tackle aisle of the store. The boats on display were smaller boats, the kind you would use for bass fishing on your local lake. They were fantastic, modern, polished, and they all had the latest features, along with high price tags too! I turned from the boats and walked up and down the racks of an endless collection of fishing tackle, poles, reels, lures, and everything else you need to go and catch a big one. It was all fantastic stuff and such a far cry from the small bait and tackle shop in our old home city of Paterson, New Jersey.

As happens so often in my life, and has allowed me to

some extent, to continue to tell these tales of adventures and life, a few of those ghosts of the past had followed me throughout the store. As I picked up a fishing rod and reel combo, I turned and looked at one of the boats on display, and I could not help but smile. The ghosts were there, sitting in the boat right in front of me. I remembered a time when Harry and I decided that a boat was just the trick to lure some pretty young women on a summer holiday getaway. A summer, when we not only bought a boat, but a summer, when I grew up quite a bit, when I learned about making life decisions and facing responsibilities.

As usual, as the adventures of Harry and Paul frequently go—things did not quite work out the way we had actually planned it.

"Youse stupid ass dopey, guys and Cocoa are going fishing? HA! HA! HA!" Cliffy the seafood delivery guy asked us one sunny Saturday afternoon in the middle of August 1976.

Harry and I were putting some tackle boxes, fishing poles, and bait cans in the back of my old custom van outside of Harry's house at 20 John Street in Haledon, New Jersey. Harry's faithful dog and our constant companion during our youth and well beyond, Cocoa followed the two of us with his favorite rubber toy; "Piggy" firmly entrenched in his mouth. Cocoa wanted to go fishing with us, too. Everyone knew Cocoa within our neighborhood circles as his well-deserved reputation for being; "the world's smartest dog" preceded him. Cliffy was hanging out in the front of Mr. Porter's house next door to Harry's house. He had spotted us loading my van, and he had wandered over to harass us a bit.

"Yeah, yeah, yeah, that's right, Cliffy. We are heading up to the Oldham Pond to fish a little. Unlike you, we worked all morning, and a little part of the afternoon until one or so, and now, we need to relax. I am still recovering from roller-skating for that charity for a bazillion hours. I need to relax for a long time. My legs have been like gelatin for weeks. Paul and I work hard. You know the drill, Cliffy. We will pass the time until it is time to go cruising for twigeons tonight." Harry did not want to answer Cliffy, but he did and he forced the answer to be long and drawn out on purpose.

Cocoa whimpered a little at the sight of Cliffy, and he tucked his tail between his legs when he heard the classic "Cliffy" words spewing from his mouth.

Now, Cliffy McWhiffy was one of the most colorful characters in our entire neighborhood, and when I pause and take a few moments to inventory in my mind, the odd cast of characters that lived within two city blocks of one another, in our home borough of Haledon, New Jersey that is saying an awful lot! Cliffy was about fifty years old, very tall, ranging in the six foot seven or so range, and he was as skinny as a pencil. He had longish, dark brown hair swirled over to the side and held in place with some greasy hair glue. He had the typical 1970s style sideburns that came down along the side of his face, and they were razor-cut into a sharp-pointed edge. He worked with Mr. Porter for years and years, delivering seafood for the Crescent Moon Seafood Company, driving one of the trucks along with Mr. Porter. Cliffy, unlike Mr. Porter, always smelled like a big, old fish. He must have lived in the fish freezers. Even when he walked away, he left a vapor trail of a fish odor that followed him around and lingered in the air behind him. We had all known Cliffy for years, and now that we were older, we hardly paid any attention to him at all.

Cliffy had not always lived in our neighborhood. If I recall correctly, he, at one time, had an apartment over near Tilted Hill. Then a few years ago, he moved over on Geyer

Street, right around the corner from Cook Street. Now that he lived closer, he would always be hanging around, drinking beer, car-pooling to and from work with Mr. Porter, and generally being annoying. He was married, however; I had never seen his wife, and he did not mention any children, but that did not mean much, because Cliffy was very difficult to understand.

Not only was he a very famous and well-known leader of the infamous, "chronic mispronunciation guys," Cliffy was also a habitual hurler of obscene words. Every single sentence spoken by Cliffy contained, at the very least, one, or usually a lot more than just one, obscene words. It did not matter if women were present, or Harry's family priest Father Mark, who was also a family friend, was visiting, or anyone else who may have objected to his cussing, nothing stopped Cliffy from littering his vocabulary with strings of continuous and colorful obscenities. He also would berate you at every opportunity with insults. His speech was always laden with extra-heavy New Jersey slang and general verbal abuse. Just to add a special touch on top of his already colorful and cryptic manner of speech, Cliffy also ended every single sentence that he ever spoke with a loud, "HA! HA! HA! It was always three short bursts of laughter, never more or less. Mrs. Porter told us when we were very little kiddies that it was a nervous habit, and she was, of course, correct in her analysis of Cliffy's strange habit. That did not stop us when we were stupid little kids, from always prompting and doing our best to make Cliffy speak, so we could hear him cuss and swear as well as the patented chuckle after every line. Mrs. Porter would scold us and chase us away, but it was worth it to hear the latest gibberish from the famous Cliffy. Now that we were older, Cliffy was just another character in the endless parade of whackos and nutcases who frequented our neighborhood.

"Ain't nuthin' friggin' worth catchin' in Oldtom Pond. Youse stupid ass guys are wasting your time. HA! HA!

HA!" Cliffy said as he stood next to us and watched us load the van.

"Oldham Pond, Cliffy . . . not Oldtom Pond," Harry made a vain attempt to correct Cliffy.

"That is what I friggin' said. HA! HA! HA!" Cliffy proposed adamantly.

True chronic mispronunciation guys did not realize their mistakes. Both Harry and I, through many years of fruitless and pointless conversations with Cliffy since we were about ten years old or thereabouts, knew that further correction was a hopeless endeavor, therefore, we moved on rather quickly.

"Whatever, Cliffy! Twenty-seven and I are going fishing and we really do not care what we catch. We just want to relax a little before we go out tonight," Harry had quickly grown annoyed with Cliffy, as well as his obscenity-laden opinion of the fishing spot that we had frequented since we were old enough to ride our bikes into the far reaches of North Haledon. Cocoa then barked twice and wagged his tail three times to indicate that he agreed with us. Poor Cocoa just wanted to leave and to go fishing!

The Oldham Pond was located about five or six miles north from where we lived, on the edge of the Borough of North Haledon. The pond was located in what was actually a surprisingly glorious backdrop of scenic beauty, along the side of a main road that led all the way to the very center of downtown Paterson, New Jersey. The towering background of High Mountain loomed above the pond in the distance. Harry and I had many glorious memories of times we spent on top of that mountain, but I will leave those stories for another time and place. If you were to close your eyes and forget where you were, a visitor could easily think the pond was located in southern Vermont or some other famous scenic location. In reality, this overlooked gem was only five or six miles away from the urban grit and all of its ambiguous glory!

The original use of the pond was to draw ice from, for use by the ice houses that lined the area many years ago, and to supply water to nearby silk mills, coloring factories, and dye factories for their manufacturing and boiler processes. The State of New Jersey, Fish and Game Department, actually stocked the Oldham Pond with trout in the springtime of the year. We felt it was the closest thing to a fishing heaven located within the pedaling distance of our bicycles and still within the confines of our urban area. When we were kids, Harry, Jeff Porter, and I would pedal our bikes to what seemed as if we were going to another state, when in reality, we were only heading to the township just north of the northern most boundaries of our own town.

It did not matter to us. All that mattered was that we were able to escape to what we felt was, "the country."

"Well, if you want to catch real damn fish you would buy a boat and head for Green Pine Lake. Ya dumb-ass jerks could pull a boat with this heap of junk truck and bring your girlfriends out on a real lake. They might think youse guys are big shots instead of the dopey-ass losers ya really are, and you could catch some not pollootoed fish if you had a boat. HA! HA! HA!" Cliffy often made up his own words, but we knew what he meant. He was correct because most of the fish in the Oldham Pond were not fit for human or any other living creature's consumption. He had offered a keen observation from Cliffy's unique world of how we could improve our fishing prowess and impress young women.

I spotted Harry's ears pop up and his attention had been gathered when he heard Cliffy mention the fact that we might be able to impress young ladies with the possession of a boat. Harry jumped up from loading the fishing gear, and his eyes flickered with interest and excitement.

Oh, oh! I knew that look all too well!

Cliffy continued, "You know, Steve Doe Springlio is

selling a leaky-ass old boat over on Clumbton Street for two hundred and fifty bucks. HA! HA! HA!"

"Who, Cliffy? Where?" I asked, while becoming puzzled by the identity of the seller.

"Youse guys know 'em. That jackass Steve Doe Springlio. HA! HA! HA!" Even for Cliffy, this convoluted name and the twisted street name was a classic mispronunciation of a new and higher magnitude. Harry and I both searched our minds for an inventory of neighbors and no one came to mind with the last name of "Doe Springlio." Suddenly, I thought of a person over on Clinton Street with a remotely sounding similar last name, which just might fit the description within the confines of Cliffy's confused language and twisted brain.

"Do you mean, Steve DelMonico, over on Clinton Street Cliffy?" I had made the pieces fit.

"Yeah, yeah, yeah, dumb-ass. That's what I just said, DelMornico over on Clifton Street. HA! HA! HA!" Cocoa whimpered again. Even the world's smartest dog was struggling to follow Cliffy today.

It was hopeless to try to have a meaningful conversation with Cliffy. The greatest cryptologist in the world, who could break any of the world's most difficult or secret codes, would scream in agony after speaking with Cliffy in a vain attempt to understand what he was saying. I felt honored to have deciphered his language, but then again, we had known him for a long time.

We had encountered an awful lot of Cliffy practice throughout the years.

"Say, thanks there, Cliffy, we will check it out," Harry said while rubbing his chin. I could tell he was intrigued, and I could see the scheming wheels spinning around in his mind. Scheming wheels spinning in Harry's mind were different from ordinary, everyday wheels. I knew this meant trouble, as Harry cleared his throat to ask Cliffy some more details.

"You say this boat is in DelMonico's backyard, Cliffy. How do you know he is selling it? No one has boats around here in this old city . . . this is not exactly a boating type neighborhood ya know."

"Sure, sure, sure I damn-well know that, Harry. That is why youse stupid lard-ass dopes should check it out. Even idiots like youse guys are should be able to work out a deal. Delborneo's uncle, or something like that, keeled over and croaked, and he left it to that jackass, Steve. He told me he would give me a twenty-buck concussion if I helped him sell it. HA! HA! HA!" We both knew the super-confused Cliffy actually meant to say commission rather than concussion, so we moved on rather quickly.

"I see now why you are pushing the boat angle there, Cliffy. You spotted us loading our fishing gear, and figured you could drop a hint or two to earn a quick twenty spot, eh?" I decided to call Cliffy out on his wheeling and dealing.

Cliffy stood back and smiled. Cliffy might have been many things, but dumb was not one of them. He had a degree in street living and he was a survivor.

"That is right, Paul, ya long-haired, mush-brained jackass hippie. It does not matter because it still is a great deal! Even if you do not keep it, even jerks like youse dopes could fix it, and sell it for a few bucks more. It is old, but it is one of those fancy, Crispy Craft boats. HA! HA! HA!"

All three of us had our maximum fill of Cliffy for today. We thanked him, said goodbye, and climbed into the van. I held the side door open for Cocoa, who grabbed his Piggy and jumped in with us.

I started the engine, and we pulled away as Cliffy yelled out to us, "Be sure you tell Delhornismo that I sent ya sorry asses over there. HA! HA! HA!" Harry leaned out the window and waved to Cliffy and he disappeared into the Porter's backyard. He was most likely going to harass Mr. Porter for the rest of the day and to drink beer with him.

I knew that I was now in hot water. I knew Harry M. Redmond Jr. as well as I knew myself, and I knew the current silence meant one thing; we were not going fishing this afternoon. We were going to go to check out the boat in Steve DelMonico's backyard.

Harry cleared his throat. Whenever he wanted to convince me of something, he would always clear his throat.

Yeah, yeah, yeah, here it comes. . ..

"You know, twenty-seven. Cliffy may be a whacked out, chronic mispronunciation guy, but this boat sounds like it might be a good deal. We should check it out. I mean, it kinda sounds really cool. As Cliffy said, we could fix it up and sell it, if we did not want to keep it. We could go halfies on it!"

Harry looked over at me to judge my reaction to his latest scheme. Two city slickers buying a boat? It sounded ridiculous to me.

"I could impress, Joyce, and maybe you would have the guts for once in your life, to ask a gal out for a big Labor Day shindig. Ya know, in thinkin' 'bout it, I think one of my uncles on my mother's side of the family has a cabin on Green Pine Lake. I bet we could borrow it or get it for some cheap rent for the holiday! Think about it! Fishing, floating around on the lake, the gals in bathing suits . . . oh yeah! Now, that is what I am talking about, twenty-seven!"

"I do not know, Harry. I think it could be a bad idea. That is an awful lot of dough to fork out for fishing and impressing young women. You know that I am saving my extra money for hockey equipment and that goalie clinic coming up in October. The boat is probably a piece of junk and Cliffy is wrong, and we will be stuck with a big hunk of junk that we cannot sell in a million years. Besides, where are we going to get that kind of money? I know you make some good jingle, but you know I am always a little short in the old cashola department."

Cocoa barked twice and wagged his tail three times to indicate that he agreed with me. Harry turned and glared at him, and Cocoa sat down and did not move a muscle.

"I do not think we asked for your opinion there, Cocoa! Remember, ya might be smart, but also ya need to remember that you're a dog, and think about whom your master around here is!"

Harry then turned his attention back towards me, and while he was shaking his head, he said, "You are such an old lady, twenty-seven. There you go, spinning off into old lady land once again. Take a chance for once! Let's check it out! Since you are such an old lady, if ya cannot dig up another chick to ask out, then don't forget that ole Maureen Zipperelli has been chasing you around for years. Other than a few dates here and there with her, and that double date when we all went to the movies in July, I have not heard you mention her lately. Can you imagine if Maureen heard of a weekend getaway with the famous number twenty-seven? Whoo weee! An older chick that is after you! I bet she looks pretty good in a bikini too! C'mon, forget the fishing, and let's turn over to Clinton Street and check it out. What can it hurt?" Harry smiled widely at me; he leaned in on the dashboard and pointed in the direction of Clinton Street.

I was doomed. I knew that Harry was now obsessed with boats and there was no turning back.

The Redmonds were legendary for their famous life phases, where they magically transformed, consumed, and shaped their lives with some wild interest. You name it, and I had seen it, everything from "baseball phase" to the now infamous, "country and western phase." Elaborations of the Redmond phases are, once more, stories that I will leave for another set of words, up and down the roads in the many adventures of Harry and Paul!

"Here is DelMonico's house. Right here, Paul, c'mon and pull the van over here."

I swung the van into an empty parking spot on Clinton Street and parked it. Before I could even shut the engine down, the now boat-crazed Harry had jumped out of the van, ran to the front of the house, and he was staring into DelMonico's backyard. I climbed out of the driver's door, walked over to the side door, and let Cocoa out. The two of us then followed Harry as he walked to the front gate of the house.

"That must be the boat over there in the back," Harry surmised as he pointed into the backyard. "Under that green tarp. Do ya see it, Paul? Back there! C'mon youse guys, let's ring the ding-dong and see if we can work a deal out for it!" Harry almost sprinted to the front door to ring the doorbell. I looked over a small wire fence and saw what appeared to be about a fifteen-foot long or so boat (it was actually difficult to determine the actual length of the boat) tucked away in the corner of the yard. It had a worn and tattered green tarp covering it, and the boat was sitting upon a very rusty trailer.

I had my immediate doubts.

"I dunno, Harry. This boat looks like a piece of junk that will sink. . .." Harry cut me off and held his hand up in the air to indicate that I needed to stop talking.

"Old Lady Syndrome, Paul. Old lady, negative attitude stuff. Take a chance for once," Harry said while he rang the doorbell repeatedly.

Now, we in a very roundabout way did know, Steve DelMonico. He was best friends with Jeff Porter's older brother, Steve Porter, and even though he was about five or six years older than we were, we did know him from around the neighborhood. He was a typical New Jersey guy of Italian descent, big and round, and very friendly. The door swung open and Steve was standing there with his father behind him.

"Geez, Harry! How many times are you going to ring the bell? How ya guys doing? Whadda ya want?" Steve was annoyed at Harry's aggressive, bell-ringing procedures. "Oh, hey, Paulie! Hey there, Cocoa!" People always spoke to Cocoa as if he was a human being. His reputation of being the world's smartest dog was well known and certainly well deserved.

"Are you still playing hockey, Paulie?"

I waved back to Steve and said, "Yeah, yeah, yeah. I am trying, Steve. I start training in a goalie clinic in the fall, right after Labor Day."

"Hey, good luck with that. I hear you are quite a good player."

Harry was in no mood for general chit chat. I could tell he wanted to get right to the negotiations. I was correct, since he dove right in and said, "Say, Steve, Cliffy told us a few minutes ago, that you have a boat for sale. Is that the boat in your yard?"

"Yeah, yeah, yeah . . . it is, Harry. What do youse two guys want with a boat?"

"Well, we are big fisherman, ya know, and well, Cliffy mentioned that it might be a cool way to attract some young twigeons. Can we take a look at it? You see, twenty-seven and I would be going half each on it."

Steve laughed, and he stepped out on the porch as he waved for us to follow him, "Sure, come take a look. Old Cliffy sucked you two bananas in with the attracting the young gal's angle, huh? The boat was my uncle's, and he passed away a few months back. We towed it down here from Pennsylvania and put it in the backyard. My old man and I are not interested in boats, so we decided to sell it. We really do not know much about it. It sat in my uncle's backyard for years and years. He had not put it in the water since he started to get old and not feel so well. I knew that blabbermouth Cliffy would spread the word. I lured him with a twenty-dollar commission, if he could sell it."

"He thinks he is getting a concussion, Steve," I corrected

Steve with the jumbled world of Cliffy.

"What? Oh yeah, that Cliffy is a piece of work." We followed Steve into his backyard and I could already tell by Harry's body posture that Harry was ready to work a deal. Harry was still in his infancy in the development of his legendary deal-making skills, in which he would hone and refine as the years passed. He would eventually become one of the greatest and legendary dealmakers of our neighborhood as well as beyond.

Those were Harry and Paul adventures, in which we could only dream about right now.

"Here it is. I doubt that it is a pretty scene underneath here. Grab an end of this tarp and we can pull it off, so youse can check it out."

My initial assessment, from farther away, seemed accurate; we now stood in front of what appeared to be a fifteen-foot, or maybe even a little longer than a fifteen-foot boat, sitting on top of a rusty trailer. You could see the bottom of the boat, but not much more, because a worn, green tarp covered the entire top of the craft. We all worked at the corners of the ropes, which held the tarp on, loosened them, and tugged and pulled until the dirty tarp slowly slid away, and it revealed a very old and dirty boat underneath.

The boat's hull was wooden, and it looked as though it was mahogany wood. The inside of the hull had collected a thick layer of muck and leaves, in fact; it smelled like an old cow's backside. The seats were all dirty, with cushions buried under mounds of dirt, leaves, and debris. The boat had two individual seats in the front, then a large cushioned console in the center of the boat, with a bench passenger seat in the back. The passenger seat took up the entire rear compartment of the boat, except for a wooden lid, which I surmised covered the inboard engine to power the boat.

Cocoa jumped up on the side of the boat and put his

paws on the edge. He tried his best to peer over the top and look inside, but he was just a little too short. He sniffed the air and caught a whiff of the rotted leaves stuck inside the passenger compartment that gave off a musty stench. Cocoa jumped down, looked over towards Harry and me, and then he sat down. It was obvious that he did not want anything else to do with the inside of the boat. I studied the boat's condition, and from a casting of a pitted, chrome metal logo, fastened to the side of the boat, I read aloud the name of the manufacturer of the boat, "Cristo Craft," I said and pointed to the logo.

I turned to Harry and laughed as I remembered Cliffy had told us it was a "Crispy Craft."

Harry pointed at the logo and laughed too, as he said, "Cliffy cannot get anything right!"

Steve was indeed correct in his description, since the boat was not very pretty at all. In fact, it was looking a bit rough.

"I love it! Now, this is what I am talking about!" Harry was now exuding his typical, over the top exuberance, at the latest whim, which happened to be the prospect of being a boat owner. Of course, since he now was embroiled into a "boating phase" of no return, it was hopeless to change his mind. He felt the boat was now the greatest thing in the world.

Steve went into a lengthy explanation and disclaimer, "Yeah, yeah, yeah. It is an old one . . . a 1949 Cristo-Craft, Sportsman model. They were an expensive boat, way back then. We found the papers and title in my uncle's files. The last time it floated was about five years ago. We do not know anything else about it. Boats are not exactly in my field of expertise, youse guys. I have to sell it as is, youse guys. I mean that the boat sale is with no guarantees of any kind. It has a motor, but I do not know if it even runs. You need to fix the trailer even to pull it over to your house. It is a rusty mess, and we barely got it home here without the trailer falling apart. I know you are in the welding business, Harry. I would think that will be the easy part. The rest of it, though. . .."

Steve finished his drawn-out speech while he shook his head in a fairly pessimistic, yet factual testimony to the boat's condition.

Harry was quickly whipping up some razz-a-ma-tazz and countering the negative attitude of Steve, "Not a problem, Steve-a-roo-ski! Paul and I can fix anything! I will weld the trailer up. Paul will fix all the wires, lights, radios, and stuff. Of course, Paul's old man can get that motor to run! We'll take it. How much?"

"Two hundred and fifty bucks there, Harry, and that is the bottom line. Now, I have to give Cliffy a few bucks too." Harry put his foot up on the trailer and the boat almost slid off as it shifted and twisted. We all ran over and steadied it, so the entire mess did not collapse in Steve's backyard.

"Oh, c'mon, Steve! Give me a few bucks off for this piece of junk trailer. Look at the work that I have to do, just to get it over to John Street!" Cocoa agreed as he gave us the two barks, followed by the three-tail wag confirmation.

"Geez, Harry. All right, two hundred and twenty-five and I need the dough by the beginning of next week." I tugged at Harry's shirt in a vain effort to pull him aside and speak with him for a moment.

"Not now, twenty-seven! You are going to pull some old lady act and tell me you do not have the dough."

I was, of course, now doomed. Guilty by association with Harry once more. Steve frowned and looked at us. He knew the real situation, and he could sense that cash for us was not exactly overflowing at this moment.

"I am sticking to it. We will take it, Steve!"

Yes, Harry confirmed it.

I was doomed.

I was about to be a part owner of some old relic of a

boat. I doubted that the thing could even float.

"You just may need to give us a few days to bring the dough over. I just had to make a payment on that new Sonicmobile that I bought this summer, and my car insurance was due. I make a lot of dough there, Steve, but payday is still a few days away. Look here, we will give you a goodwill deposit right now. I have here. . .."

Harry pulled his wallet out and counted a few dollars out.

"Ten, fifteen, eighteen. Paul, how much do you have?" I handed Harry my last five dollars. Harry grabbed it eagerly out of my hands and set it down (gently) on the end of the boat trailer. Now, it was true that Harry earned quite a bit of money as a welder, he drove a fancy, new Sonicmobile car that he had just bought in the beginning of the summer, and he had a reputation of being a guy with a few bucks stashed away. The trouble was with number twenty-seven!

Steve was still frowning, and he looked over rather suspiciously, at our meager deposit, and then at me. He piped up, "I know you make some good dough, Harry, and no offense there, Paul, but you are always broke."

Cocoa barked twice and wagged his tail three times in agreement with Steve. Even the world's smartest dog knew that I was usually broke. My reputation for being a pauper reached far and wide.

"I do not want to wait a million years for the rest of the money," Steve lamented.

Harry jumped in with his deal making skills, "Ah c'mon there, Steve-a-roo-ski. It is not exactly like folks are lining up to buy this heap of junk! We just saved ya a lot of marketing time! That must be worth something."

Harry could sell ice to an Eskimo.

Steve smiled, and he picked up the money that Harry had placed down upon the trailer. Harry had struck a chord, since Steve knew he was indeed correct in his profound observation of the limited amount of people who were currently shopping for boats in our old neighborhood.

He fingered the bills in his hand and said, "All right. I will give you a week to bring me the rest of the dough. I will write you a note for this deposit and we can all sign it and finish the deal." He picked up the dough and reached out to shake our hands.

"DEAL!" Harry shouted out. He was thrilled as he sealed the deal with Steve with a handshake. Cocoa jumped around in circles, barking and throwing Piggy into the air to celebrate. I reached out and shook Steve's hand, and he jumped back as I grasped his hand and shook it.

"Ouch! Man, oh man, Paul. You have some grip there!" Steve waved his hand in the air while he looked at me.

"Sorry, Steve. I work with my hands and pull on wires all day. Between my work and playing hockey, it must make my hands and arms fairly strong."

Steve stood back, and it appeared as if he was thinking for a few moments.

"Say, Paul, that's right. I had forgotten about where you worked. If I remember, you work in electrical and electronics. Isn't that what you do?"

"Yeah, yeah, yeah, Steve. Over in Rock Glen, at the electrical shop on Rock Road in the center of town."

I could tell that Steve was thinking about some kind of angle. I am not sure I knew where he was going with this one.

"That's what I thought. Ya know, my old man and I, we run the building maintenance for the Paterson Catholic Diocese. One of the buildings that we take care of is the big rectory and the convent up on top of the mountain there in West Paterson. We need a job done there that youse two guys may be able to handle. It will pay about one hundred and fifty bucks too. It will help you with your current, poor money situation, and help to pay off the boat."

It was obvious that Steve had an ulterior motive for mentioning the potential job.

Harry almost jumped out of his skin when he heard the pay, and he immediately answered, "Paul and Harry are in! We will do it!"

Steve laughed at Harry and his hair triggered reactions. "Now, hold on, wait a second, Harry. You have not even heard what the job is all about and believe me, this job is not very easy. My old man has had about five guys look at the job, and not one of them wants to do it. Youse guys would have to put a television antenna up on top of the roof. The roof, over on the convent end of the building. It is a steep roof and let me tell you that it is high! I do mean really, really high. We have a ladder in our shop to get ya to the lower section of the roof, but you will have to climb to the higher section where the antenna is going to be located. I thought with Paul's background in wires and stuff that ya might be interested. I would guess, Paul, that you know how to wire antennas and stuff. Don't ya?"

"Well, I am not. . .."

Harry blasted in and interrupted me, "Sure he does, Steve. Let me tell ya something there, Steve-a-roo-ski. Not only does Paul work on all that kind of stuff at work, but most every other weekend, he helps his old man fix his own television and radio antenna! He is an expert."

Steve looked at me with a strange look on his face, and I shrugged my shoulders. I guess his thought of climbing on a roof every week or so, to work on antennas, made very little sense, but I am not sure that he knew my old man. I could not argue with Harry on that point. My old man was constantly climbing on the roof, fiddling with our antenna in an endless quest to receive a better picture on our old black and white television, and we had shortwave and long wave radio antennas, too. I was always his helper on those missions.

Once again, that is a whole other story for another set of

words.

Harry shifted gears, and he instantly and magically transformed into his great blowhard role, "Oh yeah, it will be nothing for Paul to handle. He is so flexible from all that goalie stuff. He can climb like a monkey. He has no fear of anything either, since he stands in front of those wicked, hard, slap shots." Harry leaned into Steve and lowered his voice. His eyes darted over to me and with a voice just above a whisper and with his hand cupping his mouth, Harry babbled, "Between you and me, I think his head is a little scrambled from all those blows to the head."

I shrugged off the brain analysis because I suddenly realized that Harry's sales pitch centered on "he" doing all the work, climbing, and not being afraid. The, "he" was, of course, me, so I surmised that Harry was neither climbing, nor working, and I was the sucker here.

I decided to jump in here, "Hang on there, Harry, maybe we can go look at the job first and see. . .."

Of course, Harry trampled all over the top of me, "Forget about any other guys there, Steve-a-roo-ski! We will do it, and if it is not raining, we will be there right after work on this Monday. We will meet you around four in the afternoon, right in front of the building. I know where the convent is, there on the side of Paterson Mountain."

"Harry, please, I still think, we need to check it. . .."

"Relax, Paul. It will be a piece of cake. After all, how bad can it be?" Oh how, I had come to despise those words of how bad can it be because it always meant one thing and that it *was* bad.

I looked over at Cocoa, who sat down, whimpered, picked up Piggy, and gave him a loud squeak.

Sometimes, I wish that I had a Piggy too.

2

How Bad Can It Be?

Now, you would have thought after being the best buddy of Harry M. Redmond Junior for all of these years that the passage of time would have made me grow just a little wiser. A smarter person could have come up with an angle to escape his traps and lures of emotions and actions that, on occasion, turned my life upside down. Harry's twists and turns of his various phases and emotions went up and down like an elevator in a high-rise building. One minute, he was exaggerating our abilities, or describing our attributes in overblown explanations of what we were capable of, or whom we actually were. The next minute, he was a "great reducer" of a situation. He usually minimized the situation to convince me that an impossible task was nothing or very easy within reach.

I knew better.

While I stood in front of the convent and rectory building on the side of Paterson Mountain in West Paterson, New Jersey, the words, "How bad can it be" echoed throughout my mind, and resonated inside of my brain like a pair of cymbals crashing. You see, the top of the roof where the antenna had to be mounted was somewhere up there in the sky, but it was just a bit difficult to see, since it was lost in a cloud bank.

I had not brought along a telescope.

It was the Monday after Harry and I had become the almost proud owners of a dilapidated boat. We were, as promised, meeting Steve DelMonico and his father at the convent and rectory building, in hopes of installing the wire and antenna for the television for the nuns and priests who resided there.

Harry was, as always, bombastic and overconfident as he jumped out of my van, walked over to Steve and his dad, and nearly blew them over with his enthusiastic greeting, "Hey Steve! Hey there, Mr. DelMonico! How are youse two guys today? Here we are, show us the situation, and twenty-seven will scamper right on up there, and put up this antenna where others feared to tread!" Steve and Mr. DelMonico shook Harry's hand, while I wandered over towards them, and nodded to both father and son.

As I approached Steve and Mr. DelMonico, I heard Steve lean over and say to his father, "Be careful when shaking Paul's hand, Pop. He will crush your fingers like some kind of vise!"

I heeded the warning, and when I shook their hands, I was very cognizant of not crushing them. "Hello, Mr. DelMonico, Hello, Steve," I greeted them both.

"Hey, Paulie. Since Harry keeps mentioning your name, and I do not hear him saying anything about him climbing up there, then I have to ask you. Are you really going up there?" Mr. DelMonico pointed towards the clouds that covered the peak of the roof.

"Well, I think. . .."

Harry blared in, cutting me off before I could even speak the words, "Sure he is, Mr. DelMonico. Twenty-seven does not care about a little, steepy-weepy roof that some other wimps chickened out from climbing up. I am going up with him there too. I just may not exactly climb all the way with him. You see, we do this all the time and I am the rope man."

"Rope man?" I was as puzzled as both of the DelMonicos were, and furthermore, I never remembered in our endless adventures, a previous time that we climbed halfway to the moon to do a job.

I must have missed an adventure or two along the way.

"Yeah, yeah, yeah, youse see there—it is all about safety," Harry proclaimed. He walked towards the van and dragged out of the side door, a long hemp rope that we had used in the past to pull car engines out, pull Christmas trees upside down into the far reaches of oak trees in backyards, yank pool parts off the back of trucks, and various other strange missions over the years.

"Since I have legs like tree trunks, and super-powerful ass muscles, I will tie this rope around twenty-seven, and then around my waist. I will brace myself on the roof or on a chimney, or something up there, plant my legs like a tripod, and it will be a slam-dunk. That way, if by some slim chance of fate, when, I mean if, Paul slips, then I will easily just yank him on in." Harry smiled broadly while he demonstrated the "yanking on in" technique.

I have to be perfectly honest—I really felt no better about this situation after hearing of, and then witnessing the demonstration of Harry's so-called, "safety" plan.

Both Steve and his dad had a horrified look on their faces, and I did not even react. In the category of dumb Harry and Paul action plans, this one would be tough to beat.

"The only slight trouble and flaw in my plan, is that my legs are still a little shaky from skating in that crazy roller-skating marathon a few weeks back, despite that, it will all be very easy."

Oh goody, only a slight flaw this time around. Now, I really felt better.

It was true that Harry's legs were shaky. Any normal human being would be in the hospital, rather than be complaining of being, "A little shaky." Just a few weeks earlier, Harry had become an instant celebrity for skating thirty-six hours straight in a fundraising roller-skating marathon to raise money for a charity. Actually, he entered the marathon to win back the love of his latest gal, Joyce, but that is a whole other story for another set of words. Suffice it to say, he could not walk for a week due to swollen feet and legs that were as wobbly as Cliffy is after drinking a case of Big Boulder beer.

"So, show us what youse guys got cooking here," Harry said as he picked up his safety rope and waved to Steve and Mr. DelMonico to begin the project. The two men led us to a side of the building, where there was a ladder set up onto a lower roof. On the ground, there was a television antenna, a roll of about five thousand feet of old-fashioned television twin-lead wire, and some antenna mounting hardware.

"All right, Harry, and I guess, well actually, Paul. Once you climb on the lower roof here, you then will need to crawl along the roof valleys, until you reach the next section, which brings you to the higher rooftop over there," Mr. DelMonico pointed as he described where the antenna mission was going to lead us, or more specifically, lead me. I peered into the upper reaches and could faintly make out in the clouds a ridge along the top of the building.

Mr. DelMonico continued to explain the simple task, "Once you climb and crawl along a few hundred feet or so, you need to go over the top ridge, and you will see a vent pipe up there on the downward slope facing the mountain. The last time that we had to fix a roof leak up there, we dropped a repairman on the roof from a helicopter, and then airlifted him out of there. The roofing company said the helicopter was the only way to get up there. They said that it was too difficult to climb up there, and they had just laid off the Nepalese mountain climber they usually used for these types of jobs."

I looked at Harry, who, of course, had no initial reaction at all to the story in which Mr. DelMonico was telling us. When Harry, out of the corner of his eye, spotted me staring at him, he shifted gears rather quickly, and piped up in typical, Harry the hornblower fashion, "Bunch of winky-dinky, wimps! Afraid of a little climb."

I just shook my head, while we listened to Mr. DelMonico continue to explain the job, "You can mount the antenna with the hardware to the pipe, hook up the wire to the antenna, lay it along the ridge up there, and secure it with the standoff insulators. Then simply toss the wire over the edge. Oh yeah, watch out for the airplane warning lights up there. They will start flashing when it gets a little darker outside. You will be a little high up there." I could see that Mr. DelMonico had taken "minimizing" lessons from Harry. He made it sound so easy, but there was a good reason he had hired us to install the antenna and he planned to stay on the ground.

"Steve and I can take the wire from there, because we can grab it from the attic windows, and pull the wire into the building from there."

"This is a piece of cake, Mr. DelMonico! We have it covered. C'mon, twenty-seven," the overly confident, Harry exclaimed as we gathered up supplies, some tools, the wire, mast, and the antenna and started to haul it all to the lower rooftop. I had asked my boss at my job where I was apprenticed if I could borrow some of my issued tools from the shop and he had given me permission to use them tonight. I was very accustomed to climbing and performing wild installations for my job, but this was a little over the top. I put on my tool belt, pouches, and my safety belt with climbing hooks around my waist. I slipped my tool backpack on my back and tied it off. This type of climb was as if you were going into battle. However, once you were up there, you did not want to go back down, just to pick up a tool or part. I grabbed a hair tie from my pocket, tucked all my long hair behind my head, and tied it off. I did not want to have to deal with my long hair blowing around up there in the stratosphere.

"Oh yeah, one more little thing, we might have forgotten to mention and youse guys need to know that the lower roof is asphalt, but the upper rooftop is slate. That is another reason why the other guys begged out of the job. The slate can be a little tricky. It will be a little slippery up there. Please be careful and good luck!" Mr. DelMonico had strategically left the best tidbit for last.

A little slippery! I should have brought my goaltender ice skates! Let's see. Now, all I have to do is crawl a few hundred feet or so along a slate roof at the top of the world, all the while dragging a stupid television antenna and all this other junk with me. In the meantime, Mr. Blowhard Harry will have a rope around me, while he barks orders to me.

Joy, joy, and more joy.

Up we went on the ladder, hauling our ropes, supplies, tools, and the antenna to the first level. We made it to the lower roof easy enough; at least that was indeed a piece of cake.

"Here, Paul, go ahead and tie the rope around your waist really tight. Then, snap the hooks from your safety belt into the loop that I made on the end of the rope there. I will climb behind you and set up on that chimney there at the edge. I will have the rope around me and then tie it around the chimney too. You can climb the rest of the way, go over the top, and I will hold you while you go down, the other side."

"Harry, geez, this is stupid. All of this for a hundred and fifty bucks. It is not worth it! This is like climbing to the moon!" I protested.

"Nah, nah, nah, it is not as bad as I thought it was going to be."

The truth had finally come out. That was a comforting thought that Harry actually thought it was going to be worse than this.

Harry came over and put his arm around my shoulders as he waved at an imaginary scene in the air, "Now, now, now, hold on there, twenty-seven, just stop for a minute and do not go spinning off into the old lady land. Think about Maureen Zipperelli . . . in a bikini, waving to you as she sits on the end of our boat. Yeah, yeah, yeah, she will be blowing kisses to you, while you sit up in the front seat of the boat next to me. Just imagine that Joyce will be sitting next to Maureen, and Joyce will be in her skimpy bikini too. The two beautiful gals, leaning back in their revealing swimsuits . . . they are posing for us, with the wind from the boat ride blowing their hair in the air. Joyce will be making goo-goo eyes at me and blowing kisses my way. We'll have our captain's hats on, and we will be wearing smoking jackets, with pipes in our hands, sipping cognac out of fancy, snifter glasses. The wind will be in our faces, while we drive across the lake towards a lovely, golden sunset in the late summer sky."

"I am not smoking some stupid pipe, Harry! And cognac gives me a headache. I am not going up there. This is stupid."

"Oh geez! All right then. Ya are such an old lady. We will ditch the pipe, and golden sunset angle, and concentrate on the Maureen in the bikini angle. An exotic, older chick, born in a foreign land. . .."

"Maureen was born in Paterson. Her parents are from Italy. She is from New Jersey."

Harry stopped short because his inspirational speech was falling short at the moment. He screwed his face up like a corkscrew and put his hands on his hips. I could sense he was frustrated with my rebuttals to his lousy motivational tactics.

"Oh geez, for the love of Pete! You are such an old lady. Just get the hell up there, twenty-seven! Forget all the rest of that conservative mumbo jumbo, and think about Maureen's huge and amazing breasts, stuffed into a skimpy bikini top! Her gorgeous body, overflowing with appeal, and captured in some skimpy swimwear that can barely contain her various parts and pieces! One quick move and BANGO! Those giant breasts will escape and wave hello to you and plead for you to come and get 'em!" Harry cut out all the other details and fluff, and he pulled out the pinnacle of inspirational motivation for treacherous rooftop climbing with a glorious vision of Maureen's breasts and curvaceous body crammed into a skimpy bikini.

I looked at Harry for what seemed as if it was forever while pondering the incredible vision in which he had just devilishly implanted in my mind.

I had to admit that Harry had saved his best tactic for last.

I simply said, "That works for me. Make sure you hold the rope tight there, thirty-five."

Harry clapped his hands together and shouted, "Atta boy, Paul! Now, go ahead and git ya skinny, little, ass on up there!"

I picked up the antenna, which I had folded up in a small box shape, and tucked it inside my tool backpack. I slipped the mast into a hook on my belt, stuffed the tools and other supplies in my tool pouches strapped to my waist, tucked the wire from the end of the reel onto my climbing hooks, and up I went.

I did not say too much more. It seemed like as reasonable a plan as I could come up with at the moment.

I looked up, and the roof loomed a million miles above me. It was straight up, at about a sixty-degree slope that seemed virtually impossible to scale. I was a flexible guy, and a strong guy too, but this was ridiculous. Taking a deep breath, I started to climb up the side and when I reached a valley, I turned around to look at Harry. He had set up on a small section below me, and had wrapped the safety rope around the chimney, and then around his waist. He had the wire reel in front of him, and Harry monitored the wire as it peeled off the roll while I climbed.

He braced his legs on the chimney and waved for me to

continue climbing. "Keep going, twenty-seven. I got ya! Keep thinking about Maureen's breasts in a skimpy bikini top, Paul," he yelled and waved me onward.

On and on, I climbed higher and higher, as my head started to touch a cloud bank. All the time, while I was climbing, Harry was bellowing inspiration to me about boats, breasts, cognac, golden sunsets, skimpy bikinis, and other such nonsense. I reached the slate portion of the roof and slowed down as my feet skidded and slipped along the stone.

"How bad can it be? Oh, yes, by the way there, you two dummies, by the way, it is slate up there, and it could be a little tricky," and other propaganda and poppycock echoed in my mind.

I was now bijillions of miles above the surface of the Earth, and I looked down at Harry who was still waving and inspiring me to climb on. He looked like a tiny, miniature Harry. Harry was a mere speck of a human being.

Pigeons, a hawk, and a bunch of blackbirds sat on the roof ridge staring at me. They were most likely thinking, what kind of stupid idiot of a human being would actually climb up this high in the air? The wind was howling and blowing me around while I sat on my backside on the top ridge of the roof. I sat next to an airplane warning light. You have got to be kidding me? An airplane warning light! I was high enough on top of the facility to have to warn airplanes of the rooftop! I should have strapped a long-haired hippie warning light to my head. I swear, while I sat there, I saw a satellite buzz by my head.

This was nuts.

I had finally reached the top of the roof, and when I looked down the other side, it was a sheer drop of about two million feet straight down. Solid slate straight down. Oh, yes, with the vent pipe in the middle of the roof a few feet over in front of me. I started praying, crossed myself, tugged on the rope, aimed for the vent pipe, and slid my backside over the edge. The rope and Harry held me tightly around the waist, and I used it to hold me back, while I slowly made my way towards the pipe, dragging the supplies, and carrying the antenna and mast along with me. I looked down on the ground, and I spotted ten nuns who looked like tiny little specks standing there looking up at me. I saw them all cross themselves and bow their heads in prayer, while they watched me go over the side.

That sure made me feel a lot better.

While I was climbing around, I could hear Harry faintly yelling that he had me tight, and he was still spewing his stupid, inspirational speech about Maureen, Joyce, and the boat. The nuns heard him too, and when he mentioned Maureen's breasts, skimpy bikinis, smoking pipes, and the cognac, they all covered their ears with the palms of their hands.

I finally reached the vent pipe and clamped the safety hooks from my belt to the pipe. This was no time to mess around and become fancy. I wanted to get this job done and return to solid ground. I stripped the end of the wire, screwed the wire to the antenna, taped the joints with rubber tape, and installed the mounts on the vent pipe. In no time at all, I had the antenna up on the vent pipe and pointed it eastward towards New York City. I was not hanging around for any of that stupid, futile, aiming of the antenna exercise. If the antenna did not pick up signals this high up, then it was hopeless.

I could see Yonge Street in downtown Toronto, Ontario, Canada, from up here.

I worked the wire along the ridge and fitted the standoff insulators inside the edges of the slate. Now, for one last horrifying moment because I had to lean over the edge and toss the wire down to Steve and his dad, who were waiting inside a nearby attic window. Back up to the ridge at the top I went, I had to admit it was a lot easier now without the antenna and mast dragging me down. I made my way along the top of the roof and swallowed hard as I sprawled across the edge, leaned over, looked down at planet Earth, and tossed the wire down to Steve. I saw his hand grab the wire, and he waved back to me.

Thank goodness.

I made my way carefully down the other side and crawled my way back to Harry. Soon, I was standing on the lower roof next to the big oaf. Even though we still were about fifty feet in the air, it seemed as though I was back on the ground compared to the lofty heights of the upper rooftop.

"I told you that it was easy!" Harry spouted as he patted me on the back. "The world-famous, number twenty-seven and old Harry. We can do anything—right old buddy, old pal?" Harry was thrilled as we had successfully accomplished the mission and we were a step closer to being proud owners of a piece of junk boat.

"Yeah, yeah, yeah, sure, Harry. We can do anything," was all I could say. It was hard to say too much with your heart in your throat. We carried the rest of the wire reel, the tools and other supplies back down on the ground and met Steve and his father at the base of the ladder.

They were all smiles.

Steve came over and patted me on the back as he said, "Great job, Paul. I had my doubts, but youse two guys really do know what you are doing. You sure have a lot of guts to climb up there. Everyone else did quit on the job, but you made it. The nuns and priests are thrilled. Father James and Sister Bertha would come out to thank you, themselves, but they are all inside watching 'Bowling for Money' on the televisions. We hooked the wire up to a splitter just in time for the show to come on. That is their favorite show. The picture is fantastic."

"Oh, man, I am missing it tonight. I love that show too!" Harry exclaimed.

Mr. DelMonico came over and thanked us both. He then leaned in and whispered something to Steve, who nodded his head and spoke, "Say youse guys, since my dad and I feel this was a little harder than we had originally told you it was, we will pay youse guys fifty bucks more. If you can give me twenty-five bucks, then the boat is yours. We will call it a deal."

"Fantastic! We will bring the rest of the money tomorrow, and I will bring some clamps, metal braces, and other stuff to secure the trailer enough to pull it over to my house on John Street. We will see ya after work," Harry was ecstatic at the fact that we had earned the extra money and the boat was now almost ours.

Mr. Delmonico walked over and put his arm around me as I was loading my tools and other gear in the van, "Say Paul, you are a brave young man . . . or Harry was right, and that Maureen gal must look pretty good in that bikini."

I smiled, laughed, and said, "Well, I am not sure, Mr. Delmonico, but I guess after all of this, I sure will do my best to find out."

"I bet once you fix that boat all up, youse guys will have a great time with your ladies on some lake somewhere. After all, how bad could it be?"

Oh boy, there are those horrible words again. I wish people would stop saying that.

3

The Law Steps In

Right after work, on Tuesday of that same week, Harry and I met over at Steve DelMonico's house. We paid him the rest of the money in which we owed him for the boat. He signed the title over to us and the deal was final. Harry and I were the proud owners of a 1949 Cristo Craft Sportsman model, eighteen-foot boat. Well, it resembled a boat, but honesty, the jury was still out.

I had to admit that I was now a little more enthusiastic about the entire venture. I did not think it actually had anything to do with the wild and crazy Harry's obscure motivational tactics about Maureen Zipperelli. Well, actually, now in retrospect that could have had something to do with it. I think it had more to do with the actual adventure we had planned for the Labor Day weekend, and the utter shock that I was now the part owner of a boat. Never once in my entire life to this point, while growing up in this gritty, old, and urban neighborhood, did I ever consider purchasing a boat. If you had to ask me the one item that I would never guess we could buy in this neighborhood; it would be a boat. I should have known from hanging around with Harry M. Redmond Jr. all of these years, never to discount anything. Next, we will be buying a World War Two vintage surplus submarine.

Harry had brought along a supply of clamps, metal brackets, and braces, and he even had a small gas and oxygen tank welding system that he had borrowed from his old man's shop, just in case we had to make an emergency repair.

Those horrible words of "How bad can it be" still came back to haunt me. We only had to hitch it up to my van and tow it a block or two to 20 John Street, so it really did not have to go very far.

Harry had warned his father and his brother-in-law Ronnie (a.k.a. Ronzo) that we were bringing a boat to his house, and in preparation, they had moved the junk cars around in the driveway in order to allow us to slip the boat in there. Harry's family did not care. We could have told them we were bringing home a battleship, and they would be thrilled at the prospect of something new and exciting.

They were amazing. My old man would have flipped his lid if I tried to put a boat in our driveway.

We worked for an hour or two in order to secure the loose parts on the trailer, and Harry drilled a couple of metal supports on the corners of the rusty ends of the trailer where it seemed as if it would disintegrate. Harry pronounced the trailer roadworthy; I backed the van into the driveway, and we hitched the trailer up. Since my van in a previous life had been an old telephone service truck, it came fully equipped with a trailer hitch and light kit. We tested the brake lights on the trailer and, of course, they did not work.

It was now time, of course, for me to enter an element of reason and my now famous logic into the situation. I just had to do it because it was my contribution to the adventures of Harry and Paul. I knew, even before I said what I was planning to say, that Harry would trample my thoughts, and proclaim me to be acting like an "old lady." I did not care; someone had to be the voice of reason in this crazy world of Harry and Paul.

"Say Harry, don't we have to have license plates and a registration sticker for the trailer? I noticed the brake lights do not work either. The light bulbs must be out. Shouldn't we go get a few light bulbs from Vince's gas station and replace them before we roll?"

Harry dramatically dropped the tools he was carrying, and he immediately started to shake his head.

Yes indeed, here it comes!

"Ya know, the Old Lady and Mr. Nice Guy Syndrome are consuming you, Paul. You should have seen how red your ears turned yesterday when I mentioned Maureen's large and breathtaking chesty projections."

Harry waved his hands in the air as if he was duplicating a woman's bodily shape.

"Nice guys such as Paul John Henson cannot think about things like driving a few hundred feet without license plates with unregistered trailers, or dream of a gal's breasts. You have got to be kidding me, Paul! Even for you, this one is a new one in your continuous, old lady, world of worry. For the love of Pete, we are only going a block and a half over to my house. What do you think could happen?"

"Well, I thought. . .."

"Cut out the old lady and the nice guy stuff and let's get over there. It is getting dark, and we still have a ton of work to do tonight to get this pile of junk into the driveway."

Certain words and statements from Harry were prophetic. I learned over the years that he just might be one of the world's greatest soothsayers or fortune tellers, because whenever he uttered phrases such as, "What could happen," or "How bad can it be," situations that we encountered were indeed always very bad, and inevitably, something always happened.

We bid Steve goodbye, climbed in the van, and I started the engine up. I carefully pulled forward and the trailer and boat creaked and groaned, but it held together. One of the tires on the trailer was dry-rotted, and we had pumped it up with a bicycle tire pump, but it was very suspect at this point. I kept telling myself that Harry was correct, and we only had to go a block and a half or so to reach his home. I shifted gears, and carefully rolled up Clinton Street, put my right turn signal on to turn into Cook Street, when I noticed the red lights of a police car flashing behind me.

Yup, I knew it!

Harry was a soothsayer! We had officially gone about two hundred feet, and we had been nabbed.

"OH GEEZ! FOR THE LOVE OF PETE, PAUL! DO NOT SAY IT! I DO NOT WANT TO HEAR IT," Harry was ranting and raving, while he put his hand up to stop me as I was just about to tell him that I was correct, but I knew that at this point it would not change a thing.

I pulled the van over to the side of Cook Street. I still did not say a word to Harry, who had sunk deep in the passenger seat of the van in a slightly humbled posture. Instead, I reached into the glove box and pulled out the paperwork for the van. I could see in my side-view mirror that the police car was a Haledon Borough police car. That could be good news for us, because we knew many of the borough police officers who patrolled our neighborhood, as opposed to a county sheriff's officer or a Paterson, New Jersey officer, who we would more than likely not know. The policeman was remaining inside his squad car for a prolonged time, but he finally opened the door and strode out of the car. I sat lower in my driver's seat because I did not recognize the officer.

Harry turned around and asked, "Do you know him, twenty-seven? Is it, Officer Gamble?"

"Nah, Harry, I have never seen him before. It looks like a new guy to me. We are doomed." The officer was tall and lanky, and he looked quite old. He was no doubt a veteran of the force that Harry and I had just never seen around before.

I watched in the mirror while he stopped and examined the trailer and boat, and then he carefully kicked the one tire that was dry-rotted on the trailer. He shook his head, adjusted his gun belt, slowly walked over to my door, and he peered into the van. I read his name on the name tag next to his badge and noted that it said, "Officer Hough." He had a frown on his mouth, piercing dark eyes, and a grey mustache overlapping his frown.

"License, registration, and insurance card, sonny," He instructed me as I handed him the information.

"182 Belmont Avenue, huh? That is right around the corner. I am new to the Haledon Police Department, but I have been doing this for a very long time, and I have the streets and addresses down pat in this neighborhood already."

"Hello, sir. Good evening, yes, you are indeed correct, sir. It is right around the corner," I stammered and answered his questions.

The police officer handed me back the paperwork while he stared at me intently. He then said, "Polite kid for a hippie. You have long hair, a beard, and you look like a hippie, freak, weirdo." He stepped backwards and stared at me while continuing, "Now, this can go two ways. One way is that you have this van filled with illegal substances, and I will have made the best bust of my thirty-seven-year police career. Two, is that there is a fabulous explanation for you two birds towing one of the most incredible pieces of junk that I have ever seen on a trailer. A trailer that I might add, lacks a proper, New Jersey license plate, no registration, and has tail and brake lights that do not work."

Harry cleared his throat, and he went to speak when the police officer held his hand up in the air to indicate that Harry should not even try to speak.

"Aw no, no, no. Not a word or sound from you there, young man. I want to hear from the driver here first. Then, I will ask for some credentials and identification from you. Right for now, keep ya big trap shut."

Harry nodded and sunk back into the passenger seat. I

was on my own. The silken tongue, ice selling to Eskimo's voice of Harry M. Redmond Jr. was now, by the order of the law, silent.

I was going to give it my best shot, "Well, sir. I can assure you there are not going to be any illegal substances here in this old van. I do live right around the corner here, right next to Gabby's Cabin restaurant, on the corner of Belmont and Burhans Avenue. You see, my best buddy, Harry and I here, just bought this boat from Steve DelMonico on Clinton Street a few minutes ago. I will be very honest . . . I told my friend Harry here that I did not think we should move it without the brake lights, license plate, and registration, but he convinced me to do it, since we only are going right around the corner to 20 John Street. He said to me, Paul what could happen, stop being an old lady. I was wrong for listening to Harry. I will take the full responsibility for not following my instinct, for doing it anyway, and for breaking the law."

The officer leaned back, tilted his hat, and waved his hand as if he was encouraging me to continue with my sad tale of woe. I was on a roll and I was going to spill my guts.

"In my vain and futile defense—Harry is very influential. That is also what he told me yesterday when we installed a television antenna on top of the roof of the big convent in West Paterson."

Officer Hough interrupted me, "Also told you what? That you were acting like an old lady? By the way, you may address me as Officer Hough."

"Yes, that's right, Officer Hough. He always tells me that, whenever I interject logic, the law, or reason into a situation, or a stupid idea that he has come up with. You see, we landed this job to get the rest of the dough to buy this boat. I did not want to climb up there on the roof when I saw how dangerous it was. He inspired me to go about a bijillion feet in the air to climb to the top of the roof to put the antenna up there while he held me back with a rope tied around my waist."

"He inspired you to climb a bijillion feet in the air, huh? With a rope tied around your waist? How did he manage to do that?"

"Well, sir, by telling me that I was acting like an old lady again, but he also added a few other tidbits. He said we would impress all the young ladies if we had this boat. He told me to think about this gal who is a little older than me that I would like to ask out for a date, wearing a skimpy bikini with her huge breasts captured inside of her bikini top, while she was riding inside this boat along with Harry's steady gal Joyce, on a lake into a golden summer, sunset. Harry and I will be wearing some captain's hats, smoking pipes, and sipping cognac, while the gals will be blowing kisses to us and waving."

The policeman nodded, and his mouth turned up a little. He then asked, "Did you climb up the roof after he said that?"

"Yes, sir! Harry can sell ice to an Eskimo."

"I see. It is all about Harry's salesmanship. The size of this gal's chest and the skimpy bikini had nothin' at all to do with you climbing up there?"

"Well, a little . . . yes, I guess that it did eventually come down to the vision in my mind, of the gal's chest size, sir."

"And you actually climbed up to the top of the world to earn the money to buy this thing on this trailer and impress these young ladies?"

"Yes, sir."

"And you were just pulling out of the driveway with this decrepit pile of junk on a trailer, and were rolling about the equivalent of a city block, and you were nabbed by an old policeman who was on patrol, and who has heard stories like the one you just told me a million times in my career."

"I guess. . .."

Officer Hough cut me off, took his hat off, wiped his

forehead with his hand, and yelled, "Wrong! I have in all of my years, never, ever, heard a story like that one! It is the most ludicrous story and incredible explanation that I have ever heard or experienced. Therefore, option two worked. I would not have believed it, but you are either, one, a very stupid, hippie kid, or two, a very courageous hippie, or three, you're a very powerful and honest speaker. I actually think it is all three."

He looked over at Harry, pointed, and rather abruptly asked him, "Name?"

"Harry M. Redmond Junior, sir."

"Is this wild tale of lust, large breasts, stupidity, honesty, and courage actually true?"

"Yes, it is, sir."

"Do you live at 20 John Street?"

"Yes sir, I do."

"Can you really sell ice to an Eskimo?"

"Yes, sir. I can!"

"Did this hippie really climb a bijillion feet in the air with a rope tied around his waist to earn the dough for youse two dopes to buy this thing that you two think is a boat?"

"Yes, sir. Paul is fearless. Together, we can do anything. We always have since we were ten years old."

"And you did not climb with your best pal here. You let him climb all the way up there by himself?"

"Well, sir, I was the rope man. You see, my legs are still a little shaky, because I roller-skated for thirty-six hours straight in a skating marathon about two weeks ago, to impress and win back my gal Joyce, and raise a lot of dough for a charity. I could not walk for a week because my feet swelled up so badly. I just about bankrupted the entire neighborhood when it came time for them to pay off my pledges. I was on television, radio, and even the subject for the weekly homily for Father Mark."

The entire time that Harry was speaking, the police

officer was shaking his head back and forth in shock and awe.

"No kiddin' . . . I saw that on television! You were the dope that skated that long, huh! The adventures of youse two birds are incredible. You sure packed an awful lot of living in a short amount of time. Youse guys should write a book about it."

I thought about how someday, I would do exactly that.

"I guess we do, sir, but it is all true!" Harry assured the policeman.

The officer laughed, shook his head, and said, "It works for me. I will put my lights on and I will follow youse guys. I do not want some car following behind you, smashing into the back of the trailer because of the lack of brake lights and tail lights on this pile of junk. Let's move on, and put this pile of junk into your driveway, and don't ever let me see you breaking the law again!" Officer Hough handed me back my paperwork. He turned, and walked back to the patrol car, as he waved at us to indicate that we should move ahead.

Harry and I yelled out collectively, "THANK YOU, SIR!" I put the van in gear and carefully moved along the road as Officer Hough, who had turned on the red lights of the police cruiser, followed behind us. Slowly, we crept all the way of about a city block or so back to 20 John Street.

As expected, the entire neighborhood was waiting for us to return with the boat. This was big news. It had spread far and wide, and now that a police car with its lights on was following us, the audience would only increase even more. Of course, with the Redmonds, and all of John Street, any excuse for a party that came along sparked a wild celebration. Our purchase of a hunk of junk boat, qualified for dancing in the streets, cooking out on the grill, flowing beer and playing loud music.

"Oh geez, twenty-seven, the entire gang is out in front waiting for us. I will need to whip up a quick, sugar coated story of flim-flam to cover up the police thingy," Harry said as he pointed towards his house. We had spotted every member of his family, a number of the neighbors, including Mr. Porter, and Mrs. Porter, all standing in front of the house in anxious anticipation of our arrival. Mr. Redmond spotted the police escort and immediately folded his arms across his chest in a clear-cut sign that he knew we had somehow run afoul of the law. Harry's brother-in-law Ronzo opened the front gate to the driveway as Officer Hough stopped the patrol car in front of the house, and he climbed out to start a discussion with Mr. Redmond.

I announced with some revenge in my voice, "Ha! Serves ya right. Too late, Harry. Your old man already is talking to Officer Hough."

I heard Harry sigh as he jumped out of the van. Cocoa came running up to the side door with Piggy in his mouth and Harry let him jump up in the passenger seat next to me. Cocoa was upset that he did not come with us when we went to pick up the boat and he now was anxious to be involved in the action. Harry, along with Ronzo and Mr. Porter, guided me while I backed the boat and trailer into the driveway. It was a little tricky maneuvering the boat trailer into the driveway, but I managed to do a good job at backing it in after a few attempts.

When the boat was in place, I jumped out of the van along with Cocoa, who jumped down next to me. Officer Hough met me at the driver's door, and he explained to me once more the consequences of pulling another stunt of driving unregistered and defective vehicles and trailers within his jurisdiction. He smiled at me, and shook my hand when I thanked him. I knew he had sympathy for my situation, and I was very thankful for him cutting me a lucky break.

He was a good guy!

Cocoa squeaked his Piggy into the policeman's pants and it gave off a loud squeak. Cocoa was working hard to entice the nice policeman in a game of "Fetch the Piggy." I looked down at Cocoa and shook my head and he realized his error because this was a lawman! Cocoa did not want to end up in the doggie clink for playing unauthorized games and bribing an officer.

"Thank you, Officer Hough. I have learned my lesson about being influenced and making poor decisions," I said while I shook his hand.

Officer Hough was on my side now, as he relaxed his posture and said, "I know you have, sonny. Harry's old man just told me how you guide Harry, who tends to be the loose cannon at times. In reality, it was breaking the law, but it was only a few blocks. I am sure if you had to go farther, then it would have been a different story. So, are you and Harry really going to fix this thing up and put it in a lake?"

"Well sir, I was optimistic, until I saw it when we pulled it out of the DelMonico's driveway and I obtained a clearer view of it. Now, I have to admit that my confidence has faded a bit."

Ronzo came over. I introduced him to Officer Hough, and the two of them shook hands. "So, Officer Hough, you had your chance to bust these two characters, and then you went and blew it," Ronzo kidded the policeman as he patted him on the back.

"We would've bailed Paulie out, but Harry, we might have let him stew in the clinker for a few days! I would offer you a Dingleberry beer, but you are still on duty."

Officer Hough waved his hand in the air and said robustly, "Oh, thanks, but I wouldn't drink it! Those Dingleberries are way too sweet. I can't handle them!"

As we chatted, the neighbors were all drinking beer and soda, eating snacks that Harry's sister Linda had brought out, milling about, and commenting on our "wonderful" boat. Harry stood next to the boat with Cocoa, pointing out our plans to fix it up, then to go to the lake for the big weekend with the young ladies, (he thankfully skipped over the entire Maureen's breasts and bikini angle), and other typical Harry bombastic spouting. While we were standing there, I heard a familiar voice behind me and the strong odor of fish filled the air. I sighed as Cliffy had made a guest appearance. He came up behind us, carrying a beer, and he was in classic form. Cliffy did not care if there was a policeman there or not. He was always going to be Cliffy. At least, he was consistent and provided you with reasonable expectations.

"So youse stupid ass guys did buy that frig-frackin' piece of junk boat! HA! HA! HA!"

Officer Hough turned around and looked in horror at Cliffy.

"Almost got yaselves irested, ya dopey ass kids. HA! HA! HA! At least I got my constitution. That lard-ass Delpoppo gave me my dough a few minutes ago. HA! HA! HA!"

Officer Hough was still staring in horror at Cliffy when he cleared his throat, "Sir, you should mind your language here, with the women present, and please get off the sidewalk and go inside the Redmond's fence there with that open container of beer. Exactly who are you?"

"Clifford Alfred Horatio McWhiffy. Okay, I will mind my languishing. Ya know that I drive a smelly ass seafood truck and live over on Geyer Street. HA! HA! HA!"

Cliffy walked away as Officer Hough stood in frustration with his hands on his hips. Ronzo and I did our best to explain the famous Cliffy McWhiffy to him, and he listened and shook his head. In the background, Harry was still bellowing on and on about the boat, and the attributes of it as he captivated the neighbors. I was sure, when he was done with his speech, a few neighbors would be firmly convinced that they needed boats too.

Officer Hough stood next to Ronzo and me while we all listened to Harry's plans for Labor Day and of the golden sunsets of summer over Green Pine Lake. Officer Hough finally leaned over and he spoke to me in a low voice, "I see the dilemma you face there, hippie Paul. I want to run home and tell Mrs. Hough that we need to buy a boat, too. You are correct in saying that this Harry character can sell ice to an Eskimo." Officer Hough took his officer's cap off and rubbed the top of his head. "I can tell you that this is one traffic stop that I will never forget. I cannot ever recall running into such an amazing cast of whackos and unusual characters, collected in one neighborhood in my entire career, and I have been a policeman since before your old man ever even thought about you. This John Street is one special place."

"I agree with you, sir, both about Harry selling ice to an Eskimo, and about John Street being special. It is like no other place on Earth. I can guarantee you that, Officer Hough."

This was indeed a very special place. A rough and tumble, gritty, old, New Jersey neighborhood, with an unusual and strange cast of characters, nonstop fun, honesty, sincerity, and wackiness, all wrapped up into one package. I would not trade growing up here for anything and now you can add that 20 John Street even had a boat in the backyard. As we continued to listen, I just kept wishing that Harry would never bring up the source of motivation for me to climb a bijillion miles on top of a roof into the mix.

"So, youse guys, this is how it goes. I says to twenty-seven, just think about Maureen's huge breasts crammed into. . .."

Oh geez, time to get out of here. I should have known better.

4

Unreasonable Expectations

I had dropped some hints to my parents about being the proud, part owner of a boat, but I had to confess that I had never really told them the entire story. My old man was used to stories over the years, of how Harry would pull me into another wackiness vortex of his, and of the remarkable Redmond family's wild, "phases" of life. I knew that the old man would simply classify this new purchase as being another stupid idea by the crazy Harry and sucker Paul. I was eighteen years old or so now, and for the most part, I was on my own, and capable of making perfectly dumb decisions on my own. I was entering my last year in a trade school, worked a full-time job in my apprenticeship, and paid room and board, but that was not going to stop the old man from commenting on my latest whim and, "Stupid move at wasting hard earned money!"

When I provided my dear Mum and the old man the gory details over dinner on Wednesday evening, my prediction came true.

Predictably, the old man, in a very dramatic fashion, dropped his fork and shook his head as he said, "Another stupid waste of money because you two dummies, are off on another dumb idea."

I could take it. And for the most part, he was correct in his assessment of the adventures of Harry and Paul. Looking back, we sure were not boring! Mum always came to my defense, as she would proclaim how proud she was of Harry and me, and the project of restoring the boat would keep the two of us off the streets, occupied, and out of trouble. After all, she told the old man, we were both training and educating to become skilled tradesmen, and now we could apply a diversified mix of our acquired skills in the project of bringing the boat back to life. Despite the old man scoffing at her theory, I knew that deep down, he agreed.

My dear Mum was the best. No matter what adventure or crazy idea I would come up with, she would always be there to listen and support me, even if she knew in her heart that I was crazy. Mum turned out to be correct in her theory that the boat would keep us busy, but little did we realize how much it would keep us occupied!

The work on the boat had started the next day, under the occasional eye of Ronzo, Mr. Porter, Mr. Redmond, and even a guest appearance by the old man here and there. Our faithful companion, Cocoa, was always hanging around both Harry and me. We set up a wooden box next to the boat so that it was easier for him to jump up into the boat. The dog would jump up on a bench seat in the back of the boat, sit down, and watch us. The three of us worked on the boat every day after school and work. The cleanup alone took us an entire evening because of the amount of work and time it took for us to shovel out the dirt, leaves, and debris that had accumulated inside the boat from being in storage over the years.

We were lucky in the fact that we had saved a lot of money on the purchase of the boat due to the now famous antenna installation, so we could put the extra money we had saved into the restoration supplies. The materials, supplies and effort we required the most were hard work, in addition to relatively inexpensive items, such as varnish, cleaning supplies, and other common materials. The hull of the boat seemed solid enough, but until we removed the dirt and grit, we could not really assess exactly what it was that the two of us had bought. I was more concerned with the gas-powered engine that remained carefully concealed under the back of a wooden lid in the rear of the boat. I knew that I could call the old man into the mix with his world famous mechanical skills to assist us, and while I was not against doing that, in many ways this project was taking on a different angle. When it was time to, I was determined to work on this engine myself! Years of working under the sharp-eyed guidance of the old man while battling engines, and junk cars since I was old enough to carry tools, had brought me to a point where I had enough confidence that I could resurrect this old engine on my own.

I was determined to give it my best shot.

As I have mentioned, our usual support crew of Ronzo, Mr. Redmond, Mr. Porter, and my old man, stopped by to check on our progress, but in many ways, Harry and I sensed that we had reached a point in our life and training, where it was time to stand on our own feet. We did not see them helping anywhere near the amount that they did in the past. We were adults now, and it was time for us to tackle this one on our own.

Slowly, it was turning into a special project. We would set up a radio, blast some music, while Cocoa sat with Piggy and watched us work. Linda, Patty, or Mrs. Porter would come by on occasion and bring us drinks or snacks. Ronzo would sit with Mr. Redmond and Mr. Porter in lawn chairs and they would watch us work while drinking beer, and would tell us all stories, but the work was mostly ours to perform. Occasionally, one of the men would offer up a tidbit of advice, but for the most part, they were only spectators.

Amazingly, in a few days, that old hunk of junk boat actually looked like it was not a complete hunk of junk! It was an old boat, but it was made of solid mahogany wood with chrome trim framing the sides and top. The trim was old, and it had deep pits and corrosion in the metal finish, but we rubbed it, cleaned it, and polished it, and when we had finished cleaning the trim and the wood, the boat did not look half-bad at all! We scrubbed and cleaned the boat interior and seats, and once we had finished that work, we realized that under all that dirt and grit; the boat had a good-looking interior! It did not look so bad after all. The seats were not torn, ripped, or worn, and were in reasonable condition. We lightly sanded the exterior wood of the boat and then refinished it with a number of coats of a marine varnish. When the varnish dried, we rubbed the finish down with a butcher's wax and some rags.

I think the both of us were amazed at how well it all turned out. It was actually a nice-looking boat.

By the time the weekend came, Harry and I were looking forward to some decent weather and some free time to devote to our project. We had set a goal in our minds to have this boat in good shape within a few more days. Labor Day loomed ahead of us, and we knew we had a relatively short amount of time left to finish the work. We both had to work at our jobs until around noontime on Saturday, but the weather had cooperated, and we met up at Harry's house and dove into the restoration. Since most of the cleanup was now completed, we turned our focus on the wires, lights, radio, and the mechanical systems of the boat. Until now, we really did not know a thing about boats, but we put our trade skills to work, and together, we studied and figured out both the electrical systems and the mechanical systems. Once we tackled those components, then I would attempt to start the engine.

Someone had removed the main battery from the boat many years ago, but we had worked a deal with Ronzo for a used battery that he had hanging around in the garage and was a spare for one of his cars. Once I had fully charged the battery, I installed it in the boat, tested and traced out some wires that were in poor condition, and rewired the main direct current feeder wires for the entire boat. When I flipped the power switch to the "on" position and the running lights and radio came to life, we cheered so loudly and Cocoa barked along with us so hard that Ronzo and Mr. Redmond came out of the house to see what had caused the commotion.

"Well, I'll be! Good job, boys. I had my doubts, but it sure looks as if you two are going to get that boat in the water after all!" Mr. Redmond stood next to us with his hands on his hips, and the pride in our efforts was very apparent upon his face. He had taught us well over the years, going back to constructing pools in the backyard, to countless other adventures, but he knew we were now on our way to being actual tradesmen.

Harry had restored the pulleys, cables, and wires that turned the steering rudders from the steering wheel and the two rudders actually moved and followed the steering wheel back and forth! It was looking good now as darkness crept in and over us for a Saturday evening. We had made wonderful progress in a relatively short amount of time.

It was time to pack it in for the day.

Tomorrow, I would work on the inboard engine, and I knew that would be the biggest potential obstacle we were facing with the restoration of the boat. If the engine required major work, then we might be looking at purchasing an outboard motor, or perhaps some other major coin (that we did not have) in order to put the boat into the water. On the other hand, we might be dead in the water.

It had been a hot summer day, and we were both a sweaty mess. Harry had called his steady gal Joyce, and he made plans to pick her up and bring her over to see the boat. Harry was being very strategic in not showing Joyce the boat until now since he did not want her to run away screaming in horror at the initial sight of the boat before we had a chance to work on it. Now that it was looking good, he was ready to lay the groundwork for our big plans for the upcoming holiday. We both needed a shower, and while Harry was cleaning up and heading out to pick up Joyce, I went home and cleaned up, too. We both agreed to meet back at Harry's house and hang out for the rest of the evening.

By the time that I returned to Harry's house after showering and cleaning up, Joyce and Harry were already sitting on the patio in the backyard. Joyce jumped up when she saw me turn the corner and step onto the patio. She ran over to me and gave me a big hug and then a kiss on the cheek. Cocoa came running over and greeted me, too.

"Oh, twenty-seven! I am so excited about the plans for Labor Day! The boat is amazing! I can hear from Harry's description of what it used to look like and what it looks like now, that you two have done a remarkable job in such a short amount of time," Joyce was rambling on with praise and excitement about the boat and the holiday getaway that we had planned.

"Yeah, yeah, yeah, Joyce. I guess it does look very good. You are lucky that you did not see it before we worked on it, though," I offered up my honest opinion of our purchase.

I was always very fond of Joyce Dilber. I felt she was the perfect match for Harry, since she was able to withstand, to a certain extent, his annoying habits, obnoxious ways, and loudmouth tendencies. Of the constant parade of young ladies who waltzed in and out of Harry's life, I always felt as if Joyce was the one gal whom he should stick with but time would tell. Joyce also could see past all of Harry's huff and puff, and she knew that in reality, Harry was a kind and a gentle person who put up a tough guy front. She was aware of the fact that Harry would do anything for the people he loved and that he was close to in his life. Of Harry's multiple collection of gal pals, so far, Joyce was the one girlfriend, who had been able to some extent, get by his constant roaming eye, his womanizing ways, and his lewd, and at times, very inappropriate comments.

Their relationship had been on and off for a few years now, and the now famous roller-skating marathon was in fact the truth. Joyce had caught Harry in the arms of another gal while "two-timing" her, and they had a major falling out earlier this summer. What Harry told Officer Hough was one hundred percent true, as Harry did in fact enter the marathon and he was successful in winning back the heart of Joyce.

That particular event turned into another wild Harry and Paul adventure. However, as is the situation with so many of our adventures, that story will have to wait for another set of words somewhere down the road.

Joyce was tall, beautiful, funny, well spoken, and smart. She had a shapely figure, medium length brown hair, and wide, doe-like brown eyes.

I thought she was a winner!

"Well, Joyce, I do think the boat has come along a lot better than what Harry and I initially thought it would, and to our surprise, it has happened within a short amount of time. Tomorrow will be the big day since we are going to see if we can start the engine. However, if that does not start, then it could be. . .."

Harry cut me off as usual, "Old lady tendencies, twenty-seven! Old lady tendencies! Stop worryin.' You are driftin' again! Stay positive. A little tinkering, utilize the tools and skills that the old man taught you from years and years of resurrection of that 1964 Putter Classic model 200, and boom! That engine will start."

Joyce laughed, and I smiled at Harry. His forever optimistic and confident approach was something that I did lack at times.

Harry waved for me to sit down in some chairs in the center of the backyard in front of the swimming pool as he said, "Now, come on over here and relax. We will worry about the boat tomorrow. It is a gorgeous summer night, and I called to have a pizza pie and soda delivered here in a few minutes. I hoofed a few beers from Ronzo's stash for ya, and a touch of wine for Joyce, and I am going to start a fire in the metal cooker here to keep the bugs away and the chill off my fabulous, young lady. We need to make some plans for the holiday now. We are only a week or so away from Labor Day, and it is now time for some fun stuff."

"Sounds good, Harry. Hey, where is the gang tonight?"

"The old man treated all of them to the movies tonight. Ronzo, Linda, the kids, and Patty and the Big Spike, all went, so it is just us until they get back." I nodded, wandered over, and sat in a chair next to Joyce, in front of a metal cooker sitting on cinder blocks in the center of the circle of chairs. Cocoa ran over and sat down next to my chair, in between Harry and me. Cocoa always had to be involved in all of our activities.

It was one of those special, late summer evenings, with stars filtering through the urban streetlights and haze to wink at us in the darkness, a gentle breeze moving and rustling the leaves in the trees, and a whisper of autumn creeping into the picture. The heat of the day had blown away, and it had turned into a perfect night in which to dream. Harry piled some firewood in the metal cooker that Mr. Redmond had made in the shop so long ago, and soon he had a fire crackling and spitting in front of us.

I reached into a cooler, cracked open a beer, and sat back and relaxed. Technically, we were a few months away from legally enjoying a little alcohol in the great State of New Jersey, (the legal age became nineteen for a few years before it changed to twenty-one) but as long as we stayed in our own backyards, and did not go crazy, no one became upset at us stealing a sip or two of beer or wine here and there. In the Lutheran church, where the Henson family attended, it was wine in the communion cup, and Father Mark served the high test over at Saint Peter's Church where the Redmond family attended Catholic mass. This was the 1970s and things were a lot different back then because folks did not become uptight over some simple things that are major calamities nowadays. Growing up with my English Grandparents and Mum, they taught my sister and me in a different culture, likewise, Harry's dad and family, who had a heavy German and Irish heritage, raised Harry, and certain things that the modern establishment frowns upon now, were commonplace for us. I can remember how when my sister and I were very young, and the winters were long and difficult, and the sore throats, colds, and runny noses of February crept into our health, our grandfather would insist on pouring strong Irish stout in a glass for us to drink.

"A hit or two of this will not hurt you," Gramps would say, "it will build you back up and make you strong!"

Oh my, oh my, how things are different now.

Harry jumped up when he heard the pizza delivery truck pull up, and I tossed him a few dollars for the pie. Soon, we were enjoying the pie and chatting up a storm about our plans.

Harry explained about the cabin retreat we were planning to stay in. "My old man has spoken to my uncle and we can have the cabin for the weekend on the upper part of Green Pine Lake. He is not even going to soak us anything to use it. We just have to make sure we clean it when we leave. There is only one-bedroom downstairs, but there is an open sleeping loft that circles the cabin, in which we can use sleeping bags to catch some shuteye. It has a kitchenette, a fireplace, and a large, open floor plan type of living room. I was there many, many years ago, and I vaguely remember it, but I can't say that I remember too much."

"That is wonderful, Harry! I can assure you right now that you and Paul, will be in the sleeping loft, and I will share the bedroom with Paul's date. Therefore, you can vanquish any ideas out of your silly head right now about the sleeping arrangements."

I heard Harry chuckle a little. Cocoa jumped up, barked twice, and wagged his tail three times to give us the agreement signal. Harry glared at Cocoa for agreeing with Joyce, and Cocoa turned, picked up Piggy, and curled up underneath my chair for protection.

"Whose side are you on there, Cocoa? I will remember that next time you want to escape the yard when you spot that pretty, little Fife, the lady poodle over on Cook Street!"

"And that brings us to the subject of Paul's date. Exactly who is the lucky lady who will be coming with us?" Joyce had put me on the spot.

I was chewing a bite of pizza, and I covered my mouth to indicate that I was not done yet, which gave Harry the opportunity to jump in and berate me.

"He has not asked anyone yet! He wants to ask Maureen Zipperelli, but he is a chicken, plus, due to his Old Lady and Mr. Nice Guy Syndromes, he balks since she is older than him."

"Oh, Paul, c'mon and do it! I love Maureen and she is crazy about you! She is only two years or so older than you. That is nothing nowadays! Please call her. You know, and we all know, that she will be thrilled." Joyce pleaded.

Maureen and I had shared a number of double dates with Harry and Joyce, and the two gals had become acquainted. They now got along, "swimmingly" as my English Mum would say.

"Well, I am not sure."

"He won't. Even after, I planted a strategic vision of her breasts bulging inside a skimpy bikini in his nice guy mind. I bet you have not even asked her out or called her in a long time. Have you?" Harry was shaking his head as Joyce came over and sat on Harry's lap. Even Cocoa came out of hiding and sat next to me to see what my answer would be. All three of them ganged up on me.

"Well, no. I have not called her, but I have been so busy

at work," I stuttered and stammered.

"Oh, Paul, you are so funny. How can you be so confident and fearless, standing in front of the net in an ice hockey game, but are so shy and reserved with the ladies?" Joyce was moving in now for a pep talk.

She continued, "Please Paul, you are a wonderful man. Why don't you have any confidence? You are a fantastic-looking guy. The hair, the beard, and the gals all swoon at you. My friends are always begging me to introduce you to them, and then you just say hello, and never take it any farther. You are intelligent, and well mannered, and a great storyteller. I am always amazed at how well-spoken you are on all kinds of subjects. Just your knowledge of music alone is amazing. And, my oh, my that athletic body of yours . . . whoowee, wow, the gals are always checking you out, I know that I check it out!" Joyce lifted her eyebrows as if to emphasize her observation while she pointed at certain parts of my body.

She continued, "See, you are turning red now with embarrassment." Joyce was laughing at me, as I was indeed very embarrassed at the thought of her observation of my body. Joyce jumped up out of her chair; followed by Harry. They both came over to poke a little fun at me. Even Cocoa put his paws on my lap and gave the agreement signals. Harry and Joyce stood in front of me and Harry put his arm around Joyce as she shivered a little in the cold.

She stared at me as she took a sip of wine from her glass. "Well, Paul?" Joyce insisted on putting me on the spot.

Harry was now joining his gal in coaxing me on, "You mean to tell me that you have not even called Maureen, since the last time we all went out to the carnival and then hung out here until all hours of the night? We had a great time too, other than me losing my car keys under the Ferris wheel. And that was way back in July." Harry was not going to allow me to evade the questioning, and even Cocoa sat down and stared at me for my answer. The famous carnival incident with Harry's car keys was another story, but let me just say that it made for a long evening.

"No, Harry. I have already told you that I have not spoken with her since then. We did have a great time. I agree. Maureen is fun and I enjoy her company. You guys are right."

"Oh geez, Paul, for the love of Pete. You enjoy her company! Nice Guy Syndrome again! You should be all over her like a blanket. The gal drools over ya! What a nice guy loser you are! Let's see now . . . total gals to date for, twenty-seven. I can count them on my hand. Debbie Boatwright, that crazy gal Janet with that lunatic brother of hers with the weird birthmark, Maureen Zipperelli, and that gorgeous red-haired chick. I cannot remember her name, just the vision of her incredibly, perfectly formed, backside. Man, alive there Paul, ya are knocking them out here, four, total gals that you have dated! I have had hundreds of ladies. . .." Harry's voice trailed off when he spotted the evil stare that Joyce was giving him.

"Oh, Paul, please forget Harry and his blowhard speeches. You have to go inside and call Maureen right now! Labor Day is too close now. She may already have made plans."

I decided to defend the net. After all, I was a goaltender, and I specialized in defense.

"The red-haired gal's name was Glenda. Glenda Flabbergaster. Well now, I may not be exactly Harry with the number of dates, but Maureen and I went to the movies and had dinner one night a few weeks ago, without you guys. It was a nice time and we. . .. "

"Oh, whippy do! Whippy do! Geez, a nice time! Hold ya ears, Joyce! We had the time of our lives with Debbie Boatwright and Emma Whackenfuss at the dance too. What is a nice time? Man, oh man, Paul. It should be a lot more like a steamy time full of wild sex rather than a nice time. Ya should be lighting 'em up. C'mon, put the beer down, put the pizza pie down, take her number out of your wallet, and go inside and call Maureen right now."

Harry blasted me. He nodded his head violently at me and waved his hands while Joyce also followed with the same encouragement. Cocoa gave the agreement signal and they sealed my fate. I took a long sip of my beer because I knew liquid courage was going to be important, nodded my head, and leaned forward to find Maureen's telephone number inside my wallet.

"Oh, yeah! Oh, yeah!" Harry spouted as he grabbed poor Joyce, leaned her over, and gave her one of his famous, grandstanding kisses. Harry knew how to play the event like a fine fiddle. After the long kiss was over, I heard Harry shout, "Go get, Maureen, twenty-seven! See ya in about two hours!"

Harry was well aware of Maureen's penchant for talking forever.

I stood up, and with some hesitation, I walked into the back door of Harry's house to make the call. Cocoa jumped up, and he followed me into the house as if he wanted to provide some element of moral support.

I thought, while I walked into the house and approached the telephone on the wall, how my apprehension about asking Maureen for a date was ridiculous. Joyce was correct in her assessment that I was fearless enough to stand in front of blistering hockey pucks, but I trembled in fear at the thought of dialing a young woman on the telephone. It was time to call Maureen and put this all to rest.

I really did enjoy Maureen's company; she was fun, pretty, and vivacious. Maureen Zipperelli was my sister's best friend and now that my sister had finished junior college and moved to the west coast, Maureen was not over our house all the time. We had struck up a friendship many years ago, and even though she was in fact, about two years and a few months older than I was, our relationship had turned into many of what I considered to be casual dates. I had a strong and somewhat ominous feeling that Maureen never considered them casual dates at all. Maureen would turn up as a spectator and fan at many of my hockey games. She would pursue me on occasion, but for the most part, I purposely did lay quite low, and stayed under her radar. There was no doubt in my mind that Maureen wanted to turn up the relationship more, but I stayed at arm's length and just a bit more away. I was slightly uncomfortable with our age difference, but more so, I was not willing to be involved in a steady relationship at this time. I had my heart and mind focused upon a career as a professional hockey player, and my fellow players and coaches were telling me that I was good enough to make my dream a reality. At this point, I was not going to allow anything to derail my dream, especially a young woman. Therefore, I remained noncommittal.

Yet Maureen was a wonderful gal. She came from a solid family; her parents were Italian-Americans who were immigrants, and ever since the famous Thanksgiving incident at our house a few years ago (also another story) they were close to my parents too. Maureen could talk the ears off an elephant; she was an incessant chatterbox. She always smelled a little like garlic, and now that she was older, a touch of red wine, but she sure was a lot of fun to be with.

I also had to admit that Harry's observation of her figure was indeed accurate. As she grew a little older, she had lost some baby weight, and while she was still a bit on the curvy side, she was fantastically shapely and that image Harry had planted still was stuck in my mind.

Suffice it to say, Maureen Zipperelli was a very attractive, alluring, and extremely sexy young woman!

I dialed her number as Cocoa sat next to me and provided support. One ring, two rings, three rings. I breathed deeply, and I was ready to hang up, when finally, the phone was answered.

"Helloa." I recognized the fractured English language and the voice of Maureen's dad, Mr. Zipperelli.

"Hello Mr. Zipperelli. It is Paul John Henson calling. How are you, sir?"

"Younga Paulinia! It isa soa niceini toa heara youa voicea! Wherea youa beenini? Maureen shea justa saya the othera daya howa sada she isa thata youa neevra comea aroundaini ora calla hera upa!"

"Yes, well, sir, I am very sorry, Mr. Zipperelli. Harry and I have been very busy these days with projects and work. That is why I am calling now, sir. Is Maureen home? May I please speak with her?"

"Oha that isa whata Ia and Mrs. Zipperelli tella hera! Youa and Harryinia aro harda workinini youse guysa! (Some elements of New Jersey had crept into Mr. Zipperelli's vocabulary as of late) Mya wifea and Ia lovea youa younga Paulini. We thinkao youa nicestinia youngini mana fora Maureen. I willa get hera . . . shea playing thosea louda recordinins ina hera rooma. Holed onah."

I heard the phone being set down, and I sighed. A conversation with Mr. Zipperelli was always an adventure. He was very excitable, loud, and his English was a bit rough. Maureen spoke fluent Italian, and she was able to help me over some rough spots when I could not follow the conversations. Luckily, years of communicating with him, and other folks in the large Italian-American population in and around Paterson, New Jersey, had left me a good comprehension of the fractured language. I had to say that Mr. Zipperelli's English was a lot better than my Italian was.

"Paulie! Oh, wow! I am so surprised to hear from you!" Maureen screamed in the telephone so loudly that Cocoa heard her, and he jumped up, and wagged his tail.

"Hey, Maureen. How are you?"

"I am fine! Now that you have called, I am even better.

We have not spoken in a long time."

"Sorry, Maureen. It has been a busy summer with work, and some required technical school classes for my electrical apprenticeship. I apologize."

I was being a jerk and making stupid excuses.

"Have you been dating someone else, Paulie?"

"I do not really date, Maureen."

I heard her laugh loudly on the telephone and she said, "I guess, I am out of luck then!"

I realized how stupid that sounded. I stammered and tried a vain attempt at correcting my stupidity, "Sorry, that is not what I meant. In fact, I wanted to call and see . . . if you are busy on Labor Day weekend."

"You are such a cutie, Paulie. We have known each other forever, and you still stutter and your voice shakes when you ask me out for a date. No, I am not busy, and even if I was, I am not busy now. If I am correct about the reason that you are calling me for, then I can guarantee you that I have no plans. Are you asking me to go somewhere?"

"Yes, sure, sure. This may sound strange, but you did just say that you have known me forever, so maybe this will not be that rhyfedd for you to hear. Harry and I have recently bought a boat."

"Roveth? You bought a boat?"

"Sorry, I slipped a Welsh word in there. I am a bit on the nervous side, Maureen. I don't really know why. The word rhyfedd means strange. Gramps would say it about me when I drifted here and there." I had picked up some of the Welsh language from my grandfather and his relatives. Yes, another long story for some other time. In fact, it would serve me well later in my life.

"Yes, Paul John Henson. I agree that you are at times, roveth. I love your dry humor and your timing of humor is always dead on," Maureen was laughing at my obvious attempt to break the tension.

"Yes. I would never have dreamed that someday, I

would buy a boat. It is a bit of an unusual adventure."

"Unusual! A Harry and Paul adventure roveth and unusual! No! I am stunned at the mere suggestion!" Maureen was teasing me now.

"We are going to a cabin for Labor Day weekend. A cabin in the woods, which one of Harry's uncles owns on Green Pine Lake. Joyce is going to be Harry's date, and I was hoping that you . . . would go with me."

I stuttered as it occurred to me how nervous my conversation sounded. "We, we, we—will have separate rooms, Maureen. I am not suggesting any funny business or being forward by any means. Joyce and you can bunk together in a bedroom in the cabin. There is a sleeping loft for Harry, Cocoa, and me."

"Oh, you are such a cutie, Paulie. I could only dream that you would be forward or suggestive towards me. How I wish and dream that you had what you would think were unreasonable expectations for a young woman to participate in on a date. Especially a date with someone as wonderful, sexy, and handsome as Paul John Henson is! Now, I wish I were there to see how red you are turning right now! I will be thrilled to go with you. Thank you! I do not think I have ever been on a boat on a lake! I love Joyce . . . she is so nice. I am so glad to hear that she and Harry are back together. So how is Dottie doing? I miss her."

I sighed, pulled a chair from the kitchen table, and sat down. Cocoa sighed too, and he curled up around my feet. This had been a successful telephone call and now, well, Maureen was going to turn on the blabber switch. I had to listen for a long time, find a break in the action, and then bail with an excuse of some kind.

Until then, I settled in.

About an hour later, and after speaking twenty-two thousand, "Uh huhs," I finally heard Maureen pause for a fleeting second or two. I took the chance to say that I did not want to be rude and tie up Harry's telephone much longer, told Maureen that I would call her with the final plans, and somehow, managed to escape the telephone call in just under an hour and one half. I hung up and turned to Cocoa, who had jumped up on me and smiled at my good fortune in securing a date with Maureen.

"We are good to go, Cocoa. Yes! I have a date for the weekend! C'mon, boy!"

We burst through the back door into the night and the darkness of the backyard. Harry and Joyce did not even look up, or stop participating in the "activity" that they had chosen to occupy their time with, and I stopped cold in my tracks. They both were exceedingly involved with one another, oblivious to my presence, until I coughed a bit to break up the "festivities." I was embarrassed, and would have gone back into the house, except for the fact that I was dying to tell them of my good fortune. They both let go of one another. They looked up and laughed at my obvious embarrassment.

"So how did you do there, lover boy?" Harry teased me. He then looked at his watch and said, "Musta been an earthquake and the telephone lines were severed. We were not expecting you for another hour."

"Obviously, I see that. Sorry, that I interrupted. She is going!" Joyce and Harry both jumped up. They ran over and gave me a group hug.

"I am so proud of you, twenty-seven. See, other than having to talk to Maureen for quite some time, that was easy," Joyce was encouraging me.

"Yeah, yeah, yeah, it was fine." We all sat back down in the chairs in front of the fire, we all grabbed some drinks and toasted in celebration of my success.

"Say, Paul, before Joyce and I became, umm, diverted . . . (Harry could spin situations with such strategic words and phrasing) we were trying hard to come up with a name for the boat. You know, to paint on the hull. Something clever. You are so good with words. I bet you have a good idea."

"Diverted, eh? I will try to remember that one." Joyce giggled a little at my comment.

"Hmm, I never really thought of it. What did you two come up with for a name?"

"I suggested to Harry, a number rather than a name. I said to paint a three–five-two-seven on the hull for youse guy's hockey jersey numbers."

"I kinda, sorta like that Joyce-a-roo-ski, but wanted something a little more, well, supercharged. Sorta, like, hot stuff, the big-chested boat, or the backside burner!" Harry was waving his soda in the air as he touted his idea.

I leaned back, took a sip of my beer, and thought about it for a minute or two while I said, "They are good suggestions. I do like the hockey number idea there, Joyce. Hmm. . .." I then smiled, as I thought about the events of the weekend, as well as Maureen's comments, and Harry's slightly questionable and unusual motivational tactics.

"I got it! Unreasonable expectations!"

Joyce and Harry looked over at the boat and they both yelled almost simultaneously, "PERFECT!"

Harry jumped up, came over, and shook my hand while he said, "I love it, Paul! Now that is what I am talking about! That is absolutely perfect!"

Unreasonable expectations.

Yeah, yeah, yeah, I had to agree it was pretty good.

5

Cliffy Comes Along to Help

I was up very early the next morning. I usually went to church with my parents on Sunday morning, but this Sunday, I skipped out on the services. The old man and Mum understood, and they never questioned me on my plans at this point in my life.

When the old man heard, I was going to tackle the engine today; he smiled and told me, "Good luck. Be sure ya check the carburetor for spider webs inside the fuel jets. Engines that sit tend to get spider webs."

As had been consistent with this entire project, my parents, and Harry's old man and Ronzo, had offered support, but they left us alone to do battle with the boat on our own. Time was now bearing down on Harry and me. We had to get the boat finished.

The holiday was only a week away, and we not only had to have the engine running, but we had to weld and fix up the trailer. The trailer had some rusty spots, and it required removal of the rusted metal, reinforcement, and support. In order to make the repairs, it required the arduous task of actually lifting the boat off the trailer and setting it down, while Harry welded a new cross member of steel underneath the trailer. Mr. Redmond had interjected at that point, with one of his patented and creative suggestions.

He had rigged up a series of metal stands that Harry and Mr. Redmond fabricated and welded in their shop. We lined them up along the driveway, and into the backyard in a pattern to support the hull of the boat. The plan was to have a typical backyard Redmond summer shindig, and cookout this afternoon, gather up about twenty of the neighborhood men, and utilizing some slings made of heavy rope, lift the boat off the trailer and lower it onto the stands. Harry could then weld and repair the trailer, and when Harry finished the welding, we could place the boat back onto the trailer.

It seemed as if it was a good plan, but we, of course, knew there was always a chance of a little element of a Harry and Paul adventure creeping into the game.

Harry was not in the backyard when I arrived with my tools. I decided not to knock on any doors or wake anyone up if they were still sleeping. The solitude might just be exactly what I needed to get this engine running. I removed the cover off the boat and started to tinker with the engine. Cocoa was there to greet me, and he jumped up in the boat with his Piggy in his mouth while he sat down to watch me. I had removed the wooden lid to the engine and stared down inside of the compartment. I had never seen a boat engine in my life before today, but it looked as if it was not much different from any other engines that I had ever seen. My confidence was building, as I remembered all the driveway battles my old man and I had endured to resurrect the 1964 Putter Classic model 200, Harry's famous 1971 Takajunky model 10, my old van, and other junk cars in our past history.

I knew I could get this baby to run. Unlike the new name of our boat, I felt that I had some very reasonable expectations! The engine looked surprisingly clean for how old the boat was and how long it had sat without running. It was, of course, covered under the wooden and plastic lid of the engine cover, and I thought about how that had helped to preserve the aging process. I filled the gas tank with some petrol from a can we had in the garage, checked the oil level, pulled the air cleaner off, and studied the carburetor. I pumped the throttle a little and sniffed for the odor of gasoline.

Nothing.

I turned the ignition switch on, and I heard the soft whir of what I surmised to be a fuel pump, and then pumped the throttle cable again. Turning the key to the "on" position brought nothing but dry cranking, without any indication of ignition. Since it was so early, I did not want to wake the entire neighborhood, so I did not persist in cranking the engine.

Still nothing! Huh?

No gas! Bad fuel pump? No, I could hear it running. Maybe it was running but not pumping. Think, twenty-seven. Think.

I then remembered a repair battle of a long time ago, when the old man and I fought with a car of my Uncle Ed's that had been in storage for a long time. The old man told me to check the fuel filter for fuel flow at the input of the filter and then the output.

"Fuel filters always clog from sitting for years without running. They are made of cheap cardboard these days and they fall apart inside," he had told me.

Okay. I jumped down from the boat and Cocoa followed me. I traced the fuel line from the gas tank to the engine and sure enough! There was a little blocky fuel filter mounted on the side. Unlike car filters, this one was almost square in appearance. I took my wrench and loosened the fuel pump side of the filter, grabbed a bucket from the garage and set it under the loose fuel line. It was a good thing that my helper this morning was the world's smartest dog, because I told Cocoa, "Now, watch the fuel line, Cocoa. Do not go near it, but bark once, if you see fuel, come out when I turn the key on." He barked twice and wagged his tail three times to indicate that he understood my instructions.

The dog was amazing!

I climbed back in the boat, flipped the key on, and sure

enough, Cocoa barked once. I shut it down and knew the fuel pump was good, not only because of Cocoa's observation, but because a strong odor of gas now filled the air. Climbing back underneath the boat, I removed the fuel filter and turned it over to see if anything would come out of it when I tipped it. Nothing . . . not a drop, however, some big chunks of black goo dripped out of it. I knew that I had found something!

"C'mon, Cocoa! Grab Piggy and let's go see if Vince is hanging around the gas station." Cocoa grabbed his faithful Piggy, followed me to my van, and jumped in with me. A quick spin around the block, and we were at the corner Golf gas station, which was only a storefront or two, and an apartment house away from the front door of my own house. It was located exactly on the corner of Belmont Avenue and Cook Street.

Now, Vince Barroni was the owner of the gas station and he had been there for as long as I could remember. When I was just an annoying, dopey, little kid, he would let me in his shop, and I would sit on a chair and watch him and his mechanics work on cars and engines. He would allow me to borrow tools to fix my bicycle, and he gave me repair tips when I did not know what I was doing.

He was a kind and friendly soul.

Vince was a short, stocky, Italian man whose head sunk deep into his body. He seemed as if he had no discernable neck. He walked slouched over, in short, quick steps, his hands were always covered in grease, and it appeared that his hands were in a permanently clenched grip because I think years of, "knuckle busters" must have frozen his hands and fingers into that manner. Years and years of leaning over, hunching over hoods and working on cars, had also permanently bent Vince over at his waist.

Yet, he was happy, he was upbeat, and he was always working. I knew on this early Sunday morning, when most folks were still sleeping off Saturday night, or in church services, that Vince would be in his shop and gas station.

He was part of that lost breed of men who were so common in our neighborhood back then. Honest and trustworthy men who worked hard and dedicated their lives to earning a living by supporting their families and communities.

How this modern world of today misses men such as Vince Barroni.

I parked the van, jumped out along with Cocoa, and together we walked towards the side door. Sure enough, Vince was inside tinkering under the hood of some old wreck of a vehicle in his shop. The shop had a distinct odor of oil, petrol, and embedded grease. I can still smell it in my senses to this day.

"Hey, Vince. How are you?"

Vince looked up and smiled.

"Hey, Paulie. Hey, Cocoa. Where youse guys been? I have not seen youse guys around for a while."

"Busy, I guess, Vince. Are you doing, okay?"

"Man, you are one big guy. I can't believe how the years have passed me. It seems like yesterday youse was just a little kiddie bringing me your bike for repairs and asking to borrow tools."

He stood up from under the hood of the car, wiped his hands, shook my hand, and then tossed the rag over on a workbench.

"Sure, sure, sure. I am good, Paulie. Old, but good. I cannot keep up with the work, Paulie. I wish your old man would either come and work for me or fix more cars in his driveway for the neighbors just as he used to do! Too many junky cars in this old neighborhood and no one with any money to buy new ones, so they bring 'em to me to get going again. For sure, it keeps me busy! What is this I hear about you and Harry buying DelMonico's boat?"

I knew that Cliffy McWhiffy had been spreading the word.

"Yeah, yeah, yeah. It is kind of crazy, but you know Harry and me. Most of the time, we are somewhat crazy, so I guess it works for us. We did buy the boat, and that is what brought me here. Would you have any of these?" I showed Vince the fuel filter and handed it to him.

"Out of a boat, huh? Boat parts are not my specialty, but if you have enough room to mount a bigger filter, then I might have something in my bag of tricks."

"I have plenty of room, Vince," I said as Cocoa and I followed him to a corner of his shop. He pulled down a greasy box, fished through it, and pulled out a brass filter. He smiled and handed it to me. It was bigger, a little blockier, but the fittings on the ends were the same.

"That will work, Vince!"

Cocoa gave the agreement signal.

"Make sure ya have a can of carburetor cleaner, Paulie, if ya got a clogged fuel filter, then the carburetor is goin' to be dirty too. I would venture a guess that ya already know that one because your old man taught you well. Say, Paulie, if this boat is as old as what Cliffy told me, then you might also be interested in this. I have had this in my shop forever, and I will give you a deal on it. I can't even remember where I got it from!" Vince gave a wave for us to follow him to another corner of his shop, which was filled top to bottom with parts, tools, belts, hoses and a plethora of other items accumulated over years and years of repairing cars and trucks.

It was a fascinating place.

Vince pulled down a box and handed it to me. I looked inside and saw that it was some type of pump. I was a little puzzled, so I asked, "A pump, Vince?"

"Yeah, yeah, yeah. A bilge pump! You put it down inside the boat . . . just in case. You know, if you spring a leak, Paulie. It is electric." I smiled because as a hapless victim of the Old Lady Syndrome, I would always error on the safe side. I never considered a leak or the potential sinking of the boat. I liked the idea. "How much for the pump and the filter, Vince?"

"Oh, Paulie, for you, give me ten bucks and we will call it even. Good luck with getting that boat going."

I reached into my wallet and handed him the money. I thanked Vince, he petted and played with Cocoa for a few minutes, (but he did not throw Piggy because everyone who knew Cocoa, knew not to become locked into a lifelong game of, Fetch the Piggy!) and we were off in the van. A few minutes later, I was back under the boat. I had installed the filter, and Cocoa and I were back staring into the engine compartment. I crossed my fingers, turned the ignition on, and tried to crank the engine, but it spun without any ignition.

It was a bit frustrating at this point because I thought the fuel filter was the culprit. I should have known that this was not going to be so easy. I leaned over and stared down into the carburetor and sniffed. There still was no fuel. Why? Cocoa sat next to me, alternating between staring at me and down inside the engine, while he was watching me carefully for a clue as to our next move.

"Be sure to check for spider webs in the fuel jets. Engines that sit tend to get spider webs."

The words from the old man popped into my head. I grabbed my tools, loosened the fuel lines in the carburetor, and peered down into the throat of the carburetor while I stuck a thin, long screwdriver inside the fuel line input. Right on cue, Mr. Spider sprung out of the hole and walked his way out of the barrel of the carburetor.

"Man, oh man . . . geez, the old man, as usual, was dead on," I whispered as Cocoa barked once to chase Mr. Spider away. I cleaned out the holes, squirted some carburetor cleaner down inside the jets and barrel, put it all back together, and I was all set to give it another whirl. I turned to grab the key, said a little prayer for assistance, and looked at Cocoa, who had picked up Piggy, and was wagging his tail in anticipation.

I took a deep breath and gave the key a twist.

"CRANNNNNNKKKKK!"

"Oh c'mon, engine start."

"CRANNNNNNKKKK! POP! POP! POP! BRRRRRRR!" And, and, and . . . it started! The old engine kicked off, and it purred like a kitten.

Cocoa tossed Piggy into the air in joy and then ran over to me, licking my face. I hugged him around the neck and shouted out, "YES! We did it, Cocoa! We did it!" I sat back down, and said under my breath, "Thanks, Dad."

Harry, Linda, Ronzo, and Mr. Redmond, and all the nieces and nephews, came running out of the back door of the house as the noise of the engine running alerted them to my efforts. They all stood on the porch, hollering, yelling, and clapping at my efforts. I stood up in the boat, and fist pumped my grease-filled arms and hands into the air.

The old man had taught me well, and I have to say that it sure felt good.

That afternoon, brought a huge gathering of the neighbors, to not only swim in the famous pool, play horseshoes in the pits, eat hot dogs and hamburgers, drink beer and eat corn on the cob at Harry's Resort, but also to check out the boat. It was now easy to muster up enough manpower to lift the boat off the trailer.

Once we had a surplus of manpower, we encouraged the men to show their testosterone levels and show off their muscles to their ladies. Harry, Mr. Redmond, Mr. Porter, Mr. Len, Harold Clipclock, Billy Heady, Joe Hinky Doo, The Big Spike, a multitude of others, and number twenty-seven, all gathered around the boat, and with a heave and a lift, we easily lifted the boat off the trailer, and set it down upon the nest of metal stands.

Harry went to work welding, grinding, cutting, and bracing the steel on the trailer, and I worked on the wires for the trailer brake lights and tail lights so we did not run afoul of Officer Hough once again. Once we repaired the trailer, Harry rolled a coat of paint on the trailer, and soon it looked as if it was brand new.

The day had turned hot and sticky, and as the afternoon ground on, sweat, dirt and grime covered both Harry and me. We were working hard, and we were a mess. Joyce said she was going to stop by to check on our progress; she had called earlier to tell Harry that she would pick up Maureen Zipperelli on her way and bring her over to see the boat, too.

Around three in the afternoon or so, Harry pronounced the trailer good to go. I had the wires, lights, and license plate lamp back in action, and we were ready to place the boat back onto the trailer.

Now, it had been terribly hot. The men were playing horseshoes, drinking endless mugs of beer, and many of them were now half in the bag, or well on their way to being there. Lifting the boat back on the trailer was not quite as appealing as it had been earlier, and after some pleading, we finally mustered up the crew. We all spread out around the boat and were in the position to lift it back onto the trailer when. . ..

A strong fish odor filled the air, the beer-laden breath and voice of Cliffy resounded into the air, as he stood in front of the trailer and spoke, "It does not look too bad. HA! HA! HA! Youse stupid ass guys look like ya know, what the hell ya doing! Do you have the keg set up in the yard there? I need another bubbly ass beer. HA! HA! HA!"

I guess in the world of Cliffy that was as close to a compliment as we would ever hear. I was actually surprised that it had taken so long for Cliffy to show up and offer his wisdom, guidance, and advice. He must have had prior engagements, because generally when free food and beer were involved, then Cliffy would usually arrive on the scene a bit earlier. Cliffy seemed as if he was already fairly lit up as far as alcohol consumption was concerned, and I am sure if we checked his beer dipstick, it would indicate that he was way past the full mark.

Now in retrospect, it may not have been a great decision on Harry's part, and I am sure in looking back, if he had to do it over again, he would not have even considered it, but in Harry's vain and futile defense, it was at the time, a logical decision to have made. You see, we needed someone to steer us in on the trailer mounts while we "hovered" the boat back into position onto the mounts. It was impossible for us to see the underneath side of the boat, and the hull of the boat had to line up with the mounts and guides when we dropped it back into position. Since Cliffy was standing right in front of the boat, and teetering back and forth in his drunken haze, I guess Harry determined that Cliffy was in the correct spot. Therefore, he was the logical choice to be a guide.

This infamous event now comes under that fateful category of, "It seemed like a good idea at the time."

Harry shouted out, "Hey Cliffy, before you go get a beer and while you are standing there insulting us, take a look under the bottom on the boat, and guide us in for a landing. We have to land the boat on those mounts and guides on the trailer there!"

Cliffy, in the midst of his drunken stupor, wobbled, bent over, and stared under the trailer to see what the job entailed that he had just been assigned to, and then he stood up, waved and said, "I friggin' got it. HA! HA! HA! Youse muscle bound dopes pick it up, and I will watch under this heap of shit boat and tell ya when to drop it. HA! HA! HA!"

It seemed as if it was a reasonable plan.

We all gave a heave and picked the boat up in the air. Now that we were all tired, this was a bigger struggle than it had been before, and loud moans and groans echoed throughout the group. We all moved in close to the trailer and waited for Cliffy's instructions.

"C'mon the hell over! HA! HA! HA! Closer, higher, closer, closer, c'mon a little frig-frackin' higher. HA! HA! HA! Okay, move it a little lower, lower, lower, lower, no, damn turn to the far right. HA! HA! HA!"

All of us, under tremendous muscular strain, yelled out, "WHICH FAR RIGHT, CLIFFY? CLIFFY'S RIGHT OR OUR RIGHT?"

There was a long delay while he was thinking about the correct direction. Cliffy wobbled. He tilted a bit in his drunken haze, put his hand to his head while he pondered the question and finally, he said, "Towards the fence youse lard-asses. I can't figure out my damn right from my left. HA! HA! HA!" Cliffy's beer-induced haze was a bit too foggy to make heads or tails out of all of these technical things.

This was taking forever, between the obligatory cuss words and the laughs after every sentence, and all of us were about to blow our guts and the blood vessels out of our head, when Mr. Porter finally yelled out, "Geez c'mon, Cliffy! You're killing us here! Just guide us the hell in!"

"Okay, Bill, hold your damn horses! It is so hard to see this bullshit. HA! HA! HA! Lower, lower, lower . . . almost there now . . . to the fence a smidge, yes . . . lower. Perfect, now drop it the hell down. HA! HA! HA!"

We finally lowered the boat when Cliffy screamed, "NO NOT THERE! SHIT! STOP! HA! HA! HA!"

It was too late.

Disaster! A loud, sickening, "CRACCCKKKK!" filled the air. I heard Cocoa whimper and he rolled around on the ground in horror.

"Oops! I just noticed a bullshit piece of steel that some jackass left on the edge of the trailer, and the bar just went right through the bottom of the junky-ass boat! HA! HA! HA! Oh well, time for a bubbly ass beer. HA! HA! HA!" Cliffy explained as he stood up and wobbled in the direction of the beer keg, while we all leaned over and peered into the bottom of the boat. I felt like crying while I stared at a chunk of a steel bar poking through the bottom of our wooden hull. Mr. Redmond turned around and glared at Cliffy, who was drawing down a beer from the keg.

Cliffy looked over, shrugged his shoulders, and said, "Damn. I am sorry. HA! HA! HA!"

Harry was irate, and I tried my best to calm him down.

Harry was mumbling and clenching his fists, "Stupid ass Cliffy. I should have known better than to put that drunken bum in charge of the boat to trailer guidance. I am going to punch his face in!"

"Whoa, slow down, big guy . . . easy there, Harry. I am sure it was just a mistake. In his own way, Cliffy feels bad," I said as I jumped into the boat to study the damage. It was a thick hunk of steel, and it menacingly protruded right through the bottom of the boat in a grotesque display of tragedy. The steel must have been a leftover piece from a larger section of the material, in which Harry was using to repair the trailer. Harry had not noticed that he had left it on the trailer, and it had pierced right through the hull of the boat. I was suddenly glad that I had purchased that bilge pump from Vince!

Mr. Redmond and Ronzo stared into the hull of the boat too, and Mr. Redmond must have sensed our frustration, as well as our need for assistance with this repair. The other neighbors and Harry's sisters gathered around to offer encouragement that we could easily repair the boat. I looked at Harry shaking his head and I had to admit that I felt a strong feeling that all of our money, effort, and work now were for naught.

For the second time in this project, Mr. Redmond offered his expert guidance and advice, "I have an idea on how to repair this. I know it looks bad, but hang in there, boys. Do not pull the metal out yet."

Mr. Redmond walked slowly to the garage, and I could see the wheels spinning in his mind. He was a mechanical genius, and since we were little boys, he had taught us so many tricks of the trades, that we could never have thanked him enough for the knowledge of a lifetime in the trades that he had taught to both of us. Working with Mr. Redmond and my old man on a job was better than if we had earned ten technical school degrees.

We could hear him moving things around in his workshop in the garage, opening toolboxes, and supply cabinets. We then heard his table saw start up, and the sound of him cutting wood. Shortly thereafter, Mr. Redmond returned, and he was now carrying a number of supplies in a tool caddy. He placed them down next to the boat and took the supplies out of the caddy. The supplies were two small metal cans, a small piece of wood, and rubber pieces from what appeared to be an old pool liner, brass wood screws, and small, black rubber grommets. The partygoers all gathered around and stood to watch the master at work. Even Cliffy stood silently (for a change) and watched.

"Paulie, you jump up in the boat, and when we tell you, slowly push the metal back down to us. The metal must have moved and jumped up through the hull when we set the boat down. Thank goodness that we do not have to pull the boat off the trailer again. Look here, you can see that it is clear for us to work through this hole in the trailer, and we can access the wood underneath without the trailer metal blocking our work. Paulie, while you push it out, then gently push the wood fibers back into place. I am going to mix up a can of this marine epoxy that I bought a few weeks ago, to repair the pool filter tank. As you push the fibers of the wood back, you will pour the epoxy into the wood and smooth it out with this putty knife."

"Got it, Mr. Redmond," I said as I hustled into position.

"Harry, you crawl under the boat, and when Paulie

pushes the metal down to you, then pull it out, and smooth the epoxy on your side as it flows from the top to the bottom. Once it dries, which is about fifteen minutes, we will support the repair on both sides with this scrap mahogany I had in the garage, screw it with the brass screws so they do not rust, and leak proof the wood with the rubber on each side, and the grommets in the screw holes. Then another smear of epoxy over the entire sandwich, and I guarantee it will be leak proof and even stronger than it had been! During the week, you need to coat the repair with the varnish youse boys have been using on the hull and no one will ever notice it. The hole is only an inch or so wide—it is nothing. It looks bad now, but it really is not."

The man was amazing! You wonder where men, such as Mr. Redmond accumulated the knowledge they had on such a vast number of different repairs, situations, and jobs. Until now, I was sure that Mr. Redmond had never worked on a boat, but now, I was not too sure. I think between our two fathers, there was nothing that they had not actually worked on in their lives. I hope in my heart that this world someday returns to our roots, when we consider backyard ingenuity, some tool-swinging, and general, common sense to be more valuable, than the latest and greatest, whiz-bang device or endless paper degrees hung on walls.

Ronzo mixed the epoxy. We performed the repair as per Mr. Redmond's instructions, and in no time, the hull of the boat looked as good as new. We just needed the work to dry and then we would vanish it next week. Harry and I felt much better, and we thanked Mr. Redmond once more for bailing us out.

Cliffy leaned over, studied the repair, and spouted off, "Pretty damn good. HA! HA! HA! I really was just trying to help youse stupid ass guys. HA! HA! HA! I really am friggin' sorry. HA! HA! HA!"

Mr. Redmond came over, put his arm around Cliffy, and said, "I know you were trying to help there, Cliffy. C'mon, I will pour you another beer. Lord knows you do not need it, but I will pour you another one for helping us."

The next-door neighbors, the Porters, were famous in our neighborhood for their amazing creativity. The Porters lived right next door to the Redmonds at 30 John Street. Mrs. Porter was always in charge of decorations, artwork, and ideas for the big backyard cookouts, gatherings, and holiday parties. Our good friend, Jeff Porter was not around very much these days, he was always off with his girlfriend, but when we were young, Mrs. Porter would always help us with our school projects, whenever they required anything to do with art or being creative. We were just wrapping up for the day, and we were finally going to eat something, when Mrs. Porter arrived with her painting set. Mrs. Porter could paint wonderful oil paintings and portraits, and she always was working on a project in their house.

She smiled at us, and set up a little stool next to the boat as she explained, "Linny told me the name of your boat. I love it, and if you would like me to do it, then I will paint the name and some artwork on the side of the boat for youse guys."

"Sure, Mrs. Porter! Thank you!" Harry was thrilled.

The gals were coming over shortly, and Harry and I were a mess. I was soaked from head to foot with sweat and covered with a gruesome mixture of grime, epoxy, oil, grease, and as the old man would say, "Assorted schmutz." I jumped in the van to go home and wash up and Harry showered and cleaned up, too. I was going to bring back my cut-off shorts to jump in the pool and cool off after all of our hard work. It would be the perfect nightcap to a long, hot summer day. I filled my parents in on the day's activities; the old man somewhat modestly told me that he knew he would be right about the spider's web in the fuel jet. I showered, cleaned up, and stuffed a small hockey equipment bag with a towel, grabbed my cut-off shorts (a hippie's typical idea of a bathing suit) and threw them in the bag too. I was dressed in my usual attire of black dungarees, a rock-and-roll tee shirt with the name of my favorite musical band emblazoned on the front, and my canvas sneakers. I did not tie all of my shoulder length blonde hair back in a hair tie. I just let it dry in the air and headed back over to 20 John Street.

When I arrived, I spotted most of the crowd had gathered around the side of the boat, while Mrs. Porter was finishing the name and artwork on the hull of the boat.

It was an awesome display of artwork! She had painted the name, "Unreasonable Expectations" in a fancy, scroll type lettering with different colors that included reds, greens, blacks, and yellow. Underneath the name was a cartoon of artwork, which depicted a man struggling to pedal a bicycle while he was towing a large boat that resembled ours behind his bicycle. She was amazing, and the spectators praised her amazing creativity. We thanked Mrs. Porter; we all posed for pictures next to her and the boat, with her artwork in the background.

"You will just need to clear-coat the artwork with the varnish next week after it dries. Now, Bill, I want a kiss from both of youse boys in the pictures," Mrs. Porter instructed her husband as he snapped away with a camera. "I want to make you jealous, Bill. Now that these handsome young men are all cleaned up, I want hugs and then kisses for me right on the ole smacker for payment for the artwork!" Mrs. Porter had a wonderful sense of humor, and we obliged her request as we snapped a number of pictures. What memories, from such a collection of eclectic and awesome people, all living together in a wonderful time and place.

"Two-timing us as usual, I see!" We turned around to see Joyce and Maureen walking up the driveway just as

Harry and I were, "thanking" Mrs. Porter for her hard work and posing for the silly pictures. "You just cannot trust these two around the ladies," Joyce feigned anger with her hands on her hips. We all had a good laugh about it, and Joyce greeted Harry with a hug and a kiss.

I smiled and walked over to Maureen as I explained, "Hello, Maureen. You are looking wonderful. Well, you see, Mrs. Porter painted the side of the boat, and she asked us to give her a kiss for the pictures."

Maureen laughed and said, "You are all embarrassed, as usual, Paulie. You are such a cutie. Now where is my kiss?" The crowd of neighbors cheered as Maureen almost broke my lips and my face with an overzealous greeting. I could detect the slight taste of a little red wine and a touch of garlic that always was part of sharing a kiss or two with Maureen Zipperelli.

She was always so aggressive.

We showed the gals the boat, and they loved it! The excitement was building now as the two ladies climbed up into the boat, and we showed them all the efforts of our hard work. All that remained now was to register the boat, screw the license plates on, take our boating safety quiz, and obtain our boating certificates.

That would be next week's mission. Right for now, it was time to eat, swim, and relax. Harry and I were famished, and we sat down and enjoyed some hamburgers, soda, a sneak or two of cold beer, and some snacks.

Maureen had brought a jug of her family's famous homemade wine that Mr. Zipperelli and his brother made in their basement. She gave it to Mr. Redmond and Linny, along with a tray of her mother's famous homemade ziti and meatballs as a gift. Maureen's family raised her on wine; there was not a dinner, lunchtime, or event, in which wine was not a part of with her family. It was part of her heritage and presenting the wine as a gift was something she always did when she visited friends or other family.

Her parents had been born in Italy, and Mrs. Zipperelli spoke very little English, even though she had been in America for almost thirty years. Maureen was part of a different culture, in which I could also relate to, since on my mum's side we had the English and Welsh background.

While Harry and I ate some dinner, the gals decided to change into their bathing suits to jump in the pool. We would finish eating, then change, and join them.

We were just about finished when the back door to Harry's house opened and out strode the two ladies in their swimsuits. The Big Spike was just taking a big bite of a Big Bob's Griddle Frank, when he spotted Maureen and Joyce walk by. He was so stunned and dumbfounded that he dropped the hot dog on the ground, and Cocoa zoomed in and gobbled up the free snack. Patty came running over to close his mouth and cover his eyes.

Harry and I stood up. And we must have looked like shocked idiots, because neither of us could say a word. Maureen smiled and wiggled by me, and Joyce did the same to Harry. They were playing the two of us dopes as if we were fine violins.

Every male in attendance at Harry's Resort that afternoon was at a loss for words. There was a stunned silence at the appearance of the two gorgeous women. The very ground underneath our feet shook and rumbled at the passing of the young women.

I heard Cliffy mumble while he stood behind us, "Geez, youse guys are lucky ass dopes. HA! HA! HA!"

Harry's description of Maureen in a swimsuit was dead on; he had nailed it and let me tell you that Joyce was no slouch either.

Maureen was "bulging" in all the right places—just as Harry had predicted. The two of them had left a trail of men who required resuscitation and revival from the back door, all the way to the swimming pool.

As we scrambled to run inside and change into our

bathing suits and join the gals, Harry said as we ran together into the back door, "So, twenty-seven, was I right or what? Now you know why you climbed halfway to the heart of the sunrise. Now that ya see them, it is not an unreasonable expectation at all!"

I had to admit that Harry was, of course, correct, and while some folks might feel that his motivational tactics were at times somewhat questionable, I for one, was a firm believer.

6

Forever Labor Day

During the week leading up to the big holiday weekend, we registered the boat, put the license plates on, and passed our one-page examination for boating safety at the Coast Guard Auxiliary offices in downtown Paterson. We were now "officially" boating gurus!

We worked here and there at night during the week on touch ups on the boat. Officer Hough even stopped by one night when he spotted us working in the backyard from his patrol car. He was amazed at our efforts, and we thanked him again for giving us a break, rather than a difficult start to this entire adventure. We also made sure that we showed him the valid registration, the license plates, and the working brake lights and tail lights, too.

"I am very proud of you two young men. You are hardworking, solid, law-abiding citizens!" Officer Hough proudly proclaimed.

Harry roared with laughter, when he saw that I had spent my extra money that we had saved on the boat due to the antenna incident, on a two-way, Coast Guard approved walkie-talkie radio, and four, life safety inflatable vests for humans, and one doggie-sized vest for Cocoa.

"You're such an old lady, Paul. I swear you're hopeless! Those things are as useless as serving corn-on-the-cob at a barbeque picnic full of hockey players!"

In my defense, I explained, "I got a wonderful deal on them downtown in Wurtzberg Brother's sporting goods store. They were on clearance sale. I only spent fifteen bucks for all of it!"

Harry laughed even harder when I showed him the little bilge pump I had purchased from Vince and installed, wired, and tucked in under the rear compartment. I showed him how I had drilled and installed a switch on the front dashboard that controlled the pump, and I even wired a red-colored pilot light that glowed brightly when the pump turned on.

"What are you going to spend your extra dough on, Harry?" I asked him.

He smiled, and gave me a quirky and mischievous Harry response by simply saying, "You will see. It is a surprise."

Oh my, oh my. . ..

The big day finally arrived, and I was over at Harry's house right after work on Friday. It seemed as if the entire neighborhood had gathered to see us off. Joyce had driven her car over to Harry's house and met us there. We had to hitch up the boat and trailer to the van, then ride over and pick up Maureen at her house, and make our way up to Green Pine Lake.

It was around five in the afternoon, and the heat of the day had dissipated rather quickly. The summer was already giving way to autumn, and the sun was setting quicker than it had set just a few short weeks ago. It was amazing how quickly the summer had passed.

I cannot say that I was going to miss the season. I was looking forward to the end of the summer because the autumn of this year was going to be a big one for me. I enrolled a few weeks earlier in a goaltender clinic at Ice Land Arena, and I hoped that finally, I would have a chance to prove that I just may be a real goalie after all.

Oh, boy, another story. . ..

The crowd cheered and roared as Ronzo clicked the boat trailer wiring harness into the hitch on my van; we threw our gear, supplies, fishing poles and tackle, and luggage in the van, and Joyce, Harry, and Cocoa (holding his Piggy) jumped in the seats in the back.

Ronzo walked up to the driver's window and said to me, "Say, Paulie, come on back here, and make sure that I hitched the wiring harness up correctly, would you?"

"Sure, Ronnie, sure."

I met Ronzo in the back of the van, and as we bent down to double-check the harness, Ronzo bent over and he whispered to me, "I stuck two cases of Big Boulder beer under the tool compartment in the back of the van for you, and one case of Dingleberry beer."

He smiled and then winked at me.

"I was young once, and those two chicks . . . wow . . . hang on, twenty-seven. My goodness gracious. Hang on tightly, my young friend." Ronzo smiled, and I gave him a quick handshake and a smile.

"How much do I owe you, Ronzo?"

"Nothing. You have already paid me back in memories." Ronnie Boatmann was a once in a lifetime friend. He would go on later in my life to be an important guide, friend, and a special person in my life.

I climbed into the van, started it up, slowly pulled out of the driveway, and onto John Street. We left out of 20 John Street to a standing ovation of neighbors.

Need I say more about our neighborhood?

We rolled up the road, and I double-parked on Maureen's street in front of her house. We hustled through a condensed version of greetings and goodbyes with the Zipperelli family. I loaded Maureen's luggage, and three huge jugs of homemade Zipperelli wine into the van, along with numerous foil trays full of home-cooked Italian food, in which Maureen instructed me to lie flat in the van, and we were off. We needed to stop and grab a bite to eat, so we picked up some burgers and fries at a local haunt, and we were back on the road. It would take us about two hours or thereabouts to make it to Green Pine Lake. The lake was unique, because half of the lake was located in New Jersey, and the other half was in New York State. Towing the boat would slow us down a bit, but my old van had a large, six-cylinder slant-head engine that was old, but still very strong. I could feel that it was not having any trouble at all, pulling the boat up and down the roads.

Maureen was in topnotch blabber mode tonight. She sat in the passenger seat and blabbed up a storm to Harry, Joyce, and Cocoa, who were all sitting in the back seats. I had an excuse to avoid direct impact from her blabber, since I needed to keep my eyes on the road. Therefore, I would occasionally nod my head, while practicing saying, "Uh, huh."

Up and down country roads we rolled. On the top of the mountains and then back down the other sides we went, with Maureen, talking the entire way.

My ears were aching.

It was dark by the time that we made it to the lake community, and it was very hard to see the road signs. It seemed as if we left streetlights along the roadways back in Paterson because they did not exist out here in the lake communities! Harry was studying the road maps and using a flashlight in order to find road signs to check our location. It was a bit of a challenge, but soon we were in the driveway of the log cabin owned by Harry's uncle. I carefully pulled in, rolled down the gravel driveway, and parked the van and trailer.

We had made it!

I unloaded the van while Harry, Joyce, Maureen, and Cocoa went to check out the cabin. Harry knew where his uncle had hidden the key, and I was very thankful when a spotlight turned on and illuminated the driveway. Now, I could see what I was doing! I chocked the wheels to the van and boat trailer with a couple of large stones that I had found, and lugged the supplies, gear, luggage, wine, beer, food, and "stuff" into the cabin.

The cabin was incredible. I dropped our gear in the center of a wide-open, pine wood floor with a stone fireplace and an open stone hearth framing the end of the living space. There was a small kitchenette area with a stone countertop, a cooker, a refrigerator, and sink and cupboards on the one side closest to the rear door. There was a small laundry center adjacent to the kitchenette. The kitchenette faced the open first floor and had a window that opened to the deck and backyard. Extending from floor to ceiling along one side was a glass window that I surmised faced the lake. The rest of the cabin had an open floor plan on the first floor, with a loft that surrounded the open area along the entire perimeter of the second floor.

While I checked out the kitchenette, Maureen helped me ice down some beer and a jug of wine. Since it was dark, and there was no moonlight or natural light, it was nearly impossible to see the lake, but I could hear the waves lapping off in the distance when I stood on the rear deck.

"Geez, Harry, what does your uncle do to earn enough dough to own a joint like this?" I asked in stunned disbelief at the cabin.

"He owns some kind of store and was an inventor of some successful gizmo that he patented and made a ton of dough with. I do not know too much about him. He is one relative that we do not see very often, but I agree, this cabin is fantastic!"

The summer night air was cold here in the mountains and when Harry spotted firewood stacked in front of the fireplace, he quickly went to work to build a roaring fire to take the chill off the cabin. The women checked out the bedroom and dressed the beds in the room with fresh linens that were in the bedroom closet, while Harry, Cocoa, and I, prepared the sleeping loft with our sleeping bags and other necessities.

There was no television in the cabin, but a lonely table radio sat on an end table in the living room. Maureen managed to tune in a radio station playing some soft rock-and-roll, and all of us settled in front of the fire and talked while we sipped some wine and beer. We talked, and we talked, and we talked, until the fire died, and it was time to retire for the night. We said good evening with some long-winded and somewhat silly goodbyes, considering it was almost morning, anyway. I took Cocoa out in the backyard to do what doggies do, and soon we were all sleeping soundly. I must have been very tired because I woke up to a flickering of weak daylight filtering through the windows of the cabin. Harry was still next to me in his sleeping bag; sound asleep while snoring his brains out. I jumped up, made my way down the steps from the loft, and ran into Cocoa, holding his Piggy tightly in his mouth, and waiting for me at the base of the stairs. I guess he had become restless during the night and made his way downstairs to wait for me to arrive.

"C'mon, Cocoa. Let's see what is going on."

I let him out and into the backyard and tried hard to figure out exactly where I was. After Cocoa finished doing what he had to do, we went back into the cabin. I looked around and peered out into the early morning light. The floor to ceiling window did indeed face the lake, and the view was breathtaking. The window faced east. The sun was working through some heavy clouds and it was trying hard to peek over the lake. The surface of the lake was very calm, and it looked as if it was a mirror from here.

There was an outdoor shower and an outhouse at the cabin, as well as a full indoor bathroom. I showered outside, and by the time I was finished, Harry had risen, and he cleaned up outside too. Harry and I let the women utilize the more luxurious accommodations, since "roughing it" was part of the fun of the retreat atmosphere.

The women were up shortly after us, and when they were ready, I pulled the van and boat out onto the road, and with everyone's assistance, I backed into the driveway with the boat first. We now had the boat in the driveway; it was perfectly positioned and ready to put in the lake. I then unhitched the mounts and left the trailer with the boat in the driveway while we all rode down into the center of the small town at the end of the lake. There, we found a little restaurant, and we enjoyed a wonderful home-cooked country breakfast. The waitress there was very friendly, however, she warned us of inclement weather coming in for the day.

Oh no! Inclement weather! Poor weather was certainly something that we had not even considered!

We picked up some supplies at a small grocery store in town and then headed back to the cabin.

By the time we reached the cabin, the skies had let loose, and it was raining so hard, it was hard to see in front of your face.

Between downpours, I studied the situation for launching the boat. There was a boat landing with a wooden dock and you could back directly up to the driveway, and drop the boat into the lake from your trailer and tie the boat to the dock. We had hoped for a break in the rain, at least, enough to put the boat in the water, but the rain did not ease up the entire morning. It was just not worth being soaked or stuck in some mud on the landing, to see how the boat would do in the water. Most of the time, it was raining so hard and the rain and fog were so heavy that you could not even see the lake from the cabin!

We sat around and talked, played music on the radio, had fun dancing to some music here and there, and checked the weather reports every ten minutes. We went into town for lunch and ate at a small pizzeria, and browsed the small stores and shops, trying hard not to get soaked. We took silly pictures, posed with the locals, and eventually, we wandered into a little general store that we had discovered.

I rather mindlessly followed Maureen around as she

wandered up and down the aisles. Harry and Joyce grabbed some supplies that we needed, as well as some snack food. Right when we were all about to leave, Maureen suddenly tugged at my arm and she pulled me over to a small glass display counter filled with costume jewelry and other trinkets.

"Oh, Paulie, look here! Please, look at that little hockey goalie on a chain there! It reminds me of you!" Maureen pointed in the case, and she showed me a miniature replica of a silver goaltender on the end of a chain.

She smiled ear-to-ear.

"And it comes in a set too! Look, a women's version and a version for a man too! We can match." Sure enough, the men's version had a stouter chain, a larger goalie, and was five dollars more. Oh, oh! Spending money on "stuff" was not my strongpoint.

Joyce and Harry wandered over and Harry whispered to me, "Better buy it there, lover boy, twenty-seven. Maureen is guiding ya . . . no time to be a cheapo."

I folded like a cheap tourist's camera, and within minutes, I was twenty dollars poorer, Maureen was sporting a little goalie around her neck, and I had one too!

Oh well, romance was not cheap.

We thankfully left the general store, drove back to the cabin in the driving rain, and carried all of our supplies back into the cabin. After stocking our kitchen in the cabin, we returned to the living room and played card games for most of the afternoon.

It rained, and it rained some more. In fact, it rained all Saturday afternoon, and into the early evening too. It was a good thing that we had Maureen Zipperelli with us, since she was able to talk the entire time and keep us all entertained. We told some Harry and Paul adventures and laughed a lot, but to be honest, we were starting to go a bit stir crazy. There were only so many stories that you could tell!

Maureen's mom had sent her with trays of her famous baked ziti, and Joyce and Maureen heated the food up in the kitchen. Soon, we were really "roughing" it by enjoying exquisite, homemade Italian food for dinner along with wine, soda, and beer. After dinner, we sat around and talked some more, played some more card games, listened to the radio, and enjoyed each other's company. Overall, for a soggy rainy day, we had a good time, and made the most of the day.

Despite her endless chattering and energy, Maureen was a lot of fun. She was a captivating beauty, with long brown hair that was straight in nature. She always wore the larger hoop earrings that were so popular in the 1970s and they danced and glittered in the light as she moved her head. She now hung the little goalie necklace around her neck and it happily lay against her skin, within her ample cleavage, which was fantastically revealed in the plunging neckline sweater that she wore. Her typical Italian features were Mediterranean, with dark eyes that were so dark that I think they were almost black. She had perfect olive skin, which created a contrasting backdrop to the glistening earrings in which she always wore. Maureen had a straight, thin nose, with a perfect smile. She was about medium height and as I have already mentioned, her shapely female figure was, well . . . wow!

This evening, Maureen was wearing a tight, short sleeve sweater with that aforementioned neckline, hip-hugger dungarees and sandals. I was indeed a lucky young man to be in the company of such a lovely woman. She squeezed in next to me on the sofa in the living room and smiled while she took my hand in her hand. She had finally stopped talking, and Maureen rested her head upon my shoulder.

The rain had finally stopped, the night sky had cleared, and you could feel the weather changing around now. The summer breeze had picked up right after dinnertime, and now the clouds had given way to captivating silver moonlight. The moonlight streamed in through the large window and you could faintly see the lake illuminated by the backdrop of the moonlight.

Harry built another fire since the night air was considerably cooler than the humid air we had during the day and the fire helped remove the moisture from the cabin, and it was very comfortable. Harry and Joyce tossed a blanket on the floor in front of the fire, and Cocoa curled up with Piggy next to them. The radio played on with some soft rock, and before you knew it, the dancing licks of the flame had a sleep-inducing quality and we were all dozing off.

When we all finally woke up, the fire had died out, and we lazily all said goodnight and crawled off to our "real" beds. The lazy summer day, the rain, and the fire had all combined to put the five of us into a sleeping stupor!

I woke up the next morning very early, and when I saw the perfectly clear sky and admired the magnificent golden sunrise over the lake, I knew that we were in business. Harry was still sleeping in, and I knew that soon enough, the big guy would rise. For now, Cocoa and I planned to enjoy the early morning air.

We had been waiting for this day! It was time to pull the tarpaulin off the boat and hit the water!

I showered, dressed in my cut-off shorts, my favorite rock-and-roll tee shirt, sunglasses, and my canvas sneakers. Cocoa and I were off together, checking out the landing at the water's edge and formulating a game plan as to how this tricky, boat-launching process would work. It seemed simple enough. All I had to do was to hitch the trailer back up, back the van down close to the edge of the lake, tilt the trailer down, loosen the hold down straps, and crank the boat into the water, while pulling the trailer forward.

Hmm . . . that was a lot to do, yet it seemed as if we could handle it, even if we had never launched a boat before in our lives! I was happy to see that despite the heavy rain of the previous day; the rain had not washed away the gravel of the driveway leading to the boat landing. The ground was tight, and it had drained well. I would not want to risk sinking into a sea of mud and becoming stuck.

Cocoa and I stood on the edge of the lake and even though the early morning air was cool now, you could tell that it was going to be a warm day. The sun was coming up harder now, and I could see a handful of small fishing boats with fishermen on board, out on the lake here and there. We were sure a long way from John Street and Belmont Avenue now. This was a fantastic place. Green Pine Lake was very large, and it was an idyllic setting.

I was surprised when Maureen snuck up on us as we were standing there, and she joined us on the edge of the lake. She handed me a mug of coffee, gave me a warm hug, and a coffee-laden, long and passionate kiss. Maureen then knelt down, and she greeted Cocoa with a hug.

"Would you prefer tea, Paulie?" Maureen asked me.

"No, no, no, this is fine. Thank you very much, Maureen. It will hit the spot right now. It is still a bit on the cool side out here."

"A perfect day, Paulie . . . finally," she said with a smile while gazing out over the lake. Her dark eyes were somehow sparkling in the early morning sunlight, and she looked captivating. Maureen explained that she was already dressed in her bathing suit, but she had covered up with a sweatshirt and a pair of cut-off shorts over the top of it to keep the morning chill off.

"I think it is a good time to embarrass you. I have to say, I am glad it is so cool out this morning, it will take some steam off me. My goodness, before I came down here, I was on the deck watching you work, waiting for the coffee to brew. And, well, you will turn all red, but you can take a gal's breath away. All sexy, in those shorts, sunglasses, that hair and beard, moving around here, working on the boat, checking this and that."

Maureen teased me with a gentle push, followed by a warm hug.

"See, there you go, turning red! You are such a cutie, Paulie. I will stop teasing you now and leave you alone."

Maureen was so aggressive.

"Look, I am wearin my little goalie this morning to protect us. He makes all the saves." Maureen reached down into her sweatshirt; she pulled up the little charm on the end of the chain and showed me the jewelry along with a mile-wide smile.

"Do you have yours on too, Paulie?"

I nodded and pulled mine out of my shirt to show her while she giggled in delight. Amazing how a little charm set could bring such joy.

"Great! Now, let's get this boat in the water, Paulie. I will help you!"

One thing about Maureen and the rest of the Zipperellis was that they were all hard workers. Mr. Zipperelli was a stonemason and Maureen knew what hard work was, and she did not shy away from it one bit. You could tell that she was not bashful about getting her hands dirty. I was in the van backing the boat and trailer down to the water. Maureen was watching the operation, standing in the water on the edge of the lake, when Harry and Joyce arrived on the scene. After greetings and small talk, we were all working together while guiding the boat into the water.

The excitement was building! Our dream was close to fruition! The maiden voyage of the world-famous boat named; "Unreasonable Expectations" was nearby!

Joyce was snapping photographs as Harry and Maureen tilted the trailer and cranked the boat down into the water. Cocoa was running around, barking. He, too, felt the excitement. Crank, crank, crank, crank, Harry was spinning the winch, and as I watched in the rear-view mirror, I could see the water rippling underneath the boat as it slowly made its way backwards down the boat launch into the lake.

Once we had the boat right on the edge of the trailer and into the water, Harry signaled me to pull forward. I eased the clutch up, inched forward, and "plop!" She was afloat in the water, amidst cheers of joy from all of us. How exciting for two schleps from the streets of Paterson, New Jersey to be launching a boat in some fancy lake. Harry tied the boat off to the posts on the dock, and we all gathered in celebration.

The boat was floating proudly, and it looked great sitting there in the water with its little American flag mounted on the rear deck, waving gently in the breeze. Joyce snapped picture after picture, some with us in the boat, but many solo shots of "Unreasonable Expectations" on its maiden voyage.

I climbed in and checked our repair as well as the rest of the hull. And it all looked good. The boat was solid and ready to go. We all agreed to have breakfast and then head out for a ride, but first we needed to eat.

Cocoa enjoyed a dish of his favorite food; he had also worked up an early morning appetite. Maureen and Joyce prepared eggs, toast, and bacon from the supplies we had bought yesterday, and we swigged down some coffee and tea, while thoroughly enjoying the breakfast. We cleaned up the dishes, and I went down to the boat to load up for the ride. I checked the petrol and the systems on the boat and it seemed to be all in order. I put our cooler into the boat, loaded some other supplies, our fishing poles, and tackle, and of course, my emergency radios, and the life vests.

The Old Lady Syndrome was unstoppable!

The four of us were ready to go; the engine was started and purring along when we realized that Harry was missing.

"Where is, Harry? Do you know where he went, Joyce?"

"No. I do not know where the big lug is. He said he was going to grab a few things and that he would be right down."

We waited and waited and still no, Harry. I was just about to send Cocoa to retrieve him when we saw the back door to the cabin open and Harry appeared on the rear deck.

I heard Joyce sigh and groan, and she mumbled, "Oh, my goodness. . .." Cocoa sat down on the rear deck of the boat, picked up Piggy, and squeaked it loudly.

I now knew what the surprise was, and I knew what Harry had spent his extra dough on, because as often was the case with Harry, it was quite a surprise.

Harry stood on the deck and posed. He was wearing a pair of crisp white trousers, a navy-blue jacket with silver buttons and an anchor symbol stitched on the lapel. The jacket had white clapboards with silver stripes mounted upon each of his shoulders. There were even white hash marks stitched on the cuffs of the sleeves, signifying a phony symbol to signify his "years at sea." He had a white shirt underneath the jacket, with a blue bowtie. On his head, he wore a traditional white captain's hat, fully equipped with a large, silver anchor medallion attached to the front of the hat. On his feet were highly polished white shoes with traditional white laces. Being the playboy that he was, he was wearing a pair of dark, aviator type sunglasses, and he clenched in his teeth, a brown pipe with a long stem. Harry stopped halfway down the stairs, took a puff on the pipe, and he blew the dark, fragrant smoke shaped in the letter, "O" charismatically into the air.

He looked like an admiral at a dress parade.

"Unbelievable, Paulie. Harry looks like a movie star in his captain's outfit. He is more handsome than any woman could ever have imagined," Maureen said in shocked disbelief at the sight of, "Captain Redmond."

I was at a loss for words, as we watched Harry slowly and dramatically stroll towards the boat. After all the years of Harry madness, you would think that I would be used to his antics, but this one was amazing. Once you were over the shock, I had to admit that he did look good! Too bad he was not the captain of some ocean liner, and we were only going out on an eighteen-foot boat on Green Pine Lake.

I would go out on a limb here and say that he had slightly overdressed for the occasion.

When he reached the side of the boat, he motioned to Joyce for her to grab the camera next to her, and he posed for numerous shots on the side of the boat. Harry then stopped right before he stepped into the boat. He rather emphatically held his left wrist up to his face while saying, "Let me check my watch. Right on time! Top of the hour, ten hundred hours . . . hmm."

As Harry stood and proudly posed and looked at his wrist, I noticed a large wrist watch strapped to his wrist. Suddenly, the watch burst into the loud and clear melody of the song, "Anchors Aweigh."

"Yes, in-deedy, right on time," Harry announced, when the melody ended.

"Good morning, crew. Greetings and salutations, to First Officer Henson, Able Sea Women, Dilber and Zipperelli, and Chief of Naval Operations, Cocoa Redmond. I am, Captain Redmond," Harry proudly spouted as he spoofed us.

"No, you are an idiot, Harry. Now, get in the boat and let's go!" Joyce said as she stood there with her arms folded across her chest. She had her fill of Captain Redmond for today. Cocoa gave the agreement signal of two barks followed by three tail wags as Harry climbed into the boat while roaring with laughter at Joyce's very accurate assessment of his behavior and attire.

We were ready to go, and before we launched the boat, I

had to fulfill my destiny and adhere to the Old Lady Syndrome; therefore, I stood up to present my safety speech. I had read the safety manual from the United States Coast Guard, and I was going to follow the rules.

Harry rolled his eyes and laughed as he said, "Here goes the Old Lady Syndrome, after all, what could. . .." When he saw the look in my eyes, Harry stopped in mid-sentence as he remembered all too well his last criticism of me, which almost led us straight to the clinker.

"Please do not tell the ladies to wear those stupid life vests. It will cover up their fantastic chests!" Harry came out with a stupid protest.

"I think he is such a cutie. Please, go ahead, Paulie," Maureen supported me. "I would be a little more interested if you did not have your shirt on but go ahead." Maureen and Joyce giggled as she teased me.

Maureen was so aggressive.

"I think he is a cute hippie too, so please, Captain Blowhard, shut up and leave him alone," Joyce said. "We are all listening, twenty-seven. Pay no attention to the dope in the fraudulent uniform."

While Captain Redmond roared with laughter, I showed the gals and Cocoa where the life jackets were stowed, the fire extinguisher, the switch for the bilge pump, and I tucked the two-way radio on my belt with the belt clip. After my presentation, I untied the boat from the dock and signaled to Harry that we were set to go.

Harry eased the throttle up, the boat started to move, and Harry gently steered us away from the dock in reverse, while I leaned over and gently pushed us off from the dock. I watched the input and output of the water out of the pipes over the rear deck, and all looked normal.

The boat was rolling! We were underway!

Harry slowly moved out into the lake, and I darted from side-to-side, trying hard to gauge the depth of the water in the lake. The water was murky from the rain, and it was hard to see if there were any submerged obstacles.

"Go slow. Go along very slowly, Harry. This water seems shallow, and there could be stumps or something else hidden here. I cannot tell, so you need to watch with me and pay attention." Cocoa was sitting upon the rear deck with Piggy firmly entrenched in his mouth, occasionally dropping Piggy and barking in delight as we moved away from the dock.

Joyce was snapping away with her camera, capturing forever in perpetuity, the initial launch of, "Unreasonable Expectations."

"Yeah, yeah, yeah! I got it, ya, old lady. Captain Redmond is an expert pilot of this craft." Harry pushed the throttle up a little more, and the engine roared to life. The boat sped up and started to cruise into the lake. It was becoming warmer now, and the gals slipped out of their covers, revealing their fabulous figures in their swimsuits.

Harry's vision had finally come to life!

He smiled, and his eyes darted back and forth in his head as he drooled and glanced at the women in their swimsuits. He was sweating like a pig now as his hormones were bouncing more than the tachometer gauge was on the dashboard. Captain Redmond stuck his stupid pipe in his mouth, and he was nervously puffing on it like a smoke stack.

"Yaaahhhoooo! Here we go!" Harry bellowed as he pushed the throttle up a little more.

I knew Harry could not take his eyes off the women's attributes, and he was now useless to watch the water, since his attention was now clearly only upon the women and their chests. I resigned myself to the diligent mission to watch the lake surface for any hidden obstacles.

Something kept telling me that the water here was very shallow.

I leaned over, and tapped Harry on the shoulder and said, "Easy, Harry. Pay attention. I think I see some stumps here . . . slow down a little." I turned and waved Cocoa down off the deck and said, "Cocoa, go and sit down with Joyce and Maureen and get off that back deck." Cocoa immediately jumped down and sat next to the women, and just when he landed on the seat, it happened.

"BANG!"

The boat tipped and lurched a little to the side. Cocoa barked, and the women gave out a little cry while Harry fell forward a little. His stupid pipe fell out of his mouth, and it bounced on the front of the boat, made two dramatic hops, and toppled into the water.

"My pipe! Geez! Damn! My pipe went overboard! What was that big noise and bump, twenty-seven? What happened?" He eased the throttle down and the boat slowed down, and Harry then shut off the engine. I leaned over the side and swallowed hard when I saw it. It was a big, old stump. In fact, I could now see many stumps in this area because the water was a lot clearer farther out here in the lake.

"We hit a stump, Harry! Check for any water!"

"A stump! What kind of lake has stumps?" I ignored Harry. The women jumped up, and we were all checking for leaks.

"Look, Paulie, over there! Look at the warning sign in the water! On that buoy, there," Maureen said as she pointed to a sign hanging on a buoy bouncing in the waves of the lake.

In big, giant, ominous block letters the floating sign read, "WARNING! UNDERWATER OBSTACLES IN THIS AREA! PROCEED WITH EXTREME CAUTION!"

Oh geezzzz. . ..

"LOOK!" Joyce pointed to a trickle of water swirling around our feet that had entered the hull.

Suddenly, the happy maiden voyage of our beloved, "Unreasonable Expectations" was looking more like the voyage of the Titanic.

I was a problem solver, and I knew that I needed to remain calm. Harry was generally useless at times like these. "Oh boy, we have sprung a leak. The stump must have nailed the hull and gashed it. Everyone, please remain calm, we are only five hundred feet or so from shore."

Harry took his captain's hat off and tossed it in anger into the bottom of the boat while he yelled, "FRIGGIN' STUMPS!" The boat bounced and gurgled, and it felt as if it dipped a little in the water. "Geezzz, twenty-seven! I think that we are sinking!"

I jumped up and flipped the switch for the bilge pump, and the little pilot light turned red. I could hear the pump taking in water and I leaned over the side and saw the output from the pump, chucking water back into the lake.

Yup, we were sinking.

"Yes, Harry, we have a hole in the boat and technically, we are sinking. However, that is why you brought this old lady on board today. I have safeguards in place for this type of emergency. One of them is the bilge pump that you teased me about and it is now running and pumping. I hope it can stay ahead of the water long enough for us to get back to shore. Now, Harry, start the engine, and slowly push us back to shore. Stay calm, Harry."

"Stay calm, stay calm! We are sinking, Paul! We will soon all be at the bottom of this stupid lake! Davy Jones and octopuses are down there under the water."

"Now, who is acting like an old lady? Please, put your life vests on just in case, even though, I think for obvious reasons, that the water is shallow here, and we will be back to shore in a minute or two."

The women nodded, grabbed the life vests, and put them on. Joyce put the life vest on Cocoa, who grabbed his Piggy and held him tightly in his mouth. He had lost a Piggy once, and he was not risking losing another one to Green Pine Lake. I pulled my tee shirt off, tossed it aside, and put my life vest on.

Maureen, even in the middle of a tragic situation yelled, and whistled at me, "Too bad, it took us to sink for you to show us some skin, Paulie! Please, feel free to strip down some more!"

She was so aggressive.

I grabbed a vest for Harry and tossed it to him.

He picked up his captain's hat and placed it back on his head. He then stood proudly in defiance as he bellowed, "I will go down with my boat! I refuse to allow my beloved, 'Unreasonable Expectations' to sink alone!"

How dramatic. The water was only a few feet deep. He could stand up in it.

Joyce stood up and yelled at Harry, "Put the damn life vest on and steer us into shore, you big dope. If you had not been staring at our chests and listened to Paul, maybe you would have missed the stump!"

Amazingly, Harry listened to our pleas and instructions. We glided back to shore, and as we came in close to the dock, I jumped out of the boat and onto the dock. As Harry came closer, Maureen tossed me the rope, and I tied the boat off.

"Leave the boat running so the pump stays on!" I shouted, ran to the cabin, and grabbed the keys to the van. I then jumped in the van and backed it down into the water. We untied the boat, lined the boat up on the trailer, hooked it back up, and cranked it out of the water and back onto the trailer.

We had made it, and Davy Jones would have to wait for another day.

Now that the boat was on the trailer, we all peered underneath it to see where the damage was. Sure enough, there was a gash about a foot long and an inch or so wide, right along the bottom of the hull. Water was still dripping out from the hole. Our boating experience had lasted all of about five hundred feet and twenty minutes.

Harry sighed when he saw the hole, and he slowly stood

up. His wristwatch burst into the melody of "Anchors Away" and Harry tore it off his wrist and angrily tossed it on the ground. He took his hat off, shook his head, loosened his bowtie, and then tossed his hat on the ground next to the singing watch.

He put his arm around my shoulders, while he said forlornly, "No sipping of cognac, no golden sunsets over the lake, no wind in my face, no waving and blowing kisses from the ladies, whose huge breasts are jammed into skimpy bikinis, no pipe, well, I did have one but it went over the side. It is all gone. My dream is gone."

I nodded my head in agreement, slowly walked over to the side of the boat, and pointed at the name and artwork painted on the side. I said, "I guess you had, unreasonable expectations, old buddy. The boat lived up to its name!"

We did not allow the tragedy of the boat to spoil our day. It was too fabulous a day for that to have happened. Two young men, two gorgeous young women, a faithful dog, a summer holiday at a lake, a log cabin nestled in the pines, and an old boat with a gash in the bottom of it.

Yeah, yeah, yeah, well, aside from the gash in the bottom of the boat, it was a magical time to be young and to be alive.

We swam in the lake, and then we fished off the dock for hours and hours. We laughed when Joyce caught the biggest fish. Joyce reeled in a beautiful, largemouth bass that caused Cocoa to bark and scamper up and down the shoreline at the sight of the fish. I am sure that he had never seen a fish that big!

We sat on the dock and dangled our feet in the lake, and watched the boats go back and forth and waved to the occupants. Harry would yell out to each and every one that went by, "Watch out for those stupid ass stumps! They are tricky bastards!"

Even though it was not quite the golden summer sunset, in which Harry had dreamt of, the women did their best to duplicate his vision. Standing on the shoreline of the lake, with the sinking sun as a backdrop, the two gals posed for silly and slightly revealing pictures in their bathing suits, while they blew phony kisses to Harry.

That night, we cooked hot dogs and hamburgers over an open pit in the backyard next to the lake, played the radio, drank beer and wine, and shared more stories. The boat, of course, was a little easier to laugh about now. There remained little doubt that it was still painful, but now it was just another chapter in the endless parade of Harry and Paul adventures.

Soon, the day turned into a magical summer night, and I found myself in the cabin, alone with Maureen sitting on the sofa, in front of the fire. Harry and Joyce had disappeared, and we were alone.

Even Cocoa was curled up somewhere with Piggy.

Both Maureen and I had dabbled in a bit more wine and beer than we were accustomed to, and these moments have a way of advancing rather quickly, especially when you have a bit of the brew and fermented grape floating around in you. We shared in some special moments, and once she coached me over my initial embarrassment, I shared more of myself than I ever had with a woman before. Still, I realized that I had no birth control protection with me and when we came very close to reaching a point of no return; I kept my wits about me. I knew deep in my mind that these types of commitments meant a lot more than just some pent-up passion and alcohol-fueled ardor, which could have repercussions for you for an entire lifetime. I was in love with the dream of a career in professional hockey, and my dream consumed my mind and my life, too.

My own determination, despite the rather intense and passionate circumstances, remained strong, and I narrowly avoided a major commitment to a woman while I was still so young. It was not easy, there you are, a gorgeous woman next to you, both of you in various stages of undress, naked and exposed in the envelopment of passion, underneath the vague disguise of unproven love, a bit of a buzz going on, and you keep your wits about you.

I was proud of myself.

I learned a lot more at that lake that weekend than just to beware of submerged stumps. I learned about being a man, and the responsibilities that come with it. Maureen, although she was clearly disappointed, understood, and she softly whispered to me about how she always had those troublesome, "Unreasonable expectations."

Regardless, it had been a special night and Maureen was a special young woman. We shared our bodies and our passion, but, for now, we kept it all within reasonable boundaries.

The next morning, we ate breakfast, laundered the bed linens, cleaned up the cabin while making sure it was spotless, hitched up the boat, packed the van, and headed back on the rather long ride down to 20 John Street.

We returned in time to catch the enjoyment of the biggest shindig of all the summer parties at the Redmond house, which was the famous Labor Day bash. Every Labor Day, the Redmonds and the entire neighborhood went all out, in an effort to wrap up another summer with a farewell shindig to remember. These were the holiday parties, where every year, there was a different theme to the party. One year, it was Caribbean Islands; the next year was a Hawaiian Lau, and so on and so forth. This year was a country and western theme, and let me tell you that one had some major influence on our lives.

Once more, it is like a broken record but that is an entirely other story!

We told everyone the story of the boat and the sad fate, but once folks realized we were not heartbroken over the damage, and heard that we still had a great time, well then, it sure received a lot of laughs and jokes. Cliffy, of course, had a choice description for Harry's boat steering abilities!

All the women in attendance at the picnic were thrilled, and the men of the neighborhood were disappointed when Joyce and Maureen decided not to go swimming! After partying all day and a good part of the night, I took Maureen home. We shared a long, tender, and somewhat tearful goodbye, and the weekend had ended.

Autumn was now upon us, and the boat sat for a few months in Harry's driveway. We had repaired the gash the next week after the holiday with the same method that Mr. Redmond had instructed us with the "Cliffy" repair. I was quite sure the boat was solid and it would float for many more years.

For some reason, the magic was gone from the boat.

Harry traded in his captain's hat and other unused accessories, for a high-end camera with all the accessories known to man, the era of the boat had passed into perpetuity, and Harry and the rest of the Redmonds were off onto their next wild phase in life.

Our interests had changed. I was embroiled in my hockey goalie clinic, and Harry was into being a photographer now, therefore, Harry and I decided to sell the boat. It was clogging up the Redmond's driveway, and we knew we would not have the time or the money to keep it maintained.

Officer Hough came along one day and offered us eight hundred dollars for it, and it was gone. Ironically, Cliffy's prediction of turning a profit on it had turned out to be quite accurate!

The boat was past history for us, a closed era, and it was now just a memory, another adventure in the seemingly endless adventures of Harry and Paul.

Maureen Zipperelli and I dated quite often, and she came to most of my hockey games. We eventually shared a number of other very special moments and with the proper protection and responsibilities in place, we shared our bodies and our love, too. Maureen always hinted for us to make some plans for our future, but I would never promise her anything, nor make any firm commitments. Hockey was my life now, and I had this dream to play professionally that just would not let go of me. Maureen had been attending a beauty school to become a hairdresser; she had finished her education, and she now had a very good job at a local hair salon.

One Friday night, in late November of that same year, when I had some free time, I called Maureen up to ask her out for dinner and a movie.

"No, Paulie . . . I am sorry, but I cannot go out."

Maureen's voice and tone were sad and very subdued. Her usual exuberance was missing. Over the telephone, I sensed some type of significant unhappiness inside of Maureen Zipperelli.

"I have to tell you that I am going with my family over to Italy for quite a long time. We are leaving next week. I was going to call you in a few days, you know, to let you know of my plans. My dad and my uncle have a good job lined up with a large, stone restoration project, which will keep them both very busy for a year or more. I want to stay with our family and learn about my roots, you know, see the country, and see what my heritage is all about."

"Wow! That is very exciting, Maureen. Someday, I want to go to England and Wales and do the same."

"Yes, you should, but you will not be escaping lost love, Paulie, as I am."

I paused, because I was too stupid to realize where the conversation was going.

"I need to escape from you, Paul John Henson. I can never compete with the dream you have of becoming a professional hockey player, and I wonder if you will ever be able to escape it too. I have loved you since we were little kids growing up together, and maybe, no, not maybe, but I know that I always will. An ocean might be far enough to dull that pain, but honestly, I doubt it. While I can never have you, I still have my little goalie on the chain to hold near and dear to my heart, and to remind me of you. He will be just as you are, hanging near my heart forever, protecting me and making all the saves. He is in many ways, just as you are. He always makes all the saves. I thank you again for that wonderful weekend we spent together, and for me, it will be forever Labor Day in my mind. We shared our love and our bodies in many special moments, but that weekend was beyond words. It remains in my heart forever. I wish you all the best, Paulie. Guys like you, are far and few between, and some lucky gal might be able to break the grip of ice hockey on your soul."

Maureen paused for a long time. I could tell she was collecting herself, and that this conversation was going to end rather painfully.

"Perhaps, some fortunate gal, someday, will do better than I was able to do. It is about so much more than just the sport of hockey for you, Paulie. It is about playing the position of goalie, in how you can face challenges of not only the game, but of your life, and what it brings to your spirit when you win, and in some cases, when you lose. You are such a deep thinker, and a caring and wonderful person, as well as a complex, young man, Paul John Henson. The ice is where you are always the most comfortable, Paul, it is where you can hide behind that goalie mask, and no one really knows who the real Paul John Henson is. You are a wonderful young man, and such a cutie, but how do you say in Welsh . . . a revoth man too. I wish you all the luck and love in the world."

Her voice now choked off, and it filled with strong emotions. And it was one of the few times that I could recall in which Maureen was unable to speak.

She finally managed to say, "Sometimes, it is so amazing how hard it is to achieve your dreams, Paulie. I love you, Paul John Henson, now, and I always will, because to me, in my mind, it will be forever Labor Day. Goodbye."

"Click."

The telephone line went dead before I could even say anything. Looking back, I am not sure that I would have even known what to say, anyway. I reached into my tee shirt, pulled out the goalie on the chain, and stared at it for quite a long time.

I never saw or heard from Maureen Zipperelli ever again.

"May I help you, sir? That is one fine looking boat! It is on clearance today. You know, the summer is over now, so we will give you a fabulous deal on it!"

A young salesman had wandered over and I came back to reality. I realized that I was actually sitting inside one of the display boats, when my mind had wandered away, and my memories had captured me once again. I was a bit embarrassed and perhaps even a little red-faced at my incessant daydreaming. I looked down in my hands at the little hockey goalie hanging from the chain, that I was, for some reason, turning over and over in my hands, while I had been lost in my thoughts.

"No, no, no, I am sorry. I am not in the market for a boat, sir. Thank you for the offer, though," I said as I climbed out of the boat and stood next to the salesman.

"Hey, cool goalie jewelry there. I guess ya played some hockey. I have never seen anythin' like that before." He pointed at the goalie necklace, but I did not answer him. Instead, I hid the charm once again behind my shirt. He seemed to sense that it was for some reason . . . a sore spot. Therefore, he did not dwell upon the necklace; instead, he continued the sales pitch.

"Well, okay about the boat. Too bad, they are a real blast, and you sure looked good sitting in there."

"No, I have been there once before, and while they are

fun, they do have a strange way of giving you some nasty, unreasonable expectations," I said with a smile.

The salesman shrugged his shoulders because he was clearly puzzled, while he mumbled, "I guess."

I went to walk away when I suddenly had an impulsive thought. I turned and asked him, "You would not happen to have in this section—any captain's hats on clearance sale now would you, sir?"

He looked at me and smiled. "Sure, right over here. We need to unload them for the season too."

Then, I suddenly remembered the finishing touch to it all, and I asked him, "How about a wristwatch that plays the song, 'Anchors Aweigh' at the top of the hour? Do you sell those?"

The salesman stopped, looked at me with a puzzled look on his face, and he said, "No, we do not have one of them. In fact, I have never even heard of such a thing."

"I did not think so. That one will be difficult to find. I guess it would be an unreasonable expectation for you to stock those. I will settle for the hat though."

The salesman waved for me to follow him.

I followed him and while we walked along, I said, "Now one of them hats I sure could go for, meant to get one a long time ago, and never got around to it. Yeah, yeah, yeah, I need a captain's hat, a snifter of cognac, and a golden, summer sunset over a lake, a smoking jacket, and a pipe. Oh yes, I need to include a pretty gal stuffed into a skimpy bikini, waving and blowing kisses to me. Now that is a reasonable expectation."

The salesman turned and pointed at the hats on the shelf and laughed.

"Well, we have the hats. As far as the rest of it goes, you are on your own, pal."

He was a rather helpful salesman, especially considering that he just lost out on a "concussion" on the sale of a boat.

"Thank you," I said, while I pushed all my long hair out

of the way, picked out a hat and I put the hat on my head. I checked out how I looked in a mirror mounted on the wall in the store. I did not look as good as Harry had looked, but the hat did not look too bad.

Forever, Labor Day, in our minds.

Yes, I think that was quite a reasonable expectation indeed.

THE END

The Old Chair

The telephone rang in my office in Newark, New Jersey, late in the afternoon on a hot July day. We were currently embroiled in one of those typical summer heat waves that seemed to go on and on for weeks at a time with temperatures every day up near one hundred degrees. It had been a brutal stretch of weather, and the heat and humidity drain the energy out of your body and eventually drags you down.

I picked the telephone up on the second ring, "Hello, this is Pastor Paul Henson."

"Hello, Bishop Henson. It is Henry Whipley Junior calling."

"Hello, Henry. Please call me, Pastor Paul. Even after a few years in this job, I still struggle with the bishop title." After the initial happy greeting, I sensed this conversation had an ominous purpose. Henry's voice suddenly started to quiver and shake.

"Oh yes, sorry, Pastor Paul. I needed to call you with some very bad news. We, we, well—we lost my mother last night, pastor. She went to be with the Lord. . .." His voice trailed off, and I felt my heart sink.

"I am so sorry, Henry. I am so sorry. Your mother was a wonderful, loving woman, who loved the Lord with all of her heart. I loved her too, with all my heart. We spent many wonderful times together, studying scripture, laughing and discussing our faith and sharing stories. She was very special to me, and when I needed the support at

Reunion Lutheran Church, she was one of my strongest supporters. I know you and everyone, will miss her terribly, but take consolation in the fact that I know there is a celebration in Heaven today of a joyous magnitude. The gates were wide open for her. I have never known a person who had greater faith. She is in a wonderful place, Henry."

"Thank you, Pastor Paul. Thank you for your kind words about Mom. She went quietly in her sleep, and I found her this morning so peaceful in her bed with the most wonderful smile on her face. There was no long sickness, no pain, just a peaceful passing for her, Pastor Paul. She was one of a kind and I miss her already, more than I ever realized that I would. She loved you too, pastor. She always spoke about you with such admiration and pride. Even though she cried the day, you left the pastor's office at Reunion Lutheran Church, she was so proud of you when you became the bishop. She talked about it forever. And as we both know—my mother sure could talk."

Henry sounded as if he was choking back tears but in between, he managed to laugh at the comment about Mrs. Whipley's proclivity for non stop chattering. I joined in the laughter and Henry was correct. Mrs. Whipley could really wear your ears out.

"Yes, she could sure talk it up a bit, Henry, but I always felt that was part of her magic."

"Yes, it was, Pastor Paul. She had left specific instructions for you to conduct her funeral. I mean no disrespect toward Pastor Braun Jr. at Reunion Lutheran Church, but my mother, well. . .."

I cut him off in his conversation to make it a bit easier for him to explain, "I will be honored, Henry. I will be glad to explain the situation to Pastor Braun Junior. I can assure you that he will understand."

"Thank you, Pastor Paul. I will call you with the details as soon as the arrangements have been finalized." After some more small talk, we hung up, and I felt the pangs of sorrow deep in my heart. The memories of the times I spent with Mrs. Whipley came rushing back to me in a wave. She had been such a staunch supporter of my mission and ministry. I was sure that without her faith, honesty, and support that I would have been a complete failure in my first assignment as a Lutheran pastor at Reunion Lutheran Church.

She owned a Dutch colonial style home on the edge of the property of Reunion Lutheran Church, and as far as I knew, she lived in that house the majority of her entire life. She also was the largest donor of money and maybe even personal time to Reunion, but that was not her greatest attribute.

Her greatest attribute was her faith.

She was unique in her unwavering faith and the glimmer in her eye whenever it was fortified was very special to witness. Most people considered her an eccentric quack, but many folks just did not know her as well as I did. She often told wild stories of how she saw angels hovering above the church, and spaceships carrying visitors from Heaven, and she was never afraid to tell anyone that they were a big part of her life. Her faith would not allow these unusual elements not to exist. There was no question to her that it was all very real.

She also was a key person in an event in my life that I would never forget or would even have a chance at forgetting. A time when I knew that Mrs. Whipley was correct in believing that God had intervened, to teach all of us that when everything else is lost, hope, faith, and miracles are sent our way to reassure us that we should never, ever, give up. I also knew that although many people considered her an eccentric whacko, I knew better. Her quiet insight, her intelligence, and her unique ability of seeing deep into a person's mind and soul, made her very special.

I bowed my head at my desk and prayed. I said a prayer of thankfulness for God for having sent such a wonderful person as Mrs. Whipley into my life. I said a prayer of praise for her life, and I knew that someday, we would reunite together in heaven, and she would most likely talk my ears off to catch up on all that I had missed!

The heat wave continued, on and on, day after day, the same weather.

It was a terrible, hot July day, when Pastor Braun Jr. and I conducted the funeral for Mrs. Whipley at Reunion Lutheran Church. Indeed, it was the type of day that will make you drip with sweat from the top of your head, all the way to the very tip of your toes. There, the two of us were dressed in black suits and heavy, black robes. My goodness!

I had wished that it were under happier circumstances for me to return to Reunion Lutheran Church, but it was certainly enjoyable to return to such familiar surroundings, to preach from the pulpit that I had grown up in, and return to where I learned how to be a pastor.

In addition, my lovely wife Binky Henson told me, "This funeral is a celebration of a life, rather than a solemn occasion. Mrs. Whipley was all about joy. She was not about sorrow."

My wonderful wife, of course, was once more correct in her accurate analysis. After the service and the graveside burial, there was a family gathering at a local restaurant. There, Binky and I had the chance to meet so many familiar parishioners of Reunion Lutheran Church, as well as some new ones, and celebrate a remarkable life along with the Whipley family. Binky was correct. This was a celebration of a life, not a solemn service, and it sure was nice to get out of the heat, out of my robe, and into an air-conditioned environment.

"Pastor Paul, Mrs. Henson, it is so nice to see you again, and thank you for the wonderful service for Mom. It was remarkable, and as usual, you were such a powerful speaker. I know Mom is smiling down from Heaven watching all of us," Henry Whipley Jr. said as he came over and greeted me at the restaurant. "It is not every day that a bishop comes and conducts a funeral service, but I know Mom, as well as my entire family appreciated it."

"Oh, please, Henry. I am nothing special, and besides, I would not have had it any other way!"

"Pastor Paul, I know how busy you are, and I am sure your schedule is jammed these days, but we had the reading of Mom's will, and she left quite a large sum to Reunion Lutheran Church, as well as funds that were designated to you at the Lutheran District offices. Our family attorney will be in contact with Pastor Braun Junior and with you for the details on the disbursements of the funds. As you know, my father was quite successful in business and our estate is a little large."

I nodded my head in acknowledgment of the funds in which the Whipleys always were faithfully donating to the church.

"Thank you, Henry. Thank you, so very much." I shook his hand again to thank him for his family's generosity.

Henry continued, "I also have to tell you that she left something for you at the house. She also has a sealed envelope with your name on it, and specific instructions that you should receive the item and the envelope at the same time. I am sorry to impose upon you, but you will need to bring your jeep with that old trailer, if you still have it, and some plastic tarps, ropes, and hold-down straps to put the item in the trailer. I am hesitant to say anything else since Mother was very specific in her instructions that this needed to be a surprise."

I was a bit puzzled, as was Binky, but of course; I agreed to meet Henry at the house when I had some free time to ride out there. I told him that I would check my calendar and give him a telephone call in the next few days to arrange the appointment.

A few days later, I had a break in my schedule, and I arranged with Henry to meet him at the house and procure whatever it was that Mrs. Whipley had wanted me to have.

Thankfully, the heat wave had finally broken, and the day we decided to drive out to Mrs. Whipley's house was sunny and with considerably milder temperatures. It is funny how when a prolonged heat wave does finally end, a summer day with temperatures in the high eighties seems mild.

Binky rode with me, and I must say that the memories came flooding back for both of us. The entire ride out there was a trip down memory lane. We had lived there in the parsonage at Reunion Lutheran Church for many years; our children were born there, and to a certain extent, everyone all grew up there.

It was a very emotional outing.

Binky and I arrived at the Whipley home and Henry and his wife, Karen Whipley, greeted us. After some small talk and greetings, Henry led us into the living room of the home. The surroundings were so familiar to me, it seemed so strange, not to see Mrs. Whipley sitting in this room, in her old chair next to the side window, sipping tea, and chatting away to me on some Biblical subject or the latest concern of hers. In many ways, it was very sad, but in other ways, it was uplifting to know how full a life she had enjoyed.

"Pastor Paul, did the attorney contact your office with regard to the financial endowment from Mother's estate?"

"Yes, he did, Henry. Thank you so much. We are working with him on the transfer process. It was a fabulous amount of money and a wonderful, thoroughly, thought-out plan. The church will move forward as per your mother's instructions with the investment and the principle. Thank you again so very much. I have my assistant working on a proper thank you and dedication. I also know how appreciative the congregation of Reunion Lutheran Church and Pastor Braun Junior are of the endowment left for the church. Even in all my years here, I am somewhat embarrassed to admit that I never knew your family owned the property adjacent to the house. You know . . . the property that the endowment papers mention and detail. It is our wish to be able to expand Reunion Lutheran Church even more, and I know that it was your mother's wish too."

"Oh, good, Pastor Paul. Yes, it is wonderful indeed. Now, I will need to decide exactly what to do with the house, but that is down the road a little. Well, I am almost embarrassed to show you what Mother has left specifically for you, but it is right here in the living room. She also had given very exact instructions on providing you with this letter, in which you needed to read before taking away the gift."

Henry looked at me, then at Binky, and he pointed to the chair in which Mrs. Whipley always sat during our meetings.

"Here it is, Pastor Paul. Mother left to you—her old chair! Yes, her old chair right there. The chair that she always sat in next to the side window facing the church. Mother was a bit unusual, but she always had a purpose to her eccentric behavior. Here is the envelope." Henry handed me a large, sealed brown envelope.

"A chair, dear Paul?" Binky held my hand as she saw the puzzled look upon my face. I looked at Binky and nodded, then to Henry and his wife, and I smiled.

"Well, I am very happy to receive it, but I am not exactly sure of why. Perhaps, we need to read the contents of this envelope to find out," I said as I turned the envelope over and examined the address on the front. It was simply addressed to, "Pastor Paul John Henson."

"We will leave you and Mrs. Henson alone to read the contents, Pastor Paul," Henry said as he gently took his wife by her hand to lead her into the other room.

"No, no, no, please, I want you to share in this. I think that I knew your mother well enough, to say that there is much more to this than just her old chair. Please stay. I will read the contents aloud to everyone."

Henry invited me to sit down, and I decided to sit in the old chair as I opened the envelope. Henry carried some chairs from the dining room into the living room, and Binky, Henry, and Karen sat down in a circle facing me. I carefully opened the seal on the envelope and pulled out a handwritten letter. I recognized the handwriting as being that of Mrs. Whipley's writing. Even in her advanced age, she had such wonderful handwriting. The date on the letter was about one year earlier than today's date.

I began to read aloud to the group. . ..

"Dear Pastor Paul,

If you are reading this letter, then I have left this planet and gone to be with our Lord. Oh, the joy of what I am experiencing! I am sure that the joy of my glorious entrance to Heaven will overshadow the sorrow of my leaving Earth! We had spoken so many times of the wonder of it all, and it is with open arms that I go to meet the Lord Jesus, and be reunited with my dear Henry and my wonderful Timothy! The joy of faith and the message of hope and peace is something that I have so looked forward to seeing in person. Please do not be sad at my demise, but be joyous in knowing that our faith has restored us all.

If you are reading this, then you will also be aware of the fact that I have left to you my old chair. If I know you well enough, my dear Pastor Paul, then you will be sitting in it right now, while you read this letter."

I could not suppress a laugh at her prediction of my behavior, and the rest of the group joined in. I continued to read the letter.

"You see, of all the people whom I know, you were the one person who I knew that I could leave that old chair to, and who would understand why I did so. Because of your remarkable ability to see things, not so much for what they are now, but for what they may have been at one time, you would be the one person who would understand that it is not just an old chair.

My dear Pastor Paul, it is a memory bank.

The chair was my mother's chair and before that, it was my grandmother's chair. It is very old, but the heritage that the chair brings is only part of the story. The most important part of this story is where the chair has been, and where it brought me in my life. It was always there in the corner, waiting for me with open arms to accept me, to hold me and support me, and to a great extent, it was there to comfort me. It was very reliable, it was very faithful, and it never spoke poorly of me, or failed to hold me up. In many ways that old chair represented my faith in God and Jesus."

I paused as I looked and smiled at Binky and the Whipleys.

"She has used quite an analogy here," I said.

I continued to read, "It was here in this chair that I was sitting, when my dear Henry got down on one knee in front of me and proposed to me. Here in this chair when we were young, my dear Henry, and I kissed, hugged, and well, you know, the rest. It was here in this chair that I wept until my tears were gone, when I read a letter from the United States Marine Corps telling me that my oldest son, Timothy, died in action in Vietnam. I also sat here and wept, until I had no more tears left to cry, on the night that I buried my dear husband, and when I buried my mother, and my father, and a son, and two brothers. I also jumped for joy while sitting in this chair when my water broke, and I rushed to the hospital to give birth to my beloved Henry Junior. I sat right here and breastfed my babies, held them and comforted them when they were sick or hurt, and shared in their laughter and joy. It was here in this chair, my old cat Missy climbed into, she gave birth to a litter of kittens, and then later on, I held the smallest of them as she struggled to hold on to life. I cried my eyes out, as the little kitten died in my arms, while I prayed, right here in this chair. It was here in this chair that I listened to my Harvey Crooner records, and watched men land on the moon on the television, and enjoyed the twinkle of Christmas lights from our Christmas tree standing in front of me. While I sat here, I read my Bible cover to cover at least a thousand times, and I sang songs to my children and to myself when I was alone.

However, I was never alone, Pastor Paul, because this old chair was always here with me, to hold me and support me.

Now, Pastor Paul, I have to admit that I spilled some tea, and some coffee, and even a spot or two of wine on this old chair while I sat here, but I know you will not mind. After all, it is part of the character of the chair. Battle scars of a lifetime of support for me! It was here in this chair, I watched out my window, when an old jeep pulled up in the parking lot of Reunion Lutheran Church. I sat in silence, watching as a young, long-haired, hippie pastor held his wife by her hand. And together, they walked into the church to face the mission that the Lord had sent them to do. It was here in this chair that I wept with joy, when I knew that God had sent you to save our beloved church, and I knew you were the one person who could do it. In this chair, I watched as the parking lot for Sunday worship services filled with cars from end to end, as the members returned, and our church grew and grew.

I sat here, and you sat opposite me many a time, while we took turns reading from scripture together. Then you told me your wonderful stories of time bombs in cupboards, swimming pools that exploded, exciting ice hockey games and the championships of the past, and many of those wonderful, heartwarming, and crazy adventures of Harry and Paul.

It was here in this chair that I watched the lights glowing in your office late into the night, and then they would click off. I would then watch you slowly walk across the parking lot to the parsonage, your head down, hands in your pockets while you were pondering your day and your next quest in the mission of our Lord. It was here in this chair that I watched you leave with your beloved Binky as you carefully placed her in your jeep to go to the hospital for the birth of your first child. I watched from this chair as your children came home in your arms. I watched from here as they grew up before my eyes, and I watched as the love between you and your wonderful wife grew to fill the world with joy. I sat here and watched while you decorated the parsonage porch for Christmas, and as you and that wonderful Mr. Redmond taught your son how to play hockey in the parking lot in front of me. I watched from here as you held Heather Sarah as she took her first pedals of her bicycle, and while you and Mr. Redmond held little Blue Cloud's hands, as she tried to walk up your driveway. In addition, yes, I do confess; I watched from this chair as you held Mrs. Henson in your arms, and you two kissed in front of the parsonage, and you held onto each other's bodies in wonderful locations, as if you were lovers on your first date."

I looked at Binky and smiled as I saw the tears rolling down her cheeks.

"And most of all Pastor Paul, it was while I sat in this chair that I saw the signs sent from Heaven and from God to our lives, and to our church, and you believed in me and my faith enough to confirm that miracles do, in fact, exist in this tired, old, world. Here is where I sat in this chair, the night that I heard you were going to leave us, and become the next Lutheran Bishop. I wept with happiness for you and with sadness at our loss. There were countless other memories, both happy and sad, while I sat in this chair my dear Pastor Paul. Countless memories.

Now, Pastor Paul, many folks would look at the old chair you are sitting in now, and say it is just an old chair. You and I know that it is so much more than just an old chair.

It is an old friend in which to share memories with, in your own life. The upholstery will hold your tears and accidental spills without complaint. The arms will be steady, hold you tight, and keep you warm. The old wooden frame is still strong, and it will keep you straight and true when you are shaky, and no matter what, it will be there for you, in the corner of some room like a faithful friend that you can always count on to be there. I know in my heart that you will share and create your own memories with it to last another lifetime.

Yours in faith and the Lord's love,

Mrs. Henry Whipley."

I stopped reading and looked up at Binky and the Whipleys. No one in the room had dry eyes, and I smiled at theirs and my own tears of joy. I carefully folded the letter and stood up.

"Shall we pray?" was all I asked as I held out my hands. We all stood in a circle and I prayed for the group, "Thank you, Lord, for the life and the times of Mrs. Henry Whipley. Thank you for her quiet insight, and her love and hope that all of us can better understand all the wonderful things that you have given to us all. Amen."

Henry helped me load the chair onto the trailer. Binky and I thanked the Whipleys for all they had done for us, and we promised to stay in touch.

I placed the old chair in a corner of my study in my suite

of offices, in a place of honor. I would sit in it and read the Bible, or ponder ideas for a sermon, or for one of my latest writings.

I had to admit that the old chair did have a comforting influence on me.

It was in early September, right after Labor Day, and I had an old friend of mine, Pastor Jim O'Malley, stop by to see what I was doing and share some old memories. Jim and I went back a long way, in fact, too long. He and I were both professional hockey players a long time ago, and we were at one-time, mortal enemies on opposite teams vying for a league championship.

However, that is a long story for another time and place. Now, ironically, we had both come full circle, and we were great friends, and both working in the same professions once more.

Life is so full of twists and turns.

I met Jim in my office, we decided to sit in the study and have a cup of coffee together. I offered Jim the old chair to sit in, and I chose a chair next to him. As Jim sat down with the coffee in his hand, some of it spilled onto the seat of the chair.

"Oh boy . . . I am sorry, twenty-seven. I am becoming clumsy in my old age. I am so sorry. I spilled coffee on this old chair. Please, let me clean it off."

I handed Jim a cleaning rag from a drawer in my office and he dabbed at the coffee to soak it up.

"Don't worry about it, Jim. I can tell you that chair has seen its share of spilled tea, and some coffee, and even a spot or two of wine. It is part of the character of the chair. Battle scars of a lifetime of support for folks!"

Jim handed me the rag back and smiled as he said, "I bet, Paul. Sort of like you and me, my old friend. Battle scarred, but we are still standing, huh? In its own way, it is a beautiful chair, Paul. But I guess that it is just an old chair."

I smiled as I sat back down and said, "No, Jim, it is not just an old chair. It is actually a memory bank. It is an old friend in which to share memories with, in your own life. The upholstery will hold your tears and accidental spills without complaint. The arms will be steady, hold you tight, and keep you warm. The old wooden frame is still strong, and it will keep you straight and true when you are shaky, and no matter what, it will be there for you, in the corner of some room like a faithful friend that you can always count on to be there. It is many things, Jim, but an old chair is not one of them."

Jim nodded, smiled, and he sat down and started to unravel memories of our past. "Well now, that sounds good to me, twenty-seven. In many ways, then, this chair is like you and me. Old friends to share memories and spilled coffee with on occasion. Say, do you remember that backhand shot I took on you in that game in 1978? How did you ever stop that one? Boy, oh boy, twenty-seven, I will never forget that save. That one might have been the greatest save that I ever saw. I still think about how I had the whole top o' the net. . .."

THE END

Once in a Lifetime on a Summer Night

Bittersweet memories of a summer night.
Once in a lifetime, you meet a person such as you.
Sparkling eyes, and brown hair tumbling down over your shoulders.
A soft voice, a whisper in the night.
Once in a lifetime on a summer night.

Hush! Be still. A soft sigh in the night.
Choking back tears, I hear you call my name, or maybe not.
The wind in the trees, the sounds of the night are here.
The heat of the day has passed.

The drink has made me soft, made me hazy, made me weak.
I still see your face whenever I open my eyes.
When the heat of the day has ended, when the sun has sunk so low.

Bittersweet memories of a summer night.
Once in a lifetime, you meet a person such as you.
Sparkling eyes, brown hair tumbling down over your shoulders.
A soft voice, a whisper in the night.
Once in a lifetime on a summer night.

Will it ever end? The road you and I travel every day.
Rolling on forever, on a hot summer night.
Words that start and never come.
Up and down, toying with our souls, and tearing at our minds.

Memories of you and I tear away at my mind, dance in the garden in time with the wind in the trees, and cry at my door.
Am I the only one they haunt?
Can you hear and see them too?

Bittersweet memories of a summer night.
Once in a lifetime, you meet a person such as you are.
Sparkling eyes, brown hair tumbling down over your shoulders.
A soft voice, a whisper in the night.
Once in a lifetime on a summer night.

You are my wish, and you are my dream.
No one can ever replace you.
No one can ever tell me the truth like you can.
A dream caught in a haze, our love in a summer breeze,
You and I together.
Since the day when we first met, and since the day we first spoke.

Once in a lifetime on a summer night.
So long ago, when we were young, and when time flashed by us.
You are a soft whisper in my ear forever more.
Your smile and your face, I cannot forget since we first met.
Once in a lifetime on a summer night.
Once in a lifetime on a summer night.

Epilogue

September finally arrives, and the stifling heat and humidity gradually give up and fades away. It does not go without a fight, and in some cases, it leaves and returns with a last-minute fury once more. Gradually, hot winds switch places with gentle breezes, and you can cut the grass and walk to the corner store without checking into the hospital for an intravenous treatment of fluids.

Summer; wonderful, glorious summer!

All too soon, the wonder of summer is gone, and with it goes another chapter in our lives.

Autumn knocks at the door, and the sounds of splashes in swimming pools, and the cheers of fan-packed baseball stadiums fade away . . . slowly replaced by the rustling of the wind chasing the dried leaves along the street, and the cheers of football fans rooting on their favorite teams.

Summer; wonderful, glorious summer!

No more hot dogs on the grill, no more smell of suntan lotion on my shirt, no more endless droning of the air-conditioner.

Where did it all go so soon?

Open the windows! Shut off the air-conditioner! Autumn is finally here!

I set my folding chair up on my porch on an early September evening. A sunset full of blues and reds, and a little touch of gold, flashed in the western sky in front of me. The beauty that you see in a sunset is really a promise of hope and joy for a new day.

I spun the top off an ice-cold bottle of beer, poured the beer into a frosty mug, and took a long swig. A gentle, late summer breeze moved some leaves in the trees above my head, and as the trees moved, I suddenly heard the cries of the ghosts of past summers in the air. I tilted my head. And they were there, loud and clear! A splash in a swimming pool, the pop, bang, and fizzle of fireworks above my head, the whisper of a gorgeous young woman's voice, and an image of the sparkle in her eyes on a summer day. I heard the crack of a baseball hitting the bat, and the smell of a grill full of wonderful hot dogs, hamburgers, and chickens cooking over some hot coals. I could hear the ocean waves lapping at the shore, and the sounds of the boardwalk activities along the New Jersey shore.

I tried very hard to remember all the memories of summers in my past, but the thoughts overwhelmed me. I realized there were just too many of them. It would be impossible to remember them all.

However, I sure could try.

I lifted my beer to the sunset, made a toast to summer and the glorious memories of the past.

Summer; wonderful, glorious summer!

"We knew that in the world of Harry and Paul, there would be another adventure right around the corner. There always will be, you see Harry and Paul adventures never really end. The years may pass, but they go on forever, as long as there are memories, dreams to dream, fun-loving people who enjoy life and care for one another in special ways, stories to tell, roads to travel, music to hear, dances to dance, and love to give.

They go on and on until the end of all time."

ABOUT THE AUTHOR

If you ask Paul John Hausleben, he will tell you that he is not an author, he is just a storyteller. His mission is to continue to write and tell stories to warm your heart, make you laugh, and sometimes make you cry, just a little. Most of all, he deals in memories, and helps you to remember the good times of your own life, and the special people who touched you along the way. Paul was born and raised in Paterson, and then nearby Haledon, New Jersey, and began writing at an early age. He revisited a writing career later in his life, and he now is the author of a number of novels, compilations, short stories and audio and video works. Most of his work touches upon nostalgic remembrances of simpler times, and tells the stories of heartfelt, humorous, and special human relationships. Other than writing, among many careers both paid and unpaid, he is a former semi-professional hockey goaltender, a former military radio operator, a music fan and music reviewer, an avid sports fan, photographer, and an amateur radio operator. He now resides in Somewhere, U.S.A., but his heart always remains along Belmont Avenue in good old Paterson, and Haledon, New Jersey.

Titles by Mr. Hausleben that you also will enjoy:

The Time Bomb in The Cupboard and Other Adventures of Harry and Paul.

The Night Always Comes, Another story from the Adventures of Harry and Paul.

Reunion, A sequel to the Night Always Comes and Another story from the Adventures of Harry and Paul

The Autumn Collection

The Christmas Tree and Other Christmas Stories. Tales for a Christmas Evening

Crows on a High Wire

The Miracle Tree, Another story from the Adventures of Harry and Paul

And many others

Coming Soon?

You may contact us via email at ctte27@gmail.com

www.ingramcontent.com/pod-product-compliance
Lightning Source LLC
LaVergne TN
LVHW041106080826
845145LV00007B/1696

* 9 7 8 0 9 8 8 6 3 3 6 7 4 *